THE WAY OF BEAUTY

ALSO BY CAMILLE DI MAIO

The Memory of Us

Before the Rain Falls

THE WAY OF BEAUTY

Camille Di Maio

This is a work of fiction. Names, characters, organizations, places, events, and incidents are either products of the author's imagination or are used fictitiously.

Text copyright © 2018 by Camille Di Maio
All rights reserved.

No part of this book may be reproduced, or stored in a retrieval system, or transmitted in any form or by any means, electronic, mechanical, photocopying, recording, or otherwise, without express written permission of the publisher.

Published by Lake Union Publishing, Seattle

www.apub.com

Amazon, the Amazon logo, and Lake Union Publishing are trademarks of Amazon.com, Inc., or its affiliates.

ISBN-13: 9781503950122
ISBN-10: 1503950123

Cover design by PEPE *nymi*

Printed in the United States of America

The railroad, second only to religion, has been the greatest civilizing and enlightening force in the world.

—Frank A. Munsey, publisher of *Railroad Man's Magazine*, 1906

To Julie Williams, who does so much for so many.
And because you love New York!
To Elmie Lopez, my beloved friend. We'll make it to the city together someday.
And to Kristen Saglimbeni, one of my favorite New Yorkers.

Prologue

October 28, 1963

The stone birds stood at attention, as they had for more than fifty years. Their gray wings stretched in majestic neglect, aching to embrace whoever would venture to climb atop their perch over the entryway to the train station. Although a bustling Thirty-Third Street separated them from her third-story apartment window, Vera could see every detail. The scrolls of their chest feathers. The fierce grip of their claws.

Eagles, historic symbols of courage.

Did they know that their reign had come to an untimely end?

"Mama." The word cut through the room's silence. "Come away from the window. You shouldn't watch this."

Vera didn't turn. There were only minutes left before the ordeal started, and she couldn't tear herself away. Her hands clung to the peeling white paint of the sill, her bony fingers losing all color with every passing second. When she looked into the faces of the eagles, eye to eye, she saw her father, victim of the tunnels that ran underneath the station, and missed the way he used to make her laugh with one of his magic tricks. She remembered Angelo and how they'd met near those steps.

Now they were covered with construction workers in yellow hard hats.

Paid traitors to Manhattan, as far as she was concerned.

And her granddaughter was somewhere in that throng, cheering it all on.

Alice's steps were light on the knotty oak floor. She dragged over one chair and then a second. She took her mother's hand, patted the seat, and whispered, "Let's do this together."

Vera accepted the assistance. She sat down and rested her forehead against the single-paned glass of her prewar home. The heat of her breath created a small fog that grew and recessed with each movement. It was cold on the other side. Unseasonable. Like everything today.

Down on the street, protesters marched, workers waited, and police attempted to keep the peace.

The first of the jackhammers began, shooting sparks of fire that looked like tears. Then others followed, forming a raucous and discordant symphony. Black dust flew from their deadly iron drills, revealing the blush-colored granite that lay below the exterior of the regal birds, enshrouded with decades of grime. Their original beauty was uncovered in a final, futile attempt at salvation.

The two women gasped and held on to each other. Half a century of the city's dreams resided within the station's Doric columns.

Vera had jumped rope among the shadows that grew daily as the magnificent station was built. Her first real kiss had taken place underneath its cathedral-like glass ceiling. Her father had lost his life to it.

She knew Alice had her own memories. The ones she never spoke about.

Only Libby was missing from this requiem. Vera wished she didn't think of her granddaughter with such disappointment. But it couldn't be helped. The girl was infected with the same youthful fervor for *New! New! New!* that had plagued the city council.

Now they watched as the first of the twenty-two eagles descended on ropes and pulleys, slated to end their days wallowing in a swamp in

New Jersey. The politicians stood next to it and grinned for the photographers like big-game hunters with a slaughtered prize.

Progress. All in the name of Progress, the newest god birthed in America.

The legislators were not alone in their guilt, though. There were other executioners. Airplanes and cars had replaced the profitability of train travel. The demand for a basketball court and concert venue for a vacuous public, ever hungry for showy entertainment, surpassed the regard for the hallowed spot where loved ones had once said their goodbyes to the men going off to war.

Nothing seemed sacred these days.

Vera couldn't bear to watch any longer. It was like burying a piece of herself. She rose on shaky knees and asked Alice to help her to the bedroom, where she could close her eyes and be alone with her memories.

Alice adjusted the pillows as they both heard a knock at the door. Vera sat up to answer.

"I'll get that," her daughter whispered, giving her a kiss on the forehead before leaving the room.

Vera heard the unlatching of the chain and a young boy saying, "A message for someone named Alice." Her daughter let out a gasp loud enough for Vera to hear from her bed.

"I'll be right back!" Alice shouted.

The sound of the slammed door echoed down the hallway.

But she was gone for a very long time. When Vera woke up and sauntered into the hallway, she found a telegram on the floor.

My dreamer, it said. *It's been too many years. But I must see you. E.*

So he was back.

Part One: Vera

Chapter One

1900

The tangle of laundry lines reminded five-year-old Vera of the spiderweb that stretched across a corner above her mattress in the one-room apartment where she lived with Mutter and Vater.

No, not Mutter and Vater. Mother and Father. Mama and Papa. Her English was strong, but some words still slipped out of habit. Mutter—no, *Mama*—told her that she would soon start a new program called *kindergarten* while Mama went to work in a shirtwaist factory. Vera would learn to speak English better when she was with other children.

Why was it all right to say a German word like *kindergarten* but not a German word like *mutter*? New York was confusing.

Mama took her out early for errands, and already they'd visited the produce stand and the bakery that sold Papa's favorite pumpernickel. Mama walked in long strides, and Vera's little legs had to run to keep up.

The bright sun was blocked by the crisscrossed rows of trousers and undergarments and bedclothes that created a canopy over the streets.

Vera danced around their moving shadows, sidestepping litter and rat droppings to tiptoe among the brief patches of light that burst through.

"Beeil dich," said Mama, which Vera knew to mean *hurry*, and she wondered again why the adults could get away with not speaking English.

Her mother was not always as ill-tempered as she had been lately. Mama was usually sweet and sang lullabies and told stories to Vera. But not for the past few weeks. Something was different, not only with her parents but also with all the adults she encountered.

They arrived at the butcher shop, always the last stop so that the meat wouldn't spoil. Mama ran her finger down the advertisements posted on the window until she found the one that cost the least amount of money.

"Chuck eye," she said to her daughter. "I'll ask Mr. Severino to grind it." That meant that she would shape it into patties, which Vera especially loved with cheese on top of them. But cheese was saved for special occasions. Like her birthday. Sometimes a chuck eye meant that Mama would let it *marinieren*—marinate—which meant that they gave it a bath in vinegar and spices.

The bell dinged as they walked into the shop. She gripped her mother's hand tighter as she looked around the room. This was her least favorite errand.

The ceiling was lined with skinned carcasses suspended from rusted hooks. Exposed ribs hung encircled with marblelike sinew. Vera squeezed her eyes tight and imagined streaks of color shooting through the blackness of her lids. But nothing could keep out the stench, nor the sounds of the men and women arguing as they waited their turn.

"He is tall. Long black coat. Brown hair and a long nose."

"No, he's shorter than I am. Black hair. Shiny shoes."

Mr. Severino turned from behind the counter. His long apron stretched to its limits across his belly and was smeared with fresh streaks of red and brown layered over darker, older ones. He wielded a cleaver and slammed it down onto the wooden counter. Vera buried her head in her mother's hip and held in a scream. They were all speaking so quickly, but she understood most of it.

"You're a bunch of damn fools, all of you," the butcher shouted. No one dared to argue with him. "Yes, he's tall. But he's got red hair and freckles. Jesus Christ, you're all seeing things." He wiped his hands over his sweaty, hairless head. "And it doesn't matter what he looks like. He's up to some kind of no good."

His wife put down the waxed paper roll and twine that she'd just pulled from the storeroom and feverishly crossed herself. Vera's mother pulled her daughter closer and covered her ears.

The rumor was that a man was walking around the Tenderloin carrying "more cash than God." Papa had told Mama that the man was buying buildings like they were candy. Businesses were shutting down, and tenants were being evicted. Panic had immigrated to Midtown New York. Vera didn't understand what all those words meant, but they didn't sound good.

"Let's go, Vera," her mother said, holding her by the wrist and hurrying toward the entrance.

"Aw, Mrs. Keller," the butcher shouted after them. "*Mi dispiace.* I'm sorry. Come on, come on, come on." He waved his fleshy hand in the air. But whatever he said next was drowned by the sound of the bell as she closed the door behind them.

Vera was relieved to be out of that place, even it if meant they would have only bread and peas for dinner. Mama stood under the green awning, glanced at the large clock on the building across the street, and looked right and left. She told Vera that there was just enough time for a small detour.

They walked two blocks to Thirty-Fourth and Fifth, where Mama said she could choose a piece of candy from the sweets shop. As they rounded the corner, Vera smiled when her favorite window came into view. It was decorated with towers made from bags of nuts and glass jars that were filled with every sort of candy. The colors reminded her of the box of twelve wax crayons that her parents had given to her for her birthday. Just a couple of months later, they were already worn down to nubs. The two rooms of their apartment were lined with drawings that Vera had copied out of borrowed books.

Mama pulled some coins out of her pocket and frowned as she counted them. "Never enough," she whispered under her breath. But she smiled when she looked at Vera. "Just one piece today. A small one."

This place was so much better than Mr. Severino's. It smelled like marshmallows and caramel and chocolate, and the lady behind the counter was pretty, although even she wore the same nervous look that had taken up residence on the faces of the people who lived in the neighborhood. Her white apron was clean and had lace trim. Vera reached for a large lollipop, swirled like a cinnamon bun. But Mama guided her instead toward the thin sugar sticks near the register.

While Vera could identify her letters, she knew very few combinations that made words. Instead, she could differentiate the flavors by the various light and dark shades.

Dark red was cherry. Light red was watermelon. Dark green was apple. Light green was lime.

Her mother read them off anyway. "Grape, lemon, apricot," she finished as they got to the last jar. She'd slipped into German for some of the words. She waited for her daughter to select one.

"Erdbeere."

"In English," said Mama.

Vera thought for a moment, discarding the words that didn't sound right.

"Strawberry," she said at last. The shopgirl nodded.

Mama held out the coins in her hand. "Try to pick the penny," she said.

Vera looked them over, copper and silver, and recognized the correct one by the laurel wreath on the back. She pointed to it and looked up. Her mother smiled and slid it across the counter. She handed the sweet to her daughter.

Vera removed the wrapper, savoring the crinkly sound it made as it shimmied down the sugar stick.

They stepped outside. The sun was beginning the descent that would still take a few hours to complete. Mama had to cook supper in time for Papa to go to the meeting. They turned down a street that they had always avoided before. Mama said, "Close your eyes," but didn't say why. She clutched Vera's hand tighter, saying nothing about its stickiness, and quickened the pace.

In their haste, Vera dropped her sugar stick and cried out. Mama picked it up, but the red swirled candy was covered in wet dirt. She began to reach for it but jumped away when a horse carriage raced by, its wheel crushing the treat. "I'm sorry, darling. But we can't go back now."

Vera's face melted into a frown.

"How about this? I'll put a little honey on your bread when we get home."

She could feel her mother's pulse beating rapidly and didn't want to be the cause of an argument. There were too many of those lately in their neighborhood.

It seemed as if even the sun knew to stay away from the crime-riddled Tenderloin, because the sky had become cloudier than it was just moments ago. The street was littered with trash, and the smell of the sewer was overwhelming as it wafted on the back of the wind through the streets of Midtown. Pictures with women wearing nearly no clothing were plastered on brick walls, one poster laid on top of another. Vera thought they looked strangely beautiful and admired the pinkness of the women's cheeks and the fullness of their hair. She saw many signs that said **G-I-R-L-S** and **B-A-R**, and when Vera remembered to close her eyes again, she worked out the sounds of the letters the way that her mother had taught her. "B-A-R" was easy, but she didn't understand why that word was on signs, unless they sold soap, which was the only time she'd ever heard the term. "G-I-R" was not so hard, but it took her the rest of the way home to work out the sound of the "L-S," and before she had a chance to wonder why a store would say "girls," they'd arrived at their building.

Papa and the neighbors were already gathered outside. Their voices were loud.

Everyone was talking about the man who had been walking around the area, paying cash for buildings. Just like the butcher shop, no one could agree on what he looked like. Some said he was tall, with a brown trench coat and a black hat, and others said that he was short and wore a cap like a newspaper boy. Old, young, fat, thin—everyone said something else.

The next day, the confusion ended as it was discovered that there were, in fact, three men buying buildings. But it only created new problems. Some were saying that it didn't matter why the men wanted to purchase them, at least the brothels and the bars and the casinos were closing, and the place would finally be cleaned up. And others argued that people had to earn a living somehow, and the landlords were just greedy for the quick money.

The adults were anxious, and with good reason. It was not long after that Vera's parents came home to find a large paper pinned to the front door of the building. Mama cried out and held her hand to her face, and Papa's cheeks became inflamed as he hung his head. He said, "Well, you're getting your wish; looks like we have to move somewhere else."

Vera knew what it meant to move. She'd once had a friend named Cecilia who lived across the hall, but she had moved to Staten Island just a few months ago. Vera knew from her mother telling her that islands had palm trees and oceans and beaches and sunshine all year, so she imagined that it must be quite an adventure for Cecilia to live in such a place. Maybe they would move to Staten Island, too, although she thought her parents would look more excited if that were the case.

Her parents were awake all that night, and Vera peeked out from under a blanket to see Mama pulling dishes from the cupboard, saying, "Where are we going to go?" and "Why aren't you helping me?" while Papa sat with his head on the table and his arms covering it. The next day Mama's eyes were red, and she wore the kind of smile that Vera was old enough to know was a fake, but she played along when Mama said that they were going to do something new and exciting. They weren't going to Staten Island after all; they were going to a boardinghouse until they could figure things out.

The date of eviction was immediate. They had four carpetbags and a suitcase and a promise from Papa that he would go back for the cuckoo clock that Mama's grandfather had made years ago when she was a child in Germany—the one with the little girl who danced through a doorway while a bird chirped at the change of the hour.

But he never did, as far as Vera knew.

Outside, the street looked different than it ever had before. People spilled out onto the sidewalk, where they had to maneuver around putrid piles of horse droppings. Everyone had as much as they could carry—bags, trunks, crates. Some had pitched in to share carriages so they could load furniture, but Papa said that since they were going to a boardinghouse, they wouldn't need what little furniture they had. Mama hugged some of her friends, not knowing where the evictions would scatter everyone. Papa and the other men shook hands, and the landlord, Mr. Percy, stood on the stoop with his arms folded, surveying this mass goodbye, while even one block away the sounds of demolition could already be heard.

Months later, when errands took them nearby once again, Mama held Vera's hand, and they walked toward the old neighborhood. But instead of the rotten bricks of the tenements, the corroded iron of the fire escapes, the signs that said **G-I-R-L-S** and **B-A-R**, there was nothing. For blocks and blocks, the sun shone down onto the sandy-colored dirt, and it was like a cavity in the landscape that Dr. Rankin's Dental Parlor might need to fill.

Then it was learned that the three men with all the cash worked for the Pennsylvania Railroad. That they'd quietly bought every building in that part of the Tenderloin.

And that a magnificent train station was to be built on this very spot.

Chapter Two

1912

Vera slung the market bag over her shoulder and began the five-story walk up to their apartment. Usually her legs felt leaden as she neared the top, and her breath became heavy from the effort.

But today she could fly.

Today was the day it would happen.

She was still getting used to the vendors on Twenty-Ninth, having recently moved several blocks south when the boardinghouse they'd lived in burned down. The official report indicated an errant candle flame, but Vera was certain that it had been intentional. Their landlord refused to modify the dwelling to the new plumbing codes and was about to be fined. Now he'd likely collect his insurance money and gamble it away within a week.

It was the one good thing about having little—there was little to lose.

The only mercy was that the landlord had waited until all the residents were out of the building. Vera had taken her father out for a stroll on a rare morning when his legs didn't betray him with the excruciating pain he'd first endured as a sandhog. Digging 135 feet underneath the East River for a decade did that and more to most of the men who'd been the manpower behind the tunnels of the Pennsylvania Railroad.

The bends. Such a wretched ailment.

Over the years, it had manifested itself in many horrible ways. Rashes. Memory loss. Paralysis. Fatigue. Every day was different, and Vera never knew what her father would suffer on any given day. Like a cruel roulette wheel.

She had to be prepared for it all, as the sole caregiver of her father ever since Mama died.

A few years ago, S. Pearson and Sons, the management company for the railroad station, laid off its air-lock tenders in an attempt to control costs. The tenders were responsible for monitoring the hydraulic shields and volatile explosives as well as the air pressure for the workers. But their absence left hundreds of men to fend for themselves in the compressed-air caissons, and more than fifty of them died in mere months. To avoid bad publicity, their bodies were secretly transported to other boroughs, and their death certificates indicated "natural causes."

All to save one hundred twelve dollars a day.

A newspaper headline shouted:

DEATH STALKS ALONGSIDE THE TUNNELS

But what was the value of the life of a man when thousands of immigrants were desperate to take his place? Her father had been lucky to have any work at all.

The straps of Vera's bag cut into her shoulders. It was heavier than usual. The fruit seller made no secret of his interest in her, slipping extra apples without bruises into her bag along with the ones that she'd selected from the bin with the damaged offerings.

But kind as he was, it was not the fruit seller she loved.

Vera had become adept at choosing produce that was only moderately browned, cutting off what was truly rotten, salvaging what was merely softened. She'd learned from her mother to muddle the marginal parts into a juice, which tasted different day to day depending on the season and availability.

She opened the bag, putting a strap across each shoulder, creating more of a knapsack as she started up the stairs.

They'd been fortunate to get a place in this new building. It had one bedroom, a window, a sink, and a water closet. Luxury indeed. She whispered a prayer of thanks each evening for the legislators who had put new ordinances into place requiring those items. There were people living in the southern tip of Manhattan who were still sharing facilities with twenty others and whose faucets ran brown sludge.

Park Avenue it wasn't, but this was a place they could finally call home—twelve years after leaving the Tenderloin. She wished her mother had lived long enough to see it.

As much as Angelo feigned innocence, Vera was certain that he must have arranged for them to have a place in this building. Angelo. Her angel ever since the first day they'd met.

She checked her wristwatch. Two hours until she'd see him. Two hours until her life changed forever.

He'd left a note by her door this morning.

Meet me at our spot on the steps of Penn Station. 3:00 p.m. I have something important to tell you.

It could mean only one thing. What she'd dreamed of ever since first meeting him when she was a little girl. *I love you, Vera,* she imagined him saying. *I want to marry you.*

What once seemed impossible had, of late, appeared imminent. Angelo had begun to say things about the future. Even telling her that he wanted to buy an apartment that looked right over Penn Station, with a second bedroom for children.

A man didn't talk to a girl like that unless he was planning to share it with her. The certainty of this had warmed her through the frigid winter.

She'd turned seventeen just two weeks ago and had begun wearing her hair in a loose bun. Surely he'd noticed that she was no longer the child in braids who'd scraped her knee in front of his family's newspaper stand all those years ago. He'd finally seen her for the woman she was becoming.

Vera Bellavia, she'd write out on scraps of paper. *Mrs. Angelo Bellavia. Angelo and Vera Bellavia.*

It was so much prettier than *Keller*. It meant "beautiful way" in Italian. A harbinger of their future together.

Vera arrived at her door and slipped the key into the lock. That was another luxury. The boardinghouse had had no locks, and more than once the lecherous landlord had *accidentally* made his way into the apartment as she dressed for the day.

Something blocked the door. She gave it a shove, toppling a chair that had apparently been tipped underneath the handle.

A sense of dread flooded her stomach. Papa must be having one of his spells of paranoia, another manifestation of the bends. There was no part of the body that it didn't affect.

She dropped the bag of produce on the wooden floor and called out to him.

"Papa," she said, knowing that he must be in the bedroom, for he wasn't in the small parlor that functioned as sitting area, dining area, and kitchen. The sink water ran furiously, a violation of their tight restrictions. He'd forgotten to turn it off three other times this week, and she feared they'd receive a hefty fine for it. It was miraculous that it hadn't flooded anything.

"Gehen Sie weg!" he shouted. Which she recognized as *Go away!* But she was relieved just to hear his voice. She flew to the bedroom, where he huddled with his knees pulled to his chin.

"Shh," she comforted, gently rubbing a hand across his bony shoulders. She felt him flinch, but only a bit. A good sign. His episodes had worsened since they moved to this apartment, but she hoped that they would subside as he became familiar with their new surroundings. She'd drawn him a picture of the cathedral in Munich after seeing a picture of his hometown in a book. It was pinned above his bed in the hopes that he would recognize it. Any sense of sameness.

Vera laid her head against her father's back as soon as she felt she could do so without alarming him. Even if staying with him meant missing her appointment with Angelo, she would. She didn't know what her father might do if left alone in this state.

"Vater," she whispered in his native German. *"Ich liebe dich." I love you.* She repeated the words until his breathing returned to normal, and she wiped away the wetness that pooled around his eyes.

"Prinzessin," he responded at last, calling her his princess as if she were still five years old. That told her that everything was all right. Her own heartbeat slowed.

Papa looked at her with apology etched across the untimely crevices of his skin. "Vera," he said as he placed his hands on her cheeks. "Vera, my darling, it happened again, didn't it?"

The English was an even better sign. He was returning to himself.

Vera nodded. She might cry if she spoke too soon.

"Second time this week?"

"Third," she whispered.

His shoulders slumped. "I'm too much of a burden on you."

Vera pursed her lips and shook her head, still encased in his rough worker's hands. "Never."

"It will pass," he promised. "I—I just need to get used to being here."

"That's what I thought." She pulled a small package out of her bag. "Look. I brought you your favorite. Pumpernickel." Another touch of the familiar.

His face brightened, and he took the bread from her hands before bringing it to his nose. He closed his eyes as he inhaled its pungent scent. That variety had never appealed to Vera, but it always seemed to remind him of the old country. She'd even been experimenting lately with her mother's *Rouladen* recipe, but she never seemed to cut the flank steak thin enough. And pickled gherkins were expensive and difficult to find.

Papa pulled back the waxed paper delicately, as if it were worth more than the spare coins Vera had used for it. He held it out for her, but she declined.

Crumbs got caught in his ever-graying beard. "Weren't you going somewhere this afternoon?"

He remembered. All was well at last.

"Yes. I'm meeting a friend."

She'd never told him about Angelo, who was nine years older than Vera. And though she loved her father, it was times like this when she felt most acutely the lack of having a mother.

Just a year ago, Vera had feared that any romantic thoughts about Angelo lay squarely in her imagination. But recently his hand would brush against hers and he would not pull away. Maybe it was her naïveté—he was Italian, after all, and from a family that was overtly physical in their affection for one another.

She went back and forth, convincing herself that every gesture meant something, or, alternatively, that it was merely in her head. For all she knew, Angelo might still see her as the child she was when they'd met.

He had done what any kind person would do faced with a little girl with a scraped knee. When she'd told him through sobs that she and her parents had just moved to the boardinghouse across the street, he'd seemed to understand how that might be frightening. When she returned from school the following day, Angelo had called over to her from his post behind the magazines. A boy stood steps away—a younger sibling, she guessed—bellowing headlines that Vera didn't understand: "McKinley wins reelection in landslide victory!"

Angelo had shouted her name again, and Vera could still feel the flush that had come over her when she realized that he'd remembered it at all. She'd stepped in a mud puddle racing over to him, dirtying the brown leather boots she'd received in the charity box full of castoffs. But she didn't care. They were two sizes too big for her, anyway, and the laces were frayed at the ends.

"Ah, Kid," he'd said in the accent that she immediately loved. "Your knee. It's better today?"

She'd lifted up the hem of her dress to show him.

"Bene," he'd said, inspecting it. "But you know what would make it heal faster?"

"Nein," she'd answered, slipping into her native tongue.

"*Gelato!* You've had ice cream, right?"

She'd nodded.

"*Eccellente.* Then you have to try gelato. Italian ice cream. Much better. Come?"

He'd held out his hand, and she slipped her tiny palm into his large one. Angelo told the boy to mind the newsstand and walked Vera around the corner where he said his *nonna* made the best ice cream she would ever taste.

And he'd been right. She'd tried the pistachio like he suggested while he told her about the first time he'd had gelato, right around her age. In the Piazza Navona in *Roma*, where he'd grown up before coming to America. He'd made it sound so exotic and told her that she would have to go someday.

As they exited the shop, Angelo had stopped in front of a large pebble that lay on the sidewalk. He kicked it down the street and invited

Vera to take a turn. Her little legs carried her swiftly to where it rested, and she gave it a try, sending it only a few feet. Angelo caught up and sent it soaring, grazing the top hat of a man walking toward them, garnering an ugly retort. Vera stifled a giggle, mirrored by Angelo, and they'd continued their game until returning to his stand.

"Here we are, Kid," he'd said. She'd winced at the nickname, already wishing that she were fourteen just like him. Practically an adult. "Back to work for me, and home for you. Glad your knee is better. Come back and see me sometime. You'll have to try the *stracciatella*. No one makes it like my nonna."

"Thank you," she whispered.

"And how do you say that in German?"

Her eyes widened at his encouragement of the language she knew so well. Everyone else tried to make it go away. As if there were something bad about it. Bad about her.

"Danke."

"Danke," he'd repeated. "And it's *grazie* in Italian."

Vera remembered how she'd had to strain her neck to look all the way up at him. How tall he'd once seemed to her, although now she'd nearly caught up.

Meet me at our spot on the steps of Penn Station. 3:00 p.m. I have something important to tell you.

Today might be the first time he would kiss her, and she would only need to raise herself slightly on her tiptoes to meet him. She'd pictured this moment for so long, and now it was upon her. Them.

The pumpernickel nearly slipped out of her father's hand as he began to fall asleep. Vera took it from him and laid it on the bureau. She guided him down to his pillow and tucked a blanket around his sides. She glanced at the clock. Two thirty-five. He should be good for a few hours.

Vera brushed her fingers through her hair and rearranged the silver clip. She'd always liked how it looked against her blonde hair. In contrast, Angelo seemed so exotic to her, with his dark wavy hair and deep brown eyes.

What might their children look like?

She smiled. She was getting ahead of herself.

Vera pinched her cheeks, a poor girl's rouge. She bit her lips to redden them and slipped on a wool sweater. Her feet barely touched the wood stairs as she hurried down to the street.

It was only four blocks and one avenue to the other side of the train station. Penn was a microcosm of the city with its ocean of steps, towering columns, hurrying commuters. It had allowed people with money to move out of the city into Long Island and Connecticut. It was the fourth-largest building in the world, seventy acres of floor space. And people who knew about such things said that its grand concourse was the size of the nave of Saint Peter's church in Rome. Vera enjoyed watching the well-dressed men sidestep the flower sellers and the coiffed women cling to their handbags as they walked next to beggars.

She might never be able to see the world, but all the world came to her through the tunnels of Penn Station. She and Angelo liked to sit on the steps and guess the nationalities of the people who would walk by speaking languages they couldn't decipher. Sometimes they spoke in British accents or made up words altogether just to pretend that they were from somewhere else, and it was among her favorite of their games.

Angelo understood this about Vera, and they had this in common—that as big as they could dream, they could be just as happy amusing themselves with these simple pastimes.

As Vera approached the station, she saw one of the elegant sorts of ladies from afar. Her long pale-pink coat screamed quality even from this distance. She wore tall boots and a hat with lace trim that stopped just short of her eyes. Vera was about to look for Angelo when he suddenly appeared near the woman. Vera quickened her steps, tingling with anticipation.

She raised her arm to wave, but Angelo wasn't looking at her. He was still looking at the woman. Walking toward her.

Why wasn't he walking toward Vera?

The woman smiled when she saw Angelo and slipped her gloved hand through his arm. His smile matched hers—wider, even. Only then did he turn and see Vera.

Her heart sank like lead. Something was wrong. Very wrong.

"Hey, Kid," he shouted. She cringed.

"Kid," he repeated as she walked up to them. The woman had not let go of his arm, and Vera was appalled to see that she was even more beautiful up close. Perfect white skin, lips that looked as if a gifted artist had stenciled them. Eyes that seemed translucent.

"There you are. *Va bene.* I can always count on my German friend to be right on time."

It was an old joke. Vera arrived five minutes early everywhere she went. Angelo would be at least ten minutes late.

"Angelo," she said, hoping her voice didn't shake. She avoided looking at the woman.

"Thanks for meeting me here today. I told you I had something important to tell you."

There was a look in his eyes that she didn't recognize and couldn't begin to interpret as he went on.

"I want you to meet Pearl Pilkington. My fiancée."

Chapter Three

Vera gathered her collection of rocks from the box underneath the sofa that served as her bed. There were twenty-nine of them, each one etched with a memory. She pulled a coat from a hook by the front door and filled its pockets with the stones, weighing her down more than she'd expected.

Or maybe it was just her mood after meeting Angelo's fiancée yesterday.

How could she have gotten it all so wrong?

Vera's brisk steps kept her warm in weather that created icicles that dripped from the edges of the buildings. There was a time she'd thought they were magical. Crystal fingers reaching out from an unseen world. Angelo had encouraged those kinds of fantasies, telling her stories of *Beppo Pipetta* and *Sir Fiorante, Magician*. She knew them better than any of the Brothers Grimm stories from her own homeland. She'd clung to every word that Angelo had ever said to her.

But those days were over. Vera hurried along to the fountain at Madison Square Park. She scrunched her toes, willing the blood to flow. The temperature hovered just above freezing, and she was counting on the water to have not iced over just yet.

She reached the fountain. It was not magnificent, not like ones north of here, but it blended into the background, almost unnoticed. Just like her.

The concrete was chilled, but she'd worn enough layers that she barely felt its wintry bite as she sat along the fountain's edge. She opened her bag and pulled out the first stone. Round with a sharp point that jutted out as if it were pointing to something.

Carefully scratched into its gray surface, she'd written out a simple code.

3-20-07-39

March 20, 1907. Thirty-Ninth Street.

She'd been twelve years old. It was the day of her mother's funeral. There had been few attendees at the church and then the cemetery. Not one of the foremen or the other women who worked in the factory attended. To them she was another nameless cog, collapsing from exhaustion and no doubt replaced within hours by another immigrant eager for a stipend. Mama and Papa were some of the last Germans who had not moved to the Upper East Side when the migration went that way. And it was a difficult thing for people to get away to remember the dead when it meant a day without earning much-needed wages.

What few had been there looked upon Vera with pity that penetrated her broken heart, and she could not bear their eyes looking at her as if they thought they could read what she felt.

When they'd returned home, Papa had retreated into the bedroom, neither knowing nor caring where she might get off to. She'd stayed in her black dress and walked by Angelo's newsstand. He was always there, not far from their doorstep.

"Hey, Kid," he'd said, lowering his tone nearly an octave. Why did people change their voices when speaking to someone in sorrow? As if death were played on the left side of a piano while life was played on the right. "I'm sorry about your mother. Want to take a walk and talk about it?"

Vera shook her head.

"What about some *cannoli*? Guaranteed to put at least a tiny smile on your face. I know of a new place just a few blocks away."

The thought of the ricotta-filled dessert did sound good. She hadn't eaten anything since before dawn.

She'd walked a step behind Angelo through narrow paths made between hills of snow. For once she was grateful not to wear the long skirts of grown women. The ones she walked past struggled to avoid the growing puddles of slush. It was the first day that it wasn't frigid, and her breath no longer crystallized in the air.

One patch had thawed all the way down to the pavement. Angelo stooped to pick up an errant rock, a habit they'd continued. He waited until a group of top-hatted men passed them, and then he set the large pebble in front of his foot.

"Over there. Just in front of the lamppost," he said, pointing out his target. He waited once more, this time for a woman carrying a laundry bundle. As she left, he kicked his heel up and the rock went flying, exactly where he'd predicted.

"Goal!" he shouted, waving his fist in the air. Vera felt her cheeks flush with pride.

This was the signal that it was Vera's turn. She ran up to the lamppost, noting its peeling green paint, and positioned herself in front of it. She looked east on Thirty-Ninth toward the opera house across the street.

The arches of the building made a wide target she was unlikely to miss.

"There." She pointed, intentionally vague. She waited until there was a break in people crossing and gripped her black skirt in her hands. She gave the rock a good, hard kick. But she slipped on a patch of ice that stubbornly refused to melt with the rest of it. She lurched forward to find her balance, stepping right into a large puddle and soaking her shoes and stockings past her ankles, spraying her only coat with dirty water.

"Goal!" shouted Angelo, who only then looked behind him to see her in this sorry state. Vera felt his pity—the same pity that she'd seen in the eyes of people at the funeral this morning—and she burned with embarrassment.

"Aw, Kid," he said. "That's some bad luck right there. Here. Let me help you."

He took off his own jacket and wrapped it around her shoulders. She inhaled its warm, smoky scent, traces of tobacco tickling her nose. It smelled like Angelo's newsstand. Like heaven.

"Let's get you home. We'll buy some cannoli another time." He put his arm around her in a gesture that she knew was only meant to extend his own heat to her shivering body.

But it was just as lovely as she'd dreamed.

Later, after he'd closed up his stand for the evening and Papa was deep in sleep, she'd stolen out into the night with a candle. She'd had to go through a window in the basement, as the landlord kept the front door locked according to his strict curfew. Vera walked gingerly so as not to extinguish its flame. She made her way to the opera house, peering into the dark and looking across the steps until at last she found it.

The round stone with the edge that jutted out. She picked it up with near-frozen fingers and slipped it into her pocket. When she returned home, she would grab Papa's razor—the one he'd always complained was duller than it should be—and scratch out the date and the street number.

She slipped back into the building unnoticed—she hoped—and entered their rented room. It still smelled of Mama's rosewater. Sadness stopped her momentarily as she wished that she could tell her mother all the things in her heart. Angelo's family was very religious—Roman Catholic—and he believed that you could talk to the dead and that they could see you. Maybe Mama could see her and Vera could tell her the things that she'd never been brave enough to say in person.

Like how being with Angelo made her feel.

Vera held the rock in her hand, carefully carving out her code and replacing Papa's razor next to the steel plate that served as a mirror. She crossed the room to her little basket of stones and added it to her collection.

Mama, she whispered into the silence. *I love him. I'm going to marry him someday.*

Now, just five years later, Vera the woman thought back to Vera the girl and shuddered at the thought that such innocent years were now behind her for good. She was not going to marry Angelo. She was not going to cook his supper and give him babies and kiss him and grow old with him. He'd found himself a dandy rich girl, and how could the daughter of a dead factory worker and an ailing sandhog ever measure up to a woman as elegant as Pearl Pilkington?

Plink.

The stone fell to the bottom of the fountain, sending lethargic ripples across its thinly iced surface.

Plink.

Another one. From the day they'd kicked a stone down Thirty-Third to Penn Station to watch the opening ceremonies.

Plink.

From the day they'd gone down Fourteenth in Chelsea and joined the tenement children playing baseball in an alley.

She emptied them into the water, watching them sink to the bottom along with all her hopes. She held the last one in her hand. The last, but the first. The one from the day she'd met him. The day she'd scraped her knee in front of his newsstand and first looked into his compassionate eyes and read more into them than she knew was real. They'd not kicked stones that day—it was a game they started just after that. But she'd taken a rock that was in place to keep a pile of newspapers from scattering in the wind. As a memento. He hadn't seen her—she'd been careful about it—but that night she'd kept it balled up in her hands and slept well for the first time since she and Mama and Papa had come to the wretched boardinghouse.

Vera considered dropping that one, too, into the water. She felt heat in her hand pulsing to her heart as she held it. She placed her hand over the fountain, spreading her fingers slowly.

She heard footsteps and then her name.

"Vera?"

She gripped the rock before it could slip out and hastily shoved it onto her lap, covering it with her coat.

The sun obscured the face of the person in front of her, but she noticed the expensive boots.

"Vera, correct?"

She'd hoped it couldn't be true, but strangely it was. Bad luck, Angelo might have said.

"We met yesterday. I'm Pearl Pilkington."

Chapter Four

Never had Vera thought that she would find herself sitting at a restaurant like Maioglio Brothers. But she'd discovered within minutes of her second encounter with Miss Pilkington that the woman had a beguiling air about her from which emanated an invitation to agree to anything she might suggest. She was alarmingly beautiful yet somehow approachable. Wealthy yet somehow common. No, not common. But she made Vera feel as if they were equals, though nothing could have been further from the truth.

So when the woman who had captured Angelo's heart invited her to lunch, Vera heard a *yes* escape from her mouth, despite every other part of her being saying the opposite.

The disparity between the two became even more pronounced when Miss Pilkington extended a graceful, gloved hand and led Vera to one of the many mansions that lined Madison Avenue. Miss Pilkington stopped in front of one made of white stone. Light gleamed from a three-story turret, creating tiny beams of rainbows that leaped from leaded-glass windows. It didn't flicker, though, with the dance of candles that kept Vera company at night. It was steady. No doubt from bulbs that were only now becoming commonplace in public buildings.

What a luxury to cast away darkness with a mere touch. To avoid the danger of fire if one fell asleep before snuffing it out. The rich didn't know difficulty. Miss Pilkington would never know hardship.

Would Angelo be living in this palace once they were married?

Vera shuddered. She could not imagine him leaving behind his beloved newsstand for gilded rooms and crystal doorknobs.

She slipped her hand into her pocket and rubbed the cold stone that had not been drowned in the icy waters of the fountain.

"Here we are," said Miss Pilkington as they approached a sleek black automobile parked in front of them. A short-statured chauffeur smiled and tipped his hat before opening the door.

Vera let out a gasp that she hoped was inaudible. She'd sworn to herself years ago at the advent of the automobile that she would never step foot into one of the contraptions. Her father had nearly given his life for the tunnels that crisscrossed the city deep below them. The least the residents of Manhattan could do was use them as they were intended. Or maybe that was another hallmark of the Pilkingtons of the world: never to be one of the moles who burrowed into darkness and shot across the terrain in metal compartments purchased by the blood of sandhogs like her father.

Their loss. Vera found such beauty underground in the stations lined with tiles of all colors. Art for the everyday man. She imagined herself to be a great mosaic artist—or any kind of artist—and kept under the sofa a box of drawings in which she'd penciled miniature rectangles that came together to form scenes.

"Miss?" the chauffeur asked, interrupting her silent soliloquy. Miss Pilkington had already seated herself inside the automobile and gestured for Vera to join her.

Maybe one ride wouldn't do any harm. She was still a subway girl.

She slid into the seat next to Miss Pilkington and couldn't help but run her hands along the supple leather. Her fingers explored the embroidered grooves that seemed to serve no purpose other than beautifying the compartment.

The chauffeur shut the door behind her and walked to the front of the car. His seat was on the exterior, exposed to the elements. He rubbed his hands and blew into them before placing them on the polished wood steering wheel. Vera wondered if Miss Pilkington noticed such things.

"You'll have to excuse me," she said in the lyrical voice that matched everything else about her. "I prefer to walk, as it isn't such a long way. But Maioglio's closes in just over an hour, and I thought that this might save us some time."

Vera could have told her which line would take them there quite quickly, but she had to admit some respect for a woman who openly eschewed the casual use of the vehicle.

They turned onto Sixth Avenue, bypassing the always-busy Broadway. The driver made a left at Herald Square. Buttoned-up shoppers carried packages as they walked out of Macy's. Remnants of snow lingered on the awnings, creating sagging pools. Vera had once seen one rip after a rainstorm, drenching a passerby just in front of her. She watched to see if it might happen again, but everyone escaped intact.

Penn Station arose in her view just a moment later, making her heart skip as it always did. Its majestic columns. The twenty-two stone eagles. Angelo's newspaper stand.

It wasn't visible from this side, and even if it had been, they were moving at a pace many times faster than her normal walk. But he was surely there.

And no longer hers to hope for.

"I'm terribly glad I found you today. Angelo told me that you often walk in that park, and there you were on my first try. Have you ever taken a drive in an automobile?" asked Miss Pilkington, breaking the lullaby of street sounds that were muffled by the glass.

Vera looked down at her hands. Her chewed nails, bitten last night as she cried herself to sleep over this unexpected turn of events. If she had elegant gloves like the lady next to her, she could have hidden them. Just as she wanted to hide all of herself in this moment. She still didn't know what she was doing here or why the lady would have wanted to seek her out.

"No, Miss Pilkington. This is my first time." *Nein,* she thought. Her native German had largely been forgotten. But she felt like a child after weeks of believing she was a woman. What did putting her hair up in a bun signify except the pretense of something hoped for?

"Never mind the 'Miss Pilkington' bit. If we are to be friends, you must call me Pearl."

"Pearl," whispered Vera.

"Yes. And may I call you Vera? I have only known you through Angelo as 'Kid,' but a young woman such as yourself deserves to be addressed by her name."

Vera looked away from the window for the first time, expecting to find a condescending look on her companion's face. But instead Miss Pilkington was the epitome of sincerity.

A wellspring of pride rose in Vera's heart at the notion that such a stylish person had just called her a young woman. Miss Pilkington's—Pearl's—eyes seemed earnest.

"Of course."

"And what is your surname?"

"Keller."

"Vera Keller. What a lovely name for an equally lovely woman."

Had she read the words on the page, Vera would have been convinced that she was now being patronized, but still no such hint appeared on Pearl's face.

Pearl placed her hands on Vera's, warming them in an instant.

"I do hope that you will consider me a friend. You mean a great deal to Angelo, so naturally you mean a great deal to me."

Vera felt the first tingle of tears but held them back. “Yes, Miss Pilkington.”

“Pearl.”

“Yes, Pearl. I do hope that we can become friends.”

“Excellent. And what perfect timing. Here we are coming up to Maioglio’s now.”

The row of brownstones seemed ordinary enough. Eight steps to the landing. But the stoops were vacant. They looked different from the ones on her street. Where she lived, there was almost always a crowd of people spilling out from the inside. Children playing jumping games. Adults playing cards. And when all the room was taken up, they would sit on orange crates or any other container that could be found, smoking cigarettes and complaining about politics or the weather.

These stoops were gloriously silent. Enough that she could feel the stillness of the snow that was expected this evening.

“Come, my dear,” said Pearl. She placed her hand on Vera’s back as they started up to the restaurant. “Let’s get inside. I have something to ask you.”

Chapter Five

"Miss Pilkington, hello. Welcome again to Maioglio's. Such a delight to see you."

A thin, mustached man took Pearl's hands in his and kissed her on the cheek.

"Sebastiano," she said. "This is my friend Miss Vera Keller."

The man greeted Vera in the same way. The stubble on his face felt coarse against her skin but not unpleasant. It must be how fashionable people greeted one another.

"Miss Keller. You are most welcome here."

The man spoke with an accent that reminded her of Angelo's, though it had a slightly different lilt.

"Is Vincenzo here today?" asked Pearl. "He promised to make me an *espresso* on your new machine next time I was in."

"No, my brother is off looking at new locations with an estate agent."

"Don't tell me you're moving."

"Well, not yet, at least. But he is always thinking about expanding either into a second location or just a bigger one. Maybe near Broadway where all the theaters are going in or maybe on the west side."

"I'll follow you anywhere, Sebastiano. You know that. No one makes risotto like you."

"Ah, you are in luck, then, Miss Pilkington. We have the most delicious truffles that came in, and we're serving them with large prawns over risotto."

"Perfect." She turned to Vera. "I assume you don't mind if I order one for each of us?"

Vera did not know what risotto was, let alone truffles, and trusted Pearl to make the selection. She'd never eaten in a restaurant like this, though she'd gazed through windows at diners who laughed and conversed over glasses of wine. A world so close but one that might as well have been thousands of miles away.

Sebastiano led them to a small table in the back. Vera followed Pearl's lead in placing the cloth napkin across her lap. Pearl slipped her gloves off by pinching the tips of the fingers one by one and loosening them first. Vera watched every detail, every movement, marveling at the ease with which Pearl made such gestures. Vera was certain that she would fumble over such things.

When her routine was complete, Pearl leaned in. "Caruso dines here when he is in town."

"Caruso?" Vera asked.

"The opera singer. The Metropolitan Opera is not too far. He never fails to stop at Maioglio's. I've seen him here twice already."

Vera remembered now. Posters of *Rigoletto* years ago and others since. She wondered what it would be like to go inside. She'd seen pictures of the grand balconies and golden proscenium. To be dining in the room that such people would come to made her nervous. She clasped her hands together, staving off the instinct to bite her nails.

"Want a bit of gossip?" Pearl leaned in as she spoke. "Some years ago, Caruso was arrested at the zoo. He pinched the behind of a woman in the monkey exhibit. He blamed it on a monkey but was fined ten dollars when no one believed him."

Vera gasped audibly both at the image and at someone like Pearl Pilkington relaying such a tale.

Pearl's smile was wide, and Vera had the feeling that she might have told the story as a means of breaking the ice. Their eyes met, and Vera relaxed.

Pearl grew serious. "You may be wondering why I asked you here."

Vera nodded with the intimidation of a schoolgirl. She did indeed think that it was unusual.

"Of most importance, of course, is the fact that you are very dear to Angelo. He says you're like a little sister to him."

The word stung Vera's ears. She didn't want to be his sister. But how could she expect to be anything else?

Pearl continued, possibly noticing her confusion. "He's told you about Stephania, didn't he?"

"No." Vera's heart beat with a sense of foreboding.

Pearl put a hand to her mouth. "Oh, dear. I didn't mean to say something I shouldn't. But now that I've started, I hope Angelo can forgive me. You see, Stephania was his sister. His *real* little sister. She would be just a bit older than you are now. She drowned at Brighton Beach when she was just five years old. Angelo had taken her out for a swim, but she got caught in a current. He still weeps just talking about her. I imagine you came along not too many months after it had happened. Sweet young girl with a scraped knee. And Angelo so thoroughly remorseful for what had occurred."

It was all she could do to stay composed. Vera had known none of this. She'd never heard the name Stephania. Or known that he'd had a sister. She'd always assumed that Angelo saw her as a friend. Someone to have adventures with and break the boredom with during slow times during his shift at the family newsstand. But that wasn't it at all.

Vera had been no more than a proxy for a dead girl he couldn't save. A substitute. She'd basked in his affections, thinking that they were real, but they were probably no more than guilt-filled attempts to pour attention onto the first child to come along.

She felt deceived.

Although maybe that wasn't fair. What friendship existed that didn't fill a need of some kind? Friendships might be built on a desire for companionship, company, laughter, solace. Was it really so terrible that Vera was some kind of alternate for a beloved sibling? Had she not felt love and regard from Angelo? It was her own fault for ever hoping for more, for something that was so obviously impossible. He had never given her a reason to hope for more.

"So you see," Pearl said, breaking into her thoughts, "you're like family in a way. And as I am not close to my own, I am grateful for any opportunity to create one for myself."

Vera wrung her hands under the table. Besides her parents, Angelo was the only family she had known. Why not include Pearl in her small circle?

"Of course," Vera answered timidly. Sometimes conviction followed the saying of things.

Pearl clapped her hands in a ladylike way. "Excellent." She smiled. "I have no sister of my own, so you will be mine as well. And now, my second reason for seeking you out."

Vera couldn't imagine what more there could be.

"I don't mean to be indelicate," Pearl said, "but Angelo told me how your mother died."

"My mother?" Vera whispered. That had not been what she expected. If anything, she thought that Pearl might have been luring her here to this luncheon with the intention of telling her to stay away from Angelo now that they were engaged. Though how she would think that Vera could ever be some kind of competition, she didn't know.

"Yes. At a shirtwaist factory, if I am correct?"

"Yes, but not in the fire at Triangle last year. It was long before that."

"Exactly. Angelo told me that she died of exhaustion. Long hours. Bad working conditions. Collapsed on the floor and never woke up."

Vera nodded again, holding back tears.

Pearl reached across to her. "Oh, dear. I *was* indelicate, wasn't I? I'm always being told that I speak without thinking, that I'm hopelessly brash, but it's just because life is too short to waste it away on social pleasantries when there is so much work to be done."

Vera looked up. "Work?"

"Yes. That is why I wanted to speak with you today. Your mother was one of many poor women who died in factories. Unfortunately, they didn't get the attention that they so desperately deserved, and then it took a tragedy like what happened at Triangle and the loss of a hundred forty-six souls to draw attention to the deplorable conditions that exist all over Manhattan. You see, Vera"—Pearl pulled a handkerchief from her purse and dabbed her eyes—"I was there."

Vera sat up straight. "You were there? At the Triangle?"

Pearl nodded. "Not at the building itself. I was lunching not far away at Washington Square Park when we heard the alarms. I could see smoke from the restaurant windows. I ran outside to see what was happening, and it was the stuff of nightmares. Flames, screams, and—" She paused and took a deep breath. "Women jumping."

Vera's own heart clenched. She had heard the stories, but not from one who had been there to see it. "Women jumping," she echoed under her breath. It was too terrible to think of, let alone to have seen.

How did one decide in that moment that falling to one's death was a better option than facing the fire?

Pearl's voice quavered. "Here I was enjoying a lunch that I didn't have to work for, served on china, and tea in silver, and suddenly there was the horror of watching fifty women—can you even imagine?—plummeting from the ninth floor."

She wiped her eyes again, this time with a buttoned sleeve. "I won't say any more. I didn't even mean to go into that, especially when we are enjoying such a nice day out together. But sometimes I can't help myself. I will never forget them, Vera, crumpled as they landed on one another. And I knew then that this life of privilege that I enjoyed—much due to workers just like them—was over as I knew it. I could not live with myself if I didn't try to do something."

Vera nearly reached out her hand to comfort Pearl but held back, fearing that their friendship was too new for such a gesture. She wanted, too, to know what Pearl's family thought but dared not ask. Pearl raised the subject on her own, though.

"I joined other women who had already been fighting for unions and safety. Clara Lemlich and Rose Schneiderman and Pauline Newman. Much to the embarrassment of my family, I might add. Big businessmen like to watch out for one another. My father told me to stay out of their company, but I've never been one to listen well."

The names meant nothing to Vera, though she'd heard the word *union* spoken in her home years ago.

Pearl took a breath. "There I go again. Vera, if we are to be friends, do not hesitate to interrupt me. My mother tells me that I speak faster than a locomotive, and I daresay she's right."

Sebastiano approached holding two small cups on saucers. "Espresso for the ladies, my compliments." He set them on the table. "Your risotto will be ready any moment." He walked back toward the kitchen.

Vera watched the genteel way Pearl picked up the cup and did the same. It was hot, but Vera didn't flinch. She inhaled the steam that rose from it and felt immediately intoxicated by the aroma. Surely it tasted as good as it smelled. She put it to her lips and grimaced at the surprise of its bitterness.

Pearl laughed. "Espresso isn't for the beginner. I should have warned you. You might want to order it in the future with steamed milk foam. Angelo likes it that way. He calls it *cappuccino*. It's named for the Capuchin monks with the brown robes and their shaved white heads."

One could always rely on Angelo knowing little things like that. But Vera did not interject to point out the obvious: it was unlikely that she would ever be able to afford to dine in such a place again.

"I advise you to finish it, though," Pearl continued. "Stiffens you up and gives you fortitude for hours and hours. And as I said, there's a lot of work to be done, so you'll need the reinforcement."

Vera sipped at it again, letting it just brush her lips until she got used to the taste. It felt like a rite of passage—this was a drink for a woman, not a girl.

"Anyway, let me tell you about the work and how you fit into it." Pearl finished the last of her espresso before Vera was even a quarter of the way done. "Basically, the horrifying working conditions in factories—not just the shirtwaist ones—became too much to ignore, and it brought about the oddest marriage of people. Clara, for example. She's a socialist from Ukraine, and one of my good friends." Pearl pulled a cigarette out of her purse and held a match to it. She curled her lips in a rosebud manner and made a nearly perfect circle out of the smoke.

It was such a glamorous gesture, and Vera thought that perhaps she might buy some and try to imitate it. Cigarettes were not too much of an extravagance, and Vera allowed herself so little as it was.

Pearl tapped her ashes into a tray. "Clara introduced me to my first husband, may his soul rest in peace. The man was a socialist at heart, and although I'm born of blue-blooded capitalists, I did learn a thing or two about bridging the two worlds."

The espresso caught in Vera's throat, and she coughed. "Husband?"

"Yes, I'm sorry. I must have given you a shock. I'm a widow, and the mother of a little boy to boot, but I don't suppose there's any way you would have known that, as we only just met. So, here's the story briefly. Ready to keep up? Dear old Owen Bower captured my heart when Clara took me to see him on his soapbox, railing against Tammany Hall. He'd once been a ward boss for them, gathering votes from immigrants, but he grew tired of the corruption he saw. He was what people call *charismatic*, and I was not the only young woman enthralled by him. I'd like to think that I stood out for more than my beautiful clothes, but I think he was intrigued by a society girl who liked his message. We married, I argued with my parents, then I had a baby, and shortly after . . . Owen was killed by a passing motorcar."

"Pearl, I'm so sorry! How awful!" Vera reached a hand across the table. There was a sisterhood to grief. She'd seen enough of it with her parents to know what it felt like to force a smile through the pain of loss.

"It *was* awful. The motorist didn't stop and was never found, but it was a luxurious vehicle, according to witnesses, so I suppose it's only fitting that he died at the hands of the very people he spoke out against. It made a martyr of him. My grandmother saw me through that time, and it's her house that I live in on Madison Park. Wanted to rehabilitate me from my pedestrian ways. My parents barely spoke to me, and we've only just begun to talk again."

She took a final long drag of her cigarette and ground the end into a tray. "Well, that will probably change now that I'm marrying Angelo. Dear Angelo. He's nothing like Owen. The absolute opposite, in fact. My husband was brash and passionate and sometimes reckless." A look that could only be described as wistful passed across her face, though Vera could not tell if it was meant for her former husband or her future one. "Angelo is just goodness through and through without the chip on his shoulder."

Vera's heart beat faster at the sound of his name. She'd almost forgotten about Angelo during their exchange, enthralled as she was by her companion. Pearl's description indeed sounded like the Angelo she knew. He sold newspapers to everyone who came by his stall. The rich, the not so rich. He treated them all the same, and more than once she'd seen him slip a chocolate bar into the hand of a passing child who couldn't afford it. She smiled at the thought.

But there was one question that had been weighing on her. She'd thought she knew everything there was to know about Angelo. He'd worked at the family newsstand ever since he was her age. Served at Mass on Sundays. Played bat-and-ball games with his cousins in his free time.

How had he met Pearl?

She asked, hoping the wobble she felt in her voice wouldn't betray what she felt.

Pearl explained. "Well, the Italians are usually reluctant to join unions. Most of them plan to go back to Italy when conditions are right, or they're just here to send money back to Mama. So they work hard and don't get involved in politics. But people like Angelo want to change that and convince them of the opportunities here. It starts with unionizing and later voting. He was volunteering at an event, and I met him there. My Lord, my family's going to call me a slummer when they find out about him. Maybe they'll hope for another automobile accident and pray that the third time's the charm."

She must have noticed the horror that Vera felt rise from her chest.

"Oh, my, I was being uncouth again. Please don't think I feel so casually about dear Angelo. I love him dearly. Lost my head about him. He came along just as I was feeling so lost without Owen."

Remorse pierced Vera as sharply as any sword over not knowing about this side of Angelo. How many chances had she missed in all these years to ask him about his interests? She'd assumed that he was as plain in his pursuits as she was—eking out a living, taking care of family. She mourned the loss of not having joined him in such endeavors. Maybe she would have liked to do noble things, too.

But how could one afford to be noble when their kind could barely afford to prepare the next meal?

She wanted to know more, but she couldn't ask Pearl about Angelo without fighting tears. So she changed the direction of the conversation.

"And doesn't the estrangement from your parents bother you?" Vera couldn't imagine being separated from Mutter and Vater by choice.

"Please don't misunderstand what I'm going to say," said Pearl. "But this is just one of the things that divides our given, well, classes."

Vera tried not to wince. There were a thousand reminders every day of the division of the haves and have-nots. Adding to that litany was not necessary.

Pearl lowered her voice. "There is no true comparison to be had here, and I know that. Please know that I am not trivializing of those less fortunate than I have been. They are what I am giving my life for. But growing up wealthy isn't everything you might imagine. Our house is so large that my parents' bedrooms were on separate floors even from one another. They never stopped calling my room 'the nursery,' and I had a nanny until I left home and married Owen. Father was away for business most of the time, and Mother is a socialite with a calendar that rivals the president's. If I had been a son, it would have been different. But I wasn't born with the correct parts, I suppose. We women have lost that lucky coin toss. So I grew up lonely. Loneliness is its own poverty."

Vera wanted to point out that loneliness didn't make you go to bed with an ache in your belly from having to skip a meal, but Pearl seemed earnest in her words.

"So now you can see why I was drawn to Owen and then Angelo. I created my *own* family. Working together for a cause is a bond tighter than blood, in my opinion. Clara and Rose saw me through my childbirth, while my own mother didn't even send flowers."

It was heartbreaking that a woman would shut out her daughter and grandchild so thoroughly. Maybe there *was* a certain poverty in riches. Maybe this kind of understanding that Pearl was trying to create across the classes was exactly what would heal the divide.

"And this is where you come in," she continued, sitting up straight. "I want to ask you to join this sisterhood. The stakes are higher than they've ever been, and I'm going to be called away more and more to help. I thought of something that might benefit us both."

Pearl leaned in, and Vera responded in kind. She held her breath, anticipating what Pearl might be asking of her. To join the cause? To attend rallies and register voters? It might be exciting. And she warmed at the thought of a lady like Pearl Pilkington choosing her among so many to assist in the work.

"You see, Angelo runs the newsstand, and my boy, William, is too young to attend school. Angelo doesn't want to live in my grandmother's house, and I agree with him on this point. But I've insisted that we accept the stipend she's offering us. Without it, I would have to stay at home with William, and I wouldn't be much use in the field. I'm offering you a job, Vera. It will get you out of the factory and put my son in the hands of someone Angelo trusts."

A wave of disappointment washed over her as she understood she was being offered a job as a nanny. Was she not meant for any more than staying at home with someone else's child?

Then again, there were ten thousand girls in factories all around the city who would sell their souls to trade places with her for this kind of opportunity. To get out of the appalling conditions of heat and sweat and fatigue. To have one charge who probably napped half the day. Maybe in the free time she could take up painting in earnest. Or read books.

It wasn't heroic, but it sounded far more comfortable than the life she had.

Maybe deliverance came incrementally. The first step for her was getting out of the toil of a factory. The daughters of her future might dare to get an education. And the generations beyond that? It wasn't even possible to imagine.

Those things might be out of her reach, but she could do her small part now.

And it would mean seeing Angelo every day. Though she feared that this might be more than she could bear, watching him with his new wife. But the hours, the cold, the heat in the factory. It could not be turned down.

"I would love to," she found herself saying with sincerity. "I am very grateful that you thought of me."

Pearl clapped her hands. "*Benissimo!* As Angelo would say. You've made me truly happy, Vera. I know William will be well cared for, and it will free me up to work on the votes."

"The votes?" Vera asked.

"Votes for women."

She'd read headlines about it. It was such a thing to hope for—that women might one day be considered equal to men. But it seemed impossible to go up against centuries of convention. Pearl spoke as if it were an inevitable thing, though. And in her company, Vera could almost believe it.

Sebastiano reappeared with piping-hot bowls of something that looked like rice. It smelled unlike anything Vera had ever encountered.

"Thank you," she said.

He spoke in that accent that reminded her again of Angelo. "The house specialty. Have you ever eaten Italian cuisine?"

She remembered the cannoli and gelato she'd shared with Angelo over the years. "Only the desserts."

"Ah, the young lady has a sweet tooth? When you are finished, I will bring you a *bonet*. Guaranteed to be the best dessert you've ever tried. *Delizioso*." He kissed his fingers.

Pearl smiled. "If you keep spoiling us like this, Sebastiano, you may quickly become my favorite of the Maioglio brothers."

"At least there are only the two of us. And I can overtake Vincenzo in my sleep."

"We'll see about that."

He shrugged his shoulders as he returned to the kitchen, and Pearl turned to Vera once again.

"So where was I? Ah, yes. Votes for women. The next stage in our cause."

Chapter Six

"What do you think your papa would like for Christmas?"

Pearl and Angelo had married just weeks ago, and in Vera's short time working for them, she admired how Angelo had taken on the role of father to little William Pilkington.

Vera finished buttoning the boy's coat. It seemed expensive—probably a gift from Pearl's grandmother. Though spending so much on something that a child of his age would outgrow in months was unfathomable to her.

"T-t-train."

"A train? I like that idea. Maybe we can find a wooden one so we can sand it down and paint it for him."

He remained silent, so she pressed on. "Do you have a favorite color? Mine is yellow. Like the sunshine. But we can make it any color you like."

The boy gave a hesitant smile. It was not like Pearl's—her mouth was wide and her son's was thin. Vera could just see the tiny teeth peek through his lips. Maybe he took after Pearl's first husband, Owen.

"B-blue."

"Blue? A wonderful choice. My second favorite. Then that's what we will do."

Now that Pearl had gone down to the market and Vera was alone with William, she had a chance to look around. Pink curtains framed the two windows that faced Thirty-Third Street. A teakettle with rose-shaped decorations sat on the stove top, and a white lace cloth lay over the table. It was not merely tidy—there was an aroma of perfect cleanliness that smelled of lemon and lavender.

There was scant evidence that two boys lived here as well—William and Angelo.

Vera put her hand out, and after some thought, William took it. Poor thing. To have moved so recently from the comforts of his great-grandmother's home on Madison Park to this apartment and to have a stranger hired to look after him must seem bewildering to one so young. She had no experience with children, but Vera wanted desperately to give him the kind of love she'd received from her own parents.

She wriggled the yarn from the zipper with no noticeable damage to the sweater. "All done, William. Aren't you handsome? Shall we go downstairs and meet up with your mother?"

Pearl had suggested that they join her at the Christmas market a few blocks north. The suffragettes planned to stand at every entrance and hand out brochures and sashes to anyone who would take them. She'd hoped that Vera could bring William down to see the tree lighting and join her for a cup of hot cider.

Vera locked the door behind them and tightened her grip on William's hand.

The walk would have been brief, save for the boy's slow pace and his wonder at the things around him. To Vera's delight, he pointed out the stone eagles atop Penn Station. "There are twenty-two of them," she told him. "I've always loved them, too. Ever since I was around your age."

Maybe the eagles held a bit of magic that entranced children, and the lucky few who did not become jaded with time still retained fascination with their stone charms.

"G-g-go w-walk around?" he asked.

She'd noticed his stutter from the start but followed Pearl's lead in overlooking it. Maybe it was something he would outgrow.

"Not today, William. But let's do that sometime, shall we?"

A double-decker bus drove past them. Its open top was sparsely filled, and people gripped their coats to stave off the cold. William looked up and waved, and a few kind souls waved back, delighting him.

After stops to watch a window washer, a woman's parasol getting swept away in a breeze, and the steam of a smokestack, they reached Forty-Fourth, and Vera saw her new friend right away. Pearl's white sash almost disappeared against her cream-colored jacket, but there was no mistaking her. Her very presence lit up her surroundings.

"There you are!" Pearl caught sight of Vera and William and called them over. "Hello, darling," she said as she stooped down to kiss her son on the cheek. To Vera, she asked, "Did you find the money I left on the table so that William can buy a present for Angelo?"

"I did. Thank you. He wants to buy him a wooden train that we can paint together."

Pearl laughed. "How funny. And I was thinking something like new mittens or a scarf. Angelo needs a new scarf. His wool one is frayed beyond repair, but he still insists that it has years left in it."

Vera could have knitted either of those for him and rather liked little William's idea. It was heartfelt, though not practical.

"We can get something like that instead," she agreed.

Pearl didn't answer, as she had turned to a table full of Votes for Women sashes and pulled one from a pile before facing Vera again.

"For you. I think this pink one brings out the rosiness of your cheeks." She placed it over Vera's head, adjusting it so that the words were perfectly visible. "There you are. You're an official suffragette now."

Vera warmed at the gesture. A sisterhood that she'd never imagined for herself. She didn't know how someone like her could really contribute, but it was nice for someone else to think so.

Pearl spoke to her companion at the table. "Miss Voorhees, I'm going to walk around the market for a bit. I'll be back before lunchtime."

She linked arms with Vera and held William's hand on her other side. "I know I promised apple cider, and we will find some, but I saw the most darling chestnut seller a few booths over. He looks like Santa Claus with his full white beard. There—can you smell them roasting?"

The scent indeed preceded them, and Vera looked longingly at the stalls they walked past until they got there. Not because she wished to have enough money to buy anything. Instead, she envied the ability of these artists to create so freely and sell their wares. Beaded evening bags with colorful flowers, framed canvases depicting scenes of faraway places, ceramic pottery with items both useful and decorative. The people looked happy as they discussed their work with prospective buyers.

But there was a glaring disparity. The artists were almost exclusively men. The purchasers women.

Vera traced her finger down the Votes for Women banner and believed in it for the first time. Getting the vote might not have an immediate impact on her, but what if it opened the way for women to be the artists behind those tables? The men to be the ones to shell out coins for their creations?

Maybe—dare she hope?—she could be one of those vendors someday.

"N-n-nuts," stammered William as they approached the Santa-like seller. Vera thought he might have even better sales if he donned a red suit and hat. But Pearl had promised that Santa Claus himself would make an appearance later that afternoon, and perhaps the effect would have been spoiled if there were more than one.

"Yes, dearest," said Pearl. "We'll take three."

She handed six cents to the man and passed out the bags.

Vera held the paper bag to her nose and inhaled its hearty warmth, a memory overcoming her of Mama holding her hand the week before she died as they shared a bag of roasted chestnuts from a vendor outside their apartment.

It was the last time she got to be alone with her mother.

"Thank you," she said to Pearl.

She closed her eyes, bit into the hot softness of the nutmeat, and nearly cried. It was beautiful how a taste could stir up your emotions. But maybe it no longer represented loss. Maybe instead it promised hope. When she opened her eyes again, Pearl was looking at her.

Pearl. Her new friend. Recently married to Angelo.

Such a recipe for jealousy. But it was impossible not to like Pearl, despite the circumstance.

"What do you think?"

Vera smiled. "I love them. They're delicious."

A woman who seemed to know Pearl stopped her to ask a question, so Vera crouched down to William's level and noticed that he was just staring at his bag.

"Are they too hot for you?"

William looked forlorn, and Vera wanted to leap in and rescue him.

"Here. Let me help you." She pulled one from its bag and pried her finger through the crack in a shell. A flood of steam burst forth, and she blew on the chestnut until it cooled.

"There we go."

The hint of a grin began to grow on his face as he took the nutmeat from her and popped it into his mouth. It spread into a full smile that reached up to his eyes, and with this one gesture, Pearl's son won her over thoroughly.

They got through half the bag of chestnuts this way before Pearl turned to them again, the other woman having walked on.

Pearl grabbed Vera's hand and looked at her with earnest eyes. "This is how it happens, Vera. Every woman counts. Every single one. You see, by asking about this sash, that woman now knows about the rally we're planning in Greenwich Village, and she will invite friends. If she invites five friends and they invite five friends, it spreads. We're not yet a wildfire, but we are a kindling that is quickly being fanned across the city. And the city is only the beginning. We plan to secure votes for women all around the country."

Vera's chest swelled. Pearl had a way of making her feel as if she were every bit as important as the next person, even in a world that said she was lesser than most. She stroked her sash again, and she understood then why Pearl could walk away from so much opulence.

No diamond around her neck could shine brighter than this simple ribbon draped across her.

"Thank you," whispered Vera.

"For what?" Pearl pried open a chestnut and popped it in her mouth. She made a face at William that caused him to giggle.

"For—for everything."

Pearl put her arms around Vera's shoulders. "This is only the beginning, my friend. The world is changing, and we're going to hurry it along."

They were fortunate to have found one perfect wooden train engine in the vast Christmas market. Vera had begun to despair that they could find the toy that William wanted to give to Angelo. Pearl suggested many other things they passed—a felt hat, a pocket-watch chain, a shoe-shine brush. But William was adamant, and at last they found a carpenter who made not only chairs and tables but also toys out of odd remnants from his bigger work.

The man put the train into a paper sack, which William clutched to his chest.

"Would you like me to hold that for you?" asked Vera, fearing that he would lose it in the crowd.

"No."

"Don't mind him," whispered Pearl into her ear. "He's reached the age where *no* is his favorite word. Let's let him win this one. It's Christmas."

A voice behind them spoke, the one that Vera had loved for most of her life. "Well, well. Who are these two beauties illuminating an otherwise gray day?"

Pearl and Vera turned to find Angelo grinning at them.

He kissed his wife on the cheek and hoisted William onto his shoulders. Vera slid the paper bag from William's hand, as he was now occupied by the arrival of his new papa.

"You're just in time, Angelo," said Pearl. "We were going to grab a little lunch before I head back to the booth. Would you like to join us?"

A nearby stall advertised hot clam chowder, and they each bought a bowl and found a bench under a snow-laden tree. William grimaced at the steam, so once again, Vera blew on his food to cool it. But he grew restless while waiting and pulled at her to go see the carousel.

Angelo winked and came to Vera's rescue. "Will, do you see this bag here?" He held up a sack and waved it around. "One of my regular clients came by today and brought this as a gift. I was going to wait until we got home, but I think you should see it now."

He opened the bag and pulled out a long popcorn garland.

"It's for our tree," he said. "But I think you could take a few bites if you like."

William looked at him with an expression that said that he thought popcorn on a string was a ridiculous thing. But he put a hand out and yanked one of the kernels from it. He held it in his hand and turned it around. Then a smile grew on his face, and he threw it at Angelo.

"William, no—" Vera started, but Angelo put a hand up. Never losing William's gaze, he pulled a popcorn bite off the string and threw it at the boy's forehead. William giggled.

Pearl spoke up. "No reason the boys should have all the fun, Vera." She pulled off a piece and threw it at Vera. It bounced off her nose and into her soup, sending William into a fit of laughter.

"That's what we're doing?" asked Vera. Without their seeing it, she'd already been untangling several pieces from the string and collecting them in her hands. "Then let's do this right!" She threw them in an arc, hitting Pearl, Angelo, and Will nearly at the same time.

"I'm going to get you back," said Angelo. He tossed a handful at Vera, and she pulled a piece from her perfectly constructed bun.

Back and forth, they dismantled the garland and ignored the stares of people around them. There were more than four million people in New York, but right now, it was only the four of them—Pearl, Angelo, William, and Vera—launching popcorn at one another. Upping the stakes with the oyster crackers that had been served with their soup. Pearl took a handful of those, ground them into dust, and sprinkled them into everyone's hair.

It was the most fun Vera could remember having in months. She'd been so burdened by her confusing feelings and sense of place among them, but it felt wonderful to be a part of something. To have a sense of family, since hers had broken so long ago.

When they'd run out of food and finished their soup, Pearl stood up and wiped the crumbs off her jacket.

"Well, darlings, this has been a delight. But I have to get back to the booth. I told Miss Voorhees that I'd switch off so that she can get lunch. I doubt anyone will have as nice a time as we did, though."

"One cup of hot chocolate," insisted Angelo. "We haven't tried that yet."

Pearl grinned. "There's always 'one more' in your book, isn't there?"

"The key to happiness. One more chapter. One more minute. One more cup of hot chocolate."

"Some of us have important things to do," she said.

Her cheeks were red from cold and laughter, but Vera had seen this exchange between the two of them before: Angelo making light of things, Pearl never straying from her mission.

"T-t-tree," William said, pointing from the perch he'd just taken on Angelo's shoulders. Vera looked in that direction and saw an enormous tree in the circle.

"Join us," said Angelo to his wife. "Just for half an hour." But Pearl declined.

"I promised I'd get back. You all have a wonderful time and tell me about it when you're finished." She turned and disappeared as the crowd of people closed in on where she'd been standing.

"It's just you and me, then, Kid." Angelo winked at Vera and then looked up. "And you, little buddy. Shall we go see the tree with *Zia* Vera?"

Zia. Angelo had begun using the Italian name for *aunt* ever since introducing her to the boy.

Vera forced a smile. She could do this. She could figure out how to be just friends with Angelo again.

They pushed through people who were stopping at the various stalls and made their way to the Christmas tree. It would not be lit for many hours, but already, men on ladders were clipping on the candle-holders. William wiggled until Angelo set him on the ground, and then the boy ran over to a box of the metal clips and picked one up.

"No," Vera started, reaching for him.

"It's all right, ma'am." One of the workers put a hand up. Vera had not yet been called "ma'am" over "miss," and she felt quite grown-up next to Angelo.

"What a handsome young man. Would you like to help me with these?" The man took the clip from the box and showed William how to fix it onto a branch. Wonder struck, the boy repeated the action until he got it right and looked back at Angelo and Vera for approval.

They applauded. "Wonderful!" And Vera felt for a moment like they were their own family. That William and Angelo were hers and it was a glimpse of what her life might have looked like if he had never met Pearl.

"You must be mighty proud of him," said the man.

"We are," said Angelo. And Vera silently agreed that there was no need to offer more explanation.

"Can I get a photograph of him? It would make a good picture for the newspaper. Young boy helping to ready the Christmas tree."

Vera looked at Angelo, uncertain whether she was able to give this kind of permission, but Angelo had already shaken the man's hand and said yes.

The man opened his satchel and pulled out a black case. He unlatched it, and an accordionlike stem stretched out. At the end was a lens. He held it still and pressed the lever that made a clicking sound, which Vera assumed meant that the job was done.

"Why don't you two stand on either side of him?"

Vera hesitated, but Angelo grabbed her hand and pulled her toward the tree. William sat by their feet, engrossed in his task.

"A little closer together."

Angelo and Vera were shoulder to shoulder, and she felt nervous next to him, as if she had not ever been so close to him before.

She glanced at him once as the man snapped a photo, then hurriedly looked back at the camera.

"Mighty good. Going to be a lovely photo," he said.

Angelo started to bend over to pick William up. The man walked over to the tree with a pair of scissors and snipped one of the decorations off it.

"Mistletoe. For you and your lovely missus here. May you have a lifetime of love and an abundance of children like this one."

With Christmas less than a week away, Pearl had fewer activities with the suffragettes and insisted that Vera spend the time with her father, while still giving her the same pay.

"A Christmas bonus," she'd said. No such thing had ever been offered at the factory, and the best one could hope for was to come in a few hours late on Christmas Day. Vera accepted gratefully.

She was glad to not have to see Angelo after the incident with the mistletoe. She hadn't been able to look in his eyes after it had been said, so she wasn't sure how to even read his expression. He had grown silent, though, and the rest of their outing was quite perfunctory as they let William select a gift for Pearl. A velvet jewelry box that was intended to go along with a necklace or some such thing. But William had found a rock that he wanted his mother to have and begged to put it in such a case. It had cost half of what Angelo gave him to find a present, so they spent the remainder on warm muffins that they ate in almost complete silence.

She had left with a promise to visit his newsstand on Christmas Eve, as had always been their tradition.

Vera sidestepped a patch of ice, one of many that were stubbornly staying put despite a rare day of sun. She had three parcels under her arms. She'd made good use of her week, reading to Vater as he took his many naps and listening to music on the radio as she knitted, knitted, knitted. Three sets of scarves and mittens. Green for Angelo, white for

Pearl, blue for William. She'd made a set for Vater and planned to give it to him tonight, following the German custom of opening presents on Christmas Eve.

There was just enough space in their apartment for a tiny tree, and she saved every year for some toffee and yarn and a fresh strudel. There were never any presents underneath it for her—not since Mama died. Though Angelo always thought of her and gave his Kid a gift. But he liked to see her open it. Hair ribbons when she was younger, books as she got older.

Angelo planned to close up early today and was just starting to put away his stock as she approached.

He beamed when he saw her, and she was glad that their freeze had thawed. "*Eccoti!* There you are, Kid. I was losing hope."

"I'm sorry. A neighbor came by, Mrs. Sullivan. She checks in on my father when I'm with William. She'd made a fruitcake, and it was difficult to pull away."

"Of course I understand. I was going to head up that way and find you. We wanted to ask if you'd like to spend the evening with us. Pearl is trying to make a ham. And I do say *trying* because, poor girl, she was not raised in a kitchen, and the first one burned. But the second one seems to be coming along."

A lump formed in Vera's throat. She imagined sitting with the three of them, dinner set on the table. A fire in the fireplace. How absolutely cozy. But it felt like an intrusion to consider it.

"Thank you, but no. That is time with your family. It's your first Christmas together. And don't you usually go to Mass in the evening?" She'd joined him and his parents for midnight Mass several times, and once for the *Festa di Ceppo*, where they joined other Italian immigrants for the burning of the Yule log.

Would Pearl participate in these events now that she was his wife? Or would they spend Christmas Day at Madison Park with Pearl's grandmother?

"Not this year," he said with no explanation. "But come to the apartment tonight. You *are* family, Kid. You always have been."

She had always envisioned being part of his family in such a different way.

"I should be with Vater," she said, though she wanted with all her heart to say yes.

"*Va bene.* You'll be missed. But you'll have to think of us, because these are for you to put under your tree."

He handed her three packages, all wrapped in white paper and tied with red ribbons. One said, *To Mr. Keller*, and Vera was grateful that he'd remembered her father.

"It's not much," he said, watching her look at it. "Some handkerchiefs for him. The other two are for you. William picked out that one, and the one with the silk flower in the ribbon is from Pearl."

Both were oddly shaped.

He pulled out another from under the counter. This one was wrapped in newspaper and tied with green string. "And this," he said as he placed it in her hands, "is from me."

Vera smiled inwardly.

His finger brushed against the side of her hand as he gave the package to her, and a shiver ran through her body, though it was an innocent enough gesture.

The gift was rectangular in shape, the size of a book but much lighter.

"Should I open it now?" she asked.

"Nah. Put it under your tree. Save it for the morning."

She said her goodbyes and handed him the gifts she'd made, running off before he could give her a friendly hug that would make her cry.

She couldn't wait until morning. She opened the gifts when she returned home. Not because she was impatient—gifts meant little to her. But because she needed to recapture the joy of the holiday after feeling a sense of loss all day.

Each one brought a smile to her face.

A set of watercolors from Pearl. A wooden eagle from William, presumably from the same toy maker at the market.

And from Angelo, a framed picture of a newspaper cutout. There they were, in front of the Christmas tree. The mistletoe, not yet plucked, was hanging above their heads. And the two of them were looking at each other, the camera having captured expressions in a moment so brief that an onlooker might not have seen it. But here it was, immortalized. A look of love on each of their faces.

Or was she only imagining it?

Chapter Seven

March 1913

"V-V-V-era!"

Little William Pilkington threw his arms out wide as soon as he saw Vera. In the few months that Vera had known Pearl's young son, his stutter had not improved. Pearl paid it no mind, saying he'd outgrow it. Vera kept her doubts to herself. She spent far more time with him, but she believed that despite Pearl's frequent absences, a mother knew what was best.

She dismissed any thoughts to the contrary by reminding herself that Pearl was fighting for a higher cause. What was one little boy in comparison with the millions of women who needed someone like Pearl to be their beacon? Their savior? And it wasn't as if Pearl had abandoned William. Leaving him in the care of Vera put him in doting arms that showed him love every day. Vera swelled with pride at the gift of supporting the cause in this way—and in escaping the work of the factory.

At Pearl and Angelo's apartment, if she was cold, she would just layer on another blanket or pull William's warm body next to hers as she read him stories. In the factory, the foreman griped about the cost of coal, and she didn't own enough sweaters to fight the chill. Just before she'd left, a girl one table over had caught pneumonia and never returned.

She especially appreciated the additional time she got to spend with Angelo, who stopped into the apartment nearly every day for a short lunch. It was easy to imagine, when the three of them sat at the table over a soup she'd just made, that they were the family—husband, wife, child. But every time she allowed herself an indulgence in that illusion, it was quickly pierced by the reality that brought a fresh pain. If things were any other way, it would bring heartache to Pearl, whom she loved and admired. So Vera tried to detach her emotions from it all and think of it as a job. A nice one that had gotten her out of the factory. Nothing more.

But whenever Angelo walked by her, when she saw the affection he had for his stepson, Vera's heart tightened almost to the point of breaking. Sometimes his gaze seemed to linger on her, and his touch lasted just a second longer than necessary. Or did she just hope that to be the case?

Vera noticed that Pearl's fine clothes had begun to show wear. The tips of her pastel skirts were now colored by thin coats of dust from the streets, no longer hand-washed by meticulous servants. The lace frayed in places; missing buttons were not generally replaced, and if they were, it was with inexpensive mismatches.

Whatever stipend she received from her grandmother, it didn't go toward personal luxuries. But Pearl always had a spare coin to leave for Vera to take William out for an ice cream or a new book.

He was the sunshine in Vera's world. And today, they had a big outing planned.

"Will!" she responded when she'd closed the door behind her. The boy threw himself into her arms, and she spun around as she picked him up. It had been four days since they'd seen each other. Vera's father had taken a turn for the worse and she'd been forced to stay home with him. The dementia released horrible profanities that she didn't want William to hear.

"How's your papa doing? What did you do together yesterday?"

"L-l-l-lollipop," he said, holding up five fingers caked in stickiness.

"I can see that." Vera laughed. "Looks like strawberry. That was my favorite when I was your age. Although I called it by its German name. *Erdbeere.* Your papa calls it *fragola*."

Vera loved how Angelo always encouraged her to practice her German and even to learn Italian. It was uncommon in the immigrant communities as they struggled to be seen as Americans.

She leaned over and smiled. "Your papa gives you lollipops when you go out with him?" She was happy for his sake that Angelo had so enthusiastically taken on the role of father.

William nodded.

"Let's go wash up before breakfast," she said, leading the boy over to a basin on the bureau.

The bedroom door was cracked open. William must have crept into bed with Angelo again in Pearl's latest absence. The boy was afraid of the dark and wanted to sleep near him whenever possible.

She saw Angelo stir under a mountain of blankets. It was early March. Vera's shoes were wet from walking here in last night's snow, and the chill of the basement apartment made her shiver.

How warm it seemed in there.

If she'd been a great beauty or a witty conversationalist or a heroine like Pearl, perhaps the empty side of that bed would have been hers instead. But she was just plain Vera Keller.

Her hand rested on the doorframe, and she knew that no matter how hard she tried not to, she did love him. She loved him more than breathing—but she also loved Pearl too much to ever do anything about it.

Crash! Vera turned and saw that William had knocked over the water basin.

"Shh, shh, shh," she said, placing a finger over her lips and racing to him. He'd soaked himself in water and wailed until she made her way to him.

She curled him into her arms. His plump legs wrapped around her, and she thought once again that he fit her like a puzzle piece.

"Don't cry, Will. Zia Vera's here." She whispered this so that Angelo wouldn't wake.

As she rocked the boy back and forth, the rise of maternal feelings rushed through her and she worried, as she had of late, that she might be taking Pearl's place in Will's heart. She knew she'd been hired because Pearl planned to be away frequently—marches, legislative sessions, rallies. Maybe Vera just didn't know enough about the world. Maybe that was what all this meant for women. That they could be in the home with their children or choose to be somewhere else.

Vera knew what her choice would be. Home.

But she'd met women through Pearl who seemed to want something different, and it excited her to be part of these changing times. Vera attended rallies when she could, staying in the background with Will while his mother shone like the light she was. She taught him to applaud when Pearl spoke, wave when she walked by.

Today was March 2. Pearl had now been gone for nineteen days, having left from Hudson Terminal with a contingent of men and women who intended to walk all the way to Washington, DC, to preach Votes for Women at the inauguration of Woodrow Wilson. Angelo, Vera, and William had joined Pearl at the station. They blew kisses into the air as she passed. She looked regal in her long wool coat, her sable stole, and her wide-brimmed hat. Vestiges of her old life that proved useful armor in this battle, tucked away for special occasions. She wore a white Votes for Women sash across her chest and a yellow rosette on her lapel. Angelo had handed her a walking stick that he'd purchased for her journey.

They'd received postcards from Princeton and Philadelphia and Baltimore as she made her way down the 225 miles.

The general is a warhorse if there ever was one, Pearl wrote, referring to Rosalie Jones, just one of the fixtures of the movement. *We'll be meeting up with the colored women's suffrage group in Laurel. The cause is for everyone, and I am happy to march with my sisters from all over. Our feet are blistered, our hands are red and bare from the terrible cold, but our mission is just and right, and it is our very suffering that we hope will convince the president to consider our message.*

Vera loved receiving these notes. The newspapers were filled with editorials written by men who opposed the rise of the women and the friendship between races. Pearl's postcards offered hope for a world that didn't differentiate between Germans or Italians or coloreds or Poles or Russians. Pearl had explained that votes for women would open the door to votes for all.

And maybe that would mean that immigrants like her father could be employed in work that put them behind desks and not below the river's sludge. It was too late for him. But not for those who would come after.

Today Vera and the boys would travel by train down to the capital to join Pearl in time for the march. William was going to love it. She couldn't wait to see his face when he saw the real train engine. Just like the one he'd bought for Angelo.

She rubbed a hand across Will's wet arm and pulled a towel off the counter to dry him off.

"It's a bit early for a swim."

Vera turned to see Angelo standing behind her, arms crossed. His shirt was only buttoned partway, and the sight of him made her feel more like a woman than she ever had. If there were no Pearl, she might be so bold as to walk over to him and press her body against his and kiss him the way she did in her imagination.

"Someone was sticky," she said. "I'll change his clothes before we leave."

"You don't have to do that. Come to Papa, William." The boy reached out to Angelo and grinned in his arms. "Remember that blue sweater that Zia Vera knit for you? You look so handsome in it. Let's show her how handsome you are."

While they went into the bedroom to get ready, Vera looked around at all that had been left undone. Plates and cups and laundry sat waiting for washing. Jam was smeared across the table as if Will had used it as an art palette. She smiled. It was good to be needed, and her boys needed her.

In no time she'd washed down all the surfaces, cleaned the dishes, and even shelled some walnuts to pack as a snack. They were going on an adventure to meet Pearl in Washington, DC.

"Well, well, well," Angelo said as he and Will returned. "What do we say to Zia Vera for taking care of us?"

"Ta tu, V-V-Vera." Will's smile never ceased to warm her.

He reached his arms out to her, and she set him on her hip as if he'd always belonged there.

"You don't have to do this," Angelo said. He placed a hand on hers, and her skin felt warm where he touched it. "I know your pops hasn't been doing well. Not that we don't want you, though. Of course . . . we want you."

She had to remind herself to take those words at face value. The vision of someone in love could distort things like a prism, refracting the tiniest of lights into hundreds of beautiful rainbows. But it was an illusion. A parlor trick.

Vera didn't tell Angelo that she'd skimped on her own meals for weeks and endured runs in her stockings to save the money to have the woman across the hall check in on her father every few hours while she was away.

"I want to go," she assured him. "You know you'll need help with William. Especially if you want to spend time with Pearl. I've never been to Washington, DC, but I can only imagine that it's amazing." She paused. "You should take your wife to dinner."

The more she said it, the more she would convince herself.

The trio walked into the crisp air and Vera wondered, as she had every morning recently, how Pearl could endure the long walk. It was cold—the kind where your nose felt raw and your toes would no longer wiggle in your shoes. Perhaps the very act of walking kept them warm enough. She hoped.

And for Pearl, at least, the drive of justice seemed an elixir more intoxicating than any brandy that could warm the bones. Her cause, yes. But maybe her addiction as well. An absinthe of advocacy. Vera suspected that Pearl would trade her very life for suffrage.

Just four blocks later, Angelo, Will, and Vera ascended the first of the steps that led up to Penn Station. Its grandeur never ceased to amaze her. Angelo had given her a gift on her fourteenth birthday—a copy of each newspaper that bore headlines about its opening—and she'd read every word until they were memorized. From how it was fashioned after the opulent Gare d'Orsay in Paris (whatever that entailed, but it sounded wonderful) to how they'd sent a twenty-three-foot piece of tunnel to Jamestown, Virginia, to show it off at the three hundredth anniversary celebration of the colony's founding. She'd read elsewhere that when the railroad first dared to construct tunnels under the shifting silt and bedrock of the rivers, people thought that they were as likely to go to the moon as they were to be successful.

The moon, indeed.

To love Penn Station the way Vera did seemed, at first, a betrayal of her father. After all, he'd lost his life—or the wholeness of it, anyway—to its marbled halls. But when she confessed this to Angelo, he assured her that her love for Penn Station was, instead, a testament to her father. He gave his youth so that people like them could marvel at the station's beauty and follow its tracks to places that had been mere pinpoints on maps. Angelo was so good at making ugly things sound resplendent. Maybe because he lived around printed words, he knew how to say them so well.

Vera felt differently. Her father hadn't had the luxury of appreciating beauty. He'd taken the job as a sandhog because there were few others for "Krauts," and it was an act of desperation to feed his family.

Even as he'd begun to show the symptoms of the bends, he insisted that it had been worth it. "Long after we are all gone, princess, this station will stand. And I had a little something to do with that."

Optimism. It was something her father and Angelo had in common. Something she loved about them both.

Something she missed lately from her father.

For her fifteenth birthday—just a few years ago—Angelo had given her a sketchbook and pencils and encouraged her to draw every last corner of the place they loved so much.

In only three months, she'd covered every sheet, and there was not a corner or surface of the station that she didn't know.

The following Christmas, he'd bought her more paper—"for painting," he'd said—and one jar of red paint.

"I'll buy you the rainbow as I can afford it, Kid," he'd told her. And he followed through weeks later with a blue the shade of the evening sky. After blue had come yellow, and with the three colors she was able to mix them and begin to paint in purples and oranges and greens.

Which became a necessity, because there were no more paints after that.

After that, he'd met Pearl.

She'd spilled tears over the half-finished piece she'd been working on, depicting the sun setting behind the station. She had planned to give it to Angelo, but it was now relegated to a corner of her apartment, covered with a sheet so that she didn't have to look at it.

As they approached the steps, Angelo managed to put Will over one shoulder while carrying a bag for each of them.

"Look over there," he said to Will. "There's Papa's newsstand across the street. Your cousin Marco is going to look after it while we're gone. Did you know that that's where I met your zia Vera when she was just a few years older than you?"

Will just sucked on his fingers and buried his head in Angelo's shoulder.

"You remember that, Kid?" he asked, reverting to the nickname she loathed. "And the rocks. Remember how we used to kick the rocks down the street? You were pretty good."

Vera thought of the rocks that she'd plunked into the bottom of the fountain. But the action had not dulled the memories, as she'd hoped in that fervent moment. She'd gone back a week later to retrieve them, but they were gone. She had only the one left.

But she could start a new collection.

"Maybe when Will's older, we can teach him how to do it," she suggested.

"*Una buona* idea, Kid." He grinned. "I'll bet we'll get him up to speed as soon as his legs are just a little longer."

She warmed instantly at Angelo's smile.

"After you." They'd reached the top of the stairs, and he was holding one of the heavy doors open for her. She looked up at the eagles atop the building—a practice that had nearly become a superstition after her father once told her that they were his favorite part of the station. A mother gone in body, a father in spirit. But the granite eagles would stand forever on their perches, and no one could take them away from her.

"Can you walk for me, big man?" Angelo set Will on the ground, and he and Vera each took one of the child's hands. *A happy little family,* Vera thought. At least for the next few hours until they arrived in Washington.

Will looked up as soon as they entered the main waiting room, reflecting the awe that still stunned Vera to this day. From the first time she'd seen it, the vastness of Penn Station made her feel her own smallness, as if she were standing in front of an immense ocean. Knowing that long after her time on earth, this place would be here to be enjoyed by the many generations after her. If an embrace could be built in marble, it would look like this.

Her parents had taken her here for her birthday before her mother died. They went to the café to order sandwiches and hot chocolate that poured like lava and was served in metal teacups. Papa let her pick a flower from one of the stalls. She chose a rose. And the three of them read off the names of the cities on the departure board and picked which ones they'd like to see someday.

Cathedral-like ceilings were adorned with concentric stone octagons, each one recessing deeper and deeper. A bronze statue of the railroad's late president, Alexander Johnston Cassatt, loomed over them. Vera remembered her father saying that Cassatt had died four years before the station was complete, the latest in a long line of railroad presidents who died while in office.

Cursed, her father had always said. But then, that could be the bends talking. Depending on the day, he either loved Penn Station for its grandeur or hated it for all that it had taken from him.

Vera didn't believe that such a place could be cursed, though. To her, the station represented beauty. Majesty. Sacrifice. Love.

It was no accident that it had been built by someone with the heart of an artist. Alexander Cassatt was the brother of Mary Cassatt, the painter known for her depictions of mothers and children. Vera had never seen one in person—it was her dearest wish to—but she'd read about them and tried her hand at sketching similar pieces.

She liked to imagine what it must have been like to grow up in the Cassatt home. Surely artistry and beauty must have been encouraged if the family produced two such accomplished people.

If Vera ever had children of her own, she would encourage them to pursue what they loved. It reminded her again of the importance of the suffrage work. So that her sons wouldn't have to toil in deathly conditions like her father had and her daughters might be able to paint if they so wished. Or do anything else they liked.

Was it possible that such a world could exist for them?

Pearl seemed to think so.

Light streamed through abundant windows in beams that showcased a flurry of dust specks. Will reached for them as if they were some kind of fairy powder. Like the stardust that made Peter Pan fly.

Her feet indeed left the ground, but not as she had hoped. A man carrying a large satchel knocked her over, mumbling an insincere "Pardon" as he hurried to his gate.

"Watch it," Angelo shouted in retort before putting out a hand to pull Vera up. She stumbled against his chest. He wrapped his arms around her and held her. She smelled his cologne. Sprayed, perhaps, for the benefit of his wife, but enjoyed in this moment by her.

It almost broke her. She'd been so good. So careful. Perfectly proper. But a thought she'd been pushing away raced to the surface as he consoled her.

Being near him was becoming too hard for her to endure.

"I should go pummel that man," Angelo told her. His face had reddened, and Vera felt herself blush at his defensive sentiments on her behalf.

"It was an accident," she assured him, pulling away. "We might do the same thing if we were late in catching the train."

He laughed. "Must be an Italian, then. Always rushing to get there at the last minute. But not my little German friend. I can always depend on you to keep me on schedule, Kid." He checked his watch. "Early, in fact. Are you hungry?"

"I packed snacks for us."

"Let's save that for the train and get a proper breakfast instead."

Vera thought of the coins in her bag. There were so few. *Never enough.* Her mother's words echoed in her head. A sit-down breakfast was an unnecessary extravagance.

"My treat," said Angelo, as if he could read her thoughts. "How about the counter over there?"

It was the same café where she'd eaten with her parents.

Vera's stomach rumbled at the delicious smells wafting from the restaurant under the arches. She nodded. Angelo picked Will up and took Vera's hand in his. *It's just a protective gesture,* she told herself. So that she wouldn't get knocked over again. But his touch sent a shiver through her body despite the gloves that each of them wore.

He didn't let go until they'd arrived.

A tuxedoed waiter brought them menus. The last time she'd sat in a restaurant and was handed a menu was when she went to Maioglio Brothers with Pearl.

Pearl, whose feet were probably blistered. She might be limping along the last few miles as far as anyone knew.

Traitor, Vera accused herself.

Friend, she replied.

He's married.

You loved him first.

But he loves her now.

Her interior debate raged back and forth throughout the meal, stealing her attention from Angelo's small talk. She smiled and agreed every time he paused to take a breath. But her heart wasn't in it.

Pearl.

Will.

Angelo.

After this trip, Vera had to consider that distance from them all might be the only thing to do to save herself from the daily wrestling of her mind. At best, the nearness created heartache. At worst, temptation.

She'd get a job in another part of town. Even go back to factory work. It was the only way she could be a friend to Pearl. The only way to properly love Angelo.

Because as she observed him now, the way he was smiling at her, the feel of his hand on hers, the feel of his arms when they'd just been around her—she wasn't sure that being a friend was going to be enough any longer.

Chapter Eight

Angelo and Vera gathered their bags. Vera felt as if she could barely move after such a meal. Eggs, bacon, biscuits, fresh fruit. In March! She was a queen.

Will looked drowsy, and this time Vera lifted him over her own shoulder. She felt his heartbeat against her chest, and hers beat with his, as if they were one. She thought of rousing him as they walked into the grand concourse but decided against it. There would be another day to share this magnificence with him.

The concourse looked as if it had been constructed from an oversize Erector set. Steel frames ran from ceiling to floor like giant metal stalactites. Stairs leading passengers from floor to floor were adorned with decorative trellises. Arches supported the weighty structure but resembled thunderclouds against the sky that oversaw it all through the glass ceiling. As if it were trying to compete with the room that they'd just come from.

Grand upon grand.

It wasn't enough to merely look up. Looking out, Vera saw the bustle of New York, even more frenzied than what one saw every day on the street. A clock hung in the center, a common meeting place for people who might otherwise get lost in the throngs. "Meet me at the clock" became a catchphrase between friends, lovers, coworkers.

The letters on the board were changed every few minutes to announce arriving and departing trains, heading to places that Vera could only dream of going. Places far away like Boston or Chicago. Places closer in like Poughkeepsie or Hartford.

And Washington, DC.

Vera's heart leaped when she saw that board. She'd been distracted all morning with Angelo and Will, but two truths remained, overwhelming her as she stood there.

She had never left New York. And she had never been on a train.

The subway, yes. But a train, no.

She had never walked down to the deepest bowels of Penn Station. Never stood next to the wheels that were nearly as tall as she was. The endless tracks. The smells tickling her nose. Her father once told her that the new electric engines were why Penn Station even existed. Prior to that there had been only coal-fed steam, but those engines had to be outdoors to vent the smoke. The routes had ended in Jersey City, where passengers would then need to board ferries to make it into New York. It was not uncommon for people to get sick on the choppy waters of the Hudson River. And Papa had told her that the river was dangerously congested with ferry traffic and other crafts. The Pennsylvania Railroad attempted to partner with its New Jersey counterparts to build bridges into the city, but no one was interested. So the advent of electricity created the engineering opportunities to dig tunnels deep underwater and save travelers from the uncomfortable commute. Sandhogs had existed long before her father came to it, tunneling under the streets to build the subway. But to do so under the water had been an entirely new and even more dangerous venture.

The statue in honor of Mr. Cassatt was well and good. But Vera thought the workers like her father deserved to be immortalized as well. Far beneath the opulent offices of its administrators, men labored in the dirt and muck carrying buckets of sludge from the rivers, constructing steel rings inch by inch over ten years. For what? So passengers could travel in and out of the city in grand ignorance of the undertaking that had given them that privilege. Did they know how lucky they were to move into other boroughs, where they could have large houses and gardens and fly under the water in their suits to their offices in the city, returning home in comfort to a warm meal prepared by a wife who hadn't died from overwork?

Vera didn't resent them for it. They were the very things she aspired to for her own children. But when she heard the commuters complain about the lateness of a train or the bruising on an apple or the lackluster performance of a dancer at the ballet, she wanted to grab them by their vicuña lapels and shout, "Do you understand what has been sacrificed to make all this possible for you?"

Vera understood why Pearl did what she did, and she was grateful to be included in it. It was not merely for women. It was for the voiceless to be heard over the cacophony of boardroom gavels.

She would travel through her father's tunnels today, returning home to him in a few days with new appreciation for what he'd given to her. What he'd given to this city.

"Andiamo." Vera shook off her thoughts at the sound of Angelo's voice. He'd loaded their bags and was holding out his arms to take Will from her. The boy awoke as he was passed between them. Vera stepped into the second-class car and followed Angelo to their seats.

"And here we are," he announced, pointing out two backward-facing seats. "William can sit on my lap. And, son, let's give Zia Vera the window."

Will stretched almost to the point of falling. "W-w-widow," he wailed.

Vera didn't mind relinquishing her seat to the boy. "Really, Angelo. Please give him the window. Will wants it more than I do."

"Are you sure?"

"I'm sure. But thank you anyway."

They configured themselves this way, but not for long. Will was too excited to sit on Angelo's lap. He wanted the seat all to himself. He squirmed out of Angelo's arms and placed himself right next to the cold panes.

Angelo apologized. "He knows what he likes. I'm sorry, Kid. We'll have to squeeze together unless we get lucky and no one takes their place across from us."

As it happened, two riders did indeed claim their spots, and Vera pulled her feet under herself so as to avoid touching them. *Sardines,* she thought. That was second class.

Will, Angelo, and Vera were hip to hip in the two-passenger row. She had never been this close to Angelo for this length of time, and her heart beat faster than ever. Her leg touched his; her arm, his arm. Her head sat at his shoulder. She was flushed with warmth.

It was sweet and it was unbearable.

He turned to her, his face so close that it would have been romantic if it weren't tragic. She saw every perfect imperfection, every bit of his beard that he'd shaved away this morning, only to peek through, darkening his skin. He called it the Italian Scourge, but she thought it made him look unbelievably handsome. She smelled his cologne again and it overwhelmed her, shooting sensations throughout her body that were unrecognizable but not unwelcome.

"Cozy?" he asked. He leaned his forehead against hers before pulling away.

"Mmm-hmm."

Vera wished that she understood the language of love. These kinds of affections seemed so intimate, as if his thoughts matched her own, but her father had done the same thing often enough—so maybe it was just a familial gesture that meant nothing more.

"Would you like tea from the dining car?" she asked Angelo, standing up before she could feel any more overwhelmed, and was relieved when he said yes.

Will grew weary of the view only an hour in, and Vera didn't blame him. The excitement that had built in her chest as the engine roared to life and the awe at watching the city disappear gave way to a blurred tedium as the train sped through an endless countryside. The starts and stops along the way became routine, save for a delay in Philadelphia when she thought, *I am only blocks away from Independence Hall.* How proud it would make her father to know that his daughter was so near to where the American dream was born. Though he was a poorly educated man, he used to read every night before going to sleep—usually the works of Benjamin Franklin or Thomas Jefferson. Sometimes he would recite a passage to Vera or her mother. In his states of delirium, Vera would read to him now, though she doubted that he understood it anymore.

Will became restless.

"Shh, shh," Angelo said, trying to comfort him. He took a metal toy train from his pocket. "I've been saving this for the right moment."

"I think that moment is now," Vera whispered.

"Me too." He held the train out to Will, but the boy swatted it with his hand. His face turned red, and a stench began to encompass the small space.

Vera and Angelo looked at each other with wide eyes.

"Is that . . . ?" he said.

"Yes," she responded. She took Will from Angelo's arms before either could protest and slung her bag over her shoulder. She rocked Will in her arms as she hurried down the aisle and through two cars to the nearest washroom.

These spaces had definitely been designed by men who never had to consider such situations. The tiny compartment barely fit the two of them, and she couldn't even close the door all the way. She turned around, deciding that it would be best to lay him across the sink.

He wailed as she placed his back against its metal edge. "I'm so sorry, darling," she cooed. "I wouldn't like that, either, but it can't be helped. Zia Vera will go as quickly as she can so we can get out of here."

She'd come prepared for such an incident and pulled the cloth diapers from her bag. She wet one of them, maneuvering Will away from the faucet, and wiped him down before replacing the soiled one with the new one. When she'd finished, she looked around but could not find a place to dispose of it. She considered the toilet, noting the sign that was hung above it: **Do not flush while train is standing at the station.** She wondered why.

We're not at a station, she thought, and put the diaper into the bowl and sat Will on the sink. As she pulled the lever above, a hole opened, exposing the rapid speed of the tracks below. The diaper fell to the ground. Horrified, Vera wondered if she'd made a mistake, but there was nothing else she could have done. It would have been unseemly to return such a thing to her bag.

She thought of Pearl, marching for women's votes. Maybe that would lead to women in industry. A woman knew how a women's bathroom should be designed. And this was not it, despite the token nod to femininity from the pink floral wallpaper that adorned the wall.

"Well, look at you!"

Vera jumped at the sound. Angelo stood in the doorway, his frame nearly filling it up.

"What are you doing here? This is the ladies' facility!"

"I came here to help, but I think I'm too late."

"Thank goodness for that. You would not want to see what I just saw."

"That wouldn't be the first time I've changed his diaper. My boy really is a champion, believe me."

Vera laughed. "Well, not just that, but look." She pointed to the toilet and pulled the lever. "It goes right down to the *track*!"

Angelo stepped forward to look, taking up all of what little space there was.

It was Angelo's turn to smile. "Well, of course it does. Where else would it go?"

She stood there and considered the options. "I—I guess I don't know."

"People romanticize train travel. But it's not all glamorous, is it?" Angelo asked.

The idea of *romance* when they were standing in such a confined place made her dizzy.

"No, it isn't," she lied and maneuvered herself away from the door to put some space between them.

Angelo took Will in his arms, and they walked back to their seats. Once again she sat arm to arm, leg to leg, shoulder to shoulder with Angelo, pushed together so tightly that they might have been one person.

He turned to her and said, "I really owe you. Thank you for taking care of that, Kid."

How she'd hoped that he would have said her name at last. "It was nothing."

Angelo looked in her eyes then, and she saw them widen. They seemed to get softer. "You don't like being called 'Kid,' do you?"

She didn't answer.

He placed his hand over hers, and she trembled at his nearness. He was so very close.

"I'm sorry," he said. "I think that name is long outdated. Look at you." His eyes glanced over the crest of her head as if he'd never seen her before. She felt her cheeks flush. "You're a woman now, Vera," he whispered. "A beautiful one."

They looked at each other, and she saw an expression in him that she had never seen before.

He pulled back suddenly, as much as the seating arrangement would allow. "I mean, sure you are. You can't be a kid forever, I guess." He stared out the window and didn't speak again.

She felt her blood pulse, announcing its might through every bit of her body, and she thought she might die from it. A blissful, enraptured death.

Although she had no experience with men, Vera knew with the intuition of a woman that this was no brotherly affection that had passed between them.

She rubbed her temples. *No, no, no,* she said to herself. *You can't think like this.*

But the bliss that he had noticed her. That he saw her as she was now, not as she had once been. In a way, it was all she wanted. This acknowledgment. Even if nothing more could ever come from it.

The train took a sharp curve, and Will wailed from bumping his head against the window, breaking the magic.

Vera busied herself with comforting Will. She could not look at Angelo. She feared that his eyes would reflect the longing that she felt so deeply, and she wasn't sure that she was strong enough to withstand it.

It was only right. It was only fair to Pearl.

Neither spoke again for the short duration, but she felt the rigidity of his body next to hers and heard him sigh a deep breath that sounded like an ache, a sound that echoed what she felt inside.

His resistance made her love him all the more. If either gave in to what she suspected they were both feeling, they wouldn't be themselves anymore. They would be the kind of people whom she had little respect for. It was their mutual sense of kindness, honesty, simplicity that had made their friendship so enduring. It was what they admired in Pearl.

But how long could such a thing last?

When her father read to her from the Declaration of Independence, he'd extolled upon the importance of *life*, *liberty*, and the *pursuit of happiness*. The beautiful formula that made America. He said that if you took away even one of those hallmarks, the whole country would crumble. Like a stool with only two legs.

She hadn't understood it at a much younger age. But she did now.

Pearl, Angelo, Vera. An evenly proportioned spirit of friendship among them could be something everlasting. But the weakening of any of the sides, the hint of imbalance, would collapse the whole thing.

Removing herself from the little family would give them the best chance to remain intact. Perhaps it wasn't supposed to be Pearl, Angelo, Vera.

It should be Pearl, Angelo, William.

Though she'd wrestled with the idea before, it was clear as day to her. To let them thrive, she needed to step away.

The realization frightened her. It would send her back to factory work. She would miss them all terribly. But it had to be done.

Already, she felt the loneliness of it swallowing her.

None too soon, the conductor shouted, "Union Station, Washington, DC." As the train pulled in, Angelo and Vera gathered their bags and stood. Their actions were perfunctory, as if this new recognition made them strangers rather than the dear friends they'd been. Vera sensed the shift in Angelo's demeanor. She would give anything to be "Kid" again, because at least he'd laugh with her and buy her gelato.

But it didn't matter, anyway. She looked over to the window and saw Pearl waving to them from the platform. Beautiful Pearl who looked just as fresh and regal as if she'd taken the train as well and not *walked* for weeks as she had.

Vera had little to give to Pearl.

But she had much she could give up.

Chapter Nine

"Darling!" Pearl's voice pealed like tiny icicles glistening through the brisk weather. Vera took Will from Angelo's arms. He gathered the bags and hurried down the steps of the train onto the platform. He embraced his wife and kissed her cheek before looking back.

Will squirmed and used his feet to push himself down Vera's body until she could no longer hold him. She supposed that he, too, would run to Pearl, but he did not. He held firmly on to Vera's hand, merely wanting to walk on his own. This little man chose her company while the bigger one rightfully loved his wife.

"William!" Pearl finally noticed her son, but he only gripped Vera's hand tighter at his mother's approach. Pearl's smile straightened at the rebuff, but she turned to Angelo and slipped her hand into his.

Angelo voiced what Vera was thinking. "How is our favorite suffragette? You don't look like you walked here all the way from New York."

"You might not have said that yesterday," she answered, smoothing her hair. Vera noticed that her hands were red and raw. "And I'm not going to show you my feet. They're quite blistered. But some donors put their money together and rented hotel rooms last night for all the walkers. A soft bed and a hot bath, and I felt as if I were living at my grandmother's house on Madison Park once again."

Angelo asked, "Is there space in your fancy room for a weary husband and eager son and a friend? Or will we be staying at the hostel where I reserved some rooms?"

The friend comment was a welcome thing. It reassured her that, despite the moment of tacit honesty that had passed between them on the train, Angelo knew his place as much as she did. That would make it easier. She worried that she couldn't be strong enough for both of them.

"Wouldn't that be a dilly, my lovelies?" Pearl said. "How grand it would be for us all to stay here. I've been offered the room for two more nights, and if it were mine alone there is nothing that I would want more than to have my family join me. But as it is, we are four women to a room, having asked the donors to economize and give the remaining money to the cause instead."

Of course she would have done that. Saintly, perfect Pearl. Vera immediately admonished herself for her fleeting resentment. Pearl had been nothing but kind to her. Mama had always said that jealousy was like a monster that ate up your insides, and Vera had realized over the past few months how true that statement was.

She didn't want to envy Pearl, who deserved every bit of support and kindness that could be given. To stay might turn Vera into a person she didn't want to be.

Angelo said, "Don't let us rob you of your place there. You've earned it. I can take Vera and Will to the hostel, and you can rest up for the big day tomorrow."

Vera held her breath. What was he thinking? This was the very time that he and his wife needed to be together.

Pearl touched his cheek. "And that makes you a dear. But no, I plan to join you at the hostel." She clapped her hands together and said that she had an idea. "I think we all deserve a little treat, though. The hotel has the most charming dining room where they serve ice cream in crystal bowls. Would you like that, Will?"

The child didn't hear her, as his attention was set on the man who was changing the letters on the arrival and departure board.

"B-b-b," he started. He closed his eyes and took a breath. "B." He opened his eyes and pointed to the word *Baltimore*. Vera looked up at Pearl, waiting for her to lavish praise at his accomplishment, but she had already turned around and was sweeping her arm across the cityscape, narrating to Angelo, stopping at the view of the milky-white Capitol building. It was indeed breathtaking, and Vera had never seen anything like it. But this was the first time that Will had identified a letter or slowed down enough to deliberately overcome his stutter. Vera found that to be an even more marvelous thing.

She crouched down to his height and took her hands in his. "That was so good, sweet boy. Zia Vera is very proud of you." She decided to distract him from Pearl's preoccupation by continuing the lesson. "And what about that one? Can you tell me that letter on top?"

She pointed to the next column on the board. *New York.*

Will pursed his lips and wrinkled his little brow. "M," he said on the first try without stumbling.

"So close, my love. It nearly does look like an *M*, doesn't it? But it's *M*'s neighbor, *N*. Can you try saying that one?" Her own mother had patiently taught Vera her letters and numbers and coins in much the same way.

He quieted once again before saying the letter with perfection. Vera squeezed his hands. Pearl and Angelo were watching by this time.

"How wonderful, William," Pearl said. "What a smart boy for learning your alphabet. Can you say that one?" She pointed to the top of the departure board.

Philadelphia.

"P-p-p-p-p-p." Will's sounds stumbled as if he weren't really giving the same effort.

"Almost, William. Keep trying."

"P-p-p-p-p-p," he repeated. Vera saw his face go red and recognized the look of anger that flickered in his eyes. Was it possible that for Vera he tried and for Pearl he didn't? Vera again chastised herself for her vice—Will's dual responses tempted her to feel superior, if only on this one tiny point.

"It's a *P*. But don't worry, William. You'll get it soon enough. Shall we go get some ice cream?"

What he probably wanted was a hug, some sign of affection from his mother. But as soon as Vera caught herself making such a judgment of Pearl, she engaged a method that she'd learned about in a Sunday sermon: replace a thought of bitterness with one of gratitude. It was much like the Glad Game, an idea in a new book out called *Pollyanna*. Vera sympathized with the character.

I am thankful, she told herself, *that while I had a mother for too little a time, she was affectionate toward me. Poor Pearl had only the example of a mother who required a proper silence around adults. She is trying. I know she loves Will.*

The thought immediately warmed her.

Pearl held her hand out to Will, and at Vera's hidden nudging against his back, he tottered over to her. Angelo took his other hand, and Vera walked behind the proper family of three.

They are not mine. But I am theirs, she thought. *I will be lost without them when I go.*

Vera kept a few paces behind them as they walked more than a mile to the Willard Hotel. Sometimes she caught a word that Pearl said to Angelo; sometimes the breeze carried it in another direction. Pearl seemed to know quite a lot about the city in so short a time.

"The Smithsonian," Vera heard as Pearl pointed to a building far to their left. It looked like a redbrick castle, complete with a glass turret that seemed befitting of royalty. She imagined that a lonely princess lived in it. A girl awaiting her one true love to overcome every obstacle.

But before her thoughts could get away from her, Pearl was on to the next item on the tour.

"The White House."

Vera looked ahead of her.

She'd seen many marvels growing up in New York City, but besides Penn Station, none caught her breath quite as much as the White House in DC did. It was simple in its design—a long rectangle with columns in front. It was not the ornate palace she'd imagined but a building of quiet humility. The Vanderbilts and the Rockefellers and the Pilkingtons of the world all lived in much grander mansions that were inaccessible to all but those of their class or those who served them. Yet the White House, though large in scale, seemed like it was constructed so that all people—even the Kellers and the Bellavias—might feel welcome in its presence.

Vera owned so little. But she felt as if she owned a piece of this. Hard-won for her by her immigrant parents.

Her mother died providing an income for her family. Pearl rallied to improve working conditions for people like Mutter and Vater. They were here today to give voice to the women both now and in future generations so that they could all make use of the opportunity that the White House represented. If someone like Abraham Lincoln could be born in a one-room cabin and go on to become the president, then maybe anyone could. Vera's future daughters or granddaughters. The notion exhilarated her. In New York, Pearl's ardent work sometimes seemed futile to Vera. But here it all made sense. This was possible.

She owed her loyalty to Pearl more than she'd ever realized.

Pearl had taken Will in her arms as they turned to the right. "That's where the president lives, darling. And tomorrow we'll have a new president. Woodrow Wilson. That's why we're all here. To tell him we want votes for women."

Will turned to Vera. "Votes for women," she repeated, lifting a loose fist in the air. He grinned.

"And here we are," Pearl announced. "Who wants ice cream?"

Vera looked up at a stunning white building, twelve stories high. It looked like a wedding cake rising above the ground. Or something like pictures she'd seen of Paris. The American flag was the only thing that belied that particular fantasy. It sat atop the building, its tips unfurling just enough to see it. She wondered if it was a new flag—the one that included all forty-eight stars since Arizona and New Mexico had joined the United States last year.

An idea struck her. She wanted to get a small, inexpensive gift for Papa. A memento of this trip. She would look for a flag to replace the one he kept pinned by his bed. That one was quite old—it had only forty-five stars, purchased when they first came to this county and Oklahoma was a mere territory. Now the country spanned ocean to ocean, uninterrupted. It was complete. There was nowhere else the nation could grow.

"Where's my Vera right now? Head in the clouds?"

She turned away from looking up to find Angelo standing in front of her, the frost from the train ride seeming to thaw. Pearl and Will had gone ahead up the stairs, Pearl hoisting him on her hip in motherly fashion and pointing out things that Vera could not yet see from here.

The words *my Vera* were not lost on her as she took Angelo's arm and climbed the steps at the front of the hotel.

She would always be his Vera, no matter what directions their lives took them.

Two attendants opened the double doors, and Vera felt as if she'd stepped into a dream. Or inside a jewelry box. The great hall dazzled with chandeliers dripping with crystals. Mosaic marble floors inlaid with flowers. Ceilings painted with scroll upon scroll. Velvet sofas. Stained glass. She almost didn't know where to look first.

Angelo placed his hand on hers and squeezed it. She looked in his eyes and felt in this moment that he was a little more hers than he was Pearl's. He would understand the awe of such a scene.

He leaned in, confirming her thoughts. "Quite a different world from the one we know. The street in front of Penn Station. No four-cent frankfurters from the roach coaches here," he said, referring to the nickname for the less reputable street food vendors. "These people must eat caviar and roast beef."

"And gold-plated chocolates." She giggled.

"Platinum-crusted steaks!" he added.

"Diamond-topped petits fours!" Vera felt her heart quicken as if she'd sprinted here from the train station. Angelo could always do that to her. She was grateful that her heart wasn't audible. It might roar like the train itself.

He grinned. "It would cost me ten years' work to buy something like that."

"And a lifetime for me."

They looked at each other, their smiles melting in unison. A wave of regret dimmed the sparkle that had temporarily illuminated Angelo's face. She wondered what he was thinking. Did it match her own thoughts—that they would be so well suited to each other, if only things were different? They came from the same place. They wanted the same things.

They lingered there, the children of immigrants scraping by an existence, standing in worn-out shoes on mirrorlike marble floors in a country that was theirs only by the charity of a copper woman in New York Harbor who welcomed the tired, the poor, the huddled masses. Vera wondered if Angelo felt the enormity of what it took for each of them to be right there, right in that moment.

The sacrifices of their parents. Enduring weeks on ships across a boundless Atlantic, praying that they would not be turned away from the land of milk and honey, only to find that it took seven days of backbreaking work to eke out a living that could only occasionally offer such simple items. Milk and honey were not promises. They were luxuries.

Vera looked up at Pearl, who had stopped and motioned for them to join her. She blended seamlessly into the opulent surroundings. She had given up much to marry Angelo and to march for causes she believed in. But it was the world she came from. She hadn't grown up with the ache of hunger, the freeze that could paralyze you in the winter, the heat that made you beg for death to come early.

Then again, she'd willingly descended to it. And that had to count for much.

In America, not only could the poor become rich but also the rich could become poor. Even by choice. And Pearl had chosen this. For love? For rebellion? For justice? Her motives didn't matter. She'd done it.

Vera, too, had a choice. She was choosing to leave them. Her part in the cosmic drama that intertwined true love with true sacrifice, almost to the point where they were indistinguishable from each other.

Wasn't that what both her parents had done? Sacrificed themselves to provide for the family?

Pearl was still holding Will's hand, and she'd crouched next to him to point out the ceiling. It warmed Vera's heart to see her make such a motherly gesture.

Angelo's words broke into her thoughts. "We'd better catch up. Besides, we vagabonds don't want to keep the ruby-coated ice cream waiting."

Vera wondered silently how they would be able to afford to eat anything here. She imagined having to scrub the kitchen floors when the management found out that they had no money.

The ice cream did not have rubies on it. But Angelo had not been far off in his jest. Vera ordered what she thought would be a simple dish of chocolate. But it came out in a large crystal bowl, as Pearl had somehow known it would. Three scoops. Topped with mountains of what Pearl told her was "European cream" and sprinkled with little red gems that reflected the light of the chandelier that shone above them.

"They're pomegranate seeds," Pearl explained when she saw Vera rolling one around on her spoon and staring at it.

"Yes," Angelo agreed. "I remember those from my childhood. We had a pomegranate bush in our town square. *Melograno.* It would start out as a red blossom. As it grew, it became harder and harder at the stem until it was a ball about the size of a fist. We'd crack them open, and inside you'd find hundreds and hundreds of those seeds. Just like what you're holding."

"Hundreds?" asked Vera, imagining what it might have looked like.

He nodded. "They were surrounded by this fibrous maze, and you'd dig them out a few at a time. It wasn't like eating any other fruit. It could take you an hour to eat a pomegranate. Halfway through, though, we'd get tired of the seeds, and my cousins and I used to spit them at one another. Or across a field to see who could spit the farthest. My cousin shot one right into my eye once."

Pearl laughed. "And I'm sure you're just waiting until Will is older so that you can teach the same things to our son."

"Of course! A boy needs to learn good aim."

Pearl leaned over and kissed Angelo on the cheek. Vera fumbled with her napkin, tracing her finger along its scalloped lines so as to avoid watching their intimacy.

Maybe there was a man in her future. She wouldn't shut the door on it. But the bar had been set high. Angelo was not only woven into her childhood but also offered her comfort and laughter and joy. As certain as she was that he belonged to someone else, she knew what it felt like to love a man as she did him, and she was not going to settle for a substitute.

Vera heard a bustling roar approach behind her. Pearl looked up and smiled.

"Ladies, how good to see you!"

Three women approached the table. Pearl made introductions, saying that they had been on the walk with her all the way from its start in

New York. Angelo used his napkin to wipe a dot of ice cream from his lip and stood to greet each of them.

"This is my husband, Angelo Bellavia. My son, William, and our dear friend Vera Keller."

Angelo rose and picked Will up in his arms. "Stand up, son. Let's shake hands with your mother's friends."

"Dianne Voorhees."

"Emily Banker."

"Irina Katalova." The last woman said her name with a thick accent like some of the Russian girls whom Vera worked with at the factory.

Each woman shook Will's hand.

"What a gentleman you have there, Mrs. Bellavia," said the one named Dianne. Vera remembered her from the Christmas market, of course, but was unsurprised that Miss Voorhees didn't recognize her in return.

Vera thought that the distance they'd covered in the suffragette march might have allowed formalities to drop and Christian names to be used, but perhaps the old habits of the upper class never really died. It was a luxury, perhaps, to speak that way. Not so in the kind of shirtwaist factory that Vera had worked in. On a good day, Vera could sit and sew buttonholes by hand. On a bad day, sweat from the summer sun pooled on their benches and pitchers of water were passed around from which everyone drank. You didn't share water and working conditions with someone and call them anything other than Fiona. Hedwig. Rebekah. In fact, Vera hadn't even known her coworkers' surnames, let alone used them.

It occurred to her that to know someone's whole name was like knowing the whole person. A surname implied history. Family. Geography. A given name implied intimacy. Familiarity. Shared hardship. The lower classes understood this. Family history meant nothing when you were fanning the girl across from you so that she didn't faint after twelve hours in an unventilated workroom. No one had ever called her "Miss Keller" except for the fruit seller, but at least she was no longer "Kid" to Angelo.

She realized she'd been musing while the women talked, and she caught the end of their conversation.

"What do you think that means for women," asked Pearl, "if our new president cancels the inaugural ball because he doesn't think dancing is 'appropriate'?"

"Well, not all dancing," said Dianne. "Apparently he doesn't like what he considers modern. You know, the turkey trot. Or the honey bug."

"Those wouldn't have had a place at a ball like that, though, would they?" said Pearl.

"I'd think a new president could have any type of ball he wants."

"Or none at all," suggested Angelo, who had been silent until now. "I suppose he can do whatever he wants."

Pearl nodded. "Well, so long as he supports votes for women, he can celebrate any way he likes."

The women voiced their agreement.

"But what that means, Mrs. Bellavia," Miss Voorhees continued, "is that the three of us are going to start back to New York right after the march, since the festivities are concluding earlier than expected. So the bedroom here at the Willard will be free for your own use tomorrow night."

Dianne Voorhees looked at Angelo as she said this and then back at Pearl. Vera thought she might have seen her wink but dismissed the thought. It seemed too inappropriate a gesture for a lady to make, but Vera did not pretend to know all the inner workings of that class of people.

"That sounds like great fun." Pearl pressed her hands together. "But I'm afraid I couldn't leave poor Vera all alone with Will in the hostel. It wouldn't be fair after they came all this way."

The eyes of the three other women landed on Vera as if a challenge had been given and was awaiting acceptance.

She took a deep breath. She wouldn't deny Pearl and Angelo this opportunity, but the women had robbed her of the chance to suggest it first. And she would have. She put on a smile that she hoped seemed gracious.

Vera turned to Pearl. "Of course you should take the room. You and Angelo never got to go away after your wedding. Let this be my gift to you. I'd be happy to keep Will so you can stay at the Willard together."

She tried to avoid any images of what this might mean, which was not terribly difficult, as she did not have any personal experience with the subject.

Pearl accepted without hesitation.

"Oh, Vera, you are too much of a darling. How sweet of you to offer." She linked her arm through her husband's and smiled at him. "We'll join you at the hostel tonight and then head back here tomorrow."

Dianne Voorhees intervened and put a manicured hand on Pearl's shoulder. "Mrs. Bellavia, do you really think that's wise? You've come all this way on foot, and we have the march first thing in the morning. I would think you'd want to be well rested."

She could tell that the woman was appalled at the idea of a lady like Pearl staying in such humble housing. Vera looked at her friend. Pearl's lips were tight. As if she wanted to say yes but felt that it wasn't right to do so.

Vera didn't know what to do, either. Pearl had more than earned the right to stay in the luxury of this place, but in doing so, it would cast Vera with Angelo and Will, prolonging the little fantasy she'd had of them as a family. And that felt like a betrayal of her friend.

But, added to the fact that Miss Voorhees was one of the most intimidating people she'd ever met and she didn't dare speak out against her insistence, Vera couldn't exactly voice that objection.

Vera glanced at Angelo, hoping for guidance. He stared right back at her, but she couldn't read his expression. Did he feel the same precipice that she did?

Here she had made the decision to remove herself from all temptation, and yet she was being thrown into it despite her best efforts.

Before she could speak, Angelo rubbed his chin and turned to Pearl. "Of course she's right. Vera and I are scrappers. We'll manage just fine with Will. In fact, I'll take him to the room in the men's wing tonight, and Vera can even enjoy a night off to herself."

Vera let go of a breath she hadn't known she was holding. Of course. He'd said that he had reserved two rooms. And it made sense that hostels separated the men's rooms from the women's. Maybe there was little to worry about.

"Then it's settled?" Miss Voorhees asked.

Pearl smiled. "I suppose it is! Thank you, darling."

"Excellent," said Miss Voorhees. "I'm sure you'll want to show your family around the city, but do be back by dinnertime if you can. Alice Paul is giving a reception in one of the salons here at the Willard. She's just moved here to Washington, and it would be so wonderful if you could join us."

Even Vera knew who Alice Paul was. A giant in the suffragette movement both in the United States and in Britain. Her heart skipped a beat at the thought of being able to meet such a formidable woman.

Pearl had the same thought and grasped Vera's hand. "Of course we'll join you. Thank you for the invitation."

The woman frowned. "I'm afraid it's only for ladies."

"I understand. I meant that Miss Keller and I will join you."

Miss Voorhees's eyes looked Vera over, up and down. "And how lovely that would be indeed. But unfortunately there is a certain attire that is required."

"I'll lend one of my dresses to her. I sent a trunk ahead on one of the escort cars."

But the woman shook her head. "You're much taller than her, Mrs. Bellavia, and I'm afraid she'd be uncomfortable in such a setting."

Vera felt as if she were back in Mr. Severino's butcher shop. She was clearly too sinewy for the company of people such as Miss Voorhees. Her companions, Miss Banker and Miss Katalova, were silent the whole time. Mousy in the shadow of a cat like Dianne Voorhees.

Pearl began to open her mouth, and Vera had no doubt that her friend would refuse the invitation in protest. To spare her the confrontation, Vera responded instead. "How kind of you to consider my feelings, Miss Voorhees, and I agree that it might be a better setting for Mrs. Bellavia to attend alone."

The woman smiled thinly. "Precisely. Wise girl. Here—here's a lipstick." She opened her drawstring purse and pulled out one of many pink containers.

A consolation prize. Like a coin thrown to a beggar.

It was red. Elizabeth Arden red lipstick. Ever since the cosmetics company founder donated hundreds of tubes to the suffragettes last year, the bright stain had become a symbol of the cause. Pearl only wore it during rallies. It looked artificial against her porcelain-white skin. And Vera had never even tried it.

She put her hand out to accept it in politeness, and Miss Voorhees turned back toward Pearl, Vera already forgotten. "Well then, we must be off. Don't worry about the ice-cream tab. Just charge it to the room. The benefactors were specific in their wishes to cover all the expenses at the hotel."

Angelo caught Vera's eye. Both were relieved, as neither had brought enough money for such an extravagance.

Light waned as Pearl, Angelo, Will, and Vera finished a small dinner near the Capitol building. Vera held Will's hand and lingered several paces behind the others. Pearl and Angelo were silhouetted against the glow of the streetlights. They walked closely but not touching, as they each folded their arms to brace against the ever-decreasing temperature. Vera pulled her thin coat around her neck and glanced down at Will to make sure that he was warm enough.

The scarf she'd knitted for him was holding its place, and he seemed to be unaffected by the chill. Children had such a talent for adjusting to the circumstances.

They stopped at the steps of the Willard, and Vera stooped down to Will's level. "Say good night to your mother," she whispered. She tapped his back to encourage him forward.

Pearl turned around and looked back down at them as she approached the doors to the hotel. "Are you sure about this? I feel so inconsiderate staying here and sending you all to the hostel."

"You deserve this," Angelo assured her. "We'll be just fine. It will be like you're home again."

He turned to Vera, and she couldn't help but agree. Pearl indeed belonged in a posh bedroom. And Vera would have Angelo to herself for the brief walk to the hostel, for the last time. Her chance to say goodbye, though she wasn't going to voice it.

The Hooley House sat three blocks north of the Willard, which might have been across the world, considering the chasm between the two. Where the Willard was illuminated at every window, the Hooley House was dark save for a rusted gaslight at the front door. Vera scooped Will into her arms. He nestled into her shoulder and sank limply into a quick sleep.

"Here you go, Vera," Angelo said as he opened a door on squeaky hinges. The use of her name made her feel guarded, though it was what she'd always wanted to hear from him. But given the day's events, it put them on an even playing field for the first time. Man and woman.

They stepped into a dim parlor. A burly man with sleeves rolled to his elbows sat surrounded by a cloud of cigarette smoke.

"Whaddaya want?" he asked.

"Two rooms, please," said Angelo, pulling out his wallet. "I've reserved them under the name Angelo Bellavia."

The man pulled out a file box and shook his head. "Ain't got nothing under that name. And we're all booked up."

Vera grew still. She had visions of them sleeping under the arches of Union Station.

"But I wrote ahead three weeks ago," Angelo protested.

"That's the postal system for you." The man shrugged and offered no apologies.

"Is there anything available? We could sleep on the couches over there."

"It's against fire code. Ain't nothing but one room, and that's for married folks. And only 'cause we got a cancellation."

Vera's heart stopped. It was one thing to sit on the train together. Another to have two rooms in the same hostel. But to share a room—nearly alone, save for a sleeping Will—she hadn't envisioned this.

"We're married," Angelo responded firmly. He took Vera's hand and squeezed it. She hoped that her face didn't flinch at this lie. What was he doing?

But Angelo's voice remained composed, though she felt his pulse racing through his tight grip. She didn't need him to speak to know what he was telling her.

Stay quiet. Let me handle this.

"Then why d'ya want two rooms?" The man crossed his arms.

"For the boy. I snore, and I don't want to wake him. Big days ahead. Historic times."

The man pulled eyeglasses from the top of his head and peered at Vera.

"I don't see no ring."

Angelo continued the charade and didn't slip out of character once. "She insisted that a plain aluminum band would make her happy, but I want nothing less than gold for my sweet wife. I just can't afford that yet."

Wife. For a fleeting moment, she let herself indulge in the word. Because it wasn't real. It was a means to an end. Surely it couldn't hurt Pearl to pretend for a minute that this was true.

"That's all you got? No proof? We do not tolerate any tomfoolery under this roof. *My* wife and I are God-fearing people. Not that it's my business who you go with, but if anything less than savory is what you're after, there's plenty of establishments that will welcome you."

"Please, sir," Vera said, deciding to support the playacting. Because she understood now what Angelo was doing—keeping them off the street for the night. It was cold out there, and flurries were predicted. "My husband is telling the truth. This is our child, William. We've traveled here to celebrate the new president, God bless him, and our son is so tired after taking him around to see the sights today."

The man hesitated, drumming his fingers on his counter. Vera turned so that he could see Will's peaceful face.

He nodded. "I suppose that will do. Just make sure the boy stays quiet. We aren't running a kindergarten here."

"Absolutely," said Angelo. "He's a good *bambino*."

Vera was certain she heard the man mutter the words *filthy Italians* under his breath, but as long as he would give them a room, it didn't matter.

The man pulled out a register, and Angelo wrote *Mr. and Mrs. Angelo Bellavia*.

Vera's heart raced at the idea of playing the role of Mrs. Bellavia in this farce. A silent send-off before she left him. The written record would probably be stored in an attic once it was filled, but she would know forever that somewhere, even under inches of cobwebs, she was listed as Angelo's wife.

She followed Angelo down a long hallway until they reached their room. The man had stepped in ahead of them and turned up the kerosene in a lamp near the bed.

One bed.

One. Bed.

Of course that's all there would be. This was a room for "marrieds."

She couldn't put what she felt into words. But if she had to paint it, it would be full of blacks and grays. Or a green shade made ashen by mixing in something darker.

She felt sick to her stomach. Was this a betrayal of Pearl? Did the sacrifice need to go so far as to sleep in the winter air? Did it count for anything that she and Angelo had not asked for this?

"Look, darling," said Angelo, never once betraying his part. But she knew him well enough to sense the tension underneath his words. "You can see the White House from the window. Won't Will be excited to see that in the morning?"

She avoided his eyes, fearing that she might confess the truth to the innkeeper in a rapid storm of apologies. She nodded instead and stepped forward to put the child on the bed.

The man mumbled a few instructions—water closet three doors down, no unnecessary noise, don't use too much kerosene.

When he'd left, Vera collapsed on the bed next to Will, making sure to position him squarely in the middle. But she shot straight up when Angelo sat down on the other side while he removed his boots. Goose bumps ran up and down her arms.

"Sorry about all that back there, *Mrs. Bellavia.*" He laughed but sounded nervous. "I didn't think either one of us wanted to sleep out on the street tonight. Will you forgive me?" He lay down on his side, propping himself up on an elbow. But he didn't look at her. He looked only at William, brushing the sleeping boy's hair with his hand.

"There's nothing to forgive. I don't think there was any other choice." She knew her own voice sounded stilted. Would Angelo think she was angry?

Or worse, would he suspect why she was uneasy with this dilemma?

And lead us not into temptation. She didn't go to church often, but she knew the prayers that everyone was supposed to know. It felt divinely unfair to be led right into the heart of the very thing she needed to resist.

"You were masterful," Vera said at last. She stood and walked over to the window. "As good as if you were an actor for a living instead of a newspaper salesman."

He hesitated before answering. "I convince people that they need the day's news or a cigarette or chewing gum. I convinced him that we needed the vacant room that he had available. Sales."

She laughed. That was her Angelo. Always making light of something so as not to worry her. "If that's what you want to call it."

"Call it anything else and I'd need to go to confession." His voice lowered.

She turned around and looked at him. "Angelo! I don't want to do anything that gets you into trouble."

"It was a small thing, Vera. And a necessary one. I won't go to hell for it. For other things, maybe, but not for that."

"I doubt very much that you're heading in that direction. You're—you're the best man I know, Angelo." She looked down at her hands. She couldn't say that straight to his face.

"Oh, Kid." He sighed, growing even more serious. "You give me more credit than I deserve. I haven't darkened the door of a confessional since—well, it's been a few months." He sat up and looked down at the floor. "I'm sorry. Vera. Not Kid. Sit down. Please." He spoke the words slowly and then reached for her hand. He pulled her toward him, sitting up and moving over so that she could have a place to sit. But he left plenty of space between them, no longer confined by a second-class train car.

"It's okay." She leaned on the bed's edge just enough to support herself and clutched the coverlet. She wondered at his admission but didn't press it. She knew Angelo to be a weekly attendee in the confession line, almost scrupulously devout, and thought it was odd that he had stopped.

"No, it's not." He grew very silent, enough that she finally looked at him in the dim light provided by an outside streetlamp. He had the strangest expression on his face. Like he was in pain. "I didn't realize, Vera. You're all grown up. I've only begun to see it lately. Too—um, too late, perhaps. But there it is."

Her breathing grew labored, and her head hurt. He was so close to saying the things she'd always wanted to hear. But she didn't want to hear them now. It would only make it harder. More confusing.

He didn't press on. Just left that small statement, that almost admission, hanging between them.

"Don't think anything of it, Angelo. When you see someone nearly every day, it's difficult to notice the changes."

"Don't be too nice to me. I don't deserve it." He was being unnecessarily harsh with himself. It wasn't as if they'd sought out this situation intentionally. And they were two adults who were perfectly capable of conducting themselves appropriately.

Yet here they were. She was sitting on a bed in a hostel room with a married man. One who had been as a brother to her despite her wildest hopes for more. She was the very definition of a libertine.

"Pearl told me about Stephania." Vera hurried the words out and regretted them right away. She hadn't intended to bring up his sister or open an old wound, but she was desperate to say something that deflected from the path they'd begun to touch on.

Because of Pearl. And Will. She had to put them first.

"She did." Angelo said it like a statement.

He sighed. Not the sigh of a man tired after a long day but of a person carrying a burden for far too long. Vera saw tears well in his eyes, but he wiped them away before they could fall.

She scooted closer, no longer thinking about what it meant to be a man and a woman sitting on a bed in a room far away from their home. She thought only of comforting her friend. For he was that above anything else.

"Angelo," she whispered. "I'm so sorry. You don't have to say anything."

He didn't speak at first, and she watched his shoulders roll into themselves before straightening. He took her hand, and she decided to ignore whatever that implied.

"You deserve to know. I should have told you before. But why tell that sadness to a child? And then here you are, no longer a child, so I suppose there's nothing standing in the way of talking about her."

Angelo looked into her eyes, and Vera felt as if her heart might shatter. With love. With pity. With concern. With anticipation. It was as painful as it was pleasurable.

"Stephania," he said, and held her hand a little tighter. "Yes. I had a little sister. I suppose Pearl told you what happened."

"She—she did," said Vera, not wanting to reveal too much and betray Pearl—even as she sat here with her husband. She understood the irony. "Pearl said that she drowned."

He ran his fingers through his hair. "It was all my fault. I was supposed to watch her. But she'd always been such a strong little swimmer. She said she was hungry, and a pretzel seller came by. He had only three left on his cart, and I knew that if I didn't buy any for us right then, we wouldn't have anything to eat until we got home."

He took a deep breath. Vera held on to his hand. It must be very difficult for him to talk about this. And it was the most vulnerable he'd ever been in front of her. "I told her to stay put, and she agreed. We were only a few feet from the shore, and the water came to just above her knees. I ran up to where we'd laid our towels to get the money, looking back with every step. But as I was giving the nickels to the pretzel seller, I couldn't see her. The sun was just starting to set and it was right in my eyes, so I didn't think much of it. I paid the man and ran back to the water, but she wasn't there."

Vera felt her eyes well up. She looked at William. The thought that—no, it was too much to imagine. How had Angelo managed to overcome this?

Because he'd met her. She'd become his new Stephania. His chance at redemption. If he could be kind to this other little girl, it might mitigate his guilt over losing his sister. She couldn't resent him for seeing her in that way. It was only natural. It was the only way to survive.

And for her, he'd become the family she was quickly losing—her mother to death, her father to illness.

They'd needed each other.

Angelo's shoulders stiffened, holding back sobs. "She wasn't there. She wasn't there. I looked. I shouted her name. People were starting to watch, and several men raced into the water to help."

The air in the room seemed to grow thick, as if the past could conjure the ghosts who lingered in old buildings like this, whispering their secrets. As if the mention of death awakened them.

Angelo pulled his hand away and crossed himself as Vera had seen Catholics do. Hand to forehead, heart, side to side. "I swear, Vera. I would do anything—*anything*— to take that day back. If I could only have gone in her place. Sent her with the money. Not gone to Brighton Beach at all."

Vera spoke softly. "Was she ever found?"

Will shifted on the bed, curling into a fetal position in his sleep. It gave space for Vera to slide all the way next to Angelo. She had not forgotten who they were or where they were, but her friend was feeling broken right now.

"Yes."

Vera's heart ached for the pain he must have felt.

He paused before speaking again. "Hours later. It was dark. So dark. Except for the full moon that cast a reflection over the water. That's how we saw her. I ran in and I held her and her skin was so blue and she was so cold and . . ."

He couldn't speak anymore. He'd given way to a full cry. Vera moved in closer, pulling his head to her shoulder, casting aside all regard for boundaries. He was in anguish, and she had caused it by bringing the subject up. She brushed her hand across his back, up and down, smoothing out the ripples caused from his tears. They remained silent, and he grew still, resting against Vera.

She was overwhelmed with love, more than she had been before. This was new. Not the love of an infatuated schoolgirl but of a woman who wanted nothing more than to take care of this man.

He pulled away at last but remained close enough that there were just inches between their faces. She was finally ready to look into his eyes without hesitation. A girl would be shy. A woman would be steady. They held each other's gazes and paused. Vera could feel a pull toward him, like a string connected them. She imagined kissing him. It would be so easy.

"I've never spoken about this to anyone," he whispered, moving closer.

"You told Pearl." She pulled herself back. Being alone in this room did not mean that everything else didn't exist. But she didn't let go of his hand.

"Yes. Not as much as all that, though. Odd, how when I've said even a little bit about it, it was so factual. So clinical. I haven't cried about this since that moment when I held Stephania in my arms on that beach. But you—well, I believe I can tell you anything."

Vera cleared her throat. "Pearl suggested that I came along and reminded you of her. Maybe it's only that." It was her duty to mention his wife's name. It might be the one thing that would keep a space between them so that in this moment of tenderness neither did something they'd regret.

Angelo reached for a lock of her hair from the bun that had almost entirely loosened. Vera froze, not knowing how to react. "You did. There you were with your hair in braids. Just like Stephania wore it.

And your scraped knee. I guess helping you let me do something that I could no longer do for her."

"Did you call her 'Kid'?"

Angelo leaned back and laughed, and Vera was grateful. It was better when the tone was not so serious. Because she was afraid that her resolve had begun to erode.

"No, 'Kid' was all yours. I called her *bambina*. It means 'little girl' in Italian. Or sometimes, *cara betta*."

"Dear one, right?"

"You're learning!"

"You've taught me more than a few words over the years. I pay attention."

Angelo's face grew soft. He looked down at their hands, one resting in the other. He entwined his fingers with hers.

She didn't pull away. This tug-of-war was agonizing.

"It has been years, hasn't it?" he whispered. "Where have they gone?"

He looked in her eyes. She felt her cheeks flush and her chest grow heavy. Angelo leaned in until they were once again so very close. She'd heard love described as intoxicating, and though she'd never been drunk or in love, the word seemed to apply. She had to pull back.

She started to just as he spoke again.

"Where has the little girl gone who used to kick rocks with me and sample gelato and make up stories about the people walking into Penn Station?"

"She's all grown up now," Vera whispered.

"All grown up," he repeated slowly. He raised a hand to her cheek and stroked it.

Angelo was hurting too much after talking about Stephania to see the wrongness of this direction. She couldn't be responsible for something they would regret.

She didn't pull away. But she didn't get closer. It was as if her head were in conflict with her body. And her heart was stuck somewhere in the middle, paralyzing her.

A light outside flickered and then went dark.

"Vera," he said.

"Yes?" Flashes of nerves began to shoot through her body. How could something that would be so wrong feel as if it were supposed to happen?

"I have something to tell you."

"Tell me, Angelo."

His lips brushed hers so lightly that it was not quite a kiss.

Drowning. She was drowning. And the surface was getting farther away.

"I'm not married."

Chapter Ten

"Angelo!" Vera leaped off the bed. She could not believe that he had just spoken these words. He *wasn't* married? She'd seen the ring on Pearl's finger. "What are you talking about?"

"Oh, Vera," he pleaded, burying his face in his hands. "I've made a mess of things, and I don't know what to do."

She wanted to go to him in his suffering, but she stayed rooted against the window.

"Angelo, you are not making any sense. Of course you are married. Which makes this—" She gestured around the room and then crossed her arms around herself. She had to say the word out loud. To draw the line so thoroughly that they wouldn't get within a mile of it. "*Wrong.* Or are you just telling me something you think I want to hear? Angelo, tell me!"

Please tell me, she begged again in her mind. She had to hold firm on the exterior. Inside, she was shattering and didn't know how to pick up the pieces.

The room was spinning. She slid down the wall onto the floor so as not to faint.

He looked up but didn't approach her. "Oh, Vera, *is* that something you'd want to hear? Would that be good news to you?" He began to stand but looked at William asleep on the bed and sat back down.

She put her face in her hands. She didn't know how to answer.

"No, don't answer that," he said quietly. "Because I don't think I want to hear your answer, whichever way it might be."

Yes, it would be good news, she thought. But she wouldn't say it.

Angelo seemed to deflate like a balloon that had lost its air. This trip that was supposed to be so exciting—they were in the nation's capital!—had brought nothing but strife. She didn't know who she, he, they were anymore.

Her instinct was to run. To run sooner than she'd expected to.

But what did he mean—that he wasn't married?

Angelo crept off the bed and sat next to her on the floor. He moved like one who was tiptoeing around glass. She didn't move away. It was far less romantic to be in this spot than on the bed, and she felt like she could keep her head about her.

"Yes, I think it's best. Because what I feel is irrelevant unless you're telling me the truth, and if you *are*, then there is a lot more that you need to tell me."

He ran his fingers through his hair and exhaled a deep breath. "Oh, I know. I know. I'm confused, Vera."

She folded her arms. "Angelo, this is not a difficult question. Are you married or are you not? There are only two possible answers."

"I don't know."

He stood up before offering an explanation. She had never seen Angelo like this. He was always so unflappable. But then, they'd never been alone like this. She could understand now all the taboos placed on the conduct of unmarried men and women. It guarded them against the kind of proximity that could tempt you to lose yourself in the moment.

He paced around the room and rubbed his hand across his cheeks. His stubble was thicker than she'd ever seen it, and her heart ached for how handsome he looked.

"Vera, I know I am risking any regard you might have for me, but we have been friends for a long time, and you deserve the truth."

Angelo's words made her tremble. What terrible thing was he going to confess?

"You're worrying me," she said.

He stopped moving and looked at her.

"I don't mean to." He crouched down until they were eye to eye but still kept his distance. "I'm sorry."

"I think you had better just say whatever it is you have to say. I'm not a child anymore, Angelo."

He attempted a smile. "I know *that*. If you only were a child."

"You're stalling."

He sat all the way down, and despite this void between them, it felt almost like old times. Like they were sitting on the steps of Penn Station and talking.

"I'm not. I promise. Vera . . . I don't know if you've ever lost your head over someone, but I lost mine over Pearl."

This much she knew.

"I could tell. You seemed pretty smitten when you first introduced us."

"Smitten. That's a good word for it. *Innamorato* in Italian."

"I don't need the lesson, Angelo."

"You're right. You're right. So. I met Pearl at the voter registration down on the Lower East Side. She was dazzling. I probably don't need to tell you that."

"No. I think just about anyone with eyes might say that about her."

"Imagine this, Vera. You're the first son born to an Italian immigrant. I don't know how it is in Germany, but in Italy, that is a role that comes with a lot of responsibility. My father started the newsstand when I was a kid myself, and when I was old enough to take over, he gave it to me and started another of his own ten blocks up."

She didn't know what this had to do with Pearl.

"All your life, you're told that this is what you are going to do. You are going to run a newsstand. You don't even get a chance to imagine that you will go to college, and there is no time to think about anything else you might be interested in doing."

Vera could understand this. She was a factory girl. Her mother was a factory girl. When you were born five paces behind the rest of the world, you weren't going to catch up quickly.

"Then you read an article during a slow hour. It talks about registering voters. It convinces you that no matter what else holds you down, being able to vote puts you on equal footing with the millionaires of the world. They have one vote. You have one vote. And every one counts."

Her sweet Angelo, always the optimist. Even she knew that ballot boxes got stuffed and those millionaires could buy votes. But she liked his idealism.

"It excited me, Vera. I hadn't been excited about anything in a while. I'd just been running the newsstand, and except for when you would come by to visit, the day was pretty mundane. But I read this article, and I thought for the first time that I could be someone. That I could matter."

"You always mattered to me." She had to say that. Soon, she would be leaving, and she wanted him to know this much. "You saved me, Angelo."

You've been everything to me for most of my life, she thought. But she dared not say that. She might cry.

"Aw, Kid—Vera."

Kid. It was the first time she liked hearing it from his lips. It put them back in their old places. It made it easier to continue this conversation.

"Anyway, I told my old man that I was going to play bat-and-ball with some guys one night. But instead, I went to the meeting that I'd read about. And there was Pearl. Running the show, as she does. She handed me a registration form before she even said hello."

Vera couldn't help a laugh. "That does sound like her."

"Yeah, it does, doesn't it?" He grinned. It was nice to talk like this again. She could pretend things were as before.

"So, she hands you the form, she doesn't say hello, and you decide you need to marry her?"

"That's below the belt, Kid!"

"Well, you're taking an awfully long time to get to the point."

"But it's important. I had to set the scene for you. Besides the newsstand, I was supposed to marry a nice Catholic Italian girl. They even had one picked out for me—Constanza Benapoli. Yeah, it's not only the rich folks who get set up like that. Not that there were any firm expectations. We Italians don't go for the arranged marriages like the Greeks do. But still. It was made known that it would make the family very, very happy if I settled down with her. Good birthing hips, my grandmother would say."

Vera blushed. She'd never heard anything like that before.

"So there we are," he continued. "Me and Pearl. I start helping her with the forms. I can speak Italian and she can't, so afterward, she offers to buy me a drink to say thanks. We registered thirty people that night. Twice what she's done at that same location previously. It was heady, I'm telling you. I didn't need the drink. I was already feeling pretty high just from the excitement of it."

Vera could understand that. To do something that mattered. She'd started to feel some of that when she worked alongside Pearl. Pearl made you feel like what you were doing was important.

"What happened next?"

"I was head over heels, like I said. We went out a few more times, usually after a rally or some event. My pops was at home riding me to work more hours, bring in more money, get married, start a family. And Pearl was telling me that I could do more than that. That I could make a difference in the world."

"It's what you've always told me," said Vera. "You didn't believe that for yourself?"

"Not when your pops is saying the opposite. I'm telling you, Vera. You don't want to be the disappointing son of an Italian father. So, no. I didn't believe it about myself."

He stretched his legs out and looked up at the ceiling. "Anyway, I'm not proud of myself for this. But things with Pearl got—*involved*, if you know what I mean."

Vera shifted on the floor. She might not know much about these things, but it was not difficult to understand what he was implying.

"I wrestled with it. Here was this beautiful woman who liked me for some reason, and we had this understanding about how our families pressured us. But maybe it's how I was raised. I didn't think we should carry on like that without being married."

"So you asked her to marry you?"

"It wasn't anything formal. Or even planned. It just kind of came out one night. To tell you the truth, it felt like I had to convince her of something. I even made the case that her son needed a father."

"But she loves you, Angelo. I can see that." It was difficult to say these persuasive words but important to stand up for Pearl.

He shrugged. "I think she just loves people. Have you noticed that about her? Don't tell me you haven't seen that, even with William, she's not the motherly type. She's restless. Always got to be doing something. Going somewhere. She's got a big heart for people in need, and she's really earnest about it. But you can't tie her down. She isn't going to stay in one place for long."

He had a point. It wasn't a character flaw so much as a trait. Pearl was made for big things. It was just who she was.

"You don't think—Angelo, she's not with someone else, is she?" It would be too hard to believe.

"No, no. It's not that I think she's with one person. It's just that she doesn't really belong to me. She belongs to the world at large. And without realizing it, I was trying to make her into something she's not. To what end? To calm my conscience? I can't say I was doing that intentionally. But deep down? Maybe. At least it makes sense."

"But this still doesn't explain what you mean. About not being married. Because you *did* marry her, right?"

"Well, yes. The state of New York recognizes our holy union. But we didn't get married in the Church. And what's the higher authority? The government or God? The state says we're married. The Church says we aren't. And that's what I grew up believing. I told you, I'm wrestling with these things. It's not an excuse. I hope you know that. I'm not looking for some kind of loophole. Some easy ticket out."

She could tell he felt the need to explain that. To convince her that this was not just a ploy. But he needn't have tried so hard. Her Angelo was honest to the bone.

"Anyway, I told her that I thought we ought to get married. I didn't want to live in sin anymore. But she resisted the idea of doing it in a *papist* church. So we compromised. We went to the courthouse and signed the licenses. It's why no one came. We didn't invite anyone. Even you."

Vera had always wondered about that, and now it made sense. They were just suddenly married. No fanfare. She'd thought it was Angelo who wouldn't have wanted all that pomp and circumstance. But it was Pearl.

What must his parents have thought? But that was not relevant right now.

She felt like there was a jigsaw puzzle in front of her and only some of the pieces were coming together. There was no good guy here, no bad guy. A marriage but not a wedding. A wife and mother but not one who was in the home. Nothing about what he was saying was part of the traditional world that they'd both grown up in.

But times were changing. Wasn't that the very point of all that Pearl advocated for?

"Angelo, are you telling me that you and Pearl fell out of love? Because that's not a reason to—to do whatever you're trying to do."

A piece of her wanted to hear this. That Angelo wasn't in love with Pearl and that she felt the same way about him and that a path was cleared for him to fall in love again. But she didn't want to be a part of something where the changing of affections was rationale enough to flit in and out of a commitment that was made. Even if it worked to her advantage.

She loved Pearl and she loved Angelo and she loved William, and whatever happened in the future, she would not be the one to change it.

"Vera, look at me." Angelo scooted a little bit closer and put his hands on her arms.

She looked at him. At the pleading in his eyes.

"I told you that I was risking any regard you have for me. Let me just say this clearly. Because I'm not the man I'm somehow portraying myself to be."

He cleared his throat. "It's not about being in love or being out of love. I pushed something that never should have been. For all the best intentions. And she said yes. Also for good reason. I think we were two people who needed to get out of what we were in at home and we liked each other, and this is just where it went. It filled in the holes that we both had. And it is a nice thing. When she comes home, we have good talks. I love her. You love her. What's not to love about her? But, no. I'm not in love with her, nor she with me. It just—happened."

Vera's heart beat faster. This morning on the train if you'd told her that Angelo would be revealing all this to her—that the door would even be open for them to have a future together—she might have done a cartwheel down the aisle. But now that it was here—almost hers for the taking if she pressed it—it didn't feel right.

"You don't slip on the ice and get up and find yourself married, Angelo. You can't say it just *happened*."

"You're right. I shouldn't have said it like that. But I guess I understand a little better why, as a Catholic, you have to go through so many months of preparation before the priest will give his approval. This is not something to undertake lightly. I get that now. I get what's important about marriage. I thought I was doing the right thing by suggesting it, by being a gentleman."

"You almost kissed me." Vera whispered this part, but she knew he'd heard her. This didn't change her plans to leave. But she couldn't leave wondering if she were some kind of next-in-line choice. It didn't work out with Pearl, and there was Kid. All grown up. That didn't sound like the Angelo she knew, but right now she didn't know anything.

She felt numb.

But the way he looked at her. It was love. She knew it without his having to say the words. And not the kind that was fleeting. The kind that had been planted years ago, disguised by the span of their age difference, pulling ever closer like gravity as the years passed. While he'd been speaking to her as the adult that she now was, she'd learned things about him that she'd never known, and she loved him all the more for his sincerity and even his naïveté.

Silence balanced between them, teetering on the pull that each felt, neither tipping it one way in their favor.

He spoke at last. "Yes. I almost kissed you." He slid his hands down to hers, and there was something in the gesture that suggested the goodbye that had haunted her all day. He knew. He knew just as she did what had to be.

The Angelo she loved would always do the right thing. And in this case, he would stick with his marriage and find a way to make it work. If he did anything less, he wouldn't be the man she knew.

He pressed her hand to his lips and closed his eyes tightly. Her own were fighting the tears that had started as an ache in her chest.

"I love you, Vera Keller, and I always have. For all my mistakes and my distractions, I can tell you that a more true thing has never been spoken."

All her life, she would hold on to these words, even if he could never speak them again.

He opened his eyes and brushed his hand down her cheek, tracing the path of the tears that would no longer be contained. They burned her skin where they fell and ached with the kind of singe that would scar if they'd been fire.

People walked around every day with wounds that were not visible, and this one would be hers.

Angelo helped her to her feet. He turned around to the bed and pulled the coverlet over William and kissed the boy on the forehead. Then he took a pillow and walked around to the other side and set it on the floor. He lay down, curled up, and didn't speak again.

Vera stood at the window, already frosting over with the coldness of the winter night. She waited until she heard his heavy breathing that told her he was asleep. She looked at the bed. How cozy it would be to cuddle up to William. But she was not his mother.

William had a mother. And Angelo had a wife.

She gathered her coat in her arms and tiptoed to the door, escaping into the cold night.

Chapter Eleven

1916

"Hold on, Vater! Please! I have to lock the door behind us."

Her father pulled at his hair and tried to rip his coat off. She had just resewn the buttons last week and was fatigued at the thought of having to do it again.

Vera's father had never been worse. It had been days since he'd resembled anything close to himself, and she'd lost precious hours at the factory to stay home with him.

"Stop. Please." She finally managed to secure the door—not that they had much to steal—and ran down the hall to pull him back toward the stairs.

"Nein! Nein!" he shouted, pushing her away. Her own father didn't even know who she was.

She had no choice but to give up.

The time between his episodes was decreasing. It used to be weeks before a really bad spell would hit him again. Then days. Hours.

Now it seemed to be here for good.

She'd let it go too long. She should have handed him over to the state years ago, but this was her *father*. He was her only family left.

She managed to link her arm through his, and one by one, they walked down the four flights of stairs. Several times he pulled and turned back up, but she never let go and got him down to the street at last.

However was she going to get him all the way to Penn Station?

She walked slowly, which seemed to calm him, but just two blocks up he started into a fit again. She found a bench next to a tea shop and spent half of what she had in her purse on a steaming mug.

Vera stroked his bearded cheek, avoiding the places where she'd nicked him trying to shave it all. It was useless. He didn't sit still long enough for her to finish the job, so now he looked like some old, wild man who had been let loose on the city.

The tragedy was that he was still fairly young. Only forty years old. And yet she felt like the parent.

"Shh. Shh. Vera is here. Your *prinzessin*. Drink the tea for your princess."

He took it from her, shaking, spilling drops of the hot liquid on his coat, but thankfully the fabric was thick enough that the liquid didn't burn him. For a few moments, having this little thing to focus on kept him silent as he sipped the tea.

Vera rubbed her hands. They were chapped and splintered. The factory where she'd worked for the last three years had changed its focus now that new owners had bought the space. She'd previously been making delicate flowers that were sold to milliners' shops, the miniature nature of the work straining her eyes. Now she was sanding wooden spindles, and the foreman demanded perfection that left the girls' hands in near ruin.

Vera felt like her bones would pop out of her skin.

She longed to get to know the other girls at the factory. To regain some sense of sisterhood that had begun during her time with Pearl. But they all came and went as marriages and babies and illness claimed what meager thread of conviviality existed among them. Russian girls who'd immigrated now dominated the workstations, and Vera wondered what they said about her in their strange tongue. What was the word for *spinster* in Russian? The pitying looks spoke their own universal language.

The foreman alone seemed to pay her any mind, and not the kind that she welcomed. He walked down the narrow rows of benches, a little too close to her side. His hand balled in a fist until her reached her, at which point it would fall to his side and brush her backside. It was always then that he turned and placed his hands on her shoulders, looking over in a pretense of checking her work. She'd long ago learned to wear a scarf or a high-necked blouse so as to rob him of the pleasure of staring down at places that no man had ever seen.

She knew that there were sacred places on a woman's body. All these years later, she understood the **G-I-R-L-S** and **B-A-R** words that had confused her childhood mind. Words that made her blush now.

Especially when she thought of it all in relation to Angelo. The only man whom she had ever wanted to invite to see these places that belonged to her. But *he* did not belong to her.

Three whole years had passed since she'd spoken to Angelo or Pearl or Will.

Three years since she'd run away into the gathering snow.

As difficult as it had been to leave, it would have hurt more to stay.

She always wondered what Angelo had told Pearl and William about her sudden departure. She hadn't intended to lay that on his shoulders, but she hadn't been thinking of anything except making the clean break that would give Angelo and Pearl the chance to be the husband and wife they'd vowed to be.

Did William ask for her? Was he too big now for the little scarf she'd knitted for him?

Immediately after returning from Washington, DC, Vera had given notice at their apartment and found a place eleven blocks south. The rent was much less than what she'd been paying, and her wages at the factory could stretch further. She wanted to save money to take art classes.

Pearl had inspired her to work toward something more.

Vera seldom had occasion to go near her beloved Penn Station. Sometimes, though, a subway shutdown would reroute her. She avoided going outside, where she knew Angelo would be manning his newsstand. But she had seen Pearl.

It had been a surprise when she saw her old friend there. Though maybe it shouldn't have been. Pearl lived right across the street. And as it was such a hub for thousands of travelers, it was natural that the suffragettes would have a near-permanent presence there passing around flyers and holding signs.

Vera had pulled her cap around the sides of her face and hurried to transfer trains before Pearl could notice her.

She'd seen her several times since then as she passed through the station. Pearl's wardrobe was simpler than it had once been. Vera noticed from the distance that as the months wore on, so did Pearl's once-fancy clothing. Maybe she'd sold her gowns, her furs, her shoes, her gloves. It would be like her to give that money to the cause.

She never got close enough to see if Pearl was still wearing her plain wedding band.

Every time, a piece of Vera wanted to abandon her avoidance and walk over to Pearl and tell her that she was sorry, so very sorry for running away like she had. But she was too scared to find out what the reception would be—would Pearl be angry with her or embrace her as a prodigal sister?

She wondered again what explanation Angelo had offered.

"Argh!" She jumped at the sound of her father, who had spilled more tea, this time on his hand.

She pulled a handkerchief from her pocket and wiped it off. The tea had cooled enough that she wasn't worried about a burn. But of course, he didn't understand this.

"It's okay, Vater. Why don't we continue walking?"

She took his arm and, mercifully, he followed her without incident.

They approached Penn Station, and her chest clenched at the sight of the place that was so dear to her. She had not been for several months, but the thought that always struck her did so now—that her smallness amid such vastness was more of a comfort than a threat. No matter her woes, they would fade someday even as these marble columns stood and would stand for hundreds of years past her own existence.

Today they were taking a train to the far north end of the city to bring her father to an institution that was willing to assess his needs and hopefully do for him what she no longer could.

That thought broke her heart. But his needs were breaking her.

She looked up at the eagles. Those majestic birds stood at their perennial sentry posts. The one thing she could rely on when so much else was lost. They might be her only remaining family, or at least they were a tie to Mama, Vater, Pearl, Angelo, Will.

The eagles wouldn't die on her. The eagles would not marry someone else. They would not get sick. They alone were her constant.

The sun was beginning its descent in the sky, and Vera urged her father to hurry his pace. A taxi fare to the northern part of Manhattan would cost a whole three dollars that she didn't have, so she was praying with everything she had that he could withstand a subway ride without panicking. It was getting late in the day, and there was no time for error before the hospital office closed.

As soon as they stepped into the station, she realized her mistake. The bustle that she found enticing—hordes of people coming and going with exciting lives and possibilities—proved overwhelming for the frail man whom she was supporting with her shoulder.

"Go away! Go away!" he shouted as travelers brushed past them. He turned to her, the cloud of bewilderment crossing over his eyes. "Who are you? Leave me alone!" He broke free of her grip and stumbled several feet, dodging luggage. He managed to get to the center of the concourse, near the clock that hung like a Christmas angel above everyone's heads. She nearly caught up with him, hindered by the bags she'd packed with his few possessions. But even then he was too fast for her, driven by an onset of madness. He turned down one of the side hallways, narrowly avoiding a porter with an overloaded cart.

"Go away!" he repeated. Vera might have been embarrassed by all the attention they were drawing if it were not for her thorough sympathy for his delirium. She'd let this go on too long. He'd needed intervention ages ago, and instead she'd kept him home, out of what? Loyalty? Selfishness? Their one meager room was going to feel haunted if she stayed there without him.

But all too quickly, there were no chances for lamentation. Her father collided with a waiter carrying a tray of water glasses, sending a fountain of shattered glass across the floor, soaking him until his feeble body was visible through his thin white shirt.

"Vater!" she shouted, reverting to the German that sometimes still slipped from her lips. Always in her most vulnerable moments.

He crumpled to the ground, covering his face with his hands and adding tears to the wetness that pooled around him on the marble floor. Vera ran to him, taking him in her arms despite the very real chance that it would only frighten him more.

"Are you hurt?" she asked, rubbing her hands along his half-bearded face to make sure that no stray shards had cut him. She moved down to his arms and held back a cry when a tiny particle pierced her palm. She ignored the drops of blood and pulled him to her, whispering reassuring words that thankfully calmed him.

She felt the back side of her long skirt grow heavier as the water permeated its threadbare fabric. But she ignored it, rocking her father back and forth, shutting out the clatter around them as people encircled their little scene. It was just Vera and Vater cocooning themselves in this vast space.

Until a familiar voice broke through: "Move aside. Let me get to them."

Her face tingled as an onslaught of unexpected tears began to gather. Vera didn't need to look up to recognize Pearl.

She felt her old friend wrap her arms around the two of them as she gently raised them off the floor.

Pearl. After all this time. Vera couldn't even begin to comprehend it, but she felt a joy that was beyond what words could describe.

"Here we go," Pearl said to Vera's father. "You're safe. We're going to get you some help." Pearl used her free arm to keep curious watchers away. She steered them down the hallway near a side exit.

The women stood on either side of a more compliant Vater as they drew closer to the door. A heavy rain had started to descend. An awning bowed above them but mercifully never broke. A bright-yellow taxicab sped past the near-antiquated horse-drawn version.

Vera pulled back even as Pearl stepped forward to open the door.

"No," whispered Vera, concerned about the fare, but she did not have any other choices. Her protest fell away with the breeze.

Her father's body became rigid. He'd never ridden in a car as far as Vera knew, and it was daunting to even the most lucid of people. *"Bitte, Vater,"* she pleaded. It took all her strength plus Pearl's to maneuver the old man into the back seat. The driver grew frustrated.

"We're paid by the mile, not by the time, girls. Hurry up or I'll drive off and find an easier fare."

Vera knew this would rankle Pearl.

"That's some way to treat the daughter of William Pilkington II," her friend huffed. Her father was a household name right along with the Vanderbilts and the Rockefellers.

"Yeah, right, and I'm the king of the Bronx. Just get your fanny in or I'm out of here."

Vera looked at Pearl's face, expecting her to be horrified, but she did not betray anything but determination to finish the job of getting Vater into the car. Vera ran around to the other side, stepping into an ever-growing puddle, but by now she was so soaked that she barely noticed.

"Bitte, Vater," she cooed, softening her voice and looking directly into his eyes. The flicker of recognition was enough that he scooted in, helped along by her guiding his arm and Pearl nudging from her side.

Vera looked up to thank Pearl before they drove off, but to her surprise, the woman shut the door behind her.

"What are you doing?"

"I'm going with you."

"You don't have to do that." Vera did not finish the rest of her thought. *Especially after I disappeared on all of you.*

"Nonsense. That's what friends do."

Was Pearl only helping because she felt that it was some kind of duty?

The driver turned around and barked, sending a cloud of cigarette smoke through the back. "Wonderful. You made it. Now you want to tell me where you're all going so that we can get out of here?"

Vera and Pearl spoke at the same time.

"Washington Heights Hospital."

"Eleven Madison Park."

Vera turned sharply. "What are you doing?"

"We're going to bring him to my grandmother's house until we can figure out what to do next."

Vera's pulse quickened. She was grateful for Pearl's help getting Vater into a taxi, but this was more than one step too far. They couldn't impose on such generosity, especially when it wasn't Pearl's to give.

And when so much time had gone by since they'd spoken.

But Vera knew that when Pearl had an idea, there was no dissuading her.

"Are you on good terms with your family again?" she asked.

"My parents maintain their silence, but I think Lady Gran can be worked on."

Vera wanted to ask about Angelo, too, but couldn't bring herself to say his name. She didn't know what had been discussed three years ago or since then. Pearl was wearing gloves, so it wasn't even possible to see if she was wearing a ring.

Not knowing what three years might have brought made her feel like she was looking through darkened glass, seeing only images moving with nothing being clear.

The driver shifted his body far enough that he could fold his arms across the seat. "If you dames don't decide right now where you are going, I'm going to drive you all the way to Albany and collect my fifty cents a mile from you just for wasting my time."

Vera's father started to shiver and let out a tremendous sneeze.

"And if you can't keep that old man quiet, I'm charging you triple."

Couldn't he see that they were frantic anyway without making them feel guilty about it?

"Madison Park," Pearl repeated, undeterred. "And if *you* don't keep quiet, I'll report you to the mayor's office. And if you think that I won't or can't do that, check with the manager at Delmonico's and ask who dined with Pearl Pilkington just yesterday. Olive Child Mitchel. The mayor's wife. That's right. We serve on a suffrage committee together, and our families have been close friends for many years. Way back further than if I sent my fist down your throat and grabbed you by the intestines and pulled them out to knit into a blanket to keep you warm on the frigid nights that you will spend on the street after you lose your position with the New York Taxicab Company. Because you know Harry Allen, your boss? He's a friend of my father's. They golfed together last week at Clearwater."

Vera stared in utter awe and amazement at the tenacity with which Pearl spoke. A whole new depth of admiration washed over her for her formidable friend.

Pearl sat back and crossed her arms. "Now. Take us to Madison Park."

The driver looked as if he'd been struck and dutifully turned around and pressed on the pedal.

Although Vera did notice one thing—Pearl had said Pilkington, not Bellavia. Had something happened between her and Angelo? Or had the powerful name Pilkington just suited the situation better than that of an Italian immigrant?

Her curiosity was insatiable. But she had to be patient. She would not get all the answers now.

Pearl leaned into Vera's ear. "I made that last part up. I have no idea if my father was even in this country last week, let alone what he did. But he *does* golf at Clearwater, so who knows?"

Pearl's easy way with a fabrication reminded Vera of the night Angelo had pretended they were married in order to get them a room. Not that she needed much reminding. The memory of her brief chance to be Mrs. Bellavia, even by farce, warmed her in wintertime. As did the memory of their near kiss. Though it also burdened her with a guilt that had never dissipated.

In less than a mile, they'd reached the front steps of the grand home. Had it really been more than three years since she had encountered Pearl in front of that fountain? Since Vera had drowned her sorrows over Angelo's engagement by discarding her precious stones into its waters?

So much had changed since then. And so little. Vera was still the same factory girl. Pearl was the same outspoken woman who somehow made Vera feel as if she were an equal.

A uniformed man stepped out holding an umbrella. He dashed back inside and returned with several more when he saw the three bedraggled figures exit the cab. He handed one to each of them.

"Miss Pilkington," he said in an astonished tone. Again Vera noticed the use of that name. But that could also be standard in this household that had never fully accepted Angelo as Pearl's husband. "We had no word of your arrival. And your grandmother is in California right now, as is her habit in the winter."

"I'm as surprised as you are, Victor, but this is an emergency, and you and I both know that she would open her doors to me."

"Of course, miss. I meant only that we would have prepared your rooms with fresh flowers and lit a fire."

"I don't need the flowers, but I will take you up on a fire if you can have one of the girls start one in the library. And prepare three bedrooms."

"Of course. Right away." He turned to go inside but stopped when she spoke again.

"And if you could please pay the cabdriver, I would be grateful. We owe him a dollar, but I'd like for you to pay him three."

Three? Vera wondered.

"Three, because if he wasn't already going to remember this day, it will teach him a lesson so that he never forgets that *girls* and *dames* are actually all *ladies* and should be treated accordingly. And a lady forgives grievances with grace and class, qualities that he could stand to learn."

"Yes, miss," said Victor, and Vera thought that she would pay a whole three dollars just to know what might be going through his mind and the driver's.

The butler turned and went inside, keeping the door ajar. The light that flowed from inside cut through the dark rain like an invitation to a different world. What were they doing here? She and her father didn't belong in this kind of place.

"I can help you," said Pearl, standing to the side of Vera's father and putting his arm around her shoulder. Surprisingly, he didn't resist. Then again, who could resist Pearl?

"Let's get him into some dry clothes," she said. "And then we need to talk."

Chapter Twelve

We need to talk. Those words rarely contained idle pleasantries and were more often omens of something difficult. Was Pearl going to reprimand Vera for disappearing from their lives three years ago? Was little Will thriving, or could something possibly be wrong? She dreamed about him sometimes. His sticky little hands. Who had wiped them when she wasn't there?

And Angelo. He was never far from her thoughts. She missed him. But she stayed away.

All worries left Vera as they stepped into the breathtaking hall of Pearl's grandmother's house. The ceilings soared three stories high, capped with stained glass capturing scenes of tangled vines. Practical as always, Vera wondered how such a thing would fare in a hailstorm, but perhaps the wealthy could replace them on a whim.

The room was lined with columns and arches on either side, and the abundant plants in the center reminded her of pictures she'd seen of jungles. Vera knew little about horticulture, but it seemed unseasonable to have such things growing. She brushed her hand along one particularly thick leaf and marveled that there was not a speck of dust on it. Nor did she see the kind of particles in the emerging sunlight that she often saw in the rays that shone through at Penn Station.

What kind of magic was it that made a place like this so idyllic in the middle of Manhattan?

Money can't buy happiness, she'd heard. But this clearly proved that an untruth. Who wouldn't be happy in a place like this? Well, except Pearl. She'd left all this of her own choice.

Pearl. Vera snapped out of her wonderment and ran after Pearl, who was now helping Vater into a room framed by tall double doors.

"The library fireplace has been started for you, Miss Pilkington," said Victor.

"Excellent. Do you have any coffee brewed?"

"I'll ask the cook to start some."

"Thank you."

The butler began to walk out, but Pearl stopped him once more. "And, Victor, do you think you'd be able to find any of my grandfather's old shirts? Mr. Keller here is soaked."

"I believe Lady Pilkington may have kept some of his things in an armoire in the attic. I will check on that for you."

The doors made no sound as he closed them, but the *thud* Vera heard must have been her own heart. She was finally alone with Pearl and her father. It might as well have been just the two women. Vera couldn't remember ever being this nervous, maybe not even when she had been alone with Angelo in that hostel room. Now that the emergency was behind them, would Pearl reprimand her for—for everything?

They sat Vater right next to the fire, leaned against a pile of plush, tasseled cushions. They unbuttoned his shirt to remove the cold, wet cloth from his skin and covered him with a sumptuous blanket made of fur. He sank into the surroundings, not really understanding where he was, and fell asleep. Vera stroked his hair and enjoyed seeing a peace in his face that had not taken residence there in weeks.

We need to talk.

Pearl said nothing, so Vera spoke first. An innocuous topic. "*Lady* Pilkington?"

"Yes." Pearl pulled a pack of cigarettes from her skirt pocket and lit one. She inhaled slowly and closed her eyes. A thin finger of smoke escaped from her lips before she spoke again. "Gran is one of those rich American women who married a titled Brit. It saved his estate and raised her status. Like a society version of a mail-order bride. She'd only met him twice before agreeing to marry him. But they were lucky ones. She genuinely loved him, and he loved her. Not all of those kinds of arrangements turned out quite so well."

"Does that make you a lady? I mean, an official one?"

As if Vera needed one more thing to make her feel inferior to Pearl.

The end of the cigarette seemed spent. An arch of ashes looked like they would disintegrate. "No. My father was the fourth son in their marriage. The other three stayed in England, but Father returned here with Gran after my grandfather died. I don't think she was ever really happy being away from New York. Grandfather's family wasn't very kind to her. So my father made his own way in business, and Gran continued to live on her own money."

"Will she mind that we are here?" Vera felt like she and her father were intruders. Not merely because they were so out of place in such opulent surroundings but because of Pearl's estrangement from her family.

"Nah. Gran has been warming to my side. Ever since William was born, she's helped me out."

She paused and ground the remains of the cigarette butt in an ashtray. Vera thought again of that sweet little boy she'd loved so much. How could she ask about his well-being?

Pearl continued. "I guess *thawing* might be the better word now that I think of it. We're not all the way there yet. I think my mother wants to be in touch, too, but Father dear swims in a moneyed set of tightwads who really, really don't believe in rights for workers and votes for women."

We need to talk.

The words still hovered in Vera's head, like a toothache that wouldn't go away no matter what else was screaming for attention. But Pearl had not yet made a move to discuss anything that seemed fitting for that kind of prologue.

A robust knock echoed through the library door, and Victor entered, followed by two servants. All were carrying large trays, Victor with a full array of silver service that he explained had a selection of coffee and hot chocolate. He also explained that he could have some tea brewed, if they preferred. The woman behind him, clad in a smartly starched white apron, set down a tray of offerings that rivaled any bakery window that Vera had ever seen—croissants, petits fours, fruit pastries of every variety. It astonished Vera that they thought three weary people could eat so much.

The third person, a man in an ink-black uniform, bore a stack of perfectly folded clothing.

Victor turned to him and took several items off the top.

Vera was grateful for the distraction.

"A set of pajamas for Mr. Keller and a robe. I've rung for a valet to come and assist with him tonight. And I took the liberty of laying out bedclothes for you and Miss Keller in your chambers and bringing an assortment of other articles for your comfort now."

"You're too good, Victor," said Pearl. "I'll be sure to write my grandmother at the California house and let her know how well you've taken care of us, and on such short notice."

Victor stoked the fire and promised that a valet should be on hand within the hour, apologizing for the wait. He helped Pearl and Vera ensure that Vater was comfortable as he slept on the cushions. Then he and the others left in silence.

Alone again. Vera's heart raced. Surely their conversation was imminent, and the things she'd worried about for three years would come to light.

The crackling of the wood burning was the most luxurious sound she could ever remember hearing, though it was little comfort to her right now.

"Dessert?"

Vera inhaled sharply. She heard *desert. You deserted us, Vera. Vera, the deserter.*

"Vera? Are you okay?" Pearl held out the plate of treats, and she chose a raspberry tart. She nodded as she took a bite. It was the most delicious thing she'd ever eaten. She just wished she could enjoy it.

"What did you want to talk to me about?" Vera blurted. She couldn't wait any longer or this night might never end. But she couldn't look her friend in the eye as she asked it.

Pearl took a bite of a chocolate-filled croissant and wiped the crumbs from her chin before speaking. Her movements were slow, and Vera felt her eyes move up and down as if she were assessing her. But her voice retained its carefree tone.

Her old friend sat back and crossed her legs. "Everything. I've missed you, Vera. We have three years of catching up to do. I was so surprised that you disappeared on us just like that."

Vera took a deep breath while trying to make it sound normal.

"Will missed you like crazy, too. He drew a picture of a train for you. I came by your apartment to deliver it, only to find that you had moved and didn't leave a forwarding address."

"I—I would like to have seen it."

A silence descended. She picked at a snag on her finger. She knew what was coming.

"Where did you go, Vera?" Pearl's eyes didn't leave hers.

What had Angelo told her? She hadn't even mentioned him. But Vera didn't want to bring him up.

She adjusted her seat and crossed her legs just like Pearl.

"I am very sorry about how I handled that. I did not mean to leave you in the lurch like that. But it just seemed better all around. At the time."

It sounded as weak as it felt. There were no words to convey the agony that she'd gone through ripping herself from the fabric of the family they'd grown to be. But she couldn't say to his wife that with one word Angelo might have been hers instead.

Pearl didn't speak, so Vera rushed on. "You made me want something more for myself. I—I started taking art classes."

She'd been able to afford exactly twelve classes in three years, but it was a start. And she didn't feel that specificity was required.

Pearl looked at her with unsure eyes. "I still have the drawing, if you want it," she said.

The drawing? Oh, yes. The one that William drew.

"How is little Will?" asked Vera.

Pearl curled her legs under her on the sofa, and Vera thought she seemed to be relaxing. "Not so little anymore. He's nearly six years old now."

"Six!"

"Yes. And he comes up to here on me." Pearl put her hand at the bottom of her rib cage.

So big. And she'd missed that. Along with countless other things.

Vera couldn't wait any longer, and this was the next natural question. A heavy breath sat in her chest as she spoke.

"And what about Angelo?" The words were so hard to say.

Pearl paused and cocked her head. "Did you ever marry, Vera?"

"Marry? No. I've been too busy for that." *And I've never stopped loving your husband.* But she couldn't say that, of course.

"Mmm-hmm." Pearl sat up straight again. "Angelo is . . . fine."

"You hesitated. Is he really okay?"

"Yes. He's fine." Pearl sighed. "We're just not seeing eye to eye on something right now."

So they were together. A part of Vera was happy. That's what she had left to do. To allow them to be a husband and wife without her interference.

But—the romantic piece of her had hoped, in the dark nights of lying alone in her bed at night, that Angelo might have come looking for her and somehow there was a way for them to be together.

Pearl looked her up and down again and then leaned forward in a gesture that made Vera think that she'd made up her mind about something.

"Vera, it's a stroke of luck to have seen you today."

Given the very real trauma that she was facing with her father, she might say the same. By this time tonight she'd expected him to be in some cold hospital bed in Washington Heights and she would be making her way home on the subway, surely crying her eyes out at the guilt of abandoning him. But that was probably not what Pearl was thinking about.

"Yes. And how kind it was of you to bring us here."

"Really, finding you again is an answer to a prayer. Several, in fact. I'm hoping that you can help me."

She was starting to sound like the old Pearl. Like the sister she'd been. It was like clouds parting to let the sun through.

"You know I'd do anything for you," said Vera.

Pearl curled her legs up again and lit another cigarette. "Angelo and I believe that it is only a matter of time before we join the war in Europe, and that means so many things. Primarily it means that women will be called into working the jobs that the men will have to leave as they go and fight. I just returned from Atlantic City and heard the most rousing speech by Carrie Chapman Catt in which she predicted that the war will be *the* event that turns the tide for us. Already, it has taken the lives of millions of men, and when we join, how many American lives will it take? Women will assume the roles of men not only when they leave but when they return home, many injured and many not coming back at all. Only then will society understand our capabilities. But we have to put a structure in place that supports this newfound independence so that we don't lose the ground we will assuredly gain."

Only someone like Pearl—or apparently this Catt woman—would think so far as to how the aftereffects of a war that the country had not even engaged in would impact women, but Vera couldn't disagree with the premise.

"Carrie said, 'The woman's hour has struck,' and it is so true, Vera. Local organizations are communicating with one another in unprecedented ways, growing into a national movement the size of which we have not yet seen. This is, indeed, the hour, and there is much need for me to travel through the states and assist with the effort."

Vera reached for another croissant to avoid the shaking she felt growing inside. She had a feeling about what Pearl might say next. And the prospect was too exciting for her to put into words first.

"What do you mean?" she asked. "You'll be away for longer?"

Pearl nodded heartily. "Exactly. I may be gone for weeks—months at a time. This is an opportunity that cannot be lost. This is why seeing you today is providential. Are you ready for a crazy proposal?"

Vera was ready for anything that might take her from the loneliness she'd fashioned for herself, but only after her father was cared for in a proper way. She could not gallivant off to adventures when she was the only person Vater had to take care of him. But if it involved being with Pearl and Angelo again, she would have to tread carefully.

"Okay." Pearl clapped her hands. "This is big, big, big. But let me know what you think." She took a deep breath. "Nothing happens without reason. I was going to return home tonight and tell Carrie about my commitment to traveling with her even without knowing who might take care of Will. But what about this—you remain here with your father for the time being. Gran will be away for another few months, so it's not as if you'd be in her way. Will can stay with you again like old times. That way your father will be in comfort, and it gives Will someone to look out after him, and you don't have to work in that factory job anymore. Assuming that is still where you are."

The same proposition as before. Only this time she wouldn't have to work under Angelo's roof, seeing him every day. Maybe not at all.

Instead they would be living here in this *palace*, and best of all—she would be able to get help and keep her own family together.

But what about Angelo? Pearl made no mention of him in this grand plan. It was not only this thought that occupied Vera. This was enticing beyond words, and maybe worth the risk if it helped her father. But it was also fraught with holes.

What if this was too much for her father to comprehend?

What would Pearl's grandmother really think of this arrangement? Vera wasn't sure that, present or not, she'd want a sick old man, a penniless girl, and a near-orphaned child landing in her home unexpectedly.

"Well, what do you think?"

Vera rubbed her hands across her face, not realizing that she had not yet voiced any response to this generous offer.

"I am overwhelmed, to be honest. Of course I want to support you, and I think what you say about this time for women makes sense. But I have so many questions, not the least of which is what I will do for money if we stay here."

Pearl waved her hand in the air as if to disregard the comment. "Nothing to worry about there. This just came to me as the perfect solution to all our problems. You won't have rent, and Victor and the staff will feed you splendidly. As for incidentals, we'll work out a stipend just like before."

It was all so tempting. But it could be history repeating itself. Would it have made the last three years a waste, as if her leaving had never happened?

There was still an unanswered question. One that, perhaps, everything else rested on.

"And where will Angelo be in all of this? Wouldn't he want Will to be at home with him?"

Pearl sighed and walked over to a nearby sofa to escape the raging heat that was now coming from the hearty flames coming from the fireplace.

"Oh, my dear, I haven't told you that part yet. Had we found each other just a few weeks ago, I might have tried to solicit your help to talk him out of his foolish plan, but we are too late for that now."

Vera gripped the arms of her chair. "What on earth do you mean? Is Angelo unwell?"

"Not at all. His medicals came back with perfect marks, I'm nearly sad to say. No, the man has gone and signed up for navy service before there is even a definite war. I told him that thirty was much too old to be expected to serve. I begged him to wait to see if there's a draft—who else might stay home with Will?—but he walked out saying something like, 'It's time to go be a man'—whatever that's supposed to mean—and he's rearing to dig into a fight."

Angelo. Going into war. Vera didn't even want to contemplate that thought. She was already afraid for him, and he hadn't even left yet.

She joined Pearl on the sofa and sank into its endless softness, taking this in. Her first thought was that this was an ideal decision on Angelo's part. He would not be the sort to shirk a chance to serve his adopted country. And for this, she was immeasurably proud of him.

"He's already been away this week for some initial training and then leaves next week for good. But I'm sure he would approve of this arrangement," said Pearl. She held Vera's gaze again in that cryptic way. "I know that he would consider finding you today to be rather opportune."

Vera wasn't sure what Pearl's meaning was. But fear for him also lurked, spreading its darkness into the pit of her stomach. Indeed, millions had already been lost overseas, as Pearl had mentioned, and despite the professional boon that entering the war might mean for women, Vera abhorred the idea of the United States entering a war that had already devastated Europe. A whole generation of young men had been killed in Great Britain alone. And for those at home? She'd read about starvation. About farms turned into battlefields. Widows. Orphans.

And a grief so devastating that a word for it didn't even exist in the English language: mothers who lost sons.

Angelo's determination would come at a price.

He was heading directly into unspeakable danger.

Chapter Thirteen

Pearl was set to leave only a week later for Albany to assist the National American Woman Suffrage Association with their efforts to gain votes for women in New York. The surprisingly progressive western states had been embracing it as one by one they granted rights long before the eastern states. Vera shared Pearl's enthusiasm for Jeannette Pickering Rankin recently being elected as the first female representative to the United States Congress, out of Montana. Montana! Could New York not have done the same sooner? The time for a united push for nationwide successes had never been so imminent.

Pearl talked about suffrage on a big stage. What it would mean for women across the world.

Especially in the absence of Angelo, Vera found herself easily swept up again in the optimism that Pearl exuded. Pearl came to her grandmother's house every evening to join them for dinner. Afterward they would lay out big rolls of paper across the vast mahogany table and paint signs and banners that Pearl could take to Albany with her.

Their conversations revolved mostly around what the future held. Sometimes in relation to the world, the war, and women. But occasionally Vera felt that Pearl's questions were more pointed. What did Vera particularly see for herself in the future?

Maybe that was just the question of a friend. But Vera had the sense that Pearl was *interrogating* her. That made no sense. Vera's only plans were immediate—care for her father. Care for Will. Save some money. The larger stage was not hers to consider for the moment, when there were more pressing needs right in this house.

That first week flew by. Vater seemed to settle in remarkably well. How could he not? Every comfort was provided for him, and he found much solace in the rooftop greenhouse. Vera worked out a routine with Will, with whom it was like starting over. The boy didn't remember her from three years ago—he'd been so little then, so she could hardly have expected more. And maybe it was better this way. If she had caused him any heartache then, he did not seem to associate it with the Vera he was getting to know now.

On the occasions that Vera could visit with others in the working class—be it the scullery maids here in this house or the wives of the merchants at the markets—she found that they held similar ambitions to herself. The idea of a woman in office was of little consequence compared with what it would take to put a meal on the table. But Pearl's forecast was intriguing. And Vera did her part to promote it in the small ways that she was able.

She was pleased with the inroads she made in encouraging these women to attend rallies and persuade their husbands to vote on their behalf. It was nothing on the scale of Pearl's work, and she often voiced this to her friend, but Pearl insisted that *every* conversation was of unimaginable importance.

Pearl made Vera feel like a vital piece of the cause, even if she didn't feel this way herself.

So much had happened in the short time since she'd arrived, and now it was already time to say goodbye to Pearl as she left for the capital.

With her father taking a nap and William in school, Vera was free to see Pearl off at the train station. But Angelo's train to Norfolk was scheduled to leave only two hours later, and she could only assume that he would be there to see his wife off.

The idea terrified her.

Twice she'd declined Pearl's invitation, but Pearl was strangely insistent that a goodbye at the house wasn't enough.

How could Vera refuse the friend who had been so good to her?

No, she must go. And if she were honest, maybe seeing Angelo would put her heart at rest. After all, it had been three whole years. She was twenty-one years old now. Much could have changed.

As she approached the station, she looked up at the eagles and asked them to wish her luck.

And then, as if wishing could breathe matter into itself, there he was.

Angelo stood near the entrance to Platform 13W, the rays through the windows encircling him as if they had been designed to do so. He wore a smart-looking uniform of the richest deep blue with a white rope collar and white cap. At first he was looking at the departure board, but when he turned and saw Vera, her heart seemed to stop. If she had thought him handsome before, it was nothing compared with the vision in front of her. Whether it was the sight of him looking so official or the accumulation of dreams over the lost time, her feelings for him came back in a rush as if not a second had passed since she'd shared that room with him.

"You angel," Pearl said to Vera as she approached them from the ladies' lounge. "What a darling you are for coming to see us off."

Vera smiled, but inside she trembled at the oddness of being here with them both. And she had yet to meet Angelo's eyes. "Of course I wouldn't miss being here. How could I not come say goodbye to my dear friends?"

Pearl continued. "Be a love, will you, and keep Angelo company while I run off to check on my ticket." And with no obvious perception of the tumultuous emotions that Vera could feel pass around the three of them, Pearl glided over to the ticket counter.

Vera was alone with Angelo. Her heart raced at a pace that seemed dangerous. Would he be angry? Tender? Or worse—would he look at her with love in his eyes, something she wasn't sure she could withstand even with three years of distance?

"Vera," he said. One word. Two syllables. A thousand unspoken sentiments.

"Yes." *Beat. Beat. Beat.*

"It's been—it's been a long time."

"Yes."

"You left us."

"Yes."

He stepped forward and whispered in a broken voice, "I've missed you desperately."

Vera felt a wave of tears accumulate. She put a tissue up against her eyes. But she could not speak. As agonizing as it had been to be away, it was worse to stand this close to him and ache for something that couldn't be.

"Please understand. I lost my best friend when you disappeared. Could we have not worked out some way to go back to being us? Angelo and Kid?"

Kid ceased to exist when you got married.

"I'm afraid not, Angelo. There's no way I could go back to being that little girl."

"Ah, she speaks." Angelo stepped closer. "How I've missed your voice. And everything else about you, Vera. You have to know that."

Vera felt the heat that rose from his skin and enveloped her. His uniform did not help things. He looked fully like the man he was. His jaw was angular. And even though he had clearly shaved this morning, his dark Italian roots cast a shadow across his face that added to the look and made her knees feel unstable.

"I—I do know."

Vera saw Pearl making her way back through the crowd toward them, and she felt guilt though she'd done nothing wrong. Angelo placed a hand on her arm. "My train does not leave for two hours. Have lunch with me. Please, Vera. Have lunch with a sailor who will surely see war. Because what if we never have that chance again?"

She looked at him at last and said words that had no meaning. "I can't."

"There you are," said Pearl, flushed. "You'd think all of Manhattan was taking the train today. I'm off, dears."

They'd only just reconnected, and now Vera was saying goodbye again to the two friends she cherished most. Why must things always change? She wanted just a little more time with both of them.

Pearl took Vera's hands in her own. "A truer friend I cannot imagine. Thank you for taking care of Will. I know that you two will pick up where you left off. In fact, I think he always favored you anyway. You were better with him than I was. I don't suppose I was designed to be the doting mother. But you—you are a natural. I hope that life brings you your own children someday. Until then, you'll have your hands full with your father and my boy. I'll see you in a few months, and I'll send lots of postcards."

Why did this goodbye feel like so much more than Pearl's simple words implied?

"You take care of yourself," said Vera. She pulled Pearl into an embrace and held on to her. She swelled with pride over all that her friend was setting out to do. "I was not designed to change the world, as you were, but if I can help in this little corner of it, I'm happy to do so. I'll read your postcards to Will and make sure he knows that his mother loves him."

"That's all I can hope for."

Pearl stepped away and turned to her husband, transferring her hands to his. Vera once again felt like a trespasser, but it seemed her lot to be the tagalong with those two, as if fate had destined her for that position. They'd slipped into old habits. Maybe that meant it was supposed to be this way.

"Please forget that I ever called this a folly," said Pearl. "You know I pray for your safety and want you to return to all of us as soon as possible."

"I will do everything I can," Angelo responded. "We'll both be fighting the good fight."

"You're a good man, Angelo Bellavia."

Vera expected them to kiss the way a husband and wife should have during such a momentous goodbye, but when she glanced away, she saw their reflection in a glass door, and Pearl merely gave him a quick peck on the cheek before picking up her baggage.

"And goodbye to you, my friend," said Pearl. In the European fashion, she placed a light kiss on each of Vera's cheeks, then pressed a note into her palm. "This is for you," she whispered.

What would Pearl need to say in a *letter*? Something she hadn't been able to say in person?

Before Vera could respond, Pearl was off, disappearing into the arch under the platform. Angelo turned to the departure board, which was being updated with track numbers.

The letter in her hand felt heavy, its unknown words weighing it down as Vera imagined what Pearl would want to say to her. Last words at a departure held almost as much meaning as those on a deathbed—only the most precious and precise of reflections could be expressed in such a moment.

She opened the page and shielded it with her coat.

Vera, it began. *I know about you and Angelo.*

Chapter Fourteen

"Lunch, then?" Angelo asked Vera as she tried to read more of Pearl's note. But she'd not gotten past that first terrible line. She stuffed it into her coat pocket. Her pulse raced at the thought of what her friend might be thinking before she left on such an important pursuit.

But if Pearl knew, why had she been so kind as to make a wonderful arrangement for Vera and her father? Why would she leave her son in Vera's care? Was she so desperate for someone to turn to that even a near Judas would suffice?

Or had she only now found out, somehow, after the fact, and the letter was a dressing-down of someone she now regretted trusting?

"Vera, are you okay? You seem like you're lost in thought." Angelo's words cut through her worries and were at once welcome and abhorrent to her.

She'd hoped that three years away would have dulled any reaction she felt to him. But it had almost the opposite effect. Their absence had concentrated all the love she felt into one overwhelming sensation.

This was a mistake. She shouldn't have accepted Pearl's generosity, no matter what it meant for Vater. And she shouldn't have come to the train station.

"Yes, I'm all right." She still wouldn't meet his eyes, fearing that they would empty her of any shred of distance she would attempt to place between them. She thought about slipping away to powder her nose—a chance to go somewhere and finish the letter before facing him. But before she could excuse herself, Angelo took her hand and led her toward the station café. Her hand disappeared into his, but it was not the tender gesture of two people in love. It was a tether to keep them from losing each other in the throng. Still, she felt protected by his grasp.

And she had not felt protected in such a very long time.

The clamor of commuters echoed through the iron-and-glass canopy that made up the top of Penn Station, their only separation from the endless blue above. For the first time, Vera felt claustrophobic within its walls. As if the ceiling were imprisoning her instead of sending her eyes skyward. Her heart rattled in her chest, vacillating between guilt, love, and the magnitude of seeing, touching Angelo for the first time in so long.

"Here we are, darling."

Darling! The word stung her ears, piercing the veneer that put a glaze of friendship over their past feelings. Her first thought was to be indignant on behalf of Pearl. Her second was that she had not been spoken to with such an endearment for as long as she could remember. Even her father had stopped calling her *prinzessin.*

Could one so starved be found guilty for accepting a morsel tossed her way? Was it wrong to taste the crumb while rejecting the whole cake?

She chastised herself once again for allowing herself to slip back into their lives. Factory work was brutal. Making the steps to leave her father at a hospital more brutal still. But at least there she knew her duty and followed it. These tugs-of-war did not exist when survival was the only goal to be attained.

Love? It was a luxury. And she had not been born into luxury.

Angelo looked right and left and pulled Vera toward the stools at the counter. With perfect timing, a couple rose to leave even as he led Vera to slide onto one of the round leather seats.

"You can't sit here. I haven't cleared the plates yet," said the bartender behind the counter.

"Please, sir, I have only an hour and a half left with this beautiful woman before I ship off, and a few dirty dishes won't deter me from every second I can spend with her. For a fellow *paesano*?"

Darling. Beautiful woman. What game was Angelo trying to play? She'd accepted a lunch invitation with an old friend, but she never would have agreed if she'd known he'd throw her into such a struggle within herself.

She read the name tag of the bartender—Giuseppe Di Gregorio. Italians stuck together. Angelo would get anything he wanted now.

I know about you and Angelo.

She wanted to be sick.

Lickety-split, as her mother used to say, the plates were cleared and the counters wiped down, and the bartender even slammed a bud vase with a single rose between the two of them.

How romantic that would have been in another circumstance. She was tempted to just give up. She didn't want to spend the little time Angelo had before he left for the train being angry with him. What if he never returned? What if this was the last time she would ever see him?

She took a deep breath and decided to let this play out. In the event of his return, this would be the last time, the *very last time*, that Vera would participate in make-believe.

Angelo slipped a dime across to Giuseppe and ordered two coffees.

"What would you like?" Angelo asked, handing her a menu. She didn't understand his lighthearted mood. He was about to be shipped off to *war*.

Vera scanned it for the least expensive item. In this case, a chicken salad on rye.

Angelo took the menu away from her. "Not today. Anything you want. Don't worry about the money. This is my treat. It's an important day." His words reminded her of how very well he knew her.

"I can't let you do that."

Angelo turned to the bartender. "The lady will have a filet mignon with roasted potatoes and asparagus on the side, and a tiramisu for dessert."

What could he be thinking? She wanted to ask him, but she was afraid of what the answer might be. Especially in light of Pearl's note.

The man put his hands on his hips and huffed. "*Mio amico*, this is just the station café. You'd have to go to the restaurant in the first-class wing for that."

"Are both restaurants owned by the Pennsylvania Railroad?"

"Si. Certo."

Yes, of course. The little Italian Vera had learned from Angelo came trickling back, reminding her of older, happier times.

"Would there be some way," Angelo said as he slid two whole dollars across the counter, "to order from there and have it delivered here?"

The man chuckled and waved a finger at Angelo. "You're not merely a *paesano*. You're a *scugnizzo*. Seeing as you're in uniform and a fellow Italian, how can I refuse?"

"Good man. *Grazie.*"

The bartender finished wiping a glass with a towel whose edges had just begun to fray. He looked at Vera and winked. He waved a busboy over and whispered to him.

"Coming right up, sailor."

Vera turned to Angelo once they were alone. "What are you doing? That's too much."

Angelo took her hand and kissed it. She pulled back, but she still felt the heat of his skin on hers. The farce was feeling more and more real. What was his endgame? His train was leaving shortly. Did he have some kind of portent of the war that emboldened him to forget restraint?

And had he forgotten that his *wife* had been with them only minutes ago?

"I remember eating a cheese sandwich on day-old bread with a little girl once. She wore her hair in braids and had eyes just like yours. I called her Kid. I asked Kid what her dreams were, and she said, 'Someday, I'd like to be a fancy lady who eats steak and potatoes and asparagus for lunch.'"

He smiled at her. Vera felt a flutter through her body. She remembered that day, that sandwich. It was so long ago—maybe she had been seven or eight. Angelo had taken her out for gelato at a place near the opera house, but they'd passed a bakery advertising discounted baguettes because they were just about to close. They had twelve pennies between them—three from her, nine from him—just enough to treat themselves. They sat on a bench across the street. Theatergoers were already starting to line up.

What do you want to be when you grow up, Kid?

I want to be a fancy lady and eat steak and potatoes and asparagus for lunch.

I want to own a newspaper company when I grow up. Maybe when I do, I'll buy you a fancy dress and I'll take you to a fancy lunch.

I'd like that, Angelo.

I'd like that, too, Kid.

Of course, those were the days when she was no more than a substitute kid sister to him and he saw it as no more than an indulgence of a child's whims. A continual filling in of the hole that guilt had left in his heart.

But it was different now. This Angelo had eyes that spoke of love for her. The look she'd always hoped for.

I know about you and Angelo.

The look that she couldn't allow herself to return.

Vera shifted in her chair. "I can't believe you remember such a silly thing."

"I remember everything we've ever talked about, Vera. How you love to draw whenever you can get enough money together for materials. How every time your mother's birthday or the anniversary of her death rolls around, you pin a flower to your collar. Even if it was just a weed—a dandelion. How you pore over every magazine that ever had a picture of an island on it. I remember, Vera."

Her heart pounded. She'd wanted to hear these kinds of things for him for as long as she could remember. But this was not the time or place.

He leaned into her and recaptured the hands that she'd pulled away. His words benumbed her, and she couldn't move or speak.

"I remember how much it hurt to be away from you for all these years. There was never a day that I didn't think of you. Ache for you, Vera."

She tried to steady her breathing. She loved him so very much. But she couldn't tell him that she felt the very same thing.

He continued. The look in his eyes made her want to break in two. "You've been a part of my fabric for half my life, and I was a fool not to see it in time. I understood your reasons for leaving, though, and I didn't pursue you. But don't think my absence meant that I haven't thought of you every time I walked by this station or kicked a stone or *breathed*."

She felt the heat of his breath as he spoke the words. She brushed her hand along his cheek and pushed him back just enough that she could look at him directly. And put an end to this.

I know about you and Angelo.

"Amore mio," she whispered. "There are days when my resolve weakened and I wanted to walk down the street just to see you. But nothing has changed. You are a married man. Pearl is my friend. We cannot continue this. And I don't know why you're making this so difficult."

"You don't understand, Vera."

The bartender arrived with a large tray. Two plates were covered with steel lids. He draped a bar rag over his arm and unveiled the food with a flair.

"First-class service at my third-class counter. How do ya like that?"

Angelo laughed. "I'm more grateful than you could know."

The bartender slid a paper across the counter. Vera saw that it came to four dollars and some change.

Four dollars! All that it could buy for Will. Had Angelo forgotten that he'd accepted the role of father?

She looked at the steak. It looked just as delicious as she'd always imagined it would. It stood an inch tall with juices pooling onto the plate, turning the white tips of the potatoes pink. She really, really wanted to try it. But guilt overwhelmed any rumblings of her stomach.

"Mangia," said Angelo, already cutting into his own.

"I—I can't," she said, hoping that the regret in her voice wasn't as audible as it felt. She put down the fork and knife she'd been holding. "I can't, Angelo. We shouldn't be here. This isn't fair to Pearl."

"But Vera—"

She smelled the steak and thought for one half second that she should eat it before she did what she was about to do. But if she was going to deny him whatever he might be wanting to ask of her, she was certainly not entitled to the generosity of this meal. She'd thought they could eat together as friends, but Angelo had made that impossible.

She stood up and pushed her plate away. "I was right to stay away for three years. This feels like no time has passed since that night in the hostel. I left then, and I'm leaving now. I'm sorry you rushed into a marriage and later regretted it, but I'm not going to play party to *adultery*."

"What are you talking about, Vera?"

What could he mean? Had he not heard himself say these things?

Because he was tearing her heart apart with longing for what couldn't be. What might have been. If she stayed a minute longer, she might just be tempted—too tempted—to walk the road he was leading down.

"Whatever game you're playing at, this is not the Angelo I knew growing up. The one who valued loyalty and tradition. If this is the man you've become, Angelo, one who would toy with the commitment to his wife while dangling false promises to another woman, then I don't want that. I don't want *you*."

Vera raced away from the counter, through the grand corridor, past the clock, and down the steps. She did not stop running until she'd made it all the way to Madison Square Park and sat on that damnable fountain edge wiping her tears with the elegant cloth napkin she'd forgotten to leave behind.

And there were tears. So many that they felt like icicles on her cheeks against the frigid weather that surrounded her. What she'd just said to Angelo was horrible.

I don't want you.

What a thing to say to a man as he was preparing to serve the country and—God forbid—fight overseas if it came to that. What if Angelo never returned and all he remembered of her were those words—those words of reproach and rejection? How could she forgive herself if something happened to him?

And of course the words weren't true. She did want him. She wanted him more than she wanted life.

She unfolded its creases and reread the devastating first line.

Dear Vera,
I know about you and Angelo.

Vera held it to her heart and let out a deep sigh before continuing on. What admonishment would these pages contain?

I should have seen it from the beginning. He talked about you incessantly when I first knew him. "Kid did this." And "Kid said that."

I suppose I believed the notion that you were like a sister to him. He said as much, and I think he believed his own fiction as well. But then I saw you that first day on the steps of Penn Station. All wide-eyed and innocent and rosy. The kind of girl who men want to marry.

Vera paused. She could not imagine that Pearl saw her as any kind of competitor for Angelo's affections. Majestic, elegant, commanding Pearl. What man wouldn't want her at his side?

But her words rang a little true. It was warm to be in the presence of the sun—until you got too close and got burned. Safer to be near a steady candle flame instead. Angelo had alluded as much. Vera was his little candle flame.

I brushed that aside, perhaps out of loneliness. I know you probably don't believe that I could be lonely, knowing as many people as I do. But believe me, it is quite a solitary life to be around people when you are so different. When I am in my family's circles, I cannot tolerate their shallow concerns about a maid who failed to wash a red-wine stain out of a white linen tablecloth. Inside, I want to shout, "Maybe you shouldn't have been so careless with your drink, you dolt!" But I cannot say such things, of course.

Instead, I engulfed my feelings about the injustices of the classes by doing something about it. But even then, I was an outsider. Never fully trusted because of the family I came from.

I didn't belong anywhere.

Until I met Owen. Owen was the first person I met who made me feel valued for myself and who cared to listen to my opinions. When he died so unexpectedly, it was as if I'd been thrown off a cliff. For all my beliefs about the capabilities of women, it does not negate the very real desire to have a man as a partner.

Then I met Angelo, and I don't have to tell you how dear he is. He filled that void of family with his kindness and charm and eagerness to help those in need. When I felt as if I'd lost my harbor, Angelo gave me a place to land and feel welcome again.

Vera thought that was so much like Angelo. That knight-in-shining-armor type. She'd experienced it herself as a child.

And so I realize my folly in all this. My role. I blindly took what made me feel safe in the moment, and in that whirlwind, I married him. And he treated my son as if he were his own.

But as I know Angelo has told you—you see, even as friends, he and I don't have any secrets—that is not the foundation for a marriage. We filled a void in each other, but we didn't really fill each other. Does that make sense? We both knew it very early on.

After you left Washington, DC, so abruptly, he told me what had happened. I encouraged him to seek you out, but as I've told you, you'd left your apartment with no forwarding address. Some efforts on our part resulted in no results. It was as if you didn't want to be found.

Angelo and I continued to live together. It was rather convenient—we each contributed to the household bills. William adored him and still does. That all sounds kind of sad now that I write it. We were both so busy that three years passed before we knew it. Angelo is trying to get a place for his newsstand inside Penn Station. And, as you know, I've been devoted to the causes for women. It wasn't until William began nearing school age that I realized just how much time had gone by!

Pearl was calling Angelo . . . a friend?

I wanted to confide this in you the moment I saw you again at Penn Station. But I didn't know your current situation—had you married? Would this be news that would disrupt a new life you'd built?

But it took only the mention of his name to see the flicker in your eyes that surely reflected the quick beat of your heart. So I am happy to write this letter.

You are a true friend, Vera. I may have made foolish decisions, but I am not a foolish woman. I see that you love him as well, and I know that it was not a small sacrifice you made to leave the man who had been yours far before he was mine for the sake of our friendship and my marriage. You are a harbor to me as well.

Vera put her hand to her mouth, holding back a sob that became a sudden knot in her chest. Pearl knew all that and could still say such things? She missed her friend right now almost as much as she missed Angelo.

But as fate would have it, we found each other again, and I believe it was predestined. How lovely to have it all work the way it's supposed to. I'm helping you with your father. You're helping me with Will.

And I'm asking now for you to be there for Angelo.

To be there for Angelo? Just as Vera had left him after saying the most horrible things.

> *You see, Vera, we initiated the proceedings for a divorce a few months ago. Not an easy thing to do in a world in which it's so uncommon, and apparently it takes much longer than we'd anticipated. But this is entirely mutual and full of friendly affection. If you will make room for me in your lives, I hope that you will still let me be a friend to both of you, as I would gladly lose my right arm before losing either my Angelo or my Vera. I won't think it odd if you won't, though. In fact, it will give my heart great happiness to know that my two dearest friends have acknowledged in each other what I have begun to see.*
>
> *If all goes according to plan, by the time you read this, Angelo will have proposed to you over lunch.*

Vera gasped.

Proposed?

> *I even helped him select a little gold band that I think you'll like. It was done in haste, I'm sorry to say. Angelo only came home yesterday from his training, and it gave me very little time to bring him up-to-date on all that had occurred this week. Finding you again. Making certain that this is what he wanted, too.*
>
> *I hope you said yes. I hope with all my heart that you said yes and that I will receive a postcard from you telling me that you have accepted and that someday when the mountains of paperwork and his deployment and my*

campaign are all over, we might celebrate together what always should have been.

So, dear Vera, my sister, go to your Angelo and give him all the love that I couldn't and that you both so richly deserve.

I remain your friend forever,
Pearl Pilkington

Vera found it difficult to breathe. There were too many things to think about in there, and she knew that she would have to read the letter a hundred times over before she could fully understand it.

But she checked her watch. Angelo's train left in ten minutes. She'd ruined everything. He planned to propose to her—*propose!*—and she'd called him an adulterer and said that she didn't want him.

It might be weeks before she could get a letter to him, and she couldn't let him go with this misunderstanding between them.

It was a fifteen-minute walk to the train station. But if she ran, she might make it in time.

Chapter Fifteen

Patches of ice blended seamlessly with the colors of the sidewalk. Vera slipped three times running up Broadway, brushing off the well-meaning efforts of strangers to help her up. Each second that she would have spent on a platitude was one second that might cost her getting to Angelo before his train pulled away. She'd been polite all her life. Today was not the day to waste time.

She resolved to be a bit more forgiving of those who demonstrated the kind of rudeness she knew she was exhibiting now. Maybe people had things worrying them that she didn't know of. Who was she to judge them by mere actions?

Thirtieth. Thirty-First. Thirty-Second. Vera was breathless and disheveled by the time she finally reached the entrance on Thirty-Third, the exact opposite end of the station from where she needed to be. She pushed past a woman with an impossible collection of luggage and sped past vendors who were offering flowers! Perfume! Newspapers!

The only newspaper salesman she wanted to see was Angelo.

She raced past the clock, refusing to believe the hand that taunted her lateness.

Suddenly she turned around in bewilderment. She didn't even know where his train might be leaving from. In her haste just to get to the station, she'd gone past the departure board. She wasn't going to take her chances trying each of the countless platforms, so she back-tracked to the center of the station and read off the names.

Baltimore	1:45	Platform	14	On Time
Chicago	2:15	Platform	7	On Time
Dover	1:53	Platform	22	On Time
Harrisburg	2:05	Platform	1	On Time
Newark	1:58	Platform	9	On Time
Norfolk	1:39	Platform	6	Delayed

She couldn't believe it. Norfolk—*delayed!*

What stars must have aligned to give her this miracle?

She ran again across the concourse to the lower platform where six was located. The train must have just come in from somewhere else, because she encountered an avalanche of people bounding upward. It was like pushing against a mountain to make any headway. She looked above the heads of the travelers, hoping to see some sign of Angelo still on the platform, but it was impossible to spot him among all the many identically dressed sailors. And shouting for him over the cacophony of bustle would be fruitless.

She continued to push inch by inch, always looking, until the throng thinned just enough that she could make her way down faster and hope that her words might be heard. She panicked as she saw the sea of uniformed sailors begin to board.

"Angelo!" she shouted. But no one looked her way or paid her any mind.

"Angelo!" She tried again three more times.

As she reached the bottom stair, one head turned her way. His hand was holding on to the bar that led to the first step on the train car.

He stopped, and even beneath his cap she saw his eyes, his squared jaw, the shadow on those Italian cheeks. In that first glance, she was elated to have found him.

But then she panicked. She'd treated him awfully just an hour ago. What if he was angry with her? She wasn't sure she could bear it.

He let go and fought past the group of sailors trying to board until at last they were eye to eye, she on the last step, he on the ground, the first time she'd been able to look at him straight on.

It overwhelmed her, waiting for him to say something.

"You came back," he whispered. His eyes looked red. She couldn't believe she'd hurt him so much.

"Angelo, my love. I am so sorry. So deeply sorry. I was wrong. Pearl told me everything."

He tapped a finger on her nose. "Of course she did. She told me that she wanted to make sure you knew that we had her blessing. But you ran out before I could tell you about it."

He held her close and kissed the top of her head.

It was the most wonderful thing that she had ever felt in her life.

She pulled back and looked at him.

"I messed everything up, Angelo. The lunch. Your beautiful lunch. I said such horrible things and I ran out on you. And my first chance to have steak! I ruined it all."

He laughed. "You haven't ruined anything. You're here. And a delay from the train coming in from Washington gave you just enough time to come back."

"I can't believe you're leaving. Just as we've found each other again."

The train whistle blew. Angelo's eyes grew serious. "Vera. I have to go. This is not how I would have hoped to do this for my girl, but this is where time has brought us."

He got down on one knee, and her first thought was how he might wrinkle those crisply ironed pants, but then she felt ridiculous for thinking that as she realized what he was doing.

This was it. The culmination of what she'd dreamed for most of her life. Her knees shook and she was afraid she might faint.

"My dearest Vera," he started, "you have been my reason for getting up every day, ever since I met you right outside the walls of this very train station. We have known each other through so many things, but now I am ready to make you my own. To love and honor and protect you for the rest of your life."

The train whistled again, and Vera looked up to see that almost all the sailors had boarded.

But Angelo only looked at her, the happiest she had ever seen him. He stood up.

"Vera, will you marry me?"

She nodded with what seemed to be her whole body and smiled so wide that it kept the tears at bay. Her fairy tale coming true. Different from how she might have imagined it, but everything came around exactly the way it was always meant to.

This, at last, was right.

She let go of a breath, feeling like she'd been holding it for too many years.

"Yes, Angelo, yes," she answered at last. She threw her arms around him as he pressed his lips against hers for the second time. Bolts of electricity shot through her as she responded in kind with more strength than she knew she had. This was *so much better* than she'd ever pictured.

"And, my darling, we're going to do this right. We'll have my family there in the church, and you'll look beautiful as you walk down the aisle to me."

"I don't care about the details. Just come back to me; that's all I ask."

They ignored the next whistles, which came not from the train but from the mass of sailors who had noticed the scene. Vera laughed, and Angelo kissed her fully and deeply and thoroughly until she felt as if his arms were the only thing that could hold her up. The stubble from his chin chafed her skin, leaving a sweet pain in its place. When at last he pulled away from her—the third and final warning had come from the conductor—she leaned against the stair railing and felt dizzy.

"I have to go," he said into her hair. He gripped it and then pulled away, holding on to her with nothing but his fingertips touching the end of a curl.

She pulled him to her, not wanting to let him go. He couldn't go, not after finally—*finally*—having this moment that was so many years in the making. She couldn't send him overseas.

What if he never made it back?

"I'll write to you," he said as he stepped away.

"I'll write back," she said. Such ordinary things to say on an extraordinary day. He turned around at last and made his way to the stairs of the train car. Catcalls from the men rained down on him, but he only grinned. As the wheels began their slow rotation, he tossed a small box at her, and she caught it.

"I forgot to give that to you! I love you, Vera Keller! You have made me a happy man today!" He waved his arm in a high arch.

She opened the box. The ring! Her heart pounded. This was really happening. It was no longer something she pined for as she slept alone in her bed. She slipped it on and held her arm in the air so he could see it as she ran after the train.

"I love you, Angelo Bellavia. Hurry back!"

Even as she said these words and watched his train disappear into the tunnel, she thought of the headlines and of all those sailors heading to Norfolk to train for a war that had already claimed millions.

She breathed a prayer that the United States wouldn't enter the war.

And that if they did, that her Angelo would return home to her.

To all of them.

Chapter Sixteen

April 1917

War posters were plastered across the sides of buildings, creating a colorful backdrop to dreary times.

From patriotic films to bond advertisements to larger-than-life women draped in flags to encourage enlistment, one could not pass a block without encountering a dozen of them.

But the one that caught Vera's attention the most shouted, "Sow the Seeds of Victory!" A woman wearing a red handkerchief on her head walked barefoot across rows of dirt, spreading seeds behind her. President Wilson had been saying, "Food will win the war!" and Vera felt that this was an opportunity to help, even in her small way.

She wrote to the National War Garden Commission, and with Victor's permission, she started a war garden in Madison Park. He'd encouraged her to create one on the massive rooftop of the house, but she thought that putting it in a public space would motivate others to participate in it.

Besides, she didn't need the food. What was provided at Pearl's grandmother's house was substantial, even in these times. What she grew could be given to others.

What she had not anticipated was how it might also help William and Vater. Neither showed interest when she dirtied her hands burying carrot seeds, but when their lacy green tops began to peek through the soil weeks later, the old man and the young boy were keen to join her.

Afternoons found the three of them in the garden, and before long they had a modest harvest. Vera thought that it was good for William to do this kind of labor, and Vater seemed to be almost himself when he sat outside with them.

With this work, she also felt she was helping Angelo.

Though war had not yet been officially declared, most felt it was imminent. American opinions about joining the fight overseas were divided. The Irish wanted to stay out of the war because involvement would only help the British. The Germans wanted to stay out of the war because it was an attack on their homeland. The hawks in Theodore Roosevelt's circles wanted in because they believed they could save the world and spread democracy. President Wilson's speeches were increasingly leaning this way.

The suffragettes were split. Half sided with most women of the day, abhorring the idea of engaging in battle. But others saw it as an opportunity for women to prove themselves in the absence of men. With all the talk of freedom and liberation being bandied about overseas, they drew parallels to the oppression of women here in the United States, being denied their chance to have an equal say.

For or against, it was a significant opportunity to capitalize on the issue.

Politics meant little to Vera, as did the ocean that separated her from Europe. While Germany was the land of her birth, the United

States was the home of her heart. And her heart belonged to Angelo Bellavia.

Who, any day, would be crossing those Atlantic waters. She had not seen him in the months that had passed since his proposal, but they'd exchanged flurries of letters that rivaled any blizzard.

All were full of the endearments that had been withheld for too long.

Darling Vera, some would start. *There is almost no corner of me that you do not know, but my days on the ship are teaching me new strengths that I would not have known myself capable of. How it feels to swelter inside metal walls even as my uniform is drenched from being in an overturned raft during a training exercise. The extent to which I can go without eating and still feel like I can perform the duties required of me. They are testing us—how far our limits are—and giving us a foretaste of what they expect we'll see in Europe.*

Dearest Angelo, she would respond. *I have never imagined leaving New York, having been happy enough in my small world. But with the very idea of you crossing the waters you crossed as a young boy, seeing the continent of both our births, something awakens in me. I wish you could see it all under better circumstances and that I could see it with you. Perhaps one day. Keep yourself safe, I beg you. And maybe someday we'll pass over the Atlantic and you will bring me to taste gelato in your Piazza Navona.*

She hoped that letters would be able to come through once he got there—wherever he was being sent. Each letter, each postcard, each touch of his handwriting was more precious to her than any treasure she could have been given.

News from Pearl was equally worrisome.

She'd just been arrested for the third time. Apparently, authorities in Albany didn't appreciate it when you chained yourself to the fence of the capitol building.

Some women were arrested for vandalism. Reports of burned mailboxes and shattered windows made headlines, but letters from Pearl insisted that those activities distracted from the very important work they had to do.

The suffragettes had gained tremendous ground as women like Alice Paul and Carrie Chapman Catt outdid the efforts of their hallowed predecessors by creating an organized structure across the country to mobilize women from sea to sea with the same message.

Efforts ranged from the awe-inspiring to the tragic.

Just a few months ago, when President Wilson sailed across the New York Harbor in the presidential yacht to switch on the first electric lights in the Statue of Liberty, a fleet of female pilots took off from Staten Island in biplanes. They crisscrossed the sky over the mighty boat, back and forth, showering him with leaflets that said, simply, "Votes for Women."

But when that was not enough to get his attention, they turned to more drastic measures.

Resisting arrest at demonstrations.

Jail sentences.

Hunger strikes.

Pearl had participated in all of them, and Vera could not have been more proud of her.

But her joy was dimmed by the fact that Pearl languished in a prison cell in the state capital, and that her letters had come to a sudden stop. Vera longed to take a train to see her and determine whether there was anything she could do to help, but she was needed elsewhere. Little Will had just turned six years old. And she didn't want to ask Victor or the rest of the staff to watch over Vater so she could go off.

Lady Pilkington, who had just returned after an extended stay in California, had not given Vera and Vater the reception that Pearl had promised.

She'd arrived only last night, prompting Victor to recommend that Vera put William to bed early so that he didn't run around the house and disturb Lady Pilkington. She'd told her staff that she would retire to bed to recover from the long journey and was not to be bothered. But after breakfast this morning, she summoned Vera to join her in the morning room.

Vera slipped into Will's room, then Vater's, listening to the peaceful breathing that she heard from each of them as they slept. Then she walked across to the north wing and knocked on the door. Her stomach tightened at this beckoning and what it might mean.

Victor opened it, and Vera thought she saw a look of despair on his face. But perhaps it was only a mirror of her own.

"Good luck, Miss Keller," he whispered before holding the door open for her and then slipping outside himself.

"Don't dawdle, young lady," an old voice said. Vera quickened her pace, though she wanted nothing more than to draw out the steps to the desk in the alcove. Even a delay of a few seconds would allow her to continue the fiction that everything was going to be all right.

Lady Pilkington sat surrounded by candles despite having spent a fortune on wiring the house for electric lights. Pearl had once told Vera that her grandmother preferred the candles because they were not harsh on her waning vision. The scene created a glow around her, as if she wore a halo. An intentional effect? Vera doubted it, but it remained unnerving.

"Sit in that chair there." The old woman pointed with a cane to a seat across from the large, scrolled desk.

Vera did as she was told and fought the temptation to let her eyes wander around this room that she had never visited. It seemed to be one of the most beautiful of all, with wispy white curtains embroidered with butterflies. But that was as much as she could see, staring straight ahead.

Lady Pilkington leaned forward, and the effect of the candles shifted from halo to jack-o'-lantern as they lit her prunelike face. Vera squeezed her hands together on her lap to keep them from shaking.

"Sit up now. You young girls have learned terrible habits, and I'll not have bad manners or bad posture in my home."

"Yes, ma'am."

"If there was one thing I appreciated about the years I lived in England, it was their social graces."

"Yes, ma'am."

Lady Pilkington displayed the kind of countenance that demanded obedience. Vera had never met anyone quite like her.

The jack-o'-lantern face peered forward as Lady Pilkington adjusted her glasses.

"You have been living under the roof of my generosity for far too long. I was happy to indulge my granddaughter when she pleaded for a friend who was in need, but I never intended for it to become a permanent situation. I myself was ill and recuperating at my home in California, so I overlooked it for the time being. But now that I am here and have my strength back, I find two strangers in my home without the company of my granddaughter, who has gotten herself *incarcerated*. I am forced to evict you."

Panic rose in her throat. Where would they go?

"Please, no." The words escaped Vera's lips, even as she knew that it was fruitless. She could tell that this was the type of woman who might donate grand amounts of money at benefits and galas to do her part for charity, but who would not tolerate the unfortunate landing on her doorstep. Or sleeping in her bedrooms.

That was not meant to discount Vera's appreciation for having stayed here.

"This is not a poorhouse, as you have well noticed."

"But Pearl said—"

"I have no interest in what my granddaughter might have told you. She once had my support in her pursuits on behalf of women, but we diverge in our ideas on how to go about it. She had the chance to use her standing in this community to bring about change in a dignified way, and instead she has chosen to marry a ragamuffin—two times over—and has continued to demonstrate her appalling lack of judgment. I'm washing my hands of her concerns."

Blessed are the meek. Mama used to read the Bible at night and explain to Vera what the words meant. *Turn the other cheek.* She'd explained to her daughter that these phrases were examples of how to live life as a gentle woman. But in this moment, Vera began to see how she had clung to these phrases not as a guide but as an excuse. It was all well and good in times of peace to live by these principles, but how did they promote change in an increasingly unfair world?

Meekness would bury the United States under overseas aggressors. She was understanding more and more why Angelo joined the war. Why Pearl rallied for rights.

Turning the other cheek wouldn't give women the right to vote. Neither would it protect her father or Will. And calling her beloved Angelo a *ragamuffin* or dismissing Pearl's very real heroics lit a raging fire in Vera where there had been only a flicker.

She stood up and placed her hands on the desk.

"I owe you a great debt for having allowed us to stay as long as you have. So I mean no disrespect when I say this, but you are gravely mistaken in your description of Pearl, who at this very moment languishes in a cold jail cell *not* out of disregard for your family but because she has the courage to sacrifice herself rather than remain cozy in surroundings where teas and lunches bring about lovely conversations about the *idea* of betterment for women but don't produce any actual *results*."

Lady Pilkington rose to her feet, supporting herself on her cane until her hands lay on the opposite side of the desk and her eyes were level with Vera's.

But Vera no longer felt afraid.

"I will not tolerate such impertinence in my household."

"Well, as you are evicting me anyway, I have nothing to lose. This has to be said. Pearl Pilkington is a hero. A *legend*. I will not stay in a place that insults her so."

"Then off with you. You and your lunatic of a father."

That word stripped away every last vestige of propriety that Vera had been inclined to maintain. She felt alive in a way that she hadn't known was possible.

"I believe I'm correct in assuming, Lady Pilkington, that you arrived back in New York by train. And if that is so, then I'll have you know that it was my father and other sandhogs like him who gave their lives and their youth and their health to build tunnels so that women such as yourself could arrive in the city in the comfort of your posh train car rather than navigate the unreliable waters of the Hudson River."

She might have hoped for a flinch—the slightest flicker of emotion at this—but the woman across from her stood like stone.

Vera leaned farther, moving her hands closer, feeling a brazenness that had, up until now, belonged only to Pearl. But it was time for other women to step up and discover their own strength. "I am grateful, Lady Pilkington, for the very real generosity that you have bestowed on us. But I quite agree. This mansion is no place for us. I have grown too comfortable here when girls my age are working themselves to the bone just blocks away. So my father and Will and I will pack up our things and be out by tomorrow."

She expected to receive ire from the formidable old woman, but it was not forthcoming. Instead, Lady Pilkington smiled a grim smile, and her eyes shone with something that made Vera tremble more than she already was.

The old woman folded her arms. "You and your father and my granddaughter may go do whatever it is you like. But you will not be taking William with you."

Oh. Vera felt as if she'd been punched. She'd never considered that Lady Pilkington would see any kind of ownership in Will's care.

Panic rose in her throat. She could not lose Will. She'd say and do whatever Lady Pilkington wanted to keep that from happening.

Vera had been his constant companion every day when he returned from school. She knew his favorite animal at the Central Park Zoo. She knew that he liked strawberry gelato rather than chocolate. She knew that he slept in the shape of an X at night and that he was afraid of spiders.

Lady Pilkington would never know or care about these kinds of things. William would probably be packed off to some kind of boarding school, where his little spirit, the one he'd inherited from Pearl, would be mutated into some uniform mold of what a proper little rich boy should be. Pearl would rather die than see her son raised like that.

And so would Vera. She needed to think of a plan. But as much as she wanted to continue this rant, it would only be detrimental to Will to continue that course. She changed her tone to one of docility.

"I understand why you might want to keep him here, Lady Pilkington. But I am like a second mother to him. And it was the express wish of his actual mother that he remain in my care until she returns."

But the woman did not retreat. "My granddaughter has given up certain privileges with the choices she's made." She tapped a leather-bound folder. "I have here the legal documents that were drawn up by my lawyers to establish custody of William. He is a Pilkington, not a pauper, and he will not be leaving with you."

Vera tried hard to control a growing tremble. She grasped at the last hope she had. "Isn't he a Bower? Like his father, Owen?"

Her question was met with a fiery glare.

"He is a Pilkington. Nothing but a Pilkington." The old woman clasped her hands together. "I have someone who will be picking him up when school is out. That gives you one hour to leave. I do not want to ever see you or your father here again. You're dismissed."

Vera felt the heat of anger and terror rise to her skin. But she knew no more words that might convince Lady Pilkington to allow her to keep the precious boy she loved.

Lady Pilkington opened the top drawer of the desk and pulled out a small envelope.

"Out of charity and what might be your initial innocence in the matter, I will send you off with a modest sum so that you may find immediate lodgings. I will not have anyone say that Abigail Pilkington did not give when it was needed."

Vera felt like she'd been slapped.

Lady Pilkington slid the envelope across the desk. Vera so badly wanted to walk out of the room without it. To make the point that she didn't need the charity of such a woman. But without a stipend, how would she find a place for her father?

How would she take care of Will? Because despite Lady Pilkington's declaration, Vera had no intention of leaving without the boy. She would throw herself into the fireplace before letting that happen.

She snatched the envelope and hurried out of the room without looking back.

Where could they go? What could she do with a mentally unfit man and a spirited little boy? Could she get into some kind of trouble with the law if she took Will against the proclamation of his great-grandmother? Or would it be on her side because of the wishes of his mother?

But Pearl had demonstrated a hundred times over the importance of principle over everything else. What happened tomorrow didn't matter if today Vera did the right thing.

First she slipped into Will's room. She riffled through his clothes and found enough for four days. She spread the remaining ones out so that it wouldn't look as if she'd taken anything.

A magnificent stuffed bear sat on his bed, sent to him by Lady Pilkington while she was in California. A birthday present that likely cost more than Vera could expect to earn in a year. But Vera knew that Will tossed the bear to the floor every night in favor of a small stitched horse that she had made for him. He was fascinated by the few remaining horses and buggies that sometimes trotted along the streets of New York, weaving in and out of the automobiles that were rapidly replacing them.

The horse went into the satchel that she packed. She put her own clothes on top of that and would follow them with the few that Vater owned.

Vater. Getting him out of here was going to be a feat.

Vera ignored the gnawing sense of fear that wanted to rise up in her chest like bile. There were things to do. She had to be brave like Pearl and Angelo.

She stood in Vater's doorway, watching him sleep. This time on Madison Square Park had been so healing for him. There were no screeching neighbors to startle him. No landlord pounding at the door for rent. No need to find Vera at the sink when he had one of his sudden bouts of illness. He didn't really understand where they were or why, but something inside him knew that it was safe.

Until now.

"Do you want some help with him?"

Vera jumped. She hadn't heard Victor walk up behind her.

"No, I can do it." But she regretted the words as soon as she'd said them. Being a strong woman didn't mean she couldn't accept assistance. Especially when she really did need it.

Thankfully, Victor disregarded it. He walked past her. "It's one o'clock and you need to pick up Will in an hour."

Vera didn't let her face betray the fact that she planned to leave early and make an excuse for getting him out of school ahead of time.

But Victor must have already thought the same thing. "Miss Vera, I have had the pleasure to get to know you all these months. You are like a mother to that little boy. Perhaps even more than Mrs. Bellavia, if I may say so. It's not right that he be separated from you."

How did he know that this was happening?

He answered her unspoken question. "I overheard Lady Pilkington instructing her lawyer to pick the boy up at two o'clock. I think it's best if you get there earlier."

"Oh, Victor!"

"Miss Keller, you're running out of time. You go get Will. I'll get your father ready."

"But where should we go? I can't come back here."

Victor was prepared. He handed a slip of paper to Vera. Four twenty-five Delancey.

"This is my sister's address. She is prepared to take all three of you in for a few nights until you can figure out what to do next. No one will find you there."

"I don't know what to say."

"Don't say anything. Sometimes we working people need to stick together. And here—" He handed her four dollars.

"Such a sum! Victor, I can't take this!"

"Miss Keller, you will take it. Consider it my small contribution to Votes for Women. This way I know it's going directly to someone who is helping."

"But—"

"Then consider it a gift in honor of Mrs. Bellavia. I've known her for many years, and whatever helps you helps her. Now, you really *must* be going."

Vera took the money and the address and nodded, nearly dazed by Victor's generosity. But he was right. Time was running out. She blew a kiss to her sleeping father and gave a quick hug to Victor.

"I don't know how I can ever repay you, but just know that I will do everything I can to help Pearl and to raise her son."

"That's all I need to hear. Now go."

Before another word could be said, she threw her satchel across her shoulder and raced out of the palace that had begun to feel like a prison.

Vera had never so much as taken an apple from an untended cart. And now she was going to abduct the descendant of one of the wealthiest and most powerful families in New York.

She felt emboldened for the first time in her entire life.

Chapter Seventeen

Vera's second-ever train ride began uneventfully. Will was far past the age of wearing diapers and was merely as curious as any boy his age would be as they settled into their seats. He positioned himself on his knees so as to see outside the window. For the moment there was nothing to look at except the darkness of the platform.

Her father was showing the first signs of agitation. He flexed his fingers back and forth, and his fidgeting grew stronger with each minute they waited. Vera had bought three of the four seats that faced one another, and she hoped that the train would not be full. She needed to seat each of them by a window, the best distraction she could think of. But if she sat by Will, her father might fall into a fit. If she sat by her father, Will might try to get up and roam around.

She could leave neither alone. She hadn't drunk any water today in order to avoid having to use the train facilities. It was not as if she could take Will and her father with her. But it left her feeling parched, as if she were wilting.

Just three hours. She had to make it three hours with them.

Otherwise it had the potential to devolve into a small circus. But women all over the country were learning to manage children and households on their own as their husbands left for war.

She had a bigger worry, though, than the seating arrangements. Vera fidgeted just like Vater but for a different reason. In taking Will, she was running from the law.

And although she'd put down false names in the train register, a simple description and inspection by authorities would make it easy to find them.

They'd spent the night at Victor's sister's apartment, but hours of bewildered wailing by her father was clearly not what their hostess had expected. Plus, Vera needed to get them all out of the city as fast as possible.

Her father began to sway back and forth, and a groan rose from the depths of his throat. "Where am I? Who are you?" And louder, "Where are you taking me?"

The poor man was shaking. Vera gently wrapped her arms around him and rocked him as well as she could, given the awkward angle of sitting next to him in a train seat. Certainly she wanted to soothe him, but she also dreaded any attention that they might draw.

What was the sentence for kidnapping?

"All aboard!"

Vera's eyes darted to each of the passengers. Who among them might be looking for a young woman, an old man, a small boy? She clutched her purse, but it nearly slid free of her hands. Her palms were sweaty with apprehension, as if each passing face posed a threat.

The conductor shouted from the door, and porters ran up and down the sides making last-minute luggage runs. The little trio had nothing on those carts, though. Vera hadn't known that stowed luggage was something you could bring on a train. She'd only ever been on that short trip to Washington and had brought just a small knapsack.

She chided herself for being ignorant. Of course you could bring larger parcels on the train. How did you expect to travel the farther distances—Chicago, Denver, San Francisco—with only what you could carry? But in the hurry, such details had not been important.

Besides, she didn't own any luggage. Why would a factory girl living in an apartment that was only a bit better than a tenement need something large enough to go away for a long time?

So all the belongings she could carry—some clothes, Will's horse, Vater's photograph of Mutter, her solitary rock from her youth with Angelo—were packed tightly into the satchel. In her small purse, she carried the remainder of the money from Lady Pilkington and Victor. And all her letters from Angelo.

If he didn't return from the war, they would be all she had of him.

The possibility made her sick, and she begged God every night to spare him.

"Your tickets, madam," said the conductor. His voice from behind her made her jump. She pulled them from her pocket and avoided his eyes. Maybe he'd been told to look out for them.

For Vater she'd used the name Arthur Smith. She avoided anything German. The war climate had made people suspicious of such names, especially since the sinking of the *Lusitania* took the lives of so many Americans.

For Will, Daniel Smith. There must be a thousand of those in New York.

For her, Dorothy Smith. Plain enough.

"Your father?" he said, pointing to an ever restless Vater.

"My husband's uncle," she lied. "I'm taking him home to his wife. He was here for a funeral."

Please keep quiet, she willed her father, as if her thoughts could make it so. A wrong word from him could crumble their story. Her heart raced at the very notion.

"And your son? He's about my boy's age. An energetic age, eh? My Fred wants to take apart everything he finds and figure out how it's built."

"My nephew," she corrected. She needed to disguise any truth of the relationship between them in case their description had been reported. But she also needed to remain in the conductor's good graces. So she smiled, clenching her teeth into a set position to settle the nerves that had her pulse racing. Was he just being nice, or was he on the alert for a group like theirs? "But, yes, he likes to take things apart and build them back up again. Especially Tinkertoys."

The conductor laughed, and his belly shook. "I bought Fred a set of those for Christmas. He's crazy about them. He's convinced that New York will someday have the tallest building in the world, and he wants to design it."

"Smart boy. Surely there are good schools for architecture in the city."

"Not on a conductor's salary."

She nodded. She knew well enough that low wages didn't go far.

"Well, you let me know if you need anything. It's about three hours to Albany."

"Thank you."

He punched their tickets and placed them on the railing overhead. He walked on, and she breathed a bit easier. Safe for now. She hoped.

The train began to roll away. As they traveled through the tunnels under the river, Vera explained to Vater that he was the reason this was possible. She spoke softly, gently, not knowing whether he even understood her words. Since their stay at Madison Park, his condition had improved greatly, but every day could be different. As soon as she could secure custody of Will and settle into an apartment in New York, she would save up to send for her father and bring him home to be in her care once again.

Because she was not only going to Albany to see Pearl but also to bring Vater to the state hospital.

She knew that when Angelo came home, they could look after the old man and the young boy together.

If he came home. The *if* that always echoed the *when*, reminding her that nothing was certain. She wondered if all waiting wives, fiancées, mothers thought this way. There was perhaps no scarier word than the unassuming *if*.

To pass through these deep tunnels with Vater at her side was as hallowed to her as any cathedral she might imagine entering. When they emerged back into the light, she was delighted to see a look of wonder on his face as the scenes raced by, a welcome change from the agitation he'd expressed earlier. He often did well when he was kept busy, just as she remembered that diversion was the best tool when Will had been a toddler.

Old men and little boys were really not so different from one another.

Before long, the faintest bit of light began to brighten the car until they were awash with the sunlight of a gorgeous spring day. Vera hoped they would be able to return to New York soon. If all went well in Albany, this day might signify the beginning of a new life.

She would take her father to the state hospital. There were some in New York City, of course, on the Upper East Side and in the Bronx. But with her hurried need to escape, she had no opportunity to bring him to either facility.

Also, in Albany, she would see if paperwork could be drafted and signed by Pearl giving Vera custody of Will. With that in hand, permission she was sure her friend would give, Vera might be able to come back to the city she and Angelo loved—without fear of arrest—and bring Vater and Will back with her.

Although people continued to board the train when it stopped at Croton-on-Hudson, Poughkeepsie, Rhinecliff, the fourth seat in their corner remained empty. Perhaps it was the fact that Will had stretched out and fallen asleep. But as passengers departed in nearly equal numbers, the seat was not needed, and Vera was able to concentrate on writing a letter to Angelo to tell him what had happened.

When he would receive it and where she would be when he did was completely unknown.

~

Vera squeezed Will's hand and took a deep breath. She realized the irony in spending the last two days hiding from any authorities that might be looking for her, and yet she stood here at the police station. Two twenty-two North Pearl, Albany.

Her Pearl was somewhere inside these redbrick walls. Somewhere on this street that bore her name.

The coincidence of it unsettled her. It felt like the name of the street was a prescient tribute to the woman waiting inside.

Vera couldn't wait to see her friend. To see if there was some way she could help. She'd bundled some bread and sausage in her knapsack but didn't know if she'd be allowed to bring them in.

A once-white stone eagle stood atop the otherwise unimaginative two-story building, peering down at her. It was different from the ones that adorned her beloved Penn Station. Those had a benevolence that emanated from their granite shoulders. This one glared as if it were a sentry positioned there to read the hearts of those who entered. An oracle of sorts. Or so it felt.

She tucked her head down and went to open the door.

"Stop," said Will.

He stepped ahead of her and opened the door, sweeping his small arm across his chest as if he were a doorman.

Vera smiled. "What a gentleman! Where did you learn that?"

His grin showed the hole where he'd lost a tooth two weeks ago. Lady Pilkington didn't know that it was a tradition to leave a small gift under the pillow of a child after they'd lost their first tooth. Vera had left a palm-size metal train for Will. He still kept it in his pocket, awed by the magic by which it had appeared while he slept.

"My daddy taught me!" he said proudly.

That was so like Angelo. Traditional enough to believe in every chivalrous notion since the beginning of time. Progressive enough to support Pearl in her political endeavors. He was, indeed, an excellent father to Will, and the fact that the boy saw him as such confirmed the errand that Vera was here to do.

William didn't belong in a cold, gilded mansion where he wouldn't be allowed to be a child.

"Thank you. You're going to be a lady-killer someday."

His innocent little face wrinkled in confusion. "Why would I kill ladies, Zia Vera?"

"It's an expression, dearest. It means that some girl will be lucky to marry you."

"C-can I marry you, Zia Vera?" His stutter had all but vanished under Vera's care, making an appearance only when he was tired or agitated. After their long ride today, she wasn't surprised to hear it slip in.

She forced a laugh so as not to worry Will about their surroundings. "No, Will. But you'll meet a wonderful girl. I'm certain of it."

Vera walked through the glass door, hoping that Lady Pilkington had not contacted this particular station yet. But there was no choice. Vera had to see Pearl.

It fortified her for the rest of the conversations she'd have to have today. She'd just come from the state hospital and filled out the copious paperwork that declared her father unfit to live alone or be cared for without professional assistance. It was agonizing to say goodbye, but she could not think of it now. She had to be strong for Pearl and Will.

She hid her tears until they sat inside her like a rock. She could barely breathe.

Her next discussion would be with the police officer who manned the desk and looked as if he were cousin to a cactus. He had untamed whiskers that sprouted in patches and a prickly demeanor that might have scared her off if this mission were not so important.

"You're not one of those crazy suffragettes who have been swarming my station all week, are you?" he asked when Vera inquired about Pearl.

The indignation that had begun at Lady Pilkington's house grew into controlled rage at yet another person demeaning someone dear to her. But she would not get anything she wanted by rising to his confrontation. Were these kinds of statements all around her and she'd been too focused on survival to recognize such affronts?

"I am a friend of one of them, yes."

"If you ladies knew what was good for you, you'd go home and find some husbands and leave things the way they are."

She felt her cheeks reddening, and her fists clenched below the counter where he could not see them.

"Sir," she said to the man undeserving of the title, "many of the western states have already passed votes for women, and it is only a matter of time before the rest follow suit. In fact, it will be on the ballot this November here in New York."

"There's no place for women in politics."

"Sir," she repeated, raising her voice a bit, "Montana has not only given women the vote, but it has elected a woman to the United States Congress."

"Yeah, and she voted against the war. What does a woman know about war?"

Vera knew that she wasn't going to convince him of anything and decided to get to the point.

"I don't know about such things, except that someone I love is on his way to fight overseas, and if there were anything I could do to prevent it, I would. But for now, someone else I love is sitting in this building being punished for trying to protect the very same freedoms as our boys overseas. And maybe there *is* something I can do about that."

He patted his stomach and let out a belch. He sighed and cocked an eyebrow at her. "If you really want to help, you can convince your friend to eat something. She's been resisting the feeding tube, and I have to tell you, it's not a pretty sight."

A feeding tube! Vera was astonished that anyone had let it come to that. The very thought of it made her throat burn.

Vera squeezed Will's hand, and as if the officer could see it, he added, "I would not take that boy in there."

"But she's his mother."

"Then you especially shouldn't take him in. In fact, I won't allow it. A boy shouldn't see his mother looking like she does."

Vera pursed her lips, bracing herself for whatever he was warning her against. It must be bad if she could not bring a child to see his own mother. She turned to Will. "Can you stay here, my love, while I go visit your mother?"

He turned from the **WANTED** posters he was looking at. "I want to see my mama," he whispered. It was sadder than a shout might have been.

Vera held back tears. "And she wants to see you, Will. Zia Vera will go talk to her first and then maybe I can bring you in."

She knew it was unlikely but wanted to give him any assurances she could.

"I want to go with you." He was louder this time.

"Please," she said, turning to the officer. "Let me take him in. It might do Pearl some good. Maybe she'll start eating if she can just see her son."

"He'll be fine here," he insisted. "Go see your friend. Tell her to start eating. Or I can't promise what will become of her."

He leaned in, and Vera felt the implied threat. Her blood raced at the injustice of this man having any say in what happened to Pearl. It defined the very reason women were marching and protesting. And starving.

She was afraid to leave William alone in the waiting room. He was so young. He could wander off if no one was looking after him.

Or worse—the police could find out that Vera had taken the boy. How far did Lady Pilkington's reach extend? The possibility terrified her.

But she had no choice. A man might have fared better by holding his ground, but a woman's thoughts did not merit the same consideration.

"I'll be right back, Will," she said. "Sit right there and be a good boy for me."

She felt her breath become leaden for the second time today. How was one expected to go from an asylum to a prison in a matter of an hour and not feel the enormity of it? But for now, she was exhausted after the train ride and mustering all she had in her to do the smallest things. She reminded herself that it was nothing in light of what Angelo and Pearl were sacrificing. She had to be a soldier for this cause: that of supporting them.

A younger officer stepped up to the counter and opened the door through to the back for Vera. She followed him down a dim hallway. He pointed to one door. "That's the visiting room, but I'm not taking you in there. Your friend is too weak to walk, so I'm taking you to her cell."

Too weak? What did that mean?

But she didn't have to wonder for long. She understood the moment she laid eyes on Pearl.

The weak, lethargic body lying on a cot behind metal bars was not the robust woman Vera had known for five years but a cruel caricature that held little resemblance.

She felt sick to her stomach and gripped the bars to keep from collapsing at the stench. The cell reeked of vomit and death. As soon as the hinges turned, she rushed in and sat beside Pearl. The officer left the door open. Pearl was in no condition to escape.

Her skin was nearly translucent in its thinness. Her once-beautiful face sagged with extra skin at the jowls, and her eyes held none of their former luminescence. Pearl's hair had probably not been pinned into a bun in weeks. Or washed.

"Pearl," she whispered. Vera clenched her hands and wanted to pound on the concrete walls in fury over this maltreatment. This *crime*.

Her friend did not move. Did not even seem to be breathing. Vera was afraid to shake her. Afraid, even, that she might be dead. The very thought was more than she could bear right now. But at last she saw the minute flicker of an eyelash, and her hopes swelled.

"Pearl," she tried a little more loudly.

Pearl turned her head just enough for Vera to see the yellowed bruises on her neck.

It was appalling.

What on earth had they done to her?

"Ver . . . ," she responded, not able to complete the last syllable.

"Oh my God, Pearl, what happened?"

A female voice came from behind a wall. "They're playing with her, that's what they're doing."

Vera ran out the cell door to the one next to Pearl's, where another woman sat on an identical cot. Pearl was not going to be able to tell her much, but maybe this woman could. Her hair was braided and her cheeks were sallow but not sunken like Pearl's.

"What do you mean, they're playing with her?"

The woman folded her arms and curled her legs onto the cot.

"Cat and Mouse. Have you heard of it?"

The sick feeling returned. Vera shook her head.

"The Cat and Mouse. I can't say for sure that it's happening here yet, but they've done it with our sisters in Britain. They let the suffragettes continue on with their hunger strikes and leave them alone just to the point where they're too weak to do any more political *damage*. They assume that once freed, they'll eat. Then, as soon as they commit the slightest infraction—which these warriors certainly will—they'll arrest them again, and the whole process starts over."

"But that's horrible!"

"Of course it is. But the force-feeding is causing too much controversy. We fear that they'll look to the British for inspiration."

"What do you mean? This isn't controversial enough?"

Poor Pearl. Vera couldn't imagine the horror.

"Well, it was the society ladies like our Pearl here who are going on the strikes. Doctors are called in to feed them with six-foot tubes that they force through the nasal passages. I've heard the screams."

"Screams," echoed Vera. She felt like she was hearing herself through a dark tunnel. Like her mind was distancing her from each fresh, terrible revelation. She dug her nails into her hands to bring herself back.

"It's no picnic. The tubes cause them to vomit over themselves, so they sprinkle them with perfume. As if that would cover everything up."

"I can't imagine." Her own words sounded stiff. But there were no more words she knew to say.

"Well, it's why your friend is covered in bruises. And why she stinks. I know it's what's going to happen to me. I was arrested while barring the door to a store whose owner is against votes for women. But I've only been in for three days. Long enough that hunger has become a commonplace feeling. But if your friend can handle it, so can I."

Vera's eyes grew wide. The woman accepted her fate so effortlessly. Or so it seemed. Had Pearl been this resolute? Of course she had.

"I have to get back to her now." Vera's tone belied the sense of urgency she felt. She'd begun to comprehend the very real possibility that Pearl might never leave this place again. That these could be her last minutes with her, and there were none to spare.

"Good luck. She hasn't spoken since I've been here. I don't know how they expect to release her tomorrow. That's the plan, at least. I think they may have let her go too long, though."

Vera could say only two words. "Thank you."

She returned to Pearl's cell and grasped her hands. Delicately. She had no idea what might hurt.

"Sweet Pearl, Vera's here."

"Ver—a." Pearl said them as if they were different words.

"Yes, yes. It's me."

"Wi—"

"Will is with me. He's in the waiting room. They, uh, they advised that he not come in for now."

She hoped her voice didn't sound as shaky as it felt.

Pearl nodded with what seemed to be great effort.

Vera stroked her matted hair and pulled the food from her bag. "Please, Pearl? Can I help you eat something? We don't have to tell them. But even a little bit might help you."

Pearl turned her head away with obvious effort.

Vera knew that it would be no use to beg. She had never seen Pearl compromise, and even now, she was not going to do so.

She was in a bind. She could not burden Pearl with everything that had happened with her grandmother. And yet she was scared that if she didn't get some kind of permission from Will's own mother to keep him for the time being, she could be in trouble with the law, and the boy might be taken away.

But looking at her friend's wretched face, once so enviable and now stained with shadows and hollowness, it seemed as if nothing Vera would tell her could make it any worse.

She had to press on for William. Dear little Will. Pearl would hate to see him grow up in such a restrictive home. One where he might become the kind of gentleman that Lady Pilkington and her ilk imagined for him. Not the kind that Angelo would model for him.

So she gave her an abbreviated description of all that had occurred in the past few days, whispering and all the while caressing Pearl's hand. It was so bony and delicate. Vera hoped she wasn't hurting her.

"I will do whatever you want. I will bring him to your grandmother if that's what you think is best. Or I will keep him until you are out and you are healthy. Just give me any kind of sign so I know what to do."

Pearl's eyelids fluttered, and her cracked lips started to open.

"You," she exhaled.

Vera pressed her forehead to Pearl's hand and nodded.

"You," she said again.

"Yes. Yes. Of course I'll take him."

Vera slipped a piece of paper out of her pocket. She'd written it at the last minute while they were on the train, not knowing how much time they might have together in the prison. She had no idea if it would be considered legal, but she didn't have the time or the money to hire an attorney to draw it all up properly.

To whom it may concern:
Until such time as I am able to reclaim my son, William Pilkington Bower, I give guardianship to Vera Keller and to my husband, Angelo Bellavia, in my place.

It was admittedly simple, and Vera resisted the inclination to add legalistic words such as *whereto* and *forthwith*, not knowing what they meant and fearing that they'd reveal her ignorance of such things. But the intent was plain, and Pearl's signature would give it as much validation as she was capable of acquiring at this time.

She read it to Pearl, reading slowly as she fought tears.

"Please know that it is my desperate prayer, Pearl, that you are able to return home quickly and recover your health. I—I am not trying to be Will's mother. He has only one irreplaceable mother—you. But with everything I have, with my very life, I will take care of him until you are able."

The corners of Pearl's mouth turned upward.

Vera pulled a fountain pen from the bottom of her bag. The ink had leaked, leaving a black stain on the fabric, but she didn't care. She pressed it into Pearl's palm, wrapping her friend's fingers around it until she made a fist. She moved slowly, so as not to cause pain to Pearl. Vera held the paper up, unavoidably flimsy with no book or table to support it. But there did not seem to be any chance that Pearl would be able to sit up and sign it against the wall.

The enormity of such a simple action, the ache that Pearl must be enduring for the sake of her son even with such small gestures, made Vera want to weep. She would tell William of this someday when he was old enough to understand.

If such a thing could be understood.

Though three holes poked as they tried, Pearl managed to sign something illegible. Vera's heart sank, knowing that what thin chance they had at this being legal was even more unlikely, but it was all she had. She folded it and returned it to her pocket.

She continued to hold Pearl's hand. She wanted to stay. To talk Pearl into eating. Or to be there for the end. But William was alone in the waiting room. And the police could be notified any minute of who they were.

"I have to go now." She laid her head on the cot and felt Pearl's fragile body against her cheek. Vera brushed her paper-thin skin and whispered incoherent apologies. "I don't want to, I don't want to, Pearl, but I have to. Find Victor when you get out. He'll know where we are."

When. Not *if.* But she didn't believe her own optimism.

She kissed her beloved friend on the forehead and squeezed her eyes tight so that the tears that wanted to come wouldn't land on Pearl.

"You are my hero," she whispered. "There is no one else like you. But please eat. I say this not as a sympathizer to your very right cause but as one who loves you. Please eat, Pearl. Please eat and come home. You are worth more to women alive than if you are—"

But she could not complete the sentence and wished to erase the unsaid word from her mind.

"Come back to us." She'd asked of Angelo the same thing before he left.

Come back to us.

Chapter Eighteen

Vera jumped at the sound of the knock.

She and Will had made their home in this one-room tenement near Houston and Second. They'd been back in New York for only a week, and she'd not met any of the other residents in this building yet. Surely no one was coming to borrow a cup of sugar that she couldn't afford to have.

She'd just gotten off a shift at her new job. She'd been lucky to find another factory position so soon. If there was one good thing to be said about the war, it was that jobs for women were more plentiful than they'd been before. She was making asbestos mattresses. Not for sleeping on but for wrapping the boilers of battleships. The work was exhausting, her fingers were worn and cut already, and the summer heat was just beginning to make its appearance. But it was worth it to be able to have daytime hours so that she could walk Will home from his new school and be with him in the evening. She left him every morning at four o'clock and had taught him how to put together a simple breakfast before letting himself out.

She would kiss his rosy cheeks one at a time before she left. He slept too deeply to know it, but she hoped that somehow, subconsciously, he felt how much she loved him.

Knock, knock.

Her muscles tightened. Only Victor knew they were here, but she didn't want to take any chances.

"A game, Will," she whispered. "Let's play a game. Slide under the bed and see how long you can stay there without making a sound."

Thankfully, he obeyed, and when she couldn't see anything but his bare heels, she covered them with a blanket and walked over to the door.

She smoothed her hair back and took a deep breath.

"Vera."

"Victor!"

She exhaled and threw the door open to invite him in, then called out to Will, "You can come out, sweetheart."

"Have a seat," she said to her guest. She wiped the table down with her apron, as she'd not yet had the time to launder the two dish towels that she owned. "Can I make you some tea?"

Victor sank into the wooden chair, his shoulders slumping.

"No. I can't stay long."

"So you got my note. About where we are."

"Yes. My sister gave it to me right away."

"Is Lady Pilkington looking for us? For Will?"

He nodded.

"The Pilkingtons—including Pearl's parents—have hired two investigators. And the staff has been questioned. No one but Angelica and I know where you are, though."

Vera's chest tightened, and she had to hold her hands together to avoid their shaking. Investigators. It would be only a matter of time until they were found.

She took a breath and steadied her voice so as not to scare William, who was driving his toy train along the threadbare arms of the sofa. "They're that determined to get him back. But it will be just a matter of time before Pearl returns, and when she does, she'll want Will to be with her."

He shook his head. Vera knew he was thinking. Her family might make a case that with Pearl's incarceration she was unfit to be a parent. They would win no matter what.

Making her scrap of paper, so pitifully signed by Pearl, even more worthless than she'd feared.

"Vera," he said in a muffled tone.

Her heart beat hard. Harder.

"Yes?"

"Miss Pearl is dead."

Vera sat next to him, placing her face in her hands.

She'd known it. She really had, even before he'd said it. Four days ago a dark rain cloud had passed over the sun, erasing the light momentarily, and Vera had thought of Pearl. She'd shuddered, then brushed it off. It didn't mean anything. Pearl would start eating and return home and all would be well.

Except that it wouldn't. The blackest of black colors invaded her vision. A color so dark that she'd never be able to paint it.

Victor told her the details, but she could have guessed easily enough.

"She was supposed to be released this week. We got a telegram at the house that we were to send someone up to Albany to get her. There was a terrible argument within the family about it. Pearl's father, he'd have just written her off. Left her there. Pearl's mother began crying. Never saw that before. But Lady Pilkington was the one who was most determined. She planned to send a car for Miss Pearl and was going to hire a nurse to restore her to health. I guess the old bird has a heart after all. Or part of one."

"Pearl wouldn't have wanted to go back to that place." Vera stood up and smoothed her skirt and paced back and forth around the room.

"You and I both know it, Vera, and I think Lady Pilkington did, too. All the time they spent arguing, there was Pearl, passing on in a jail cell."

She wanted to scream, but this was no place for it. But not just for her, for the loss of her friend.

The world had lost a light like no other.

Those tyrants couldn't win.

Vera wanted to run from the apartment to Penn Station and find the suffragettes who spent every day there and join their ranks in a bigger way, taking up the mantle that Pearl had started.

But there were more pressing concerns.

What to tell Angelo?

What to tell Will?

She reached out to him and brushed her hand along his leg.

"Oh, my darling," she said, pulling him onto her lap. He wrapped his arms around her. His angelic face looked up at her.

"M-m-m-m-my m-m-m-m-other i-i-i-i-s d-d-d-d-ead?"

Vera tightened her lips and nodded. "I'm afraid so."

It was an offense to all that was good to have to tell a child that his mother was never coming back.

She pulled him into her arms, and he wrapped his legs around her waist. He hid in her shoulder, and she stroked his hair, speaking to him in soft tones.

"I can never replace your mother, Will. But I will always be your zia Vera, who loves you so much. And I will take care of you and protect you."

His whimpers were muffled in her sweater.

"And I love you, dearest." She rubbed her nose with her sleeve as she forced out the words. It should be Pearl here saying these things.

Oh, mercy, this was difficult.

Victor stood up and walked over to her. "I'd better go. I slipped out over lunch and wanted to come tell you."

"Thank you. I know you came at great personal risk to yourself." She set Will on the bed.

"Anything for Miss Pearl, and for you, Vera. Keep the boy safe, okay? And give my regards to your father when you see him. If he'll remember me."

She placed her hand on his arm as he headed for the door. "He remembers little, Victor. But I will never forget you and how good you were to us these past few months."

"Goodbye, Vera. If I hear of anything else you should know, I'll drop by or send a note."

"I'd be most grateful."

She shut the door behind him and rested her forehead against it. She slid down its side until she sat curled in a ball. Will joined her, and together they huddled in the shadow that the door cast against the moonlight.

She wasn't sure that there would ever be light again.

The owner of the mattress factory where Vera was employed was a Jewish man.

"No one shall work on their Sabbath," he was known to say, paraphrasing the commandment in Exodus that was dear to his own faith and that of all his Christian employees.

So, according to their particular faith, they were encouraged to observe either Saturday or Sunday with their families.

If pressed, Vera might say that she was Lutheran. Not that she practiced. Her church was the parks around New York, her cathedral the grand concourse of Penn Station. It didn't cost one cent to smell the flowers or to watch the people. She memorized details so that she could draw them when she came home.

It was in these moments that she felt uplifted above the difficulty that was life and from the reminders of Pearl that seemed to be everywhere.

It was on Sundays that she and Will explored the city. If it was too hot or too cold, they would sit inside Penn Station and make a game of guessing where the passengers were going. If they carried a lot of luggage, they might be traveling far across the country to San Francisco. If it was expensive, they were probably going first class.

"Where would you go if you could?" she'd ask him.

And he'd always have the same answer: "Over the ocean to see Papa."

She'd pat his hand. "Me too, Will. Me too. Did you know that he and I used to play these games together?"

The memory saddened her, and she rubbed her hand across her chin to stop it from quivering.

She especially missed Angelo now that she could no longer receive his letters. At first she'd asked for them to be sent to Victor's sister, but with Lady Pilkington's investigators looking for them, Vera could not risk being found.

She worried every day about Angelo's safety.

After Victor's visit, Vera packed up her few possessions and moved with William to a hostel that very night without telling anyone. Maybe it was unnecessarily paranoid to do so, but she was not going to take any chances where Will was concerned.

Without any way to be comforted by Angelo, Vera would clutch the bedcovers at night and curl up with worry. Was he safe? Was he cold? Was he scared?

But the headlines offered hope that dispelled fear. Today Vera smiled at the sun and imagined that it was Pearl reading the words alongside her.

THOUSANDS OF SUFFRAGETTES MARCH DOWN 5TH AVENUE

TIDES TURNING: WOMEN WINNING

MILLIONS OF SIGNATURES COLLECTED SUPPORTING VOTES FOR WOMEN

Vera stood behind William as he placed his hands and face on the picture glass of a trinket store. There was a red caboose on display. Not too expensive. Vera was putting money aside to purchase it for him. Another two weeks should do it.

They walked along Thirty-Third Street, a route she could never resist. She enjoyed strolling past Angelo's newsstand, which was currently run by his little brother while he was overseas. She could see it from about a block away. It had a dark-blue awning. Over the years the color had changed—whenever the weather had worn it past the ability to be patched, Angelo had let Kid pick the newest color, knowing how she liked such things. She'd picked red, green, and he'd even indulged her in white. That one quickly turned brown with dirt, and they never went back to it. But for two short weeks it had looked like a cloud of cotton.

She held Will's hand as they approached from across the street and saw a small cluster of people surrounding it. She raised herself on tiptoe to see what they might be looking at, but all she could see was Angelo's brother in the middle, a tweed cap covering his head.

Vera looked both ways at the traffic and crossed the street when it was clear. As she approached, a couple walked away, and she saw the man who had looked like Angelo's brother but wasn't. Instead, a man on crutches stood facing the stand. He picked up a newspaper and turned around to hand it to a customer.

Vera's heart raced. It was not a cousin or a nephew or any of the others from his large Italian family who pitched in during his absence.

It was Angelo.

"Papa!" Will called. Angelo's head shot to the left, and his face reflected how Vera's felt. His eyes widened, his jaw dropped, and Will's hand slipped from hers as they both hurried over to him.

The customers dispersed when they saw the woman and child approaching. Vera stood in front of Angelo, her eyes taking him in. His hair was cropped in a short military cut that was just starting to sprout outgrowth. His jawline held the same dark shadow that she'd always loved.

Her chest swelled with elation at seeing him. At last! He was safe. He was safe. Nothing else mattered.

But then she looked down. His legs. One was missing at the kneecap, and she knew without him telling her that some injury—something she didn't want to even imagine—had sent him home. She blessed and cursed it at the same time.

Before she could ask him anything, she felt his arms wrap around her waist and his lips plant themselves on hers. They were so warm, and she'd missed them—oh, how she'd missed them.

"Papa," Will said, pulling on Angelo's belt.

"Un momento," replied Angelo, breathing his words next to Vera's ear, as they didn't dare pull away from each other. His lips moved to her neck, sending flutters throughout her body. He whispered, "I've missed you, *cara mia*."

"Angelo. What happened? Why are you back? Why didn't you tell me?"

"You disappeared. I found Victor, but he didn't know where you were."

"Papa," Will said more urgently. But Angelo spoke to Vera first.

"There's enough time for discussing all that. What matters is that I'm here and I'm staying and I'm yours, darling, if you'll still have me."

She placed light kisses all over his face. She never wanted to be separated from him again. "Of course. You are all I've wanted for as long as I can remember."

"Zia Vera," said Will.

"A minute, darling," said Vera.

"I want to go to the church and light a candle for Pearl," Angelo said.

Vera nodded. Pearl was already being called a martyr among the suffragettes. But Vera would cherish a moment when just she, Angelo, and William could sit in a church and remember her together.

"Papa! Zia Vera!" This time Will's impatient urgency turned into a wail, and Vera turned her head just in time to see the boy being carried off by two policemen.

Everything became a tunnel, and Vera heard herself scream.

"Will!"

Her throat burned as she called for him again.

"Zia Vera!"

She raced after him, watching his little legs get scooped off the sidewalk into a car. Her arms stretched as far as they would go, all the way through her fingertips, reaching for the car whose engine was already running.

Angelo hobbled behind her on crutches.

"Will!" he called.

Vera screamed again and pushed against the gathering crowd until she could no longer see the car. Angelo caught up with her and wrapped his arms around her waist, pulling them both to the ground. A horse whinnied as it kicked its hooves into the air, tilting the carriage it was bound to.

She heard the sound of metal crunching against a light post. Angelo pulled her onto the sidewalk just before the horse could come down on her.

William. Gone. She felt depleted.

"Shh, shh, darling," Angelo said, stroking her hair. "He's gone. But I promise you. We will find him again."

He pulled her closer.

"We'll find him again."

Part Two: Alice

Chapter Nineteen

New York City, 1942

The departure board fluttered its letters in rapid movements that reminded Alice of hummingbird wings. In seconds Baltimore moved up to the top spot, replacing Boston, whose passenger train had left ten minutes ago.

A couple scrambled to the arch that said Platform 14, from which the Baltimore train would leave any second.

Alice often wondered how people managed to slide in just in time and why they didn't plan their day around a comfortable margin of space. Better to arrive early and enjoy a cup of coffee in one of the station cafés and stroll to your platform without the frenzy of arriving just before the train rolled away.

She took after her mother, Vera, this way. From that German side, Alice inherited a strong sense of timeliness. Five minutes early was too late, according to the Bellavia women.

Her father was an entirely different story. Angelo lived as if clocks and pocket watches had never been invented. *La dolce vita,* he'd say if they ever tried to hurry him. To him, there was always one more sip of cappuccino to savor, one more cloud to observe. Magically, he managed to be *just* on time, often causing Vera and Alice to break into a panic as they were leaving anywhere. When he'd see their nervousness, he'd put on an exaggerated frown and pat the stump that was his left leg and beg pity on a poor crippled man.

Then the exchange would go like this:

Her mother would smile. "Sorry, darling. You were like that long before the war. Always five minutes late and always trying to charm me with that handsome grin of yours."

"And is it working?" he'd respond, his large Italian eyes staring at hers. This always served to break her resolve.

"Yes."

He'd kiss her cheek, and all would be well until the next time.

Alice was lucky, she supposed. Not everyone's parents got along so well after twenty or so years of marriage. More often, she observed demanding husbands and mousy wives, or the reverse. But her parents functioned as equals, though her mother had converted to her father's Catholic faith in order to marry him.

They'd endured much together. She'd grown up knowing about Pearl, about William, and the grandmother she'd never known.

Also different for them was the fact that Alice was their only child in a world where couples seemed to have them by the half dozen. They'd always said that they wanted more. Vera's heart had the capacity to stretch across countless children. But she'd lost one after another just weeks into her confinements, and they all became resigned to being a family of three. So instead Vera worked at the glove counter at Macy's and used the bit of money it brought in to buy herself art supplies.

Their simple apartment on Thirty-Third was adorned with her mother's pastel scenes of parks and flowers. It was as if they lived outside. The artwork was especially cheering during the winter months when the world outside their window was a frozen one. Alice grew up surrounded by this beauty and had absorbed it into her own soul.

She looked at her wristwatch and checked it against the station clock in the center of the grand concourse. Hers was one minute off, so she wound the dial slowly until it was precise. Today her father was actually late. A whole seven minutes. And she needed to catch the subway to her class at Barnard.

"I'll take a pack of Chesterfields and today's *Times*."

The man in front of her was young enough to look as if he should be part of the draft but old enough to look as if life had shown him some potholes. He wore a camera around his neck the way a woman might wear a necklace: an accessory that was put on out of habit. It showed a few dents on its metal casing, silver peeking through black. A bit tatty, just like the cuffs of his sleeves. But not so far gone as to be shabby.

"Lucky Strikes are on special today," she offered instead.

"ABC—Always Buy Chesterfield."

"You read too many advertisements."

He shrugged. "I like what I like."

She pulled the Chesterfields off the shelf behind her and wondered again when her father might decide to show up and relieve her at the newspaper stand so that she could get to the subway. But she shouldn't complain. When he was growing up, his stand was an outside one, open every day despite the weather. Just a few years ago he'd gotten a coveted spot inside the station, and working for him here was a world of difference from how it used to be.

"I haven't seen you here before," the man continued. Alice was often uneasy with conversations that seemed as if men were creating an opening to ask her out. They sometimes complimented her on her abundant brunette locks—a gift from her Italian side—or her large blue eyes, a gift from her German side. Most nationalities didn't mix back when her parents had gotten together. But more and more as America became the melting pot that people called it, marriages between the French and the Dutch and the Italians and the Germans and the Spaniards who immigrated were becoming acceptable.

"I could say the same of you." He was certainly someone she would have remembered.

"I don't usually smoke or read the newspaper," he answered.

"So what makes today special?"

"Would you like for me to say that it's because I saw you standing behind this counter?"

"I am hoping you don't."

"Well, good. Because that isn't why."

He'd caught her in his net with a question that begged to be asked.

"Then why?" Alice played along.

"Because today is going to be a difficult day, and difficult days should always begin with a smoke to relax you and the newspaper to help you remember your blessings."

"But you just said that you don't smoke or read the paper."

"It's my new philosophy. Untested."

She smiled. Yes, she would definitely have remembered if this man had ever visited their newsstand.

His cryptic statement intrigued her, though. "And why is today going to be difficult?"

"Because of all the kisses."

Not the answer she might have expected. "The kisses?" she asked.

"Yes," he answered. "Today, several trains of soldiers are heading out to basic training before the men get sent overseas. So there will be lots of farewell kisses and goodbye embraces. And tears, of course."

"And you are here to say goodbye to someone?" She wondered why, at his age—somewhat around hers—he was not among those shipping out.

"No, I'm here to take their photographs."

"Oh, are you a journalist?"

"Something like that. Journalist. Artist. Whatever pays the most on any given day."

This piqued her curiosity. She considered herself an artist, like her mother. But where Vera valued landscapes and flowers, Alice was drawn to man-made wonders. Buildings and bridges. The features that made a place unique, such as an arched ceiling or well-placed Doric column. It was what interested her in studying architecture, though she was only in the first-year math classes.

He continued. "I like when I get to capture the raw emotions of people. The wrinkles in a face that tell the story of hardship. The light that catches a child's eye when he sees a balloon. There's a bit of a trick to taking their picture just in the instant when their guard is down."

She'd never considered this. A photograph seemed like such a fleeting thing, while a painting required long hours of observation. But they shared a need for the moment to be just right—for her it might be the way the sun reflected on a window before being shielded by a cloud.

Alice glanced at her wristwatch once more, this time hoping that her father would continue to delay his return.

But just as she'd thought that, she saw Angelo coming down the hallway with Bertie. She smiled at the two friends. Between them, they had one good leg. Her father had one remaining after the war, and as Bertie had contracted polio as a child, he could use neither of his. He'd fashioned a board onto wheels and sat on it, close to the ground, making him look about three feet tall. He kept pencils in a bag slung across his chest and etched tiny designs into their yellow paint and sold them to passersby in the concourse.

At first people would buy pencils from Bertie because they felt sorry for him and for the way he had to propel himself across the marble floor with wooden posts in each hand. But when they discovered his talent for carving amazingly detailed miniature scenes, they sought him out to buy them as gifts. He had the wild look of a man who lived on the streets, but he made a tidy living off his regulars, and the station manager turned his eye from the knowledge that Bertie did, indeed, sleep in the men's lounge on the first floor.

He and Angelo had become fast friends when they'd first met years ago. Angelo overheard a child point out a "gimpy half man" who was rolling down the hall. That was all it took for Angelo to seek Bertie out, and they discovered not only a handicap in common but also a love of books and humor.

For as long as she could remember, they'd shared Sunday lunch with Bertie in or around Penn Station. If business had been particularly good, they ordered fountain drinks.

Alice's father always had a soft spot for the less fortunate and never considered himself to be one. That was how he'd met her mother. She'd been a small child with a scraped knee, and he'd given her some gelato to make her feel better. And he'd even taken in a little boy who wasn't his own. But that was long before Alice was born, and stories of young William had permeated her childhood.

Though every happy thing they remembered was tinged with melancholy. Her parents' sadness over losing the boy was a language Alice understood before she could speak. There was always a sense that someone was missing from the table that had four chairs.

"I'll be going now," said the man with the camera around his neck. Alice watched as her father and Bertie came closer.

"That's twenty-nine cents," she responded. He handed her a quarter and a nickel and refused the change.

"I'm Emmett, by the way."

"Alice."

"After *Alice in Wonderland*?"

"After Alice Paul of the National Woman's Party."

"If you say so, Alice in Wonderland. I'll be seeing you."

She opened her mouth in protest, proud of the name she'd been given in honor of all the work her parents' beloved friend, Pearl, had done for women's suffrage before she died. But he walked off before she could say anything.

Her father approached at that moment.

"You have that look about you, *cara mia*," he said. "I know, I know. *You're late, Papa.* I could hear you from all the way down the hall."

"I didn't say anything."

"Not with words. But I know my girl. You and your mama get riled when I don't make it to places in time. So I hear you in my head."

"But if you know that it concerns us, why don't you make an effort to get to places sooner?" It was a recurring question. A true mystery of the universe.

"Would it help if I told you that I was visiting with Bertie here about a birthday present for you?"

"Nice try. It's not for two months."

"For one who is always so early, you should be proud that I'm thinking ahead." He kissed her on the cheek, and she found it impossible, as her mother did, to be upset with him.

She leaned over the counter on her tiptoes and said hello to Bertie.

"Hiya, Alice. Who was the young man you were talking to?"

"Uncle Bertie, you sound like my mother." He always smiled at the affectionate term. After all, he didn't have any nieces—or children, for that matter—of his own.

"I've got to look out for my girl."

"Thank you, but as it happens, he was just a customer."

"Looks like he stayed awhile and didn't buy much."

"A chatty customer, then. They come along once in a while. Not everyone at the station is in a rush."

A woman arrived at the counter and asked for a pack of chewing gum.

"I'll handle this," said Angelo, stepping around Bertie. He gave the woman the pack and waved Alice away.

"Go. Go. You have a class to get to."

Alice knew that at this point she would have missed at least twenty minutes, and the professor took students to task for far smaller things. So she decided not to go today. But she didn't want to make her father feel bad.

She slung her purse over her shoulder. "Got it, Pops." She picked up a pack of Juicy Fruit and kissed her father on the cheek.

She walked in the direction of the subway until she knew that he wouldn't see her.

The subway side of the station was the part that Alice frequented most regularly, zipping north to the college on the Upper West Side. She was the only one of her extended Italian family pursuing higher education. The Bellavias valued manual labor. They were plumbers, electricians, shop clerks. Her interest in studying architecture was looked upon at the annual family gathering at Christmas as though she had an affliction of some sort. It wasn't that she was a woman going to college. It was that anyone from the family was going at all.

But she had the encouragement of her parents, and that was enough.

She stepped into the grand concourse. The great train stations of Europe inspired it, and she hoped that she might see them all someday. The Gare du Nord in Paris. Victoria Station in London. She pored over their pictures in the library and imagined standing under glass canopies. Though she could not imagine the stations being any more beautiful than this. The sun poured through one dome after another and caressed the travelers with its warmth.

She found herself scanning the room and saw that Emmett had been right. Hordes of servicemen in their unused khaki uniforms gathered under the arches leading to the platforms on the other side. Benches were placed through the halls like church pews, the people filling them like worshipful parishioners.

Alice had grown up around these halls. She'd hidden under these benches. She'd scratched her initials into the underside of one of them.

But to see them today was an altogether new vision as she watched soldiers swarmed by loved ones—mothers, fathers, siblings, girlfriends.

The families received cursory nods, perhaps the mothers a bit more, but the girlfriends and wives commanded the greatest attention. Their embraces were the last ones, the longest ones. Despite the onlookers, the soldiers would sweep their girls into their arms. The girls would wind themselves around the soldiers' necks. And their cherry-red lips would leave a mark that they'd wipe away with white-gloved fingers.

Daughter of an entrepreneur, Alice had the thought that one could make a tidy sum of money selling handkerchiefs to mop up the tears. And perhaps tea and water to resupply all that was lost.

Alice watched, mesmerized, at the scene that replayed with every couple. But something else caught her eye.

It was Emmett. He stood behind a column—not hiding yet somewhat hidden, as if he didn't want to intrude. But he held his camera against his face, stretching the accordionlike arm that contained the lens. He waited, waited, waited, and then she saw his finger tap the top of it.

Her breath paused as if it had been waiting right along with him. Steady until just the right moment lined up. She admired his patience and realized that photography *was* about observation, as much as the skill was crucial for any painter.

Then he turned, and their eyes met. Maybe it was the heightened sense of romance that permeated this space. Or the sense of urgency that a war manufactured in the hearts of people who didn't know if there would be a tomorrow.

But she knew already that she would never forget this man.

Chapter Twenty

"A pack of Lucky Strikes and a newspaper."

Alice looked up from her magazine, and her throat became tight.

It had been a week since she'd first met Emmett, although she'd thought of him ever since. She felt comfort in putting things into categories. Her books were alphabetized by title. Everything had its place in their small kitchen. And her father's haphazard newsstand had been transformed as soon as he gave her permission to reorganize it.

But Emmett rattled her. In that one encounter, he'd seemed young yet old. Casual though not ragged. And the things that came out of his mouth were just not what people said every day in conversations with those they'd just met.

She didn't even know his last name.

"I thought it was ABC. Always Buy Chesterfields."

"But you said the Lucky Strikes are on special."

"They were last week."

"Well, maybe it's time to try something new."

She turned around to the wall full of colorful boxes and selected a white package with the targetlike red circle on the front. "How's your new philosophy coming along?" she asked.

"What do you mean?"

"The one where you smoke to relax and read the newspaper to count your blessings?"

"Oh, that one." His eyes sparkled as he looked at her, but it could just have been the reflection of the light bulb that hung above the stand. "The smokes made me cough, and all the stories in the paper are sad."

"And yet you bought both again?"

"Hmm. New philosophy. Try something at least twice before deciding to give it up, especially when a beautiful woman is selling it to you."

She felt herself blush before taking a deep breath. She rubbed her hands down her cheeks before facing him again.

"Here you are. That's twenty-nine cents," she said.

He put thirty on the counter again and refused the change.

This happened for the next two Fridays as well. He always picked a different brand—Old Gold one week and Camel the next. He'd leave his coins on the counter, roll the newspaper under his arm, and saunter off, camera around his neck.

No more statements like *beautiful woman*, but she hadn't really known what to do with that anyway.

Alice never prolonged the conversation, as he always arrived just as her father came to take over her shift so that she could get to class. But she found herself thinking of the curious young man while she worked out formulas and balanced algebraic equations.

But the fifth week marked the beginning of her break for the spring, and she came prepared. She wore the checkerboard dress that her father said looked like a picnic blanket. He knew nothing about fashion.

Emmett appeared right on schedule. Ten forty-five. He laid fifty-five cents on the counter this time.

"A pack of Pall Malls, a newspaper, and a *Life* magazine."

"A magazine? That's a change in your routine." Alice remained poised despite the way her heart pounded when he was around.

He leaned in and took the *Life* magazine from her hands. "I have to show you something. I haven't been able to show anyone yet." He flipped through the pages, looking back and forth until he found what he was searching for on page thirty-two. He smiled and turned it around on the counter so that she could see it.

It was a beautifully composed photo that captured a soldier kissing his lady goodbye. But what was spectacular about it was the way the sunlight shone through the shapes of their faces pressed against each other. The rays found their way through the web of her hair and the spaces where the arches of their noses didn't quite come together, and even down to the place between their necks. It formed something that looked like a star that enveloped them and clearly exhibited the skill necessary to capture that exact moment.

"Look," he said, pointing to the bottom of the picture.

Photo credit: Emmett Adler.

Well, now she knew his last name.

"It's one of mine!"

"I see that," she said, feeling a sense of pride on his behalf—and delight that he'd shared that moment with her.

She watched his face as he beamed at the page. He looked as if he couldn't believe it. His distraction gave her a chance to observe him without knowing it.

His jaw was somewhat rectangular. His cheeks rosy, not from being flushed or warm or cold but a natural color that she'd seen on him before. His blond hair was cut near his head but was just long enough to tell that it would be curly if he let it grow. Combined with his last name and sharp blue eyes, it was easy to fit him into a category that she was familiar with: German. Like one half of herself.

But it was risky these days to mention that heritage, given that the homeland of her history was at war with the homeland of her heart. Her grandfather had been forcibly registered with the government as a German citizen and put on a travel ban merely because of the country of his birth, as if he ever even left the apartment. Her mother must have slipped through the cracks, perhaps because her last name had been Bellavia for so long or because she'd come to the United States as a very small child.

German restaurants replaced their red, gold, and black flags with American banners, and they advertised liberty cabbage and freedom sausage instead of sauerkraut and bratwurst. Even German shepherd dogs were now called Alsatians.

It was not a good time to have ties to Deutschland. She would keep her assumptions about him to herself.

"How did you manage that?" she asked him. "That's no small thing to be published there."

"I send in my pictures regularly. They've been picked up by smaller publications—a newspaper here and there. But never something on this scale."

"Will that help you in the future? Giving you a certain level of credibility?"

"I hope so," he said. "It would be nice to be able to do this for a living. But those kinds of jobs are hard to come by. Unless you want to travel to the war zones. Lots of pictures to be had there."

She wondered again why he *wasn't* overseas like others his age—their age—but there must be a reason, and she didn't know him well enough to ask.

Emmett closed the magazine and set it on the counter. She returned part of his money.

"It's on me today. You shouldn't have to pay for a copy of your first photograph in *Life* magazine. My father would say the same. In fact, he would probably go so far as to give you the entire stack so that you could hand them all out to your friends and family."

Emmett's smile faded. "Well, I haven't got either of those, so I'll just take that one."

It was an unexpected statement, laden with an unspoken history. Once again, she wanted to know more.

"I'll tell you what, though," he continued. "I'd love to celebrate. Are you free after your shift or do you have to catch the subway to school?"

She inhaled quickly. "How do you know I go to school after this?"

He grinned, and she enjoyed the shy expression that came over his face. "I—I may have asked the man on the wheel board about you."

"Bertie?" The old matchmaker. Of course he would have offered up anything if it meant being able to witness young love. She'd always suspected that he was a romantic.

"Yes. That's the one. With the pencils."

"Mmm-hmm. What else did Bertie tell you?"

Emmett looked down at his feet. "That you want to study architecture and that any man who takes you on had better be prepared to have his work cut out for him."

"He didn't!" Her blood rushed to her cheeks, and she felt chagrined.

"He did. But he said it with fondness. If that doesn't sound too confusing."

She clenched her jaw and nodded. "He's always told me that if I pursue the career I want, it will be hard to find a man who won't be jealous of it."

Emmett nodded. "How does that make you feel?"

She leaned her elbows on the counter and looked up at the dangling bulb above her head, as if it might be able to give her the right answer.

"I suppose I'd like to have a man in my life as much as the next girl. But also I want to study and restore old buildings. I don't see why it should be impossible to hope for both."

She held her breath. In her household, her father had always supported her mother's dreams, buying her new paints and canvases as he could afford them. Though her ambition to attend the Parsons School was far beyond their reach, Vera made a modest sum selling abstract pieces that depicted revolutionary subjects about women's rights and workers' unions. But those proceeds she donated to causes in Pearl Pilkington's name. For her own pleasure she painted flowers and scenes from nature.

"Well, that's pretty much what I told Bertie. I think life could be pretty interesting with a woman who will keep me on my toes."

Alice could not have been more surprised by his answer and felt a buzz in the back of her neck over the fact that he and Bertie had been having a whole conversation about her.

Or maybe the flutter was the attraction she felt toward him compounded with her satisfaction at his answer. It was unusual for a man to hold that belief.

He spoke again before she could respond. "Would you like to go somewhere with me after you get off work? There's something I want to show you."

Alice's pulse quickened at the thought of it. "What do you have in mind?"

"It's a surprise. And the fact that you have a mind of your own is a must."

"What is that supposed to mean?" He'd certainly piqued her curiosity.

"Oh, please don't misunderstand. I meant it as a compliment—in that many girls might not say yes to this, but I think you would like it. I know that you don't know me, really, but I'm asking you to trust me."

There was every reason to say no. A photograph in *Life* was a great accomplishment, but it was not a personal reference.

But she heard herself saying yes.

He said he'd meet her by the clock in the grand concourse at seven o'clock.

She wondered what the evening would bring.

As she watched him walk away, she saw him give the pack of Pall Malls to Bertie, unopened.

Chapter Twenty-One

Alice worked awhile longer before her father arrived to relieve her. Emmett had wanted to take her to wherever they were going right after that, but she told him that she had to meet up with her mother first. They had a standing appointment to catch a movie together every Friday evening, and Alice would have to tell her that she couldn't make it. She knew Vera would understand.

So she and Emmett agreed to seven o'clock. And she was already counting down the hours.

She skipped down the steps of the Thirty-Third Street exit. She looked up at the building across the street to the windows of their third-story apartment. Her father had left them open. He loved the fresh air, winter, spring, summer, fall. The clouds were light gray, and she was concerned about the possibility of rain, but if she went home to close them instead of heading straight to Macy's, she'd be late meeting her mother.

And the Bellavia women were never late.

Besides, her grandfather was at home. And although his health was poor—he'd been a sandhog who built the tunnels under the rivers—he'd be able to get up and close the windows if it rained.

She headed to Thirty-Fourth and rounded the corner to the familiar department store. It was the place of firsts. Her first black patent-leather shoes for her first day of school. Her First Communion dress. Her first brassiere.

Her mother had never forgotten her tenement years and what it had been like to work in a factory. So Vera shopped only for winter clothes in the summer and summer clothes in the winter, when the discounts were the most lucrative. And being an employee, she always knew when the best sales were coming up. Alice and Vera both dressed quite well for little money.

Angelo was more practical. He wore the same shirts he'd worn since Alice was a child and simply patched or sewed them as needed. But he loved to see his wife and daughter delighting in something new they'd brought home.

She headed through the revolving doors and into the wonderland that always took her breath away. Columns lined the room floor to ceiling, flanked with rows of glass cases offering everything an imagination could dream up. A banner hung saying "World's Largest Department Store," and though Alice had no experience outside New York City, she deemed this to be true. Brass elevators, wooden escalators, grand staircases all moving people up and down the eleven floors to purchase everything from chocolates to fur coats to radios.

The glove department was on the second floor. Alice liked to ride the escalator and watch the wooden slats consume one another step by step as it ascended. They'd been installed forty years ago—1902—and Macy's was the first building in the world to have them.

Another first. Alice beamed with pride to have a connection with such a place.

It was often said: Who needed to leave New York when the best was right here in her city?

But as much as she loved it, she ached to see more of the world.

She arrived on the second floor, where a dreamland of ladies' hats greeted her. As she approached the glove counter, she saw that her mother was working with a customer. Vera wore her usual beguiling smile, her lips colored in the red that was Angelo's favorite. "The color of the suffragettes," her mother would say. When her father thought no one was around, he'd call her *Vera, my vixen,* and pinch her rear end, and she'd squeal and kiss him. Alice had witnessed their affection all through her life and hoped that someday she'd have a marriage like that.

Her thoughts migrated to Emmett, but it was early, too early, to consider such notions.

The man at her mother's counter was holding a pair of violet leather gloves in his hands. The kind that had buttons that would run up the sides of a woman's arms. Expensive. Alice knew that much. His knee-length coat was made of a camel-colored wool that screamed of quality, and his shoes shone like the way the sun kissed the Empire State Building. Vera would be pleased with making that sale today to such an obviously wealthy gentleman.

Alice paused and stood next to a mannequin wearing a long silk robe. There was something odd about her mother's behavior, though, and Alice wanted to watch before approaching them.

The man placed the gloves on the counter as if they were unimportant and instead took Vera's hands in his. Her mother blushed to a color that Alice could see from ten feet away.

Vera smiled and rubbed the man's hands and looked at him with adoration. *Adoration*—and a beaming gaze that she usually reserved for Angelo and Alice. Who was this stranger who merited such acclaim? Alice knotted up inside at the notion that her mother—her *mother*—was captivated by this younger man. He was handsome, of that there was no doubt. And Alice thought that she herself, in her mother's shoes, probably couldn't have controlled her reaction any better.

The man was a head taller than Vera and better looking than most movie stars, with his wavy brown hair and dimpled cheeks. An *aura*—that's the word that came to Alice's mind. And Vera seemed to have been caught in it.

Alice turned around, a bit alarmed at this scene and not knowing quite how to feel about seeing her mother look at someone else that way. But she was too late.

"Alice!" she heard. Her mother's voice sounded like a tinkling bell.

She took a breath and turned back toward the counter, where her mother was waving her over. She took short steps to reach it.

"Darling," said Vera, "I've just had the most wonderful surprise. You have to come over here." Vera came around, lifting the platform that separated her from customers. She ran her hand down the arm of the stranger and looped her elbow through his. They looked at each other with a glance of familiarity that Alice didn't understand.

When Alice approached, Vera detached herself from him and locked arms with her daughter.

"My sweet boy," she said to the man. "This is my daughter, Alice. Alice, this is William Pilkington."

William Pilkington. His name had been spoken in their household for many years with a combination of reverence and regret. Alice knew the story. The son of their friend Pearl. The boy whom Vera and Angelo had loved as if he were their own. The one who had been taken from them right on the steps of Penn Station and never seen by them again.

He was a phantom brother to Alice, always remembered in evening prayer and mourned around the Christmas table. They'd known his whereabouts—that part was no mystery. A mention in the society page here and there told them that his grandparents—Pearl's parents—had raised him, and he had spent much of his youth in boarding schools overseas. But Vera always maintained that it would have broken Pearl's heart to see him absorbed into that world that she herself had renounced.

"William Pilkington," he said in deep, rich tones as he held his hand out to Alice.

"Alice Bellavia," she breathed. His formidable presence might have been intimidating were it not for a softness in his demeanor.

"I was almost a B-Bellavia." He laughed.

She was surprised by the ease with which he spoke of the tragedy that had haunted their family for so many years. Either he said it with affection or he was unaware that his absence had been felt as fully as his presence would have been.

She also noticed the trace of the stutter that her mother had described.

What did a man of his standing have to feel nervous about?

"So I've heard," said Alice, realizing that her curt response might have sounded unfriendly. But this was a whole lot to take in. A legend in flesh and bone, both within her family and in all of New York City. She'd once torn a picture of him out of a magazine and pinned it to her wall by her pillow, underneath one of Cary Grant. She didn't want her parents to see it. To them, he was a son. To her, he was among the names giggled over by her schoolmates as one of the city's dreamy bachelors.

"You are v-very lucky to have had this woman as your mother. She was mine, sort of, for part of my childhood, and she was the one I always hoped would walk into my b-bedroom when I was sick and sit with me until I was better."

That was certainly the Vera that Alice knew. Always nurturing. First her own father through his highs and lows suffering from the bends. Then Pearl through the tumult with her family and her aspirations of social justice. And as a surrogate parent to Will. Angelo, in his first years getting used to his injury. All of that before Alice was born.

So when the time came to have a child of her own, Vera was well practiced in the art of taking care of others.

But Alice knew her mother felt inadequate. As if her love could have cured her father, saved Pearl, held on to Will, grown Angelo's leg back.

As Alice looked at Vera's radiant face right now, there was a *completeness* about it. A peace that wiped away years of concern.

"I am indeed lucky to have her for a mother, and to have my father as well," Alice agreed. She considered for the first time what it might feel like to be William. To have had the love of people like Vera and Angelo and then to be snatched away from them. Had it scarred him at all?

William responded, "Dear Angelo. Of c-c-course I have also harbored memories of him being a f-father to me. How is he doing?" The question seemed directed to Vera, although he never took his eyes off Alice. She felt herself blush.

"He lost his leg during the war," said Vera.

Will's face grew dark as he turned to her. "Bad business, that war. And this one."

It struck Alice that, like Emmett, he seemed the right age to be fighting with the boys overseas. Maybe on the old side of that but still within range.

"Indeed," said Vera. "But let's talk about much happier things. Are you married, dear William? Do you have any children?"

Alice knew that her mother scanned the pages of newspapers every day in hopes of such information. They already knew the answer.

"No," he acknowledged. "My grandfather has had no shortage of suggestions in that regard, but, w-well, I j-just haven't agreed with him."

Her mother clapped her hands together and spoke in an excited tone. "William, it would make me so happy if you would join us for dinner tonight. You, Angelo, Alice, and me. It will take no persuasion for Angelo to close up shop early as soon as he hears that I have found you. Or that you found us. We have so many years to catch up on."

He smiled and turned to her. "For you, Zia Vera, anything. B-but one caveat. Let me take you all to dinner. I know what it means to have unexpected c-c-company, and I don't want to impose. But I have been craving a steak at Delmonico's and would love for you to all be my guests."

"Delmonico's!" she exclaimed. "That is too much."

"Nothing is too much for you and Angelo. And A-Alice." He looked her way again and smiled.

Alice felt her mother squeeze her arm and knew how very much Vera would want this to happen. Not because it would be at Delmonico's—a place that would take them a year to save for—but because it had been her hope for twenty years to see Will again, and here he was. Wanting to spend time with the family.

But she had already promised to meet Emmett this evening. He had a surprise for her, which intrigued her almost as much as it excited her to spend more time with him.

"I can pick you up in my car at seven o'clock."

"How can I refuse? Yes, of course!" Vera agreed on behalf of both of them.

She held out her arms to hug William. He returned it, and Alice watched as he closed his eyes and pulled her mother in tighter.

A quick pain shot through Alice's chest. Was she not enough to make her parents perfectly happy?

She pushed it away. It was foolish to feel anything like jealousy when this was the one thing she knew her parents had hoped for more than anything else. And it would be quite an evening. Getting to know the intriguing William Pilkington. Eating at Delmonico's. She just wished it weren't happening on the very night she'd planned to meet Emmett.

Will pulled back and turned toward Alice. He extended his hand, and when she put hers in his, he brought it to his lips in an old, chivalrous gesture. Her pulse quickened where he'd touched it, and she felt herself blush, leaving her confused about her feelings.

Just the gesture of a gentleman, she told herself.

But it was more than that. She felt something pass between them, unspoken and unseen but very real.

Emmett Adler. William Pilkington. Two men from entirely different worlds.

Both competing for space in her thoughts.

Alice was in trouble.

Chapter Twenty-Two

Vera dispatched Alice to return home and see that Grandfather was settled in before they all left for the evening. She would run over to the station and tell Angelo the glorious news.

Alice had hoped to reverse the tasks, as she needed to find Emmett and tell him about the change of plans. That was, if he was even around. If he thought she was standing him up, it might be the end before there was a beginning.

She trotted off to their apartment. There were two sets of doors that required two sets of keys just to get into the building, unlike the posh kind that had a doorman to tip his hat and welcome you home. Not that any of her friends lived in such places, but she had a few regular clients who tipped well if she delivered their newspapers and cigarettes and candy to them in person.

The second lock always took some jiggling to open, but she managed it despite holding the bag of bread rolls she'd stopped for on the way home. She shut the door with her hip, checked the mailbox to find it empty, and climbed up to the third story, where the usually dim hallway was even darker due to a light that had been out for two months. She had half a mind to replace it herself but didn't want to spare the change for a bulb when they already paid a ransom in rent. Her father always dreamed of buying their own place but could never save enough. All his money went to indulging his wife and daughter with scarves and earrings that they insisted they didn't need, or in spontaneous charitable contributions to the ever-growing homeless population that gathered outside the train station steps. All this gave him more joy than a mortgage payment would. And so they rented.

The door to their apartment required another two keys, and Alice had those open in no time.

"Opa," she called to her grandfather. He always found comfort when they addressed him in German. Alice's knowledge of the language was limited, but she knew enough to ask if he was comfortable and what she could get for him.

He was not entirely an invalid. A couple of decades ago, he'd lived in an institution in Albany. But as soon as her parents had married and found an apartment large enough to include him, they did so. His condition had improved, she'd been told, by the time he'd spent in the capital city. He'd suffered none of the horror stories that often came out of asylums and had been part of experimental treatments in improving the lives of those with his ailments. The oxygen recompression therapies introduced by Dr. Albert Behnke had been particularly helpful, as well as efforts to keep the patient well hydrated.

He still suffered, though, from the fundamental effects of the bends—fatigue, rashes, joint pain, confusion—but mercifully they were rarely present all at the same time and rotated, as if to not overtax him or those who cared for him.

"Aleit," he responded, using the German version of her name. Her Italian relatives pronounced it a-LEE-chay, as a "ce" in that language sounded like "ch" in English. She marveled at the many variations that existed for such a simple name.

Although *Alice in Wonderland*, spoken by the lips of Emmett Adler, might be her favorite now.

It sounded as if Opa's voice was coming from the bedroom. The lone one shared by her parents. Opa and Alice shared the living room, the sofa for her and a narrow bed for him. His snoring would often wake her, but she was also grateful for it—it meant that he was sleeping soundly. Perhaps the only time he was ever truly at peace.

Today, as she often did, she found him in a confused state, sitting on a chair in the bedroom looking out the window at the eagle atop Penn Station.

"Aleit," he said when he saw her. His bushy eyebrows were untamed, obscuring his vision, but he wouldn't let anyone near him even with the tiniest scissors. Every piece of him sagged—his jowls, his bottom lip, his shoulders. Except when Alice was in the room. Whatever piece of him had awareness brightened when she was near. Ever since she was a little girl, she could calm his terrors and soothe his pains.

She entered the room and rubbed his arm.

"What is it, Opa?"

He pointed to the train station. It was a viewpoint that always amused Alice—watching the people come and go. The concerns of life that seemed so vital when you were walking on the street dissipated once you were three stories above, looking down. Her parents had taken her, on her ninth birthday, to see the lights come on at the Empire State Building for the first time. President Hoover himself had pulled the switch all the way from Washington, DC. A few months later, they took her to its sky-high observatory, and she noted how all the little people looked like ants.

She far preferred the height of their apartment. She could make out the faces—just barely—and imagine where they might be going. She and her grandfather liked to make up stories.

She pointed out a lady who she could see just alighting the steps.

"Look, Opa. See the woman in the mauve hat? Where do you think she's going?"

"The mountains." This was a frequent answer of his. He'd never been to any, as far as she knew. Maybe he remembered them from Germany.

"The mountains?" she repeated. "Maybe the Poconos. Do you think she might be going to meet a lover in a remote cabin on a lake?"

"Die Burg!" he shouted, repeating his answer.

She sighed. "Yes, Opa. She must be going to the mountains."

On his best days, he played along with her embellishments, and on very rare days he contributed to them.

"Apple?" she offered, taking one from her bag. The word sounded the same in both English and German.

His eyes lit up. Apples were one of his favorites. As he finished it, she wiped the juices from his beard and then led him to his bed.

She knocked on the neighbor's door. The widow there could always be counted on to watch Opa if they were away as a means of making a little extra money.

She had to go find Emmett.

It was six thirty. Alice hoped with everything she had that Emmett would somehow be early and she could tell him that she couldn't be a part of his plan for tonight.

She stood under the clock in the grand concourse and glanced at every midheight man who came near. None had eyes so blue or a presence that made her pulse race the way that he did. But he wasn't there. She hurried past the platforms that took soldiers away to war, but those trains had already left for the day, and there was nothing to photograph except for businessmen catching the commuter rides back to Connecticut and Long Island.

Bertie! Maybe she could leave a message with him, but she could not find him anywhere, either. Figured. The one time she needed him, a fixture almost as permanent as the enormous statue of Alexander Cassatt, and he was nowhere to be seen. She stopped by their newsstand, hoping that Emmett would think to look for her there. If she left a note, she could explain that unexpected plans with her family had come up.

The metal gate to the newsstand was already closed. She dug through her purse and found an old receipt from a bookstore on Twenty-Third and a half-used lipstick.

> *E—I have to cancel our plans. Please understand. Try again soon?*

Alice wished that her words didn't need to be so stilted, but in the unlikely event that her parents would see it, she did not want to raise questions that she didn't know how to answer.

She slipped it into a slot in the metal grate.

She only hoped that Emmett would find it.

Alice's detour to the train station meant that she wouldn't be able to join her parents and William for the car ride. Maybe that was best. They had much catching up to do about a time before she'd ever been born.

She arrived at the narrow entrance of Delmonico's on the street side and saw the trio step out of a long maroon car with a body so glossy that she could see her distorted reflection from the corner.

Her mother noticed her first and waved to her, but it was William, currently holding the door open, who walked over to greet her. She took a deep breath. Despite her vacillating emotions of just a few hours ago, she was definitely fascinated by William Pilkington in person. To his credit, she'd always thought he looked a little uncomfortable in photographs. Like he lived in that world but wasn't really a part of it.

William held out his arm, and she took it.

"I hope you'll do me the f-favor of letting me call you Alice and dispense with the formalities, g-given our unusual association. 'Miss Bellavia' sounds so stilted after all the stories your parents just regaled me with on the way over."

She felt herself blush. "They didn't tell you—"

"About the t-time you painted the toilet seat when they'd given you some watercolors because you said that made it p-prettier?" He grinned. "No. No, they didn't tell me that. Or about the time you pretended to run away b-because you didn't want to eat the cooked carrots on the plate, but you were really just hiding in the b-bathtub and they knew it all along? No. They didn't tell me that story, either."

She put her hand on her forehead. "I can't believe they would say those things to a stranger."

Alice was a little surprised that they'd spent that time talking about *her* and wondered if William felt put out that they weren't asking all about him. She would have understood. She'd experienced those pangs over the years. But now that she'd met him, those silly worries that had nagged her as a child all but disappeared.

He tightened his hold on her arm, and she felt the luxurious wool of his coat against her skin. There was something comfortable about him. "I'm not a stranger to them, Alice. It is only you and I who are. And we'll remedy that over d-dinner."

She nodded. "I suppose we will."

He turned just as they arrived at the entrance. "I don't want to have the upper hand here. H-how about this—for every embarrassing childhood story they tell me about you, I'll make sure to match it at some time in the f-future with stories of my own for you. Believe me, there are plenty."

How good-natured he was. She heard herself agreeing to this bargain.

When William held the door open for her, Alice was enveloped in a scent that was possibly the most delicious she had ever smelled in her entire life. It was as if the spirits of filet mignon, onions, wine, and chocolate haunted the space and collaborated to create a place unlike any she'd ever been in.

She'd heard of Delmonico's, of course. It would be Tiffany if it sold diamonds. Bergdorf Goodman if it sold clothing. But they sold food. And not just any food. Banquets for gods.

The room itself seemed like it was an antechamber to some old Tudor estate. Dark paneling adorned the walls and ceiling with discreet embedded lights. Alice caught her reflection in a mirror and noticed that it created a glow on her skin that made her look better than she looked in the harsh lights of their apartment.

She thought one could live in such light and appear beautiful for many decades beyond their youth. Seeing herself this way, she felt not merely pretty but elegant.

Did the fashionable people who dined here come because of the food? Or because they looked their most captivating inside its doors?

The maître d'—Alice had read that this was the name for such a person—bowed to William.

"Mr. Pilkington. How wonderful to see you again. We have your preferred table ready."

He led them to a corner table that had its own three walls so that it looked like a private cave just for the four of them. William pulled out chairs first for Vera, then Alice, then Angelo. The menus were delivered, bound in leather.

Vera took William's and Alice's hands in each of her own. She looked back and forth at them and then at her husband.

"Angelo, can you believe that this is real? So long we've hoped that our Will might come back to us, and here he is along with our sweet Alice, the four of us together."

Alice saw a new kind of smile on her father's face. "It's a miracle. God only knows how my wife has tormented herself over losing you."

"It's not as if anything could have prevented it," said William. Alice saw the look of regret on his face that matched that of her parents. Would he really have wanted to trade all he had for a third-story walk-up on Thirty-Third?

Vera put a handkerchief to her nose, and Angelo spoke for her. "She would have left the city and gone into hiding if she had known that they would be there that day to take you."

Alice held up an empty water goblet, all that was at her disposal since they had not yet looked at the wine menu. "Here's to the future, then, where all is restored to what it should have been, and the new memories to be had."

"Hear, hear," said the group, repeating her gesture.

"Oh, please indulge me just one more thing," Vera said when they'd returned the goblets to the table. "I just wanted to thank William for bringing us all here. Will, you may not know this, but the only other time I've ever eaten at an establishment like this was with your mother."

"I didn't know that."

"Yes, it was called Maioglio Brothers, although now they've moved to another part of town and renamed it Barbetta's."

"I know the place," said William.

"They had the first espresso machine in the city, and Pearl encouraged me to try some. I nearly shot up to the moon with the jolt of it." She smiled with that thin look that remembered both fondly and sadly. "It was the first day of our friendship. She was the sun and I was in her orbit and I never really understood what she received from me, but I was grateful for the warmth she brought into my life."

Angelo raised his empty goblet this time. "To Pearl."

"To Pearl," they repeated.

Courses of oyster stew, sautéed beef kidneys, and broiled Deerfoot sausages continued as William regaled them all with stories of having grown up with his English relatives and finishing his education at Cambridge. He was now working in his grandfather's business, learning everything from manufacturing to exports.

Cambridge. Vera felt a shiver move up her spine. To actually go to school at such a place! New York was no slouch as far as cities went, but she wanted to see so much more. Her parents were content enough, but she ached to see something beyond the borders of the East and Hudson Rivers.

William ordered four Delmonico's steaks for them, as well as their famed mashed potatoes topped with Parmesan cheese and toasted bread crumbs.

Alice could never remember eating anything this delicious in her life.

Bread-and-butter pudding was brought out next. There were black speckles of vanilla bean in the sauce and a touch of rum to the taste. Alice was quite sure she would burst right through her buttons, but it looked too delicious to be ignored. By this time she'd determined that William had inherited whatever gravity his mother must have possessed, for they all found themselves enraptured by him.

Especially her.

"I remember when you wanted to be a train conductor," Vera said as she laid her spoon next to her now-spotless dessert bowl.

William sat back in his chair and set his napkin on the table. "I still do. But I'm af-fraid that's not really an option for me."

"Why not?" asked Alice, and then she bit her tongue. Of course he couldn't do that kind of thing. Certainly there were rules that the rich lived by.

He sighed. "Neither the p-poor nor the w-wealthy get to be exactly what they'd like to be. The poor must work to survive, and the wealthy are limited by things like legacy and d-duty. And please d-don't misinterpret that I th-think one equal to the other. I understand th-that I am very l-lucky."

Alice was willing to trade long hours of working on her feet for whatever confines William thought money put on him. But she didn't hold his view against him—she supposed that people of all kinds had their own type of problems, and nothing was to be gained by arguing the comparison.

"To that regard, I am t-t-trying to get our board to p-pass a philanthropic measure to fund a new school in the lower part of Manhattan, to serve the tenement community better. If they say n-no, as I th-think they will, I hope to find another way."

Vera put her hand over his. "How very good of you, William. That's just the kind of thing Pearl would have done."

"I am not as g-good as my mother. She gave her life for noble pursuits, and I have not yet found my way with it all."

Angelo spoke up. "You only returned from Europe a little more than a year ago, right?"

"Yes. I still have f-family in England, and it's become a tradition to g-go to school at Cambridge. My grandmother was reluctant to let m-me, due to the w-war, but my grandfather and I insisted."

"Brave young man. I'm sure it will take time to establish yourself in your family's company. But I agree with my wife. I see a lot of your mother in you."

William pulled a wallet from his pocket and laid some large bills on the table, more than Alice had ever seen at one time. "Well, if for now that m-means that I can treat my loved ones to a meal such as this, then I am especially g-grateful for what I've been given."

He stood, and they all followed his lead. Angelo had long ago mastered walking with his crutches and having Vera take his arm. William held his out to Alice, and she took it. The ride back to their apartment was brief at this time of night. It did not escape Alice's attention that

William stole glances at her as streetlights cast their glow through the windows.

Weeks ago, this might have made her blush. Not because he was the kind of man whom heiresses would be pleased to know but because he possessed the kinds of virtues that her parents had always valued—kindness, generosity, joviality. In one word, William Pilkington was—good.

But there was a quickness to her pulse when she thought of Emmett Adler that no one—not even William—could provoke. And it could not be dismissed so handily.

When they arrived home, a flurry of embraces and promises to see one another again passed among the four of them. Alice couldn't remember the last time she'd seen her mother so radiant. As if a candle inside that had been extinguished was now a roaring fire of joy. Now that William was no longer a vague name of lore but a real and likable man, Alice harbored no envy toward him. How wonderful it was to see her parents so thoroughly happy tonight.

She turned to follow Angelo and Vera up the stairs to the building, and William cleared his throat. She looked at him, and he stepped forward.

"I b-believe I still owe you several embarrassing stories about myself. May I take you to dinner next Friday evening to pay that debt?"

A thought of Emmett passed through her mind. What had he thought when she hadn't shown up at the station? What was he doing right now?

"Yes," she found herself answering, though. "And thank you for tonight. You made my parents so very happy."

"I owe them everything. You know, I didn't say this to Vera, but it was no c-c-coincidence that I found her at the counter at Macy's."

This surprised her. "What do you mean? She said that you were shopping for ladies' gloves and recognized one another."

William shrugged. "Well, in truth, I hired a private d-detective to help me find her. And when I discovered that she worked there, I thought it m-might be the best place to make an appearance. I was j-just going to send a n-note, but I was too impatient."

"So why didn't you tell her all this?"

He smiled. "You should have seen her face when I introduced myself. She went on about how p-providential it seemed, the coincidence of finding each other there at Macy's, and I didn't want to spoil what seemed, well, kind of m-magical to her."

Alice agreed. "That was a kindness upon kindness. How considerate of you."

"You know, she was all I had for a time in my young l-life. It was too brief, but very meaningful to m-me. I think it showed me the kind of man I try to be."

"That and the genes of your actual mother." Alice hoped it wasn't too forward to say that, but she'd always looked up to Pearl as some kind of guardian angel. Especially now that Alice was at the beginning of her own womanhood. She was going to be able to vote in her first presidential election in a couple of years, and her fingers tingled with excitement at the very thought of it.

"Without a doubt. Although to hear my family talk about Owen and Pearl, they were s-s-selfish s-socialists whose memories have been wiped under the rug along with the d-dust that they don't dare see."

"Isn't 'selfish socialist' a bit of a contrary phrase?"

He laughed. "You're right. I suppose that does sound backward."

William looked down at his hands and then up again at Alice. He had the countenance of a man but the gaze of a small boy hidden within. "I—I hope to ask Vera more about my mother, but I don't want her to feel as if my curiosity diminishes what I know she did for me as w-w-well."

Alice reached out and held his hand, a gesture that surprised her, but there was a childlike vulnerability in the man in front of her that nearly demanded an action of tenderness.

"William, to hear my parents—especially my mother—speak of Pearl, you would think that she should be a candidate for canonization. I know she would love to have a chance to talk about her."

He nodded in a way that included his shoulders. "Thank you for that. It means everything to have found her and Angelo—a-a-and you." He whispered that last part. "You were unexpected, b-b-but I am so glad to have met you, t-t-too."

She noticed his stutter becoming more pronounced. Did that mean he was nervous around her? Alice bit her lower lip to avoid smiling at the thought.

But then an image of Emmett raced through her mind again. It pricked her conscience, though she had made no promises, no commitments to him. But he hovered there, dueling for her attention.

William took her hand and kissed it once again. "It was so nice to meet you, Alice Bellavia. I can pick you up here on F-Friday evening at seven o'clock. Until then?"

"Until then," she said.

She felt like the shuttlecock of a badminton set, tossing back and forth between sides. When she was with William, there was a comfort to it that felt as easy as breathing.

But when she was with Emmett, she felt alive in a way that she hadn't known was possible.

And it was only beginning.

Chapter Twenty-Three

Bertie might have lost the use of his legs, but his eyes, mind, and ability to snoop were in perfect working order.

In this instance, it worked to Alice's advantage.

When he saw her the next day at the newsstand, he told her that Emmett had mentioned that he'd be at Coney Island today shooting photos of a parade of naval ships making their way up the coast.

"Why would I care to know that?" she asked, hoping that her feelings were not that apparent.

"Because even from down here I can tell that you drum your fingers when he's around, and your cheeks turn red when his name is even mentioned."

She sighed. "Oh, Bertie, you don't think he notices, do you?"

"Who knows, my dear? But I can tell you that he does the same thing."

And there it went. She felt the blood rush to her cheeks, her broadcast of how she felt about Emmett Adler.

"So as I was saying," he continued. "The boy is going to be at Coney Island this afternoon, and as far as I recall, your shift ends at noon today."

"Why did he mention it to you?"

"Your friend has supported my cigarette habit quite lavishly these past few weeks."

"What does that mean?"

"Let me ask you this. Have you seen our young Emmett actually open a pack of those cigarettes you sell him?"

She thought about it and couldn't say that she had.

"He never bought cigarettes before until he started noticing you at the stand. And, as he doesn't smoke himself, he's got to do something with them. And yours truly happens to be a willing charity case."

She laughed. "Oh, Bertie."

"Don't give me this 'Oh, Bertie' business. I know what I am, and I know what I have to offer. He gives me my smokes; I tell him things he wants. A beautiful partnership sprung from the heart's wish for a beautiful girl."

"And just what kind of things does he want to know?"

"Ask him yourself. He'll be at Coney Island this afternoon."

"So you said."

"But you'd better catch him today. He mentioned that he was going away for a while. Weeks, months—he didn't know. This might be your last chance to see him before then."

Where would he be going? Alice realized that she didn't know Emmett well enough to know if he had family elsewhere or a job or an apartment. He could be leaving for any number of reasons. If she didn't find him today, an untold amount of time could go by before she'd see him again. Before she could apologize for not showing up the other evening.

Before she could find out whether these things she felt might be returned.

She asked Bertie if he knew where Emmett was going.

"Can't say that I do. That boy is a mystery, if you ask me. He's hiding something, though. I'd bet on it."

It was funny that Bertie should say that. It was something that had struck Alice the few times she'd met Emmett—that there was more to him than he let on—but she'd brushed it aside, convincing herself that it was only her imagination.

But while it might have set off warning bells, it did the opposite. It intrigued her more than she wanted it to.

There was only one way to find out. She needed to see him.

The minute the clock hands aligned at the twelve, she kissed her father on the cheek and raced to Herald Square so she could catch the N train that went to Coney Island without transfers. At the Kings Highway stop, passengers entered the subway car, many bound for the beach with their sunglasses on their heads and picnic baskets in their arms. But just as the train started again, it lurched, sending those who had not yet arranged themselves in seats tumbling to the floor. A basket of sandwiches opened, and a high-heeled woman stepped on it, leaving a deep indentation in its side. An orange rolled next to Alice's feet.

Grumbling was heard from adults and whines from children as they pulled themselves up. All had questions as to what had just happened.

The doors opened, and the subway driver walked past, shouting to everyone that a small electrical fire had started in his compartment and he'd had to halt the train and extinguish it. But it would require repairs, and he was uncertain as to how long a delay they would have.

Alice felt her blood race at this setback. The naval ships would be visible for half an hour at best, and she was already concerned about being too late to find Emmett. Even if that would be possible at an event that would surely have attracted a crowd.

She couldn't wait. She stepped out of the train onto the elevated platform and raced down its rusted green metal steps into the dusty street. She looked right and left for a taxi, but the few that were present were occupied. She'd never been here before. She'd never left Manhattan.

She stepped into a maze of confusion not unlike the hubbub that existed around Penn Station. But at least that was familiar to her. Here there were also fruit stands, grocers, washers, florists.

She stopped at the latter. "Which way to Coney Island?" she asked.

The woman held a child on her left hip and pointed with her right hand.

"That way. About two miles."

Alice looked south and wondered what the long walk through an unfamiliar neighborhood might have in store for her.

"Two miles?" she asked. "Do you have a bicycle or anything I could borrow? I'm in a bit of a hurry."

The woman scowled, showing yellowed teeth. "What do you take me for, a philanthropist? I'm no fool. You'd be off and I'd never see you again."

"Please. I promise you. I'll have it back in two hours."

"Your word means as much to me as a wooden nickel. Now go away. You're blocking other customers."

Alice looked back and found that no one, in fact, was behind her, but she was not going to get anywhere with this woman. Instead, she set off down West Seventh Street, only to find it closed off. She backtracked to Fourteenth Street, where fire escapes hovered above her like macramé baskets, and patches of discarded, blackened chewing gum made her hopscotch around their sticky resting places. Brooklyn felt like Manhattan except that it didn't have the tall buildings that pierced the skyline. But the people were the same—sweeping their stoops, reprimanding their children, shaking their rugs out the windows.

Alice hurried her pace as she checked her wristwatch and noted that it was nearly one o'clock. The ships were likely just arriving on the horizon to the north, and the ideal time for photographing them would be upon her soon.

She'd never run two miles so fast. In fact, she'd never run two miles at all. But something inside told her that if she didn't find Emmett today, she might lose him forever.

As she drew closer, she heard the varied sounds of people having fun. She turned a corner and saw the arched tops of a roller coaster and Ferris wheel peeking out. She heard the rise and fall of people screaming as they sped down a ride called the Cyclone. Bright-red letters spelled out its name along its highest point. It had several turns that spiraled one on top of another, creating an illusion that must have earned it its name. She had never had the opportunity to go on such a thing, but it seemed like an adventure.

But not the parachute jump. Or at least, that's what it looked like. It appeared like a giant metal cornstalk, taller than anything else around it. People dangled from chains attached to its flowering top, rising and falling. The very thought of it made her shudder.

She could not understand why anyone would find that exciting.

Alice took a breath and smoothed her skirt. She was not here for such amusements, fascinating though many of them seemed. She was here to find Emmett, although as she looked around, she was afraid it was going to be an impossible task. She had never considered how large Coney Island might be. It wasn't so far away, but her father rarely took a day off, and if he did, there was enough to explore in Manhattan that they never left.

The idea that she would be able to find him in this bedlam was as likely as her becoming the mayor of New York. The very thought made her dizzy.

Still, she had not come this far to give up.

She bypassed the rides, and though she was hungry, she even ignored the sumptuous smells coming from food vendors. Signs promised hot dogs, popcorn, cotton candy, and the scents promised that they would taste amazing. Perhaps if she was lucky enough to find him, she and Emmett could eat a late lunch together here.

She pictured them sitting at one of the wooden picnic tables scattered around in yellow and green patterns. She might wipe mustard from his chin, and he might share his chocolate shake with her.

It would be wonderful to stroll the immense grounds with him. Although she'd never been here, she'd read so much about its colorful history. The buildings that had burned and been resurrected. The sideshows of days past with a man with parchment skin or another with a pointed head. And the animals—they had once publicly electrocuted an elephant in punishment for killing a man who'd fed it a lit cigarette.

Served the man right, in Alice's opinion.

Her love of historical buildings could be nurtured for weeks on end in a place like this.

A roar rose through the crowd, and Alice looked toward the beach. Men held children on their shoulders and pointed. She stood on her tiptoes and could not see over all the people. She looked around for some higher ground.

Finding none, she pushed forward instead. Families and couples and sunbathing girls and ogling boys stood in the sand. At first she tried to step around the colorful towels that were laid all over the beach, but it was an impossibility.

"Excuse me," she found herself saying until it seemed pointless. No one cared anyway. They were all focused on the water.

At last, she was close enough to see what everyone was watching.

A parade of naval ships turned in from the Atlantic Ocean into the Lower Bay. Their gray smokestacks rose from enormous decks where white-clad sailors waved to a crowd that waved back. From bow to stern, rows of flags were strung and flapped in the breeze.

Alice's mother had told her what a relief it was when Armistice Day came, ending the hostilities. Though Angelo was spared, more than three hundred thousand Americans were dead or wounded, and millions in Europe died. Vera was convinced that the world would never see its equal—that humanity would learn from that horror. And yet, only months ago, President Roosevelt had begun calling this new conflict the Second World War, and the predictions for it were far more devastating.

Alice looked at those sailors, who seemed so small from this distance, and wondered about their mothers, sisters, girls—all those they'd kissed goodbye at their own train stations. Some percentage of these boys would never see the shores of America again.

A nearby boy around eleven years old asked his father the questions that Alice had herself.

"Why don't the ships come closer, Daddy?"

"The bay is too shallow for them to come in all the way, son."

"Where are they going?"

"They're heading down the East Coast to Florida before going back to Europe. And they're advertising war bonds along the way."

"What are war bonds?"

"They're a way for the government to raise money for the war now and a way for citizens to invest their money. For example, your mother and I bought some bonds recently at just over eighteen dollars. In ten years, we'll be able to cash those in for twenty-five dollars."

The boy seemed satisfied. Or he became distracted, as many did, by the deep bass tones coming from one of the ship's horns.

Alice wondered if people generally bought bonds out of patriotism or for the purpose of making more money a decade later. It seemed an awfully long time, but an even bigger statement of trust. Who was to say that at that time, the government wouldn't need even more money and fail to honor the bonds?

Who was to say that this war would even be over by then?

Alice thought that if women were in charge, these wars wouldn't even happen. They would solve their differences over a glass of tea like civilized people did, instead of taking up guns and tanks and turning villages into battle stations.

She returned her attention to the bay. Six ships came through. She did not know their names, though she heard people talk about the battleship and battle cruiser and didn't know if there was a difference.

The ships circled into the bay, one by one, reminding her of a three-ring circus. The first one swung around toward Sandy Hook Bay, and she knew that she'd better find Emmett now before the ships were all out of sight and his purpose for being here was complete.

Where would I go if I wanted to photograph all these ships? she asked herself. The scope of this was daunting. She looked around at the throngs gathered on the sand. Too many people coming and going to guarantee a straight shot. If it were her, she'd want to find a view from which you could see all six ships.

There were only two possibilities. Either make it up to the roof of a nearby building. Or—the Ferris wheel.

Yes. If she were going to try to take a good picture that captured the panorama, she would ride the Ferris wheel. Its slow-moving cars would provide different intervals of height, allowing the photographer to try different views. And if she didn't find him there, maybe it would offer her a view from which to look around for him.

She raced over, once again ignoring the enticing smells of the food lanes. She saw a woman biting into an enormous turkey leg, and her stomach rumbled once again, but she had no time to consider it.

The line for the Ferris wheel was long, which was just as well. It allowed her to watch the people come and go. But Emmett was nowhere to be seen. For one relieving moment, Alice thought she'd seen him—a man with light sandy hair and glassy blue eyes—but when he turned fully in her direction, she noticed that he was older, and the resemblance was less than it had been in profile.

"Next!" shouted the carnival worker every thirty seconds, like a fatigued cuckoo clock. One after another until the wheel had made a full rotation, and then it circled around for several minutes, giving its occupants a chance to ride it without interruption. She gazed at the wheel's metal structure, which looked like a perfectly formed spiderweb. Though it was a carnival ride, its design fascinated her as one who was interested in how things were built. She wished she had a little camera. One she would use to photograph odd angles and unique decorations on buildings, printing and saving them so she could pore over their fine details.

It was distracting to look at not only the Ferris wheel—or the Wonder Wheel, as this one was named—but also at everything surrounding it. The pool house of white brick with the red roof and arched windows. Behind it stood a Moorish-looking tower of yellow tile.

But as each compartment edged to the ground, she watched the people come out. There was no sign of Emmett. Maybe she was wrong in thinking that this would have given an ideal view, and he'd found something better.

"Next!" the man grumbled when she was at the front of the line. An older couple, holding hands, stepped out of a compartment that was painted in yellow, red, blue, and green squares. He told her to hurry on in and also ushered in a couple her age who had been giggling all sorts of sappy things to each other the whole time they'd been waiting.

Lovely. Now she was going to feel like an interloper stuck with a couple of honeymooners.

They settled in on opposite benches, and the barker closed their car with the flip of a metal bar. The couple lost no time in cuddling up to each other and whispering affections as if Alice were not there. She gripped the opening that served as a window and decided to let them have their privacy as much as she could. Besides, she was going to attend to the impossible task of looking for Emmett from the air.

And then there he was. Just below her like a mirage. There was no mistaking him, though, not only for his fair features but also for that same camera that hung so carelessly around his neck. He came from nowhere and walked to the front of the line, where he seemed to slip some money to the barker, who ushered him into the latest car—just two behind hers. As they continued to move upward, she leaned out her window, hoping that he would do the same. But he didn't until he was a quarter of the way up.

Then she saw half his body bend over the opening, camera in hand. She was right! He'd also thought that this was the perfect place from which to photograph the ships. She followed his gaze and saw the resplendent parade of the ships just as the second began to exit the bay. As they cut through the water, they left a V-shaped pattern at their fronts and a foamy trail in their wakes. Sad to think how many boys aboard might be seeing the shores of this country for the last time, and she wondered again why Emmett had not joined the service. She'd figured it out for William, or at least what was likely—his sort could either buy their way out or make a case for their indispensability. Captains of industry or something like that. Maybe his grandfather had insisted upon it and made the arrangements.

Emmett. At this point, they'd made another two stops, and she was now at the highest point of the ride. The lovebirds next to her seemed entirely unaware of her existence, and out of the corner of her eye she saw the man's hand slide up the woman's thigh until Alice could see the edge of her black garter. She was amazed at their brazenness.

She leaned out the window once again and saw Emmett doing the same, two cars down. He no longer held the camera to his face and instead seemed to study the horizon as she did.

Did he think the things she thought? Did he wonder what lay beyond the water and long to see a world very different from this one?

If she didn't take this chance to talk to him, she might never know.

"Emmett!" she cried out into the open. He looked to his left and his right but nowhere else.

"Emmett!" she called again. This time, he stood a little straighter and looked down and then up.

He saw her. She could tell that he saw her. The day was bright enough to see that their eyes met. But instead of waving to her as she might have expected, he disappeared into the compartment. And didn't return.

The lovebirds had now graduated to the other thigh, the other garter, and Alice had nowhere to look but out. At this point, she was situated at the nine o'clock of the great wheel and Emmett had passed the peak to the eleven. If she leaned a certain way, she could see his left pant leg and his hand resting on it.

"Emmett!" she tried once more, knowing that it would not be difficult for him to hear her.

At last, he poked his head out. "What do you want?" he shouted.

"I had to find you. I had to apologize!"

"I don't want your apology. Just leave me be."

"Are you that upset that I missed our appointment?"

She was aware that this was now playing out like a radio soap opera for all the riders to hear. At least they weren't subjected to advertisements. And wouldn't the soaps be more fun if everyone were shouting their lines?

"The appointment? You think *that's* why I'm angry? How about, why didn't you tell me you are married?"

The lovebirds ceased their lovemaking and looked at Alice with rapt attention.

"I'm not married. Where did you get a funny idea like that?"

"When you weren't at the clock, I went by your newsstand, but it was closed."

"Didn't you see my note?"

"What note?"

"I left a note. I wrote it—" She laughed. "I wrote it in lipstick. I couldn't find a pencil."

"I can't hear you!"

Well, those kinds of details could be discussed later.

He cupped his hands. "The man at the shoeshine stand said that he hadn't seen Mrs. Bellavia all day."

Mrs. Bellavia. It must have been Mr. Szercy. He wore eyeglasses so thick that his eyes looked like large bugs. He frequently mistook her for her mother, though any resemblance was slight.

"I'm not married," she repeated, shouting down to the six o'clock position that he held. The wheel had made its cycle and now they would spin without stopping for several rotations. She wished they could step off and carry on a conversation that was less public, but she had to work with what she had.

"Then—" He said something else, but it was lost to the wind.

"What?" she shouted, cupping her hands as he had.

"THEN WHY WEREN'T YOU AT THE CLOCK?"

"My parents. It had to do with my parents. I'll tell you when we're off this thing."

They spun another cycle, staring at each other, not able to carry on the way they had in a conversation that was best suited for quiet. The male lovebird joined Alice at the window, and the delicate balance of the car tipped slightly, causing her to grip a nearby bar in panic.

"Hey, buddy," he shouted to Emmett. "You gonna kiss her when we get off this thing?" He grinned. Alice was mortified. She saw many more heads pop out of their Ferris wheel cars. Indeed, they had entertained the crowd.

Emmett said something that she couldn't hear, but she saw her unwanted companion give a thumbs-up signal into the air before popping in next to his girlfriend/wife/lover again. The car was approaching the peak, and this time Alice looked down at the landscape that was colorful Coney Island. It looked like miniature dollhouses with moving parts and tiny people. The rides spun, raised, lowered, raced in a flurry of exhilarating activity. The people milled about like lazy ants, sauntering from one fair stand to another. Food, games, prizes. It was an indescribable feeling, being so high above it all as if she weren't really one of the masses but a bird surveying a kingdom built for amusement.

Opa would enjoy this, she thought.

Two more cycles and Alice's car reached the bottom, where it slowed to a stop. She hopped off ahead of the couple and waited at the gate for Emmett's turn to come. When he stepped out of his car, she saw that a small crowd had gathered, anticipating this moment.

A quick vision of a fairy-tale kiss came to her mind. Was this where and how she wanted her first to happen? Would he step out, relieved that she wasn't married, and sweep her into his arms and delight the onlookers who were clearly hoping for the same thing Alice was?

If they were, though, it was not to happen. Emmett looked a sight as he stood in front of her. His arms were crossed over his chest, resting on the top of his camera. He was dusty with sand that had settled into the crevices of his shirt seams, and he smelled of the ocean. Alice felt dizzy with what she could now name as desire, wanting more than ever for this, indeed, to be her first kiss. But when he didn't respond, her lips, left untouched, tingled as if a ghost of what almost was.

"Emmett," she whispered, reaching for his hand.

He unfolded his arms and touched her arm only enough to lead her way.

"Let's go somewhere else," he said.

Chapter Twenty-Four

The subway again. She followed Emmett to the train station where she should have gotten off in the first place. Its round, gazebolike appearance was a fitting welcome to the circus of Coney Island that she had seen for all too brief a time. They waited on the platform silently, side by side, until the train appeared, and they entered it together. Had they wanted to talk, it would have become impossible, as the thunderous sound of the tracks was too loud to allow for conversation.

They exited at the Twenty-Eighth Street station and began walking south.

"Where are we going?" Alice asked at last. She'd tried to read his expressions on the train. Was he angry with her? Hurt?

"To my apartment, so I can show you what I wanted you to see the other day."

Her heart pounded. If you'd told her this morning that she would be alone with a man in his apartment by this afternoon, she'd have told you that it was about as true as the George Washington Bridge being in China. Maybe that was what he'd meant about her having to be up for anything. Maybe he recognized in her the hunger for something beyond what was familiar and comfortable. Her mother's generation had fought for women like Alice to have opportunities, but real, actual, tangible change was taking too long. Perhaps it would be her generation's charge to race ahead to new possibilities.

Perhaps it started with things like going to a man's apartment if she felt like it. She told herself that Pearl would have done the same thing, though she had no way of knowing if it was actually true.

So here she was, under the spell that his mystery cast, following him up three, four, five flights of stairs to a door at the end of a hallway. There was nothing to suggest that anyone lived there. Behind other doors, she heard the sounds of radios, the smells of dinner cooking. But this one seemed lonely in its quiet.

Emmett opened the door. It was a small space. A kitchen with a counter so narrow that a rolling pin would hang over its edges. A small table sat in the middle with only one chair, as if no company were expected. The sole light was a bulb hanging from the ceiling. Holes surrounded it in an even pattern, the remnants of some long-discarded fixture that must have covered them. A sofa faced the narrow window, which blocked all view save for the diagonal pattern of the fire escape.

This was not merely absent the touch of a woman. This room had a stale air about it, as if its sole purpose was to be a cemetery for unwanted furniture that went unused most of the time.

But with one stunning difference: the walls were lined with photograph after photograph, every inch covered in perfect eight-by-ten blocks as if they were wallpaper. One wall featured architecture in and around New York—some items were recognizable, such as the fountain in Central Park, and others had been taken so close that it took the eye of an artist to see the beauty in the detail over that of the whole.

Another wall showed animals, mostly dogs, captured at all stages of activity. Some were action shots and others, like the architecture wall, homed in close on eyes, paws, tails.

The third wall showed people. Old, young, but mostly young. Children playing. All joyful, with the exception of one. A small boy with light hair and light eyes with a look as if he'd just lost his puppy. It felt even sadder as those who held balloons and toys and slid down slides surrounded him. She wondered why this particular boy had touched Emmett's heart.

The final wall—the one with the window—was smaller than the others. And fittingly, it held landscapes—flowers, beaches, trees. The pictures were trimmed to fit around the window, sometimes cutting right through a photograph. She wondered why he didn't just print it in a smaller size so as to appreciate the entire image.

But when she stood back and looked at them in their totality, she saw the genius of it. So orderly that the images themselves took center stage instead of their arrangements.

She looked at Emmett, who closed the door behind him and set his camera on the counter. Only then did they face each other, and she felt an electric current pass between them that could have overpowered the lone bulb.

Her mouth felt dry. She was not as brave as she'd convinced herself. Had she been stupid to think that she could score a point for women by putting herself in this position with a man of whom she knew little?

"Something to drink?" he offered.

"Some water, thank you." She felt the rumble in her stomach again, a reminder that she hadn't eaten since dawn, when she'd left to work at the train station. But from the scant belongings in his apartment, she wasn't sure he even had anything on hand.

After he'd turned off the sink, he ushered her over to the sofa. She sank into it and thought that its softness was likely due to its age, not its construction. In fact, the slightest movement might have her falling right onto the floor.

Emmett handed her the glass of water and looked down into his own. He sighed.

"Why would the man at the shoeshine stand call you Mrs. Bellavia?"

"That was Mr. Szercy. He couldn't see his two hands if they were right in front of him. He's always confusing things. Once he asked my father what it was like growing up in Russia. My father is from Italy. If you'd talked to him for two minutes longer, you would have suspected as much. Nice man. But I think he lost three sons in the first war, same unit, and he's never been the same. Or so I was told."

Emmett leaned back into the sofa and, placing his glass on the floor, put his hands behind his head. But she was afraid that she might disappear into it if she followed suit. Not to mention that the casual situation might imply something that there wasn't. She sat stiffly with her hands on her lap and faced him.

He laughed in a way that made him sound nervous. "Then that will teach me to be brash in my reactions. I mean, you weren't where we were supposed to meet, and then he said that. It sounds pretty silly now that I think of it. But I was—"

Emmett stopped and looked intently at her. His voice became tender.

"Why *weren't* you at the clock as we'd agreed? I heard you say something about your parents, but it was too loud to hear on the Ferris wheel."

She told him a brief history about William Pilkington and her parents. He nodded without responding.

Alice smiled. "That was some way to have a conversation, wasn't it? Over there at Coney Island."

"I felt like we were on *Bachelor's Children* or something, the way everyone started watching it."

"I just—I just didn't want to miss the chance to talk to you. I felt awful about standing you up. And Bertie said—" She looked down at her hands and picked at her nails. She knew that she was revealing more than she wanted to say. "Bertie said that you are going away for several weeks, and I didn't know when I'd see you again."

"No, that got changed. It was a project that fell through."

"For *Life* magazine?"

He offered no more to his statement, and she decided not to press it for now.

Instead, she looked around the room. "Is this all your work, Emmett?"

"Yes." He stood up and reached out for her hand. She took it, and he walked close to one of the walls.

"It's spectacular. It's like a gallery in here," she said.

"Four years in New York. That's enough time to take a few pictures."

She laughed and pulled away so that she could look at the photos more closely. The shadows cast by the Brooklyn Bridge into the water. A baby with a knitted bonnet leaning over its seat to toss a piece of bread to an eager dog.

"Four years? Where did you come from before that?" she asked.

"All over."

"That's a vague answer." She turned back to him. He was grinning.

"Then take a guess. Take three guesses. If you're right, I'll show you what is behind there."

He pointed across the way to a door that had appeared invisible to her, as it, too, was plastered with photographs, along the architectural wall.

"Oh, please show me now!"

His finger traced the side of her face and rested on a tendril of hair that had escaped from the rest. She took a quick breath, and he stepped back.

"Not yet," he said softly. "What are your guesses?"

"Florida."

"You're just throwing that out. What would make you think I'm from Florida?"

"I don't know. You said to guess."

"Make a thoughtful guess. You want to see behind the door, right?"

She'd heard that girls liked the brooding types, the Mr. Rochester types, and Emmett fit that bill with the little he revealed about himself. The mystery as intoxicating as the man.

"Iowa."

He crossed his arms like hers and laughed. Her second laugh from him in mere minutes. "And where did you pull that straw from? I said make a *thoughtful* guess."

"That *was* a thoughtful guess. Iowa kind of represents the whole heartland, but I didn't know how specific you wanted me to be. See, don't many people from the middle of the country dream of coming to New York City? And if you were from the cornfields but you loved to take pictures, wouldn't you be apt to photograph everything you see—buildings, landscapes, people, animals—because it was all so new to you?"

He nodded. "I'll give you that. It was a thoughtful guess. But it was still wrong."

She sighed. "Are you from outside the United States?" She doubted it, as he had no trace of an accent.

"That's not fair. You don't get hints."

"That's not a no."

"That's not a yes."

"You're insufferable."

"I've been told as much."

She looked at his eyes, holding them there with her own gaze as if they might reveal their secrets.

"I am going to do this," she determined. And she felt its truth. "You are fair-haired, fair-skinned, and have bright-blue eyes. Your name is Emmett Adler, so you're probably not Irish."

"Unless it's really O'Adler," he suggested.

"Stop! You're distracting me!" But she smiled. "And though you appear to be able-bodied and of the right age, you are not serving in the war, so you might be foreign. All that baffles me is that you have no accent. But that's my guess. You're German."

His eyes grew dark and he turned around. "You have a good imagination. Let's go see what's behind the door."

It did not occur to her until later that he never acknowledged if she was right or wrong.

Chapter Twenty-Five

Alice followed Emmett, more curious than ever as to what he had to show her. He pulled from his pocket a key ring, which seemed to hold an inordinate number of keys, given that he just had this small apartment and apparently one locked room in it. He jostled the key into the hole and opened the door.

Immediately, a stench of chemicals tickled her nose.

He pulled a cord from the ceiling, and another solitary bulb flashed on.

"Do you know what this is?" he asked.

Photos hung on limp paper from strings spread across the room, held in place by clothespins whose grip was softened by tiny pieces of cotton. She assumed that was to avoid damaging the prints.

Below the paintings lay bins of what looked like water but must be developing chemicals.

She'd read about such places. But she never imagined she'd see one.

"It's a darkroom," she said in reverence.

"Exactly."

He pulled the cord again and then flipped a switch. A haunting red glow permeated the room. Two red bulbs were attached to the wall. As

Emmett approached them, the front of his face seemed to be illuminated while the back was still in shadows. Like a Jekyll and Hyde, interchangeable with the slightest movement. His usually pale skin grew warm with color, and she saw angles on his face that weren't otherwise so pronounced. It made him *more* attractive, if that were possible, and she wondered if it did the same for her.

He reached around her and closed the door. It felt unbearably intimate to be here with him. Not only in his apartment but also in a room that was supposed to be a bedroom. But instead of a bed, a worktable. Instead of a lamp, this otherworldly illumination.

All sense of time or place dissipated.

The room was not unusually small, but it was so full of equipment that there was little space to move about. Emmett stood very close to her, and when she turned to face him they were nearly nose to nose. He could have stepped back, but he didn't.

Instead, she felt the warmth of his breath on her skin.

"Is this what you wanted to show me the other day?" she whispered.

"Yes." He looked down at her, and she thought, as she had at the Ferris wheel, that *this* might be the moment that she received her first kiss, and she was glad that it would not be so public after all.

He put his hands on her shoulders, and she closed her eyes, preparing for him to bend down toward her. She felt goose bumps rise on her arms in anticipation.

But instead, he turned her around and guided her to one of two chairs in front of the table. Why he had two chairs in here but only one in the other room, she didn't know. Unless he took girls here regularly.

She dismissed that thought.

"Do you want to see how it all works?" he asked.

She nodded. She was conflicted—torn between disappointment at the romantic moment passing by and equal intrigue at seeing this place. There was a camaraderie among creative people that was not discernible by others. But Alice understood this room. This was his canvas, just as old buildings were hers and watercolor papers were her mother's. Letting her into this space had one of two purposes: to impress her, as maybe was his habit with women. Or to invite her into something that was meaningful to him. She hoped it was the latter.

He pulled the camera from his neck and set it on the table. He opened the back of it and removed a roll of film.

"The red bulbs are called safelights. They give off just enough light so I can see while working but not so much that it damages the negatives. Then you have the enlarger, the timer, and three trays with developing chemicals." He pointed to each one as he named them.

"And of course, funnels and tongs. The kind you'd find in a kitchen. If this were a more professional office, I might have other gadgets, like a thermometer or a scale or different sizes of enlargers."

"You seem to print in just one size, like all the photos in the other room," she said, making it sound like a question.

"Yes. I like the eight by ten. Anyone can see the details without having to squint. It helps my photographs stand out when I submit them to publications. Most people turn in four by sixes. Costs a bit more, but it's worth it, if you ask me."

He picked up a funnel and a gallon-size glass container. He poured some of the clear liquid into the first bin. "Okay. This is the developer step. The next two are the stop and the fixer. But we'll get to those."

He put the cap back on the bottle and reached for a fan on a shelf. The room cooled, and Alice shivered. It was more difficult to hear, but not impossible.

"That's quite cold," she noted.

"The superintendent controls the temperature throughout the building, but it needs to be cool in here. Twenty degrees Celsius is ideal. I mean, sixty-eight Fahrenheit."

It struck Alice as odd that he would name the European measurement of temperature. The only people she knew who did that were her paternal grandmother and some of her other Italian relatives, who always commented on weather as if it were much colder than it was. A sweltering New York summer day would find her grandmother complaining about the thirty-two-degree weather.

As Emmett poured different chemicals into the remaining two bins, Alice looked around the rest of the room, her eyes adjusting to the red illumination. A thick, dark blanket hung on the wall, covering, she assumed, a window, so as not to let in any light. A water basin stood on another table.

"Now we're ready," he said.

He opened the film and unrolled a long strand of negatives. Using scissors, he cut them into five-frame pieces. He held them up one at a time against the red light until he'd chosen the image he wanted. He put the others down and then returned the lone one to the light.

"Come closer," he said, as if there were more than a hairbreadth of space between them. She stepped in, and he put an arm around her shoulder. She shivered once again, but not from the airflow of the fan. His touch was something she'd dreamed of at night for all the weeks since she'd first met him. But again, his movement seemed perfunctory, not intimate. It merely allowed him to control how she looked at the negative.

Up close to the bulb, she saw a tiny image from Coney Island. One of those taken from the Ferris wheel. She could count six microscopic ships taking their turn in the bay and imagined that the picture would look stunning once enlarged.

"Now," he said, releasing her just as abruptly as he'd drawn her in. He pursed his lips and blew onto the negative. Tiny specks of dust flew off.

He slid it into the enlarger and adjusted it so that the correct frame was in the middle. Then he switched off the red bulbs and returned to the overhanging one. Alice rubbed her eyes at the sudden change.

"Sorry about that," he said. "We really don't need to turn off the bright light until we start the developing. I just wanted to show you what it all looked like."

She nodded in understanding.

He turned on the enlarger and adjusted it through different sizes and focuses until an eight-by-ten image of the ships appeared on its white base. She could now see more details—the small people in the foreground, the striped awnings of the food stands. It was beautiful.

He changed to the red light once again.

"I'm exposing it now," he explained. He pulled paper from a plastic sheath and laid it over the projected image. He made more tweaks to the enhancer, keeping silent as he concentrated. Then he selected one set of tongs from the table, and she noticed that he'd affixed rubber pieces to its tips.

"Want to try the next step?" he offered.

Alice shook her head. "I'd rather watch once and then do it. Do you have more negatives that need to be developed?"

He smiled knowingly in a way that she could not interpret.

"Yes. You'll see," he said.

He lifted the paper with the tongs and leaned over to the bin with the developing liquid. He rocked it gently so that the entire page could be covered and then set a timer for two minutes.

"And now we wait," he told her.

They stood side by side in the tiny space. She had no more questions other than those for herself.

Who is this man, and why am I here with him?

And she'd come up with her own answers.

Emmett Adler. You don't know why, but you love him.

It was odd that *that* word would present itself, for she knew that there was nothing on which to base it. Her own parents, Vera and Angelo, shared a love that had been built through adversity and experience. It grew over the years and carried with it the traits that one might associate with that kind of commitment—honesty, trust, loyalty. Did Emmett possess any of these traits? She had no idea. He had not been *dis*honest as far as she knew, but his omissions were common.

So did she actually love him, or did he simply fascinate her?

And yet, there he stood next to her, the hairs on her arms rising in an expectation of something that she didn't even know to describe. He'd brought her back to this crimson hideaway, and she was going to believe that it was because he wanted to share this piece of himself with her. What he didn't say with words.

For some time Alice had been restless to go places outside her neighborhood. See people who weren't familiar to her. Dream big things and actually make them happen. Her age and gender and working status confined her to certain boundaries. Then again, what had the Pearl Pilkingtons of the world died for if not to forge ways for Alice's generation to break barriers?

The fact that Emmett seemed to live according to his own agenda and that he was inviting her into it filled the void that had been growing in her.

He embodied what she wanted to be.

He stood there moving the paper now and then and humming a song under his breath that sounded both familiar and distant. Like something her mother might have sung to her.

Before she could identify it, he spoke.

"Next step is the stop liquid."

She left her daydreams aside and looked down. The image had appeared once again, this time permeating the paper instead of receiving the projection. The black-and-white tones were rich in their lines and shadows, and she thought that this was another one of his pieces that was worthy of a magazine.

He said nothing of the wonder of the picture appearing on the white page, but then again, he did this all the time.

He picked up a new set of tongs and placed the paper in the second bin.

"No need for a timer for this one. Just thirty seconds. Would you like to count with me?"

"Yes," she said.

"One, two, three, four," they said in unison. As they did, was it her imagination, or did they both step just a bit closer to each other, face-to-face?

"Nineteen, twenty, twenty-one, twenty-two . . ."

They were nearly touching by now, their breathing slowing until she was sure they'd lost the rhythm of the count. She felt his warm breath on her cheek, and just when he'd leaned in, they both said, "Thirty." He inhaled sharply and turned around.

"The last one is the fixer solution." Yet a new set of tongs was selected, and he placed the paper in the final bin and set the timer for ninety seconds.

Ninety seconds. It could fly. Or it could be the longest time of her life.

When he turned again, he raised his hand and traced it down her cheek, down her jawline, and to her chin.

"Red becomes you," he said in the dim light. "Has anyone ever told you that?"

"How could they?" she whispered. "I've never been in a place like this before."

His hand moved to her hair, which he stroked so lightly that she barely felt it.

"A darkroom is a magical place, isn't it?" His eyes were on hers. They were softer than she'd ever seen them, not because of the trick of the light but because of the tenderness they conveyed. In this moment she wanted to submerge herself in them as the paper into chemicals, getting lost until she came out a new version of herself.

He spoke again. "I love this room. When New York and all its bustle becomes too much for me, this is my haven. The little place that's all mine, where I can close out everything else that happens. And that's why I wanted to show it to you."

His hand moved down to hers, which was captive at her side, unknowing what to do. He looped a finger around one of hers, and she felt him pull her in just a bit closer.

Ding!

The timer went off, and Alice no longer gave a whit about the photograph and saw it as an intruder upon this moment, although it was the very thing that had drawn them here together in the first place.

He turned as if the fireworks launching inside her were not even a flicker in himself.

"Can you hand me the basin and pitcher, please?" he asked, and she complied. It was porcelain, painted with delicate flowers, and so out of place in this room that she wondered if he'd bought it at a thrift store merely for its function or if it was possibly sentimental. She wished he would tell her something about his past.

He poured some water into the bowl and placed the photograph in it. By this time the image had fully set in. He reached up for the string, and the room was flooded with light that caused Alice to put her hands over her face.

"I'm so sorry," he apologized, and those eyes that had already seemed gentle just minutes ago seemed even more so.

Could a man playact such a thing, or could she trust that his words and actions were that of a man who hid much but had begun to let her in through the cracks?

"I'm all right," she answered, and placed her hand on his forearm to reassure him.

"What do you think?" He held up the photograph, now complete.

"It's exquisite. How clever of you to shoot this from the Ferris wheel."

"Not any more clever than you to think that I might be there and come find me."

She smiled. It was true. They'd thought so similarly on that point, artist to artist, as if they understood each other through that language.

"Are you going to submit it anyplace?"

"I am!" he said. "Now that I can put the *Life* magazine credit in my portfolio, I'm hoping something like this might sell well in these patriotic times."

He raised his arms and pinned the picture to the clothesline.

"Your turn?" he asked.

"Only on something that you don't plan to try to sell."

He grinned again in that way that told her he wasn't saying something. "No, this one is for my eyes—our eyes—only."

She held in a breath at the way he'd said that, as if he'd thought of them as a plural as much as she had.

She thought he would continue with more of the Coney Island negatives, but instead, he pulled open a drawer under the table and selected another can of film.

He pulled it out but held it away from her, and she was unable to see what it contained. Like before, he cut the negatives at every fifth image and then held them up to the light until he found the one he wanted.

"May I see?" she asked, feeling emboldened.

"Not yet. It's a surprise."

He placed it into the enlarger and put a new piece of paper on it, switching the lights from white to red.

"Close your eyes," he said. "It's not ready for you yet."

She did as he told her, her heartbeat quickening with anticipation at yet a new mystery that was Emmett. She heard him fiddle with the device and imagined what he was doing based on having just watched him with the previous photo.

"Perfect," he said to himself, but it pleased her to hear it. "Now, open."

She opened her eyes. The paper was still white, but she understood now that whatever the image was had been exposed from the negative and was just waiting for its triple baths.

"I want you to do this one," he said. He pulled out one of the two chairs for her and then sat in the other. "Do you remember what to do?"

She nodded. "Two minutes in the developing solution."

"Exactly. You're a good pupil."

"You're a good teacher." Alice grinned. She liked talking to him like this.

She picked up the tongs and placed the paper in the bin, stirring it gently as she'd seen him do.

Lines of black and gray started to emerge until they began to reveal the image that they were hiding.

It was a picture of her. She was looking up, wistfully, it might be said, as if the answers to all the things she wanted to know were written on the ceiling. There was little background, and what there was of that was blurred so as to be unrecognizable.

She felt breathless.

"When did you take this?"

"Weeks ago. The first day I talked to you."

"Why didn't I see you?"

"It was my first day photographing the soldiers. I was walking around taking pictures of the train station before getting to the platform. If you look at my whole roll, you'll see the café, the concourse, the flower seller. And—the newsstand."

"This was taken at the newsstand?"

He nodded. "I wasn't intending to take a picture of *you*, necessarily, but as I held the camera to my eye, I noticed this beautiful woman daydreaming. And I wanted to know what she was dreaming about." He paused. "Or even become the one she dreamed of."

This last piece he said quietly. She took his hand in hers, a gesture she felt comfortable enough to make. "You have no idea," she said.

That might have been the ideal moment for her first kiss. But once again, the timer interrupted them, and she was beginning to think that maybe photography was more of a hindrance to romance than a help.

"What's next?" he asked. He had an uncanny ability to switch his emotions on and off, like the string from the bulb.

"Thirty seconds in the stopping solution."

"Excellent."

She removed the image from the first bin, marveling at how beautiful it indeed was. Not because it was herself but because of the girl it represented—the dreamer, as he'd said. Alice in Wonderland, who found her way to adventure by following a white rabbit. Emmett in a second had caught her, so real and so vulnerable, and she appreciated that he didn't plan to show it to anyone else.

It was his. Hers. Theirs.

"One, two, three," she started. But on four, his lips were on hers and the tentative dance they'd been playing at ended and this—*this*—her first kiss, was so enveloping, so much better than the girl in the picture could have expected that she wanted it to go on forever, damn the timer.

His kiss was not a gentle one. It was eager. Hungry, perhaps, if the word could describe such an action. It was as if his need for her—and hers that matched it—was bigger than both of them, and she responded with equal want.

He pulled back, breathing heavily, and said, "Thirty."

"I forgot to count," she managed to say.

She pulled the paper from the bin and laid it in the next one, not even looking at it, and setting the timer for ninety seconds.

Ninety seconds.

They didn't waste one of them. Emmett leaned in, pulling her into his arms, their knees interlocking as if they knew what to do all on their own. He kissed not only her lips but also moved to her cheek, her neck, her ear—oh, her *ear*—and she'd had no idea that the earthquake that it created in her even existed as a feeling. It inspired her to respond in kind, and she pulled away to re-create the pattern he'd left on her—lips, cheeks, neck, ear. And when she got to his ear, that innocent little place that apparently screamed with feeling, she heard him groan, and his grip on her arms tightened.

"Alice," he said eagerly.

"Emmett."

He made a raspy sound that was more eager than a sigh.

"I'm sorry," he said, pulling away as if it were the most excruciating thing he'd ever had to do.

"For what?"

His eyes looked at hers with such melancholy, but he seemed to brush it off and said, "Because the timer is about to go off."

And just like that it did, but she felt something unsettling in her stomach. That feeling that he was hiding something. Again.

Still, that language of their souls was undeniable. Something told her to believe in it.

The cold room moderated the heat they'd created, and they returned to the task at hand. She lifted the photo from the fixer solution and rinsed it with water before hanging it to dry.

"It's a marvel," she said, "that you were able to shoot this so close to me without my knowing it."

"Oh, I wasn't very close. Do you want to see how I did that?"

"Yes."

He turned toward the enlarger, and the negative image revealed itself again. But this time he turned some dials, and the girl in the photograph became smaller and her surroundings became more identifiable. Indeed, she was at the newsstand, and she could see the totality of the displays of magazines.

"How did you do that?"

"This is the full image. The picture I took. But, see?" And he turned the dials so that they closed in on her. "With this, I can focus on any part of the whole thing. And then cut it where I choose."

"I love it. Both of them. Both perspectives."

"As do I." He turned on the bright light, and she closed her eyes, only to feel his lips seal each of her lids as he pulled her into himself in an embrace. "Because they both have you in them."

Her stomach then rumbled at the most inopportune time, and he pulled back in that Jekyll and Hyde way he had of changing.

"You're hungry."

She felt embarrassed. "Well, yes."

"Then I need to let you go."

"Come with me. Is there a diner nearby or somewhere we can talk?" She did not want this afternoon to be over yet.

"I'm afraid not. Well, there *is* a diner. That's not what I meant. But I'm afraid I can't go with you. I have—I have some things I have to do."

The mystery man.

He opened the door of the darkroom, and through the other room's window she could see that it was already dusk. He walked her to the front door, and she felt a bit wounded at the unceremonious ending to an improbable day.

She turned to leave, but he held her arm. "I want you to know that you can come here anytime."

To his apartment? Alice was only just now getting used to the idea that she'd come here in the first place.

"To the darkroom," he continued, though she hadn't uttered a sound. Maybe he'd read it in her eyes.

"What are the things you think about, my dreamer?" he asked.

It pleased her that he called her this. He recognized the piece of her that imagined herself to be elsewhere. Her parents seemed so very *content* with their domestic lives when she longed to be part of something bigger.

"I—I love old buildings."

"Then get a camera—I'm sorry I only have this one at the moment, or it would be yours—but get a camera and take pictures of old buildings or anything else that you love. That room is yours to use as you need. Just—just don't open that drawer there."

He pointed to the top one on the desk.

She was stunned and full of questions. But she asked only one.

"Why?"

"I trust you, Alice." She thought it was a funny way to respond. "Now, go." He kissed her on the forehead in a way that felt like a dismissal.

But he wanted her to visit the darkroom again.

That meant she would see him soon.

Chapter Twenty-Six

When Alice arrived home, there were flowers waiting on the table.

Her mother stood in the kitchen, apron around her waist, stirring what smelled like her heavenly vegetable soup.

Vera clapped her hands when she saw her. "Oh, my dear, look what arrived for you!"

The flowers had been arranged in a brilliantly cut crystal vase that rivaled the beauty of the stems in them. The pink blossoms were paper-thin and layered in a seemingly infinite pattern. Their fragrance permeated the room. There must have been forty of them.

"What are they?" asked Alice.

"Peonies, darling," said her mother. "I've only seen them in pictures, but they are even more exquisite than I could have imagined."

She was right. Alice had never seen anything quite like them.

"Who are they from?" Alice stroked the exterior petal of one and was entranced by its softness.

"I don't know. There's a card, but I didn't want to open it. It has *your* name on it."

"My name? Who would send me flowers?" Emmett was the only one who came to mind, but it was unlikely, given his humble apartment, that he could afford a bouquet such as this. Wildflowers might be more his style, anyway.

Alice removed the card and read it.

> *Alice—*
> *I have not stopped thinking about you since our dinner together at Delmonico's. There was something so complete about the four of us sitting together like that. I believe I owe you an evening of stories, and I hope you would still like to go to dinner next Friday evening. I can come for you at seven.*
> *William Pilkington*

William Pilkington! She had not thought of him all day.

She showed the card to her mother, certain of what would happen next. Her mother lived to love and be loved. Alice ached to get out of New York and see the great buildings of the world. If she could ever do that, she might come back and get married and have children. But it was the furthest thing from her mind right now.

Vera pressed her hands to her face.

"Oh, dear Lord. My Will and my Alice. Together. Who would have thought? Oh, I cannot tell you the joy that this gives me. Wait until your father finds out."

Alice wanted to ask her not to say anything, but she knew that there were never secrets between Angelo and Vera. Maybe that was the key to their happy marriage.

"Are you going to say yes?" Alice could see the anticipation in her mother's face. How could she say no and crush her like that?

"Yes," she found herself agreeing. But as much as she had enjoyed William's company at dinner and would like to see him again, she still felt the heat of Emmett's kisses.

Could a modern woman accept the pursuit of two men who were so very different from each other? Was this part of the new era that the suffragettes had fought for?

At precisely seven o'clock on the appointed evening, the knocker on their apartment door echoed. Her father answered the door and shared a hearty handshake with William. Alice felt her cheeks redden at the sight of him.

"Will. So good of you to bless us here."

"You don't know how nice it is for me to be here. It's a welcome change from my g-grandparents' home."

Angelo slapped him on the back in that inexplicable way that men did. "It's kind of you to say so, but you wouldn't envy it if you had to sleep under five blankets in the winter and strip down to your skivvies in the summer."

Alice rolled her eyes. What a word to say in front of a gentleman.

But William laughed. "I think I'd like to sleep in my skivvies, Angelo. I'd g-give quite a shock to my valet if he found me like that in the morning."

The man had a valet? There were corners of wealth that Alice had never even considered.

After a bit more small talk with her parents, William turned to her and held out his arm. "Shall we go, Alice?"

She glanced at her mother. Vera looked as if she might burst with pride over this pairing. Alice felt that same lump in her throat that suggested guilt over having dinner with William when she'd shared a kiss with Emmett—a kiss that had kept her awake ever since. But they had no promises between them, nor had she seen him since. He hadn't come by the newsstand, and she could not bring herself to go to his apartment unannounced, despite the invitation.

Maybe she was a little more traditional than she thought.

She took William's arm, a gesture that immediately felt comfortable. Alice could feel her mother's eyes on her back as they headed to the stairwell. Vera closed the door behind them.

What must William Pilkington think of their apartment? Neat but worn, tall and without an elevator, cramped in a way that could almost be called cozy.

They stepped out into the bustle of Thirty-Third Street, where the eagles atop Penn Station looked down at her. She liked to think of them as her guardians. Her mother told her that she'd always thought the same thing. Solid, resolute, everlasting. They provided a security that the world could never promise.

A light-blue car with white-and-black tires and a folded creamy canvas top was parked right in front of the building, and William walked toward it. Alice expected a chauffeur to step out, but William opened the door next to the driver's seat for her and walked around to let himself in by the steering wheel.

He must have read her mind. "I gave the driver the evening off," he said. "I hope you d-don't mind, but I really prefer to drive myself."

"I don't mind," she answered. And in fact, she was in awe as she looked at all the different parts of the car here in the front. She'd only been in a vehicle a few times in her life—taxis, at that—and never in the front. But she would be embarrassed to let on what a treat it was.

"Have you ever driven a car?" He put leather gloves on his hands, then began to pull away from the curb.

"No, but I think I'd like to someday."

"Would you like for me to t-t-teach you?"

Teach her! The idea had never crossed her mind, but the thought intrigued her.

"I think I would like that. Yes!"

"Then let's make a plan to do just that."

They drove twelve blocks north, a distance that Alice could have easily covered in less time than it took to drive in traffic. Williams maneuvered around slower cars and waved as they passed them. Alice laughed and followed his lead, cupping her hand like Princess Elizabeth might. As they progressed, William explained the various components of the car—the clutch, the transmission, bumpers, fenders, headlights. She tried to memorize them all.

"This is one of the rare new models available," he explained, caressing the leather-clad steering wheel with obvious pride. "The war has put a halt on automobile manufacturers being able to use aluminum, so it's been replaced with c-c-cast iron for the pistons, which, of course, means that they had to make heavier crankshafts and r-rod bearings."

It was as if he were speaking something other than English, but Alice enjoyed watching him talk about something that animated him like this. By the time they arrived, she'd learned more than she'd ever expected to know about the subject—heat gauges, headlights, wind silencers.

"I'm af-fraid I've dominated the conversation," he apologized as white linen napkins were laid across their laps at the restaurant. His hair was disheveled from the drive, but the fact that he was unaware of it held a kind of charm. "I'm a b-bit n-n-nervous, as you m-might be able to tell."

"Why, William? There's no need to be nervous around me."

He took a deep breath and said each word with deliberation. "You're quite beautiful, Alice Bellavia."

"Thank you."

The waiter filled crystal goblets with ice water and presented the menus. It was only the second time Alice had eaten in such a place—Delmonico's being the first—and she found it difficult to keep the calm decorum that belied the anticipation inside her at such offerings.

"Do you know what is interesting about this restaurant?" William asked. He must be relaxing. His speech was steadier.

"What is that?"

"This is the one your mother was talking about. How she and my mother ate together at its predecessor, Maioglio Brothers, once."

How thoughtful of him to have remembered.

"I want to bring them back here." His voice quieted. "And you. I'm—I'm glad you were able to be there th-that evening. And here."

"So am I." William had kind eyes, a gentle demeanor. He was everything a girl like her was supposed to want. She looked at his lips and the hesitant smile that they hid. A kiss from William might be a lovely experience. Like a sweet bowl of cream. Whereas Emmett's kiss—Emmett's kiss was fire.

She upbraided herself for comparing the two. She tried to put Emmett out of her mind and give William her full attention.

"Do you know what the occasion was that brought our mothers to Maioglio?" Alice asked.

"I asked Vera about it later. According to her, m-my mother—Pearl—wanted her to leave her job in a factory and be a kind of nanny for me. That way Pearl would be free to fight the g-g-good fight, as they say."

She had heard that part of the story from her parents. Alice wondered if he had any resentment at being handed off to someone else. But then, in his world, that was probably a common thing.

"I know my mother cared for you like you were her own son. She often said so."

"I don't remember everything about that time. I was very young. But I have always had a sense of being well nurtured and even loved. Before I went to live with my grandparents."

Alice tore off a piece of the *rosetta* roll that had been placed before them. "She is that. All love. I'm very fortunate."

"You are. I don't remember much about my real parents. Well, nothing about my father. Little about my mother. I was old enough to go with Vera to the prison in Albany, but she d-didn't allow me to see Pearl, and maybe that was just as well. Growing up with my grandparents and great-grandmother was not an experience to be envied."

"That's a little difficult to believe, if I'm honest, William." She dipped the bread in a dish of olive oil. Was this what Italy tasted like? If so, it was delectable. "My father has to stand all day at work with only one leg. My mother works at Macy's and at our newsstand to help out and had to sacrifice her hopes of being a painter. In our position, dreams are elusive things, rarely realized."

William shifted in his chair. "I wouldn't even pretend otherwise, and when the day comes where I am in a position to direct the decisions for our company, I hope to ease the burdens of all we employ. But that d-doesn't mean that where I was raised was void of sadness. As a boy, I dreamed of having a mother and a father to come home to. Who would read to me by a fireplace and make me hot milk when I was sick. I had none of those things. Only a foul-breathed governess."

She didn't point out that he could probably buy his own railroad company and become a train conductor like he'd always wanted to. But she sensed that he was trying to find points of commonality to her, across the abyss that stretched between their very different lives.

Alice smiled. "William, I hope you don't mind my saying so, but you went quite a long time there with barely a trace of a stutter. Does it really come and go like that?" She knew it was forward to say that to someone who was still something of a stranger, but he could just as well have been her brother had things not taken the course they did.

He smiled. "You're right. I feel like I can tell you anything, dear Alice."

He reached across the table and touched her hand. It warmed her throughout her body—a gentle glow rather than a raging flame. But it was pleasant. Welcome. She didn't pull away.

"What I m-mean is that I've never felt like I fit anywhere. Those early years must have made a bigger impact than I thought. Wh-when I saw Vera and Angelo again and met you and we went to D-Delmonico's, it was—" He pulled his hand back and sighed. "It was like I found home."

Alice understood what he meant. The four of them together, seated around that table. There was a rightness to it. Like a puzzle that had been completed.

"You—you are lucky, Alice."

"Lucky?" This from the man who drove a gorgeous automobile and paid for expensive dinners and lived like few ever would.

"To have the luxury of love." His eyes looked saddened.

"You think love is a luxury?" Maybe she'd taken her family for granted. But she could think of other luxuries that she would enjoy. The opportunity to travel and to be a student who didn't have to work, and to be regarded as equal to any man despite being a woman of humble means.

"Yes. The love of a mother and a father. The love of family. The love of—w-well, the l-l-l-love of s-someone you c-care about."

His stutter was more pronounced then, and Alice had started to see its pattern. Where she was concerned, it seemed to make a frequent appearance.

She made him nervous.

It occurred to her that knowing these two men enlightened her understanding of her own femininity. With Emmett, she discovered that she could provoke intense sensual reactions in a man. With William, she was beginning to realize the very real power that womanhood wielded—his speech patterns were only a symptom of a larger influence.

It was a heady thought—that women possessed a quiet power that was a greater force than men might ever acknowledge.

William continued. "Yes, Alice. L-love is a luxury. Food and shelter may sustain a p-person, b-but what kind of life is worth h-having if it is not shared?"

She met his gaze and felt as if she could get lost in his caring eyes.

Maybe men held the balance of the power after all. What a delight true equality between partners could be.

"So, then," Alice responded, "would the perfect life be that in which there are no concerns about money and one that has the abundant love of family?"

William sat back and smiled. He rubbed his chin and looked at the ceiling before returning to face her. "Now, that does seem as if one would have no r-reason for sorrows. But wealth can be lost, loved ones can pass away, and p-perhaps the ache of having had them and then lost them is worse than never having had them at all."

"Money or family?"

"Either. Both."

There was depth to William that she was eager to discover. He was not merely the man in the fine wool coat driving the expensive automobile. She was tired enough of being judged on her own status. She owed him the same consideration.

Alice laid her hands in her lap and responded to William's words. "I wouldn't want money so that other people can do things for me that I'm quite capable of. In fact, there's a kind of satisfaction in work. But I would treasure the opportunity to have time to explore all things I am interested in if there weren't quite so many responsibilities. This is especially true for women. We have more dimensions and, I daresay, passions than what we are allowed to voice."

William leaned in. His broad shoulders were the width of the tiny table, and the thought came to her that it would be a welcome thing to be embraced by him.

"Well, although I was so little when my mother died, I know well enough the sacrifices she made for women's suffrage, and I believe my parents' causes run through my blood, though my grandparents tried their best to l-leech them out of me."

Oh, dear William. He really was born of both worlds. He didn't even seem to know quite where he fit.

Alice grinned. "And do you bear the marks of their bites?"

"My g-grandparents' or the leeches'?"

They both began to laugh loudly enough that other patrons looked over their shoulders at them, but their attempts to stifle it were half-hearted.

"Quick! Tell me something sad," said Alice through giggles.

"Something sad? Let's see. Something sad. I'm so h-happy in this moment, I don't think I can come up with anything."

"Oh, do try, please? I will fall apart laughing if you don't, and they will kick us out of here, and I haven't had my steak yet."

"We can't have that. Their steak is delicious. So—" He took a breath. "I'll tell you that in that tree outside my bedroom window, there is a nest with three eggs. There used to be five, but a breeze knocked two of them out and they cracked on the pavement before the poor babes were ready."

She felt a deep breath fill her lungs. "Oh, that is sad."

"Did it help?"

"I'm totally cured."

"Can I tell you something, then, since that seemed to help?"

"Yes."

"There are still five eggs. There nearly weren't, as the nest was in a precarious place, but I leaned out my sill and repositioned it."

"Oh, you are a hero, then, William!"

"Only to the t-tiny sparrows, I suppose."

"And to me," she said slowly.

William reached again for her hand and placed his lips on it. They were soft, tender. If they were pressed against her own, she imagined that she might sink into them as onto a down pillow. A cushion to break her fall.

With Emmett, she was afraid that he might be the fall.

But sometimes falling was like floating, and that could be exhilarating.

Chapter Twenty-Seven

"Alice."

She was leaning over the counter of the newsstand, absorbed in a news article about Princess Elizabeth registering for war service and finding it fascinating that a monarch—or a someday monarch—would descend to work among her people. Alice wondered if she would have the same grit. She'd certainly had enough examples in the stories about Pearl and in the witness of her own parents, and she wouldn't want to be the first who was not brave in some way.

She looked up at the voice that was so familiar that she heard it even when he was not there.

"Emmett."

It had been more than a week since their encounter in the darkroom. Since he'd kissed her in ways that made her feel all sorts of things she hadn't known existed.

But was it love? After dinner with William, its definition felt elusive. The two men evoked such different reactions in her.

"I've missed you," he said.

"Why haven't you come by the station?"

"I wanted to come. But there are things that pulled me away." He didn't offer any more explanation.

But even as he stood here, he consumed the very air she breathed.

"What are you doing here, Alice?" he asked.

"I work here. For my father." What a strange thing to ask.

"That's not what I mean. I mean, what are you doing selling newspapers about other people's stories when you could be creating your own?"

Her heart fluttered. No one ever spoke to her like that. As if they saw right into her truest self. She felt a magnetic pull toward him, and it made her light-headed.

"Why would you say that?"

"Your mind is elsewhere, just as it was the first time I saw you."

He could see that? She'd just been reading an article about the upcoming twentieth anniversary of the opening of the tomb of King Tutankhamen and imagining what it would be like to see such a thing.

Emmett continued. "Your eyes reflect the small piece of me that still believes that there can be something better than what we have in this world. You make me believe in that again."

"You are an enigma, Emmett Adler."

"I'm—well, I don't know what I am. Around you."

Alice didn't know how to respond to that. It might be the cocktail of war and infatuation that made him say such things, or there might be something particular in his life to which he was referring. His secrets.

"I have something to show you," he said, standing straight. "Are you free soon?"

"Yes. There's my father now."

Emmett stepped aside. "Meet me at the clock in five minutes," he whispered, and she agreed.

When she arrived, he was leaning against an iron light post that sported four white spheres on its stem. He was reading some kind of letter and had an agitated look on his face. But when he saw her, he stuffed the letter in his pocket and smiled.

"There you are," he said, holding out a hand, which she accepted. "Are you ready for an adventure?"

Alice imagined that a life with Emmett would be one adventure after another, while a life with William might be charming and enjoyable.

"Yes."

He led her down the grand concourse, and her pulse beat rapidly as his hand held hers.

It seemed as if he were leading her into the men's lounge at the end of the hall, but just before then, he turned and looked around them and then darted through a small black door. Above it, in faded letters, it read: **Lost and Found**.

She followed him in, and he shut the door behind them. And, like the darkroom, it was as if they'd entered an entirely different world. He flipped a switch, which illuminated several bulbs along a narrow metal stairway with holes perforated into its steps. "Follow me," he said, and she knew that she would agree to go anywhere he wanted to go.

When they reached the bottom, another switch showed the way to a warehouselike room that was filled floor to ceiling with rows of black metal shelves. And on the shelves sat all sorts of everyday things that were orphaned in this basement. It had the stale scent of age and mold, but it also held a kind of magic.

"Lost and found," she whispered, looking at all the items. "More lost than found, I'd say."

"Yes," he agreed. "Isn't there something haunting about such abandoned things?"

She nodded slowly, taking in the wonder of it. There were the ordinary items—suitcases, handbags, overcoats, dolls, books. And the unexpected ones—dentures, wristwatches, crutches, even a telephone with frayed wiring springing from it. Paper signs had scrawl written across them that seemed to point to a failed attempt at order.

"How did you know about this place?"

"You don't have to speak quietly in here," he said in a normal tone. "We're too far below the main level for anyone to hear us. And they don't come into this room until after hours."

"How do you know that?"

"I've been exploring the station and watching this door in particular."

"Why?"

He shrugged. "It sounded like it would be interesting. The things that get lost in a train station. Supposedly they keep items here for forty weeks before disposing of them or donating them to charity. But I'm not sure that rule sticks."

Alice wiped her hand along a shelf and uncovered a layer of dust that seemed much older than the time allotted for its residency here. She sneezed.

"I'm so sorry, Alice," Emmett said, putting his hands on her shoulders. "Should we leave?"

"No, it's just the dust. I'll be all right. I want to stay."

"Okay. You say the word. But there is one particular thing I wanted to show you."

He led her down the labyrinth of shelves, passing by more oddities—a Kurley Kew, a cigarette case with a comb sticking out from its side, a ski pole.

"Here it is." He led her to a corner that had an enormous trunk sitting half open. It had rusted buckles and scores of stickers on it showing the destinations of the owner—mostly throughout Canada. "I waited to go through it until we could do it together."

It pleased Alice that he would have thought of this.

The light here was not as bright, so Emmett took a silver Zippo from his pocket and lit it.

"Bertie told me you don't smoke." As soon as she said it, she regretted revealing that she and their mutual friend had spoken of him at all.

"That's not the only reason to have a cigarette lighter," he said.

Indeed, as long as he held it open, as he did now, above his head, it gave off a warm glow that once again reminded her of his darkroom.

"Read what it says," he told her.

A yellowed paper that seemed to have been glued to the inside lining read, "Marion Greenwood, Providence, Rhode Island."

"I wonder who she is," said Alice. "And why she didn't collect her trunk. Or why they haven't contacted her to pick it up."

"You're the dreamer. Tell me a story."

Alice thought. There could be a thousand reasons why it was here, but she enjoyed the opportunity to try to imagine it.

"Let's see what it contains first."

"How about this?" he suggested instead. "You start the story, and as I pull out each item, you add to it."

She grinned. "That sounds like fun."

"So, the first sentence?"

"Marion Greenwood had a secret life," she began.

Emmett lowered the lid of the trunk to within a few inches of closing. "Don't look at it all," he said. "Just the things I pull out. Or you'll be cheating the story."

She agreed. He drew out a string of pearls. What could she concoct with that? She thought about it and then continued. "Marion Greenwood was a housewife. A fat housewife. She wore a string of pearls around her neck that pinched her skin. But her husband had given them to her on their wedding day, and she never greeted him without wearing them."

"Very good start," said Emmett. "Let's try another."

This time he didn't look as he reached in, perhaps wanting to let the tale reveal itself to him as well.

A small pair of ladies' undergarments came out. Emmett grinned as the garment hung on his finger. It was a deep violet color with white lace trim. Alice blushed. "No, pick something else."

Emmett's eyes danced in the twinkle of the Zippo light, which he occasionally turned off and on to restart.

"That's the game, Alice. Why does our Marion own something like this if she's a fat housewife?"

Alice thought about this and began again. "Sadly, Mr. Greenwood died. He choked on a piece of pie that she'd made for him. An apple slice lodged in his throat. Or, at least, that's what the police determined. In fact, Marion had forced it there while he was drunk, so they never caught on to her crime."

"But how does it explain this?" He held up his prize again to her eye level.

"Oh, you see, Marion had lost so much weight that she was no longer fat. Her husband never looked at her much anyway, so he wouldn't have known the difference. As she grew smaller, she kept herself rounded with pillows and stuffing and began to wear turtlenecks, but all the while, she bought herself things like this."

"Why?"

"You'll have to pull out another item so that we can figure that out."

"Right." He closed his eyes and pulled out a book.

Shakespeare's Sonnets. It was bound in red leather with gold lettering across the front.

Alice continued. "You see, as Mr. Greenwood ignored her throughout the marriage, Marion befriended a bookseller. A middle-aged widower who loved to have a pretty thing like her come and read to him after the shop closed for the evening. Their favorite was this book here."

She knew the story was a bit convoluted, but the joy was in making it up as she went along.

She flipped through the book, hoping to find some kind of marking that would indicate what might be their mystery woman's favorite, but the spine cracked as if it had never been opened. She decided to ignore that fact, as it didn't fit well into the story she was weaving.

"How about my turn?" said Alice. "I want to pull an item out and you finish the story."

"That's only fair, but I can't promise that it will have a happy ending. Flowery romances are for the ladies to read."

"Poor Marion. Maybe I should finish it after all. We have to give her a happy ending. Won't you at least try?"

He shrugged. "We'll see."

Alice reached into the trunk. Some items were identifiable just by touch, many too commonplace to be useful in this game.

Until she reached something in a metal case. She felt around for it, trying to identify what might be in it, but she couldn't. She decided that would be her item.

She brought it out, and it fit just right in both her hands. She flipped its lid open, and Emmett drew closer with the light, which shot small beams across his face. He looked happy in this moment. Not pensive, as he had been up above while waiting for her.

It was a camera. Alice's first thought was that it might be some kind of providential sign, pointing her toward Emmett and away from William, but she had to acknowledge that it was a common enough item for a traveler to carry.

"A camera!" said Emmett. He pulled it from its case and looked it over. "You need one of these. I think you should keep it."

"I can't keep it. It's not mine."

"Well, it's not our Marion's. Look what else I found."

It was a card that had fallen from the case.

> *To my darling niece, Catherine. May you enjoy many years with this and send some of your photographs to your aunt Marion.*

"See?" he said. "It's not hers. It belongs to some girl named Catherine. And it's dated three years ago. I think there's some kind of finders, keepers statute at work here."

"Still." Alice hesitated. She would love to have a camera. It would take her a long time to buy one like this, and now she even had access to a place where she could develop the pictures. She could walk along the streets of New York's older buildings and photograph their arches, their tiles, their scrolls.

"It's settled," said Emmett. "I'll finish the story if you agree to keep the camera."

He placed it in her hands, and she looked at it. She didn't see the harm in keeping it, especially if it had been gone so long. If it had been important enough, someone would have come looking for it. And this trunk.

"Go on," she said.

Emmett handed the Zippo to her and crossed his arms. "The police accepted Marion's story that her husband had choked, because they already knew her and trusted her. She secretly worked as an informant for them, spending evenings in her pretty underthings in the bed of the bookseller, but also in those of mafia bosses, learning their secrets and taking pictures of their belongings while the latest don would shower after their lovemaking."

Alice blushed at this line of talk. The very word being spoken on his lips, and the way he looked at her when he said it, made her feel things she didn't have names for.

"Is that the end?" she managed to ask in a shaky voice.

"No. You wanted a happy ending, so I'll give one to you after all. There was one don among them, though, who stood out to Marion beyond the others. She knew that there were things that he could never tell her. Things that he had done, things that he might still have to do. But she loved him anyway. And so she never told anyone about him.

Not the police. Not her parents." Emmett drew nearer as he spoke each sentence, and Alice's heart felt as if it might leap from her chest.

He continued, whispering. "He was the one secret that she kept all to herself. Because she was convinced that he loved her back and was going to set about making things right in his world so that he could be with her. But until then, she forgave the things that she didn't know about and believed his promise that all would be possible for them in the end, if she would only wait. And trust."

He stood so close to her now, and she trembled. She understood that they were not talking about some fictional story but that he was asking something of her. Telling her something in parable that he couldn't—or wouldn't—say out loud. It scared her. Excited her. Everything told her to run but also to stay. Her hand gripped the trunk so that she could steady herself, as she again felt light-headed around him. It landed on something silky. She pulled it out, and it slid through the opening in the trunk. It was a long nightgown. White with white lace. Bridal. A neck in the shape of a V and capped sleeves at the shoulders. It was exquisite.

She was about to continue the story, although she wasn't sure where to take it from there. Emmett saw the item and ran his hand along it.

"Beautiful." He lowered his head. "How I would love to see it on you," he said under his breath.

Her nerves tingled at these words and their meaning, and her mind continued the back-and-forth that had heightened with every encounter she had with him.

"Okay," she said, her heart betraying her head. She laid it over her arm and tucked herself behind one of the shelves. It seemed overly modest to hide as she put it on, since it was so thin that the light from the Zippo would surely silhouette her slender shape. But she'd never held anything so elegant, let alone worn it. She felt like a Hollywood starlet.

This world down below the station gave the impression that everything above was illusion and that it only contained the two of them in this unusual room, void of rules and inviting of impetuousness.

As if the consequences of her actions here might not have any bearing on her life at street level.

She unbuttoned her dress and unrolled her stockings, shaking as she did so. The air was cold on her bare skin. She slipped the nightgown over her head, and while it offered no protection from the chill in the room, she found that she felt increasingly warm from the inside.

Alice took small steps from behind the shelf, holding on to the edge of it as if it were the last anchor to her old life on the precipice of a new one. She suddenly felt like their fictional Marion with a dual life. There, she was Alice Bellavia. Only child of Angelo and Vera Bellavia, newsstand owner and Macy's shopgirl. Here, she would belong to Emmett Adler, a man whose history she knew nothing of but whose soul read hers with fluency.

Emmett's eyes widened as he saw her.

"Beautiful," he said again, and she knew he was not speaking of the gown.

He took a step toward her, but she stopped him.

"Will you take my picture?"

"You want a picture?"

"Yes." Alice had never felt more radiant than in this moment. And she might never again. But if Emmett took her picture, she would always remember how she looked and felt here in this room, in this train station that was so dear to her. When she was old—when she was ashes—even as these walls stood above and around her, this photograph would be a testament to the woman who was emerging from her girlish shell.

"Of course." He did not use his own, though, the one that was always slung around his neck as if it were an additional limb. He opened the silver case of Marion's—Catherine's—long-forgotten camera and wound the film to its starting point. Ensuring that she would take the camera rather than leave it here for someone else to find.

She leaned against a shelf, placing herself in a position that concealed the parts that allowed her to pretend some shred of modesty.

"Put your chin down and then look up at me. No, the other way." He directed her with words, never touching her, and standing back when she was just right. "Like that. Stay exactly like that." He took several pictures—she lost count as he moved around her and told her to shift just a bit. It became more and more comfortable as he repeatedly told her that she was lovely—a vision—stunning.

At the end, he made one more request. This one in a tone that made it sound as if she would be doing him a favor.

"My darling," he breathed. "Uncross your arms. Let me take just one picture like that. But only if you are comfortable."

She nodded. She put her hands at her sides, still leaning, but she knew that the light from the distant bulbs and the tiny flame of the lighter exposed a great deal. He bent at the knees and focused the lens on her. "Look up, my dreamer. Like you were when I first saw you." She posed as she remembered how she'd looked in that photograph.

Click.

"Perfect. You are perfection."

He set the camera down on the trunk, never taking his eyes off her. He shut the Zippo lid and set that down as well. She saw only the outline of him in this light until he came closer. But this time he approached without the confidence that had emboldened him in his own apartment. She saw him tremble—perhaps not as much as her—but it was there. No swagger. No telltale sign of this being something he did on an everyday basis.

He stood at last in front of her, and every nerve in her body ached to throw her arms around him and recapture the fire of their kiss. He ran a finger down her bare arm and followed it with his eyes. "Perfect," he said again.

Then he looked at her. "Nothing more needs to happen, Alice," he said. "I did not bring you down here with this in mind."

But he corrected himself before she could respond. He smiled and looked away from her. "Well, that's not entirely true. I've had this on my mind ever since I first saw you. I've wondered what it would be like to take you in my arms and have you as mine. But I am not a cad. I did not invite you here for this purpose. Just to see if you found this strange little place as intriguing as I did."

Alice put a finger on his lips, and he stopped talking. He placed his hands on either side of her face and pulled her into him. He set a featherlight kiss on her mouth, and she gasped at the sensation of the simple gesture. This created an invitation to a kiss that grew from kindle to blaze before she knew it. Then his hands, hers, were everywhere. She felt the gown slip from her shoulders and pool around her feet, but she barely noticed as what she felt for this man overtook all reasonable thought. She sank down with him onto the cold cement floor, where he pulled a tweedy overcoat from a shelf and laid it underneath her.

Once again, in his arms, she lost all sense of time, and as they emerged from their hideaway much later, she was surprised that the clock in the grand concourse indicated that it was four o'clock and she was an hour late in returning to the newsstand.

Chapter Twenty-Eight

Alice was on Opa duty. Vera and Angelo were both at work, but her grandfather had been going through a bad spell again. Every few months the effects of the bends would overtake him, even after he'd made so much progress under her mother's gentle care. This was one of those times when he could not be left alone in the apartment.

She'd led him to the bathtub. Helped him undress. His wrinkly old buttocks displayed a sprinkling of liver spots, and he sprouted white hair from his ears that she would need to trim—if he'd let her near him with scissors. She ran her hand under the water until it was the right temperature and added the bubbles that she knew he liked.

"Danke," he said as he sank into the water.

"Bitte, Opa."

He closed his eyes and leaned back. She kissed him on the forehead and ran her fingers through his thinning hair.

Vera was afraid that he might not be with them for much longer. But she'd been saying that for as long as Alice could remember.

When he seemed content, Alice left and returned to the sofa that served as her bed. She lay down on it and closed her eyes, drumming her fingers against the skin of her stomach. She'd loved when Emmett kissed that spot—the hollow right above her belly. And the one behind her neck.

When she wasn't working or in class, they explored the city as if it were brand-new to them both. They delighted in an unspoken competition of who could find the best place to uncover a new piece of New York history.

Alice took him to the alley by the opera house where, in just the right spot, you could hear the sopranos hit their high notes. He made her laugh when he mimicked their buxom chests and exaggerated trilling.

Emmett brought her to the City Hall subway station, where the stained-glass domes looked into the sky from below the ground. Leaves would flutter onto their tops, casting shadows on the concrete platform.

Alice showed him the spot in Grand Central Terminal, under the bricked archways, where you could face the corners on opposite ends of the room and whisper things that could be heard by the other.

Unexpectedly, the place she liked the most was the Green-Wood Cemetery in Brooklyn. Its pink stone Gothic arches seemed from another era, and its tiny mausoleums were ornate houses for the dead. It was not macabre, as she'd expected when he was describing what they were going to see. But more like a fairy village and very ripe for sketching pictures.

They packed a picnic lunch and sat underneath what Emmett called a camperdown elm tree. Its branches sagged all the way to the ground in a circle around the trunk, creating a tentlike hideaway, unseen by any passersby. Emmett kissed her deeply in that place, not with the fervor of their lovemaking but in a way that conveyed things they hadn't dared to speak. When he pulled back, he traced his hand along her cheek.

"This place has a sense of eternity about it. Do you feel that, too? I want to be with you forever, Alice."

He used words like *forever*, but they never accompanied the word *marriage*, and it remained a notion rather than a proposal.

When she was with Emmett, it felt like there was no one else in the world.

But as she lay next to him under the tree, nearly all sunlight blocked by the dense leaves, she thought about this word.

What would it look like with Emmett?

Forever with Emmett would bring new adventures every day. Maybe they would not have children at all—they might exhaust all that they could do in the city and stretch their pennies to go past its borders. He would photograph and she would sketch every old building and every kind of scene and paper their apartment walls a thousand times over in an ever-changing gallery created just for them. They would find new places, new ways to reveal their love to each other.

But she could not forget William.

He'd been in Chicago with his grandfather for a while, and she smiled at the thought of him sitting in his private railroad car secretly wishing to trade places with the ones punching the tickets. He'd sent flowers, each arrangement more magnificent than the last.

They were not all for Alice. Sometimes they came addressed to Zia Vera. Even Angelo didn't escape William's generous attention—a mahogany box with red velvet lining arrived, containing shaving cream in a glass bottle and a brush made of boar hair.

Her parents appreciated the gifts, of course, but she knew that having William back in their lives provided more happiness than anything money could be spent on.

William even sent three tickets to *This Is the Army* by Irving Berlin along with a caretaker for Opa for the evening. A Broadway show! It was more than she could have ever imagined.

Alice felt like she was living two lives. Hot dogs at the ballpark in cheap seats and apple pie from the Automat with Emmett. Delmonico's and Barbetta with William.

Vera had already started making comments about how lovely it would be to make their family whole again.

Emmett started breathing deeply. Alice turned over onto her stomach and propped herself up on her elbows. She pulled an apple from her bag and bit into it. Like Eve in the garden.

It was tough on the outside, tender on the inside. Two distinct goods making up one whole.

Alice could relate to the apple. Like its skin, she wanted to be tough. Resilient. But like its inside, she also valued sweetness. Softness.

As a woman, it was hard to discover what you *wanted* to be when the world told you what you were *supposed* to be.

And was it so impossible to want both? Couldn't she crave adventure but also appreciate the idea of a Sunday dinner surrounded by family, and gathering around the fireplace afterward to listen to a radio program?

These thoughts stayed with Alice while she worked the next day. William was due back from his trip tomorrow, and she needed to figure things out.

She slung her bag over her shoulder and walked south to Emmett's apartment. Last week they'd taken a boat to Roosevelt Island between Manhattan and Queens to photograph the smallpox hospital that looked like a castle. Its turrets and pointed windows seemed like something they might find if they could afford to go all the way to England, but the East River was the only body of water they had to cross. He wanted to develop the pictures today and send them out for submission to a medical journal that was doing an article on it. He'd given her a key in case he was late getting there. With a reminder not to look into that one forbidden drawer.

She jiggled the key into the lock, and while it unlatched, the door was still blocked by a chain. That was new. Not that he'd never used it—he'd never had one to begin with that she could recall.

"Emmett?" she said through the bit she could open. She heard a muffled voice, and then it went quiet. Footsteps came closer, and she saw a sliver of Emmett as he approached.

"Sorry about that, darling. Let me get that for you." He closed the door, jostled the chain, and then opened the way fully.

"Why did you get a chain?"

"One can never be too careful."

"Have there been any robberies in the neighborhood?"

"Why the questions?" His voice said he was agitated, but his eyes said he was—afraid?

"I don't mean anything by it. It's just new. I suppose I was curious."

"Of course you are, darling. I was a brute." He pulled her close to him and kissed her forehead. "Don't mind me. I just had a difficult day."

"Do you want to tell me about it?" She set her pocketbook on the tiny counter and made her way over to the couch.

He joined her and began to nuzzle her neck. She felt the familiar tingle that shot up and down her body, but she had the impression that he was trying to distract her.

She pushed him away.

"I heard you talking to someone. Like you were on the telephone. But you don't have a telephone, do you?"

"It was the radio. That's all. I turned it down so that we don't have to hear it."

"Hmm. I suppose I didn't recognize the program."

He leaned in to the other side of her neck, and all she wanted to do was to let him keep going. Because next he would unbutton her blouse and unpin her hair and begin the routine that always felt new.

"No. Wait." She pushed him back once again.

"What's wrong, Alice? You're acting different today."

"Why do we always do this, Emmett?"

"Do what?"

"Why do you try to change the subject when I try to ask you anything serious?"

"I don't know what you're talking about." He sat back and crossed his arms over his chest.

"Sweetheart," she said, scooting in and releasing his arms until they were holding hands. "We talk about so much. But even after all this time, I don't know anything about who you really are. When I try to ask about parents or siblings or where you grew up, you change the subject or you overwhelm me with kisses until I forget. But that has to stop. If we are going to have a future together, I have to know these things about your past."

He sat up and walked over to the kitchen. He pulled a cup from the cabinet and ran the faucet. He drank it all in one swig and set it back on the counter. He didn't approach her, though. He stayed on that side of the room and leaned on the edge.

"What does all that matter? We have you. Me. What else does there need to be?"

"There is a lot more, Emmett. Wouldn't you like to get married? Have children? We don't need to do it all exactly as everyone else, but there are some things that are in place for a reason, and what if we're getting it all backward?"

"What is it you want, Alice? You want the church and the dress and the ring? You want to be Alice Adler and embroider scrolled AAs across guest room towels? We don't even have a guest room, for Christ's sake. But is that the rosy picture you want?"

She flinched at his belittlement of what she was trying to say.

"Because I sure know someone else who wants to give that to you. William Pilkington."

"William?"

"Yes. Do you think I can't read between the lines when you tell me how much he does for your family?"

They stood back, looking at each other. Emmett's arms were folded again, and it wrecked her to be at odds with him.

But did her regard for William show through more than she intended it to? This was exactly why she'd provoked this conversation. The tug-of-war stretched her to the point of hurting.

"He's like a son to them. Isn't that natural that he would be a part of our lives?"

"I'll bet. I'll bet he'd like to make that official."

She ran over to him and placed her hands to his chest, but he remained stiff. "I'm not going to try to read William's mind, Emmett. And maybe you're right. But if it came to that—if he wanted to marry me, then in saying no, that means I'm saying yes to you. To us. And I just want to know that I have your yes in return."

He sighed and pulled her into him. "You have my yes, darling. How do you not know that?"

She rested against his chest and felt the rapid beat of his heart. She just wanted all the complications to go away. It would be easy to drop the conversation. But that only prolonged what had to be discussed.

"Your yes to what?" she asked. "Marriage? Children? Shouldn't we at least discuss more seriously what our future would look like?"

"We're talking in circles. Look at me." She stepped back, and he put his hands on her arms. His eyes were as soft as she'd ever seen them. "I have not been fair to you. I see it now. In loving you the way I do while holding back a piece of myself, I have let it get this far. Selfishly. I have wanted to be with you so much that I've pressed on without thinking about the ramifications. Alice, if you are asking if I will love you forever, if I want to be with you forever, then you have my yes. If you are asking me for marriage and for children, I can't—I can't give that."

Alice felt like she'd been punched in the stomach. Tears welled up inside her until her shoulders shook and she could no longer keep them in. "What are you not telling me? Are you sick?"

"No, love, I am not sick."

"Is—is there some reason you cannot have children? Because I don't really care about that, Emmett. I was not one who spent my whole life dreaming of them. I can be happy with my drawings and taking my classes so that I can get a job. But it seems that the subject should at least be talked about."

"No, my love, I have no reason to believe that I *can't* have children."

"Then what is it?" She heard herself shout it, but he was not making any sense. "Are you already married?" Alice pulled away from him and asked quietly, "Is that it, Emmett? Do you have a wife somewhere and that's why you won't marry me or tell me anything about yourself?"

He reached out to her. "No, please, Alice, no, it is nothing like that. I'm not married. There is no one else for me. No one. Ever. But I can't marry you. Not because I'm attached in any way like that. It's because I'm protecting you. Please. I'm protecting you. I can't say anything more than that."

This was not any kind of answer she saw coming. Protecting her? From what? Maybe his little tale about Marion Greenwood and the mafia dons was autobiographical in some way. It seemed absurd, though.

"I—I don't know how to respond to that, Emmett. I don't even know what questions to ask you." She rubbed her temples. Why did he always speak in riddles?

"Don't ask me anything, sweet, sweet Alice in Wonderland." He stepped toward her and spoke into her hair even as he ran his hands through it. She felt his chest heave as he held back his own tears, and it broke her wondering what he didn't think he could say.

"Can't we just stay in Wonderland? Pretend the world out there doesn't exist?" he asked, muffled. His kisses worked their way all around her head, down her neck, back to her ears, and like they always did, they weakened her knees, and she no longer wanted to ask any more questions. She just wanted him, all of him that she could have, even if it wasn't everything.

"Why do you think the world out there so terrible?" she whispered.

He clung to her so she couldn't see his face. "I've seen things, Alice, and I've lost people I loved. I don't want anything to ever happen to you. For now, this needs to be enough. Not forever. But for now."

What could he mean by those things?

She was too exhausted to belabor it for now.

"Yes, Emmett. It's enough."

It wasn't. But to demand more might mean to lose this, and while she might have to face up to that someday, she would delay it as long as possible.

Chapter Twenty-Nine

She returned home spent—emotionally, physically. She and Emmett had never fought. And she never wanted to again. She didn't know if she was strong enough to face William tonight, but if the hot water was working, she could at least take a shower and refresh herself before dinner.

"Mama," she said as she stepped into the apartment. Vera was at the stove wearing a blue apron with red cherry designs. "You're home early."

"It was a slow day at the store, so my boss told me I could go home if I liked, and I've been dying to make some of your father's favorite minestrone. It just takes so much time, and I haven't had a chance to do it."

"Where's Opa?"

"A blessing, Alice! William has hired a woman to spend several hours a week with Opa to help us. Her name is Celeste, and he is out taking a walk with her right now. A walk! Can you believe it? She's charmed him every which way. She was a godsend, and we have William to thank for that."

Alice leaned on the counter and dipped a finger into the soup pot. "Are you at all afraid that we're taking advantage of William's generosity?"

Vera put down her wooden spoon and placed her hands on her hips. "Whatever are you talking about?"

"All this stuff he does for us. The gifts. The shows. And now a caretaker for Opa?"

"Oh, Alice. I can't believe you'd even think such a thing about your father and me. You know that just having William back in our lives is all we want. The rest is lovely. But I can do without it."

"Why do you think he does it?"

"Because we're his family."

"We're not his family. But maybe he's doing this so that he can buy his way in."

She knew even as she said it that it was grossly unfair. And it wasn't even something she believed. But things seemed so upside down, and it was all she could cling to as she tried to understand how to move forward.

It would be so much easier to lament William than to love him.

And she did love him.

"Alice Bellavia! I have a mind to wash that tongue with a soap bar, no matter how old you are. What has made you so sour today?"

Alice felt her lip quiver. When she was a child, her mother had always seemed to sense when she was afraid or confused. She would crawl into Alice's bed and sing "Wiegenlied," the lullaby by Brahms.

Vera walked over and pulled her into her arms. "What is really wrong, Alice?"

Alice nodded into her mother's shoulder and then shook her head. "I don't know."

"Love is never easy, is it?"

Alice pulled away and smiled through the start of tears. "I guess I always pictured that when I fell in love I would just know it."

She hadn't told her mother specifically about Emmett, but she also knew that Vera was perceptive enough to know more than she let on.

"Sweetheart, which is more beautiful—a summer day when you can sip lemonade and dip your feet in a fountain? Or a winter one at Christmastime when you drink hot cider and go ice-skating?"

Alice thought about this, but her mother again spoke first. "The answer is neither. They are both beautiful in their own ways. What you must do is decide which suits you better."

Alice smiled and hoped that if she ever had children, she would be as insightful as her mother was.

"Thanks, Mama." She kissed her on the cheek and put a sweater around her shoulders. She decided to go catch up to Opa and Celeste and walk with them.

When she arrived at the curb, she looked right and left but didn't see them. She was just about to go back in when the horn of a car caught her attention.

A sleek black automobile pulled up. She could see her reflection in its shiny polish, which contrasted with the stark white wheels that slowed down as it approached her.

"It's a lovely day to learn how to d-drive," said its occupant.

"William!" she said when she tipped her head away from the sun. "What are you doing here? I thought you were coming back tomorrow."

It did not escape her that her first reaction at seeing him was one of gladness.

"My grandfather wrapped up a d-d-deal sooner than we both thought, so we took an earlier train."

"It's good to see you," she said. Meaning it. She was already sorry for the way she'd spoken to her mother about William. Her agitation told her that her feelings for William were truer than she wanted to admit.

"Care to get behind the wheel?"

"You're joking. I've never driven in my life."

"I'm half-serious. Let's head out of the city and then get you started."

A grin spread across her face. He opened the passenger door, and she slid in.

"This is some car," she commented. "Red leather seats? I didn't know they came like this."

"They don't. I ordered it specially. Kind of p-perks up all the black and white."

"What happened to your other car? The blue one?"

"It's at home," he said. And she realized the silliness of her question. Surely someone like William could own two, three, four of them.

As they drove over the Williamsburg Bridge into Brooklyn, he told her that this was a Lincoln Continental.

"It was already on order before what happened at P-Pearl Harbor. They stopped p-production for the war. They squared up the f-fender for the 1942."

When they'd passed the suspension towers and reached the other side, William drove until they came to a quiet area.

"Ready?"

Alice felt her blood race with excitement at the idea of doing this.

He stopped the car and got out while she slid into the driver's seat. It was warm where he'd been sitting. She rubbed her hands along the steering wheel and began to memorize what all the white knobs and red needles said.

Air. Temperature. Hood.

"Okay," said William. He closed the door behind him, and Alice realized that this was the most alone they'd ever been together. "What you want to do is engage the clutch. That's the pedal on the l-left. There you go. And turn on the ignition."

She turned the key and heard the engine roar. She felt it vibrate throughout her body, and she had the feeling of being one with the car. It was like nothing she'd ever experienced. The power of it!

William laughed. "You're grinning, and we haven't even gone anywhere y-yet."

"I love this! I'm driving," she said, which prompted another laugh.

"Not so fast. Put your right foot there on that brake." He pointed to the other pedal. "Let's put it in first gear."

Alice looked around. She didn't know what that meant.

"Here," said William. He took her hand and put it on what he called the gearshift. He laid his hand over hers and helped her maneuver it into the lowest gear.

Maybe it was just the exhilaration of the moment, but she liked this feeling.

"N-now, slowly press on the gas while releasing the clutch."

She did just as he said, and after jerking the car once, she found the right rhythm to it. And they were off!

Not quickly, of course. In fact, a stray dog ran by them and was lost to the distance before she'd gotten very far. But William encouraged her to go a little faster. Without speaking, he took her hand and again guided it, this time into second gear.

Alice felt emboldened—she could do anything! And with the open road ahead of her, she drove to the limit of what the gear would allow. It was enough for the wind to blow her hair around. It fell in front of her eyes, and she tried to brush it away, but it was hard to do that when she needed to keep her hands on the wheel.

William noticed and leaned over to pull it back for her. But he was a second too late. She saw something streak across the car and felt a bump.

She'd hit something.

She stepped on the brake, and William helped her turn off the ignition quickly. She hurried around the car and found a dog lying on the ground. It was the same one they'd seen earlier. His fur was black and white, but red blood began to pool around one of his legs.

Alice felt her whole chest constrict as she raced to the small animal.

"No," she said. "No, no, no. Oh, I'm so sorry." She collapsed next to the dog and scooped him into her arms. He looked at her with big black eyes that seemed to forgive her even as she wanted to trade places with him rather than see him hurt.

William ran over to her side.

"Let's get him to my house."

Alice nodded and carried the pup in her arms like he was a baby. He yelped as she sat down in the passenger seat once again. Her yellow dress was filthy, but she barely noticed it as she rocked the dog and held him tightly against her.

How could this have happened? Had she been so enraptured by the excitement of the moment that she'd failed to see everything around her?

She never wanted to drive again.

William didn't talk as he turned the car around, spraying a fan of dust into the air. He raced back over the bridge, driving with one hand while the other slid over to pet the dog. He took Alice's hand and glanced at her.

"He's going to be just fine," William shouted over the wind. "And you didn't do anything wrong. He just came out of nowhere. The same thing would have happened if I were the one behind the wheel."

She appreciated his regard more than she could say. But it didn't stop her from feeling so terribly responsible for the accident.

When they got to the city, he veered around cars, driving faster than what Alice thought would be allowed, but she was grateful that he seemed to be risking a traffic ticket for the sake of this little animal.

They pulled up to a large white house on a park. A chauffeur came down the steps and took over the car from William, ignition still running. William placed a hand against Alice's back and guided her up the stairs.

"This is my great-grandmother's house," he explained. "She lives closer, so I thought we could c-come here."

"Mr. Pilkington. So good to see you."

"Victor, hello. Can you help Miss Bellavia here?"

Alice thought she saw the butler raise an eyebrow at the sound of her name, but she brushed off the thought.

"Certainly, sir. Let's go down to the first-floor kitchen. There's a large table there that rarely gets used."

The details of the house were a blur to Alice, though its extravagance was not entirely unnoticed. It was like a museum.

She followed Victor down a set of stairs to a series of rooms and halls that were much simpler than what was above. William followed behind.

Victor laid a tablecloth across a table and gently took the dog from Alice's arms. They suddenly felt so empty, but she leaned over his little body and stroked his ears while Victor and William took a look.

"It's okay, A-Alice," said William after a minute. "It's j-just a broken leg, and we can set that." Victor left the room, saying that he was going to get some clean towels.

Alice released a guttural sob that she must have been holding back. She rested her head against the dog and apologized over and over.

"Alice," said William. She turned around. He had blood on his shirt, too, his crisp white shirt. She looked down at herself and suddenly laughed. Not because anything was funny but because the tension just released itself that way.

"You're going to think I'm crazy. Crying one minute. Laughing another."

"Come here." He held out his arms, and she stepped into them. She felt his heart beat against her chest, though she didn't know if it was the adrenaline of the past hour or their own proximity.

"I wish I could get him past our landlord," she said. And as soon as she spoke the words, she knew that William would come to the rescue the way he always did.

"He can stay with me, if that's all right with you."

She pulled away and looked up at him. "You're a busy man, William. You don't need the responsibility of a puppy."

It was his turn to laugh. "I have people who help me with th-things, Alice."

Of course he did. She had to get used to how different his life was from hers.

"Although," he continued, reaching over to stroke the dog's nose, "I think I might just take care of this little guy on my own."

"Thank you," Alice mouthed. She was at a loss to voice more than that.

"He'll need a n-name, though," suggested William.

Alice thought about it. "Would it be silly to call him Lincoln, since the car is how we found him?"

"Lincoln it is."

Their hands brushed against each other as they petted Lincoln. Alice felt a shiver run up her arm. She pulled away after lingering a second longer than necessary.

"I should get home now."

He nodded. "I can drive you. Victor can take care of Lincoln until I get back."

"Thank you, but I'd like to walk." She tucked a strand of hair behind her ear. "Really, though, William. Thank you for everything today. For trying to teach me to drive. And for—him."

She looked at Lincoln one more time while William spoke. "If you'll let me, Alice, I'd like to c-continue with the driving lessons in the future. You were really good out there. I know you can do it—that you can do anything you want to."

"How can you say that after what happened?"

He held her gaze.

"B-b-because I believe in you."

There were no more tears to be had today, but William's words surrounded her heart and made her feel the kind of love that her parents shared with each other.

He followed her back up the stairs and held the door open for her. She turned back, and their eyes locked.

"See you soon?" he asked.

"See you soon.

It was a long walk home, but Alice was starting to feel like herself again when she got to the door of the building. What a day it had been. Her argument with Emmett seemed like it was ages ago, but her exhaustion reminded her that it had happened just this afternoon.

Then William had shown up. William. Lincoln. Driving.

And it was only just getting dark.

When she arrived home, Opa was asleep, and her parents were sitting down at the table eating the minestrone. She saw an envelope waiting at her place, and she opened it. Her parents said nothing about how it had gotten there or who had delivered it, but the way they averted their eyes as she read made her understand that they weren't going to ask her questions.

> *I thought about what you said. I do want those things, my dreamer. I want to marry you and have children with you and see you through college and spend every day in your company. But I have to put some things to rest that stand between us now. Things that might put you in danger. So please have faith until I can see you again.*
>
> *Please trust me. Trust us.*
>
> *Love, E.*
>
> *P.S. And, I beg you, don't come to the apartment.*

Chapter Thirty

There was no trace of Emmett. She waited for him to come by the newsstand as he always did, hoping that his absence would mean days. But it turned to weeks, and he did not come. Bertie had not seen him. She even dared to ask her father if he'd seen Emmett, describing him, although she quickly saw that Angelo's eyes had not missed anything and he knew more than he'd ever let on to her.

She was frightened with worry.

I beg you, don't come to the apartment.

Alice did as he asked, but she looked everywhere else—she even visited the offices at *Life* to see if any submissions from Emmett Adler had come in. But no one had heard from him.

At last, she tried him at the apartment despite his warnings.

But the lock had been changed. She didn't know what else to do.

In contrast, she heard from William almost daily. While he was away again on business, she received postcards from Philadelphia, Richmond, Durham, Charleston, all the way down to Miami. His grandfather was working on negotiating contracts with the government to convert some of their clothing lines into military uniforms. William had designed a pitch that outlined their ability to bring down costs per unit for the government while increasing revenue for their company due to the volume of work.

He told her—although she would have already known this of him—that it was not the profits he was concerned with so much as helping their employees keep their jobs during this economic uncertainty. He had a plan to ask them to reduce their pay across the board by 10 percent so that everyone could stay rather than letting some go.

While he was away, Alice took Lincoln out for a walk at every opportunity. He still limped, and it looked as though it might be permanent, but he leaped with excitement every time Alice came by to see him. She could barely get him on his leash and he was ready to bound down the stairs.

Lincoln and the fact that her classes would be resuming again soon gave her much joy. But as she was concerned about Emmett and thought about William, she knew one thing—she had to make a decision before anyone got hurt.

"Alice, what is the matter?" Her mother found her stewing over this one afternoon. She rubbed her hand along her daughter's back. Alice was holding Emmett's note and had not moved, frozen as she thought about all these things.

"You've looked troubled for a long time. Do you remember how we used to talk? You used to bring home flowers you'd pick along the way, and I wouldn't have the heart to tell you that you weren't supposed to take them from people's gardens. But you gave them with such innocence that I couldn't reproach you. Where has that Alice gone?"

"I'm the same Alice, Mama."

"I don't think you are, dear. Your father and I have been very worried about you."

"You don't have to worry. I'm going to be okay."

Vera sighed. "Do you remember your favorite treat as a little girl?"

Alice grinned. "The hot chocolate at the café in the station."

"It's a cold afternoon. Wouldn't it be like old times to go get some together?"

Her mother's eyes pleaded, and Alice knew that she couldn't refuse.

"Let's get our coats."

They crossed the street, always without the crosswalk, as it would have meant walking far out of their way to do it correctly. Alice had grown up dodging the cars, and it was second nature. She could always tell the New Yorkers from the tourists by where and how they got from one place to another. The locals acted as if they owned the sidewalks. The out-of-towners treated them with deadly trepidation.

They had no trouble finding a seat in the café. It was a Wednesday, and the commuters would not get off work for another hour. Then the train would be bursting, people jockeying for a table as train delays were announced, and the inevitable grumbling would begin. But in this quiet space they could hear each other without the competing noises.

As the hot chocolates were placed in front of them, both of the women held their mugs to their noses and smelled. It was one of the many points where Alice knew that she was just like her mother. And yet she'd shut her out when she needed a mother the most.

"I'm so sorry," she began. And her tale about Emmett and William began.

As Alice spoke, she wished that she had talked more to her mother about these feelings long before it all got this far.

Vera patted her daughter's hand, encumbered by the table between them. But she leaned in as close as possible.

"That is a terrible dilemma, darling," she said. "And I'm afraid that I don't have an answer. If it is an answer that you are looking for."

Alice spoke through tears, dabbing her eyes with a paper napkin that already had drops of hot chocolate saturating it. "But it would make you and Papa so happy if I were to marry William."

"Of course it would, Alice. But if that has contributed to your pain, then I hold myself solely responsible. You see, I have always loved William as if he were my own son. To have him taken from me was the most dreadful thing I would ever hope to endure. To have him return has been one of my greatest joys. Certainly seeing my William and my Alice together would be a dream I never dared to have. But not if it means you sacrificing your happiness. A mother always wants her child's happiness over her own."

"But that's just the thing, Mama. I wouldn't be unhappy with William. He is so good, and I like him very much. I would even say I love him, although I'm not sure I can totally say what kind of love that is. Do I feel about him like I feel about Emmett? No. I'm not sure that I can ever love anyone in that same way."

"You will learn, though, dear, that passion and love are not synonymous, as the world would have you believe. Love is honesty, loyalty, and putting the other first. Can you say that Emmett is all those things for you? Can you say that William is?"

Alice thought about that. There were moments when she knew that Emmett bared his soul to her in such raw, honest ways, but that knowledge couldn't be put into words. And yet he was secretive. Was that pure honesty, then? Was he loyal? If so, where was he? William sent postcards faithfully and spoke of all these places that he wanted to take her to. She had heard nothing from Emmett after receiving his note.

Trust me. Trust us.

His words compelled her to wait. But was she being a fool for doing so?

She felt smothered by the reasoning, although it was exactly the light she was hoping her mother could reveal for her.

She answered slowly. "By your definition, William's love for me is truer."

"Alice, I don't mean to pry, but there are some things you may need my advice on. Has this Emmett—has he defiled you in any way?"

She knew what her mother meant. But it was a coarse word for something that had been so beautiful between her and Emmett. It was love—love of some kind—she was sure of that.

"No."

"You don't have to be proud, Alice. We have all had our errors. Including me."

"I don't think so, Mama. You've never done a wrong thing in your life. I'm sure of it."

"I fell in love with a married man."

"What!" That, indeed, was an unexpected revelation.

Vera laughed. "Your father, Alice. I fell in love with your father. But you know he was married."

"Oh, that. Well, of course I know *that* story. But you knew him before he knew Pearl, so it doesn't really count."

"That doesn't matter. He chose her at the time, and I still harbored those feelings."

"But you didn't *act* on those feelings. And that makes you even more saintly, if you ask me. Because to deny yourself someone you feel passionate about is just—is just the most noble thing."

Even as she said these words, she knew that it was analogous to her. There was something that felt so right about being with William. Even if what she felt with Emmett was the kind of passion that people wrote books about.

They'd both reached the dregs of their mugs, and Alice needed to return to the stove, which she'd turned off while they stepped out. She was making the lasagna that her father claimed was better than his own mother's.

As they walked back down the Penn Station steps, Vera looked up at the eagles.

"Did I ever tell you what your father named the one that looks into our window?"

"I don't think you did."

"Saint Michael. Like the archangel in our faith. A protector and defender against evil. Those eagles have seen much in their thirty years and will see even more in hundreds to come. If they could talk, I wonder what wisdom they would impart?"

Alice smiled. She had always felt safe under the gaze of the eagle.

And then she stopped in her tracks. A long-ago childhood memory came to her. A German picture book from which her mother tried to teach Alice a little of her native tongue so that she could talk with her grandfather. It made him so happy to hear the German when he was in a fit with the bends.

"Mama," she said, "what is the German word for eagle?"

Vera paused and thought. "*Adler.* Yes, that's it. *Adler.* Why do you ask?"

A chill went through Alice's spine. "Oh, just because we were talking about them." But inside, she knew.

Emmett was her eagle. He'd told her that he was protecting her, and now he seemed to have disappeared. Whatever happened, whomever she chose, Alice trusted him. But she also feared that he might be in danger.

She had to find him.

Chapter Thirty-One

Something was wrong. Alice recalled her conversation with Emmett about it being dangerous for them to be together. And then he'd distracted her in the most expert of ways and the details blurred, but her pulse quickened at the feeling that his absence meant that he'd been gravely serious.

She had to try again. And this time she wouldn't give up.

She stood from the table.

"Sit down, Alice," said her mother. "Let's have another cup."

"I'm sorry, Mama. I've got to go."

She kissed her on the head and raced out the door without looking back.

Though it was just on the other side of Penn Station and down a few blocks, Alice felt like it took her forever to run to Emmett's apartment. She was angry with herself for waiting for him to come to her just because he always had.

She saw her breath as she ran. The evening chill had set in, fall was coming soon, and the sun was nearly down all the way. The streetlights would turn on at any moment.

She tripped over a bottle that had been thrown on the street and scraped her elbows on the pavement. She saw them bleed, but she had no time to stop to tend to them.

The feeling that something was wrong nagged at her and spurred her on even faster.

She pulled his keys from her purse. She'd never had a chance to give them back. She put the wrong one in first—the one that was meant for upstairs.

"Come on!" she yelled, and tried the other one. She hurried up the flights of stairs until she came to his door. She went to knock, but the door swung open at her touch.

"Emmett?" she called. But there was only silence.

And devastation.

What little he owned had been turned over. The couch on which they'd laughed and loved had been sliced open and its cotton batting pulled haphazardly out. Kitchen drawers were opened with their contents emptied onto the floor. The wallpaper gallery made up of all his glossy photographs was torn into ragged strips. No regard for their beauty.

She peeked into the bathroom. The shower door was open and its little metal grate lifted up.

Nothing there. Her heart pounded.

She went into the darkroom.

The door there was open as well, although he always kept it closed. The black curtain over the window had been shredded, revealing the window that she'd never seen. The red bulb was broken into sharp points; drawers lay scattered, even one that had always been locked. She looked at it closer. Its metal hinges had been pried open. Whoever wanted something might have found it in there. Why had she never pressed him about it?

If she'd known what it was he was secretive about, could she have helped him?

Where was he?

She needed to find something that gave her any kind of clue. But she might be looking for the very thing that someone else had—and they might have found it.

But what if they didn't? That was her only hope.

Chances were it had something to do with that drawer. She went back to the entryway to shut the door and connect the chain and then returned to the darkroom.

Whoever had been here had been thorough. The drawer was ordinary. No secret compartments, as she would have hoped. But that was probably just true in spy novels. It was empty, as was every other drawer. She looked inside the gallons of chemicals, the shelves, the few albums that he had. She pulled down the clothespins in case the pictures had been arranged so as to hide something. But there was nothing.

Either they'd found it or there was nothing to find. She sat on the floor and pulled her knees up to her chin. Her shoulders shook as she struggled to breathe.

Where was Emmett?

Who was Emmett?

The possibilities terrified her.

Someone was at the door.

Her heart raced.

The doorknob was moving, and outside it, two voices expressed some kind of frustration that it was locked. Her heart pounded. She looked around the tiny room. She might be able to fit behind the table, but she'd still be too exposed, and there was nothing with which to cover herself.

The window.

Whoever was at the door had managed to remove the doorknob, and now they were kicking it in. The chain would not hold. It was meant to keep out snooping landlords. Not whatever kind of thugs were there.

Her legs felt like jelly, but she had to hurry.

She crossed the room to the window, but its sills had been painted over several times. Old white had yellowed and new white covered it. It budged only a tiny bit, not nearly enough. She found scissors lying on the floor and opened them to use their blade to cut through the paint. It crackled as she did so, but she made progress and was able to open it enough to slip through. She closed it again and pressed her back against the brick wall outside. Thankfully this was the window with the fire escape landing. To release the ladder, three stories down, would have drawn attention she didn't want, so she waited on the small ledge.

With the window closed, she could not hear what was being said, but the muffled tones had recognizable sounds.

German. Whoever was in there was speaking German.

She saw their shadows moving across the darkroom. Her pulse raced. As the figures disappeared, she thought they must be crossing into the other room, so she let herself peek in.

Emmett! Emmett was one of the two men. Her heart leaped—but then she saw him. He looked gaunt and worn, but he stood straight and argued in effortless German with the other man.

Someone must have knocked on the door, because both their heads turned in that direction. While the stranger walked to answer it, Alice saw Emmett step over to the counter and write something down on a piece of paper. He stuck it in his back pocket.

The door closed behind the man who'd just arrived, and he spoke with the first one. They also appeared to speak quite harshly.

Then one saluted the other, tapping his heel and giving the Third Reich salute that Alice had seen in newsreels.

Emmett followed suit.

Emmett was—a Nazi?

She wanted to be sick.

Alice leaned back against the wall and covered her mouth to avoid crying out. Of course. It all made sense. The blond hair. The blue eyes. The German name. She'd suspected that he was of that descent, as she partially was, and she'd heard that trace of an accent just once and forgotten about it. And it would explain why, at his age, he was not drafted into military service. Because he wasn't American.

Could he be a spy? She didn't want to believe the horribleness of the other possibility.

It was like something out of a movie. But she had no other explanation. Why would people be looking for things in his apartment? Why had he not used his key?

Maybe because he'd wanted to delay their coming in here. Could he have smelled traces of her perfume as he entered and been trying to protect her?

But if he wasn't one of them, why was he speaking in German and returning their Nazi salute?

She dared to peek in one more time. The three stood by the door, arguing but keeping their voices down. Then the first man raised his fists and brought them down across Emmett's shoulders like a hammer.

Alice felt a scream rise in her throat, and she bit her lips to avoid it escaping.

When the second man punched him, Emmett collapsed to the floor.

They repeated their beating on his back, and she saw him spit out blood. It pooled on the floor, and as they shoved him, he landed in it, staining the knees of his pants.

Whoever he was, Alice wanted to run to Emmett and help him. Her muscles ached with the effort it took to hold herself back.

But there was one hope—if they were the bad men doing this to Emmett, maybe he wasn't one of them after all.

Her blood raced with anger and fear, desperate to help him, paralyzed with the knowledge that to reveal herself would only make things worse. She put her fist to her mouth again to avoid crying out and watched as they dragged him to his feet and smoothed his clothes, presumably to avoid a scene as they pushed him outside. One of the men took off his overcoat and put it around Emmett's shoulders.

Emmett held his hands behind his back, hunched over in obvious pain, and she winced in sympathy. Just as they exited, Alice saw him pull something from his back pocket and drop it on the floor, unnoticed. It fluttered, just missing the blood streak.

Yes, he must have known she was there.

The door shut without a noise.

Alice counted to thirty, pressing sweaty palms together in a desperate prayer, thinking that this might be how long it would take them to reach the street. She did not want to stay out here and have them look back and see her on the fire escape.

She slid back in and ran over to what he had dropped.

It was the piece of paper, and on it he'd scrawled:

Under paint.

Under paint. What could that mean? She wished he'd had even two more seconds to write more.

She looked around the room. Under paint. Under paint. It made no sense. The room was too bare to hide gallons of paint, and the only other thing it could mean was the trim. But what would be under trim? She ran her hands along the crackled baseboards as flakes fell to the floor.

Nothing.

She tried the window. But just more flakes.

She returned to the darkroom and repeated her efforts.

But then she got to the window. The discolored paint, yellowed with time. And the fresh white coat along the side.

Fresh white paint.

And then she saw it.

A small, rounded bulge, obscured unless you knew to look for it. She tried to pull it out with her fingers, but it was wedged into a niche that must have been carved for this purpose. She found the scissors that Emmett used to cut the negative strips splayed open on the floor. She used its metal tip to gently slice a line around the perimeter. That loosened the item.

She pulled again with her fingers. It was a roll of film, undeveloped. This must be what he'd originally hidden in the drawer.

What did Emmett want her to see on it?

The darkroom was bathed in light from the shredded curtain, and it was too damaged to repair. Alice looked around the apartment for anything that might serve her purpose, but her sweater was too small and thin, and the only blanket Emmett seemed to own had been similarly destroyed, though how anyone thought something could have been hidden in its wool strands, she didn't know.

She would go fetch one from her apartment and return.

Alice planned to be home for only a few minutes, but when she got there, Opa was in a state.

"Nein! Nein!" he was shouting to Celeste as she tried to coax some broth into him. He tossed it aside, splashing most of its steaming contents onto his caretaker. She screeched when it landed on her arm.

"Enough!" she cried. She turned and saw Alice. "I have looked after more ill people in my life than I care to count, but there has never, ever been anyone as cantankerous as your grandfather." She shuffled over to the countertop and wrapped a towel across her arm. She put her coat around her shoulders and slung her purse over her arm. "I don't mean to pry, Miss Bellavia, but he is not well enough to be cared for at home. He needs to be somewhere where he can be tended to round the clock. And not by you and your parents. His time may be near. I've seen it before. And it will only get more difficult for you all. Mark my words."

"Thank you, Celeste," said Alice. She felt like she would buckle under the worries of today. "I'll comfort him. I know how to. That looks like you should see a doctor."

Celeste left without another word, and Alice closed the door behind her. She remembered that her parents were at another show.

She couldn't remember the name. William had gotten a ticket for her, too, but it had slipped her mind when she ran off to Emmett's. She gripped the roll of film in her pocket.

But as urgent as it was to get back to the darkroom, she didn't think it would be safe to go tonight. In fact, it frightened her to ever go back again, but she didn't have the money to get the film developed elsewhere.

Opa threw a spoon across the room at the window, leaving a hair-thin crack. His arms flailed about, and no amount of cooing and whispering could make him recognize her.

Celeste was right. Alice had been noticing how much worse he was getting, but she had been too preoccupied to do anything about it.

A simple phone call to William would solve everything. She had no doubt that if she asked him to help put Opa into a proper facility, he would not only do it but also pick the finest in the city.

But she couldn't ask that of him. She couldn't let her feelings for him be confused with what he could do for her family. For now, they would have to make sure that one of them was always with Opa, until the end.

Alice guarded the film all night, a sleepless night, letting it out of her sight only when she had to shower. The next day she finished her shift at the newsstand and looked for Bertie.

She found him over by the women's lounge, showing some tourists the pencils into which he'd carved a miniature scene of Penn Station. He rolled the six sides of the pencil slowly, revealing how the shape of the station unfolded as he turned it. They were amazed. Although he'd asked for only three cents for his handiwork, one of the women slipped her diamond-adorned hand into her purse and pulled out two quarters. She bent her knees in order to speak to Bertie at eye level.

Alice was impatient to talk to him but couldn't interrupt his little transaction.

"I'll take four," the woman said.

Bertie's eyes grew wide. "I don't have any change for you, miss."

"No change needed. You are not charging nearly enough, if you ask me. Are you here often? I may send a friend over to see these. She's a writer, and I think she'd find these delightful."

"I'm here every day, every night, miss," he said. He grinned in the way that Alice knew would have been irresistible to women if polio had not stolen everything else from him.

"Every night? Why, where do you sleep?"

"Wherever that is, I won't be sleeping tonight. I'll be lying awake thinking of that beautiful smile of yours."

He'd avoided her question. Alice knew that he moved every evening, pretending to hide from the stationmaster, even as Bertie's residency was well known and quietly accepted.

The woman stood and put her fingertips to her mouth and giggled. "Aren't you too funny? Here is another quarter just for making me laugh today. I'll send some friends to find you."

Bertie tipped his hat as she walked away.

"You *scugnize*," said Alice. "If you were a proud man, you would reject that charity. But you actually encourage it."

He kissed the three quarters and put them in his shirt pocket. "You'd better believe it. This will keep me in cigarettes for weeks."

Just as well. Emmett had seemed to be his regular tobacco donor in all the weeks that she'd known him. And now he was . . . now he was gone.

"Bertie," she whispered, sitting down next to him. She pulled an envelope from her purse and handed it to him. "Can I trust you to hold on to this? Don't open it and don't tell anyone about it unless I don't return."

"Return from where?"

"I have an errand to run. Don't ask me what. I'll be back here at—" She checked her wristwatch. It would take several hours to develop the film and dry it. "Seven o'clock. If I haven't come and found you by then, please give this to my parents."

"I don't like this, Alice. I don't like this at all. What are you up to?"

She felt tears come on and dabbed her eyes with a wrinkled handkerchief.

"I think Emmett is in trouble, Bertie. I'm going to try to help him somehow." She broke her own resolve and told him everything that she'd witnessed the other day. His usually jovial demeanor turned to concern.

"That doesn't sound good."

"I know." She blew her nose. "I'm scared for him. For me."

Bertie looked down at the wheeled board that served as his legs. "I'd give anything to go with you, Alice, but I'm afraid I'm no help."

"Just give this to my parents if you don't see me by seven. It's Emmett's address. I hope those men haven't come back."

"Don't go there just to develop the film, Alice. Here." He took the three quarters from his pocket and put them in her hand. "Take this. Go to a studio. Get it done right."

She returned them. "It's not just the money, Bertie, although I thank you for that. I don't have any idea what is on the film. But it was something important enough for him to risk everything for, and I can't have other people seeing it until I know what it is."

He nodded. "Right enough. But you stay safe. Try to get out of there as fast as you can. I'm not sure my heart can take worrying about you for so long."

She kissed his head. "I will."

"Now go."

It was only a few short blocks to Emmett's apartment from the other side of the station, but Alice's feet felt like lead, and they seemed to be the longest blocks she'd ever walked.

In order to keep herself from going mad, she paid keen new attention to every detail she passed. The cigarette butts that lay strewn on the concrete. The very old woman walking the very small dog. The bicycle leaning against a crumbling brick wall.

Anything, anything to keep her from worrying about Emmett.

When she finally arrived, she didn't need the key for the first door, as the mailman was just leaving. He held it open for her, and she mumbled a thank-you. She climbed the stairs, and as she arrived on the landing on Emmett's floor, she paused. There was a rustling coming from down the hall, and it sounded as if it was coming from his apartment.

She tiptoed a few inches and then a few more until she was able to see that his door was wide open.

Her first thought was to flee. It could be those men again. But then, it could be Emmett. She froze, alert for any sound. And then heard a rough female voice.

"Well, he didn't leave much of value, did he? Go ahead and throw away those cushions. Ain't nothin' can be salvaged from those. Keep the cups, 'cept for the one with a crack in it. Can't get nothin' from that."

Alice let go of a breath. She approached and tapped on the door. "Hello?"

"What do you want?"

"I'm looking for Emmett Adler."

"Who?"

"Emmett Adler. The man who lived here."

She peeked in. Little had changed in three days, save for the disarray being somewhat righted.

The woman continued to look confused, so Alice explained, "The man with the blond hair and blue eyes. About so tall?" She raised her hand a few inches above her head.

"Yeah, that's the one. Didn't go by that name. Not the last name, at least. It was Fischer. But now that I think of it, it might have been Emmett. Emmett Fischer. Yeah, that sounds right."

Then where had Adler come from, and why had he lied to her? Alice felt desolate at the idea that he hadn't confided in her. That he'd deceived her.

Could she believe anything he'd ever said?

"Do you know where he's gone?" she asked the landlady.

"I don't know nothin' 'cept some man came by and said if I found—let's see, what was it—some film canister, I was to hold on to it and he'd come by and check in for it."

"Emmett would come by?"

"Ain't you hearin' what I'm saying? No. The boy is on his way overseas or somethin' like that. That's what the man said. The man's gonna come by next Tuesday in case I find what he wanted. Offered to pay good money for it, too, but I ain't seen nothin' like that. Shame. Sure could use the cash."

Alice ran her hands through her hair. None of this made sense.

"Have you cleaned out the darkroom yet?"

"The what? Speak up, girl. You're too quiet."

Alice pointed to the door. "The bedroom in there."

The woman shook her head. "Nah. Been in there, though. Bunch of junk and god-awful-smellin' jars of somethin'. I'm coming back for that tomorrow. Gotta bring buckets. Don't know what he was doin' with that stuff. Don't think I can sell any of it."

Alice opened her purse and pulled out eight dimes and two nickels. All she had on her. "I am—was—*am* his friend. Do you mind if I can be alone in here for a bit?" She held the coins in her hand and held them out.

The landlady shrugged. "Not sure there's nothin' in here worth all that. Hurry up. I gotta get new people in here as soon as possible."

"Yes," agreed Alice. She wanted to get the woman out of there. She would need a few hours in the darkroom and didn't want to worry Bertie. "I want to be alone to remember—to remember the times we shared here."

That was not far from the truth, although the thought of it was likely to make her cry again. She could not look at the shredded sofa where they'd shared their love and slept in each other's arms.

What had it all meant if it hadn't been truthful? What had she given away to someone who gave her nothing?

The woman took the money and closed the door, saying she'd be back tomorrow. Alice surveyed the room, gingerly picking up pieces of the torn photographs that had once graced the walls. They were mere fragments—a half a face here, the top of a tree there, and nearly a whole scene with a bridge. Separate, they were nothing, but together, they were the remains of what had once been.

She placed them all in her purse. And set about her work.

Alice had come prepared. She arranged a thick blanket around the window to block the light and took out a Zippo to help her see in the absence of the red bulb that had shattered. She rearranged the equipment—the enlarger, the chemicals, the bins—back into their proper places and set about to work. She cut the negatives into five-frame strips and slid the first image into the enlarger.

All Emmett had on hand were eight-by-ten pages, so she adjusted the settings to fit the page.

The light from the Zippo did little, so her eyes strained as she peered at the images. But she pressed on in near darkness, taking each frame one by one through the steps. When they were finished with their final bath, she drew them out with the tongs and pinned them to the string that she'd rehung across the room. As she pinned the last—the eighteenth—to dry, she huddled in a corner and wrapped her arms around her knees.

Maybe Emmett had his reasons. Maybe he'd really been trying to protect her. It was all so much to take in.

She didn't know what to believe.

When someone began banging on the door, she jolted awake, unaware that she'd fallen asleep. A chill ran through her body.

Had the men returned? Emmett? The landlady?

A fist pounded again. She looked around for somewhere to hide.

"Alice!"

It was her father.

She let go of a breath she didn't know she was holding.

"Alice!" he shouted again. "Are you in there? I've brought the police."

She lit the Zippo and looked at her wristwatch. It was nearly nine thirty. Bertie must have found her parents and delivered the note in which she'd told them exactly where to find her. If she hadn't returned, it had meant that she'd run into trouble.

How worried they must have been.

"I'm here!" she called as she ran out of the room. She opened it to find five people there. Angelo. Vera. Bertie. And two officers.

They were quite the ragtag bunch, her father with his crutches, Bertie with his board. She could only assume that the policemen had carried him up.

But it was her mother's face that she looked into. Her mascara had streaked down her face from tears, and they sank into each other's arms.

"Alice, we were so worried about you. What happened?"

She held her mother close before pulling back and telling them as much as she knew.

They all walked into the darkroom, the policemen leading the way. Alice pulled the blanket from the window, and the string of pictures revealed the story that Emmett must have wanted to tell.

Rallies with Nazi sympathizers—by the looks of it, twenty thousand of them, gathering at Madison Square Garden on Forty-Ninth. Swastikas as much as three stories high hung from the ceiling as people cheered for the speakers onstage. An enormous banner of George Washington hung incongruously in the middle of all of them.

Could there really be so many people right here in New York who were sympathetic to the monster overseas?

"The Bund," said one of the officers. "This was a few years ago. Your friend has been involved for a while if he was at that event."

"What is the Bund?" asked Alice.

"A group of aspiring Nazis. You had to be of German descent to join. But their goal was to make life under the Reich seem attractive to Americans. So we could all live under it someday."

"You said *had*. Are they not around anymore?"

"They're not as visible. I think they officially broke up last year."

"But they still meet privately?" she asked.

"We've heard so, though they're much harder to locate. Looks like your friend here had no problem finding them. You have to know people."

Did Emmett *know people*? And what side did that mean he was on?

While the initial photographs of the crowds were shocking, it was the remaining twelve that everyone homed in on.

These were personal. Photos of men talking over whiskey and cigars, laughing, strategizing. Maps laid out on tables before them. Documents in folders on tables.

But two showed where a folder had been opened and two handwritten letters were shot at odd angles, as if Emmett had been in a hurry. The last picture showed the shadows of two men as if they were hovering over the letters.

Emmett, presumably—and who? Someone who was trying to stop him?

"Can you read those, Vera?" asked Angelo.

"I'm sorry, darling. My German is limited to everyday things. There are few words I can make out."

"We'll have to take these, miss." One policeman stepped forward and addressed Alice.

"Of course." She nodded, still in disbelief over what she was seeing.

As far as it looked, Emmett had attended a rally.

But anyone from the public could do that.

He'd been invited into a meeting.

He'd have had to know someone. They'd have had to know him.

He'd taken a look at private documents.

And now he was missing.

Either Emmett was a sympathizer. Or he was a spy.

But the photographs did not show anything that might tell her all that she really wanted to know.

Where was he?

The policemen took the pictures and exchanged information with the Bellavia family. The prints would be passed along to higher authorities, of course, but if Alice had any questions, she could get in touch, and they would see what they could find out for her.

She was the last one out, and she locked the door for what she hoped was not the last time.

Even while knowing that it was. She felt with that deep certainty of women's intuition that Emmett was not coming back to her.

They spoke little on the walk home. Bertie had gone on ahead, returning to Penn Station in spite of Vera's promise of a freshly cooked lasagna if he came with them.

"And disappoint my date?" he asked. "I left a dame waiting for me over by the ladies' lounge."

Bertie always said such things, though they all knew it not to be true. He belonged to the station and the station belonged to him, and he never seemed to want more.

Vera stepped ahead of Angelo and looped her arm through Alice's. "Darling, I can't even imagine what you must be feeling right now. And we will have to sit down and talk about it. But there is something you must know before we get home."

"What?" she asked with no enthusiasm. The only thing she wanted to know was where Emmett was. That he was safe. And that he loved her.

But she might never have that chance.

"William is there. And he wants to talk to you."

"What do you mean, William is there?"

She hadn't looked at a calendar in days, but she did a quick calculation in her head. Of course. He was supposed to be arriving home from his trip today.

"I don't know about that, Alice, but his timing could not have been better. He showed up a few hours ago and helped me make the noodles while we waited for you to come home. And then when your father came home instead and told us about the note you gave to Bertie and Bertie's fear that you were in danger, he offered to stay with Opa so that I could help find you. Oh, he wanted to come. He is terribly worried about you, Alice. Why don't you run ahead?"

William was as good a man as was ever made, and she did love him. But to not know where Emmett was felt like she'd inhaled a poison that was slowly burning her up inside. She couldn't fathom seeing gentle, caring William while this darkness swirled in and around her.

But Alice did as her mother suggested. As she approached, she saw the doors to their building flung open and William's blue car parked in front. A white ambulance had pulled alongside it, blocking the street, and she saw two men in white outfits rush through the doors carrying a stretcher.

"Opa!" she called. William followed behind them and pulled Alice into his arms.

"Alice, sweetheart, you're all right. I've been so desperately worried."

She pulled away a bit and pointed toward her grandfather. "What happened? Where are they taking him?"

"He collapsed. I was helping him to the restroom, and his knees gave out. He fell to the floor and hit his head against the table. They're going to take him to the hospital—I'll drive you over there."

She hadn't been there. In chasing after Emmett, she'd neglected to be there for her grandfather. What if she could have helped him?

"Alice." He looked at her with concern. "It is not safe for him here. He needs medical help. He needs to be in a facility that is experienced in how to care for him."

She ran her hands through her hair. It had been coming for some time. But now that it was here, she couldn't bear the thought of Opa being put away somewhere. Opa had been a constant presence, and she knew better than anyone how to coax lucidity out of him.

She shook her head. "Mother won't hear of it. And—and we just can't."

Alice didn't finish saying what was on her mind. Even if they ate beans every day and stopped buying paints and no longer gave to the causes they supported, they could not afford the expense. And she knew her mother never wanted to abandon him to the state again.

William removed his wool overcoat and put it around her shoulders. He drew her into his arms once more and rested his head against hers as they watched the ambulance doors close on her grandfather.

"My dear, you know that you don't need to worry about such things. I'm going to take care of it all."

She didn't protest. Being wrapped in William's arms felt like a harbor in the storm surrounding her. She was too tired to think of what that might imply right now.

"Where are Angelo and Vera?" he asked without moving.

"She's walking with him. It takes him much longer on crutches, you know." She knew that they had only to say the word, and William would arrange for the finest prosthesis available to be made for him. But not one of them would have ever asked.

"They love each other very much, don't they?"

She managed a smile, despite the circumstances. "Yes, they do. They really do."

Alice realized that William had not let go of her and she had not pulled away. And that he had not stuttered once.

In this moment when she felt as if she had nothing to hold on to, she was being held up.

Chapter Thirty-Two

"Here you go, Opa."

Alice put a pillow behind her grandfather's head, taking care to avoid the white bandage that a nurse had just changed.

"Danke, Aleit," he said, and she was pleased to realize that he knew who she was.

Thanks to William, her mother had been able to spend these past two weeks by Opa's side. He'd offered to cover any losses she might have from requesting a leave of absence from her post at Macy's.

At first she refused, but he offered this explanation.

"Zia Vera, you and I both know that he won't be with us for much longer. You have this time, and time is precious. You gave me so much of yourself when I was a young boy, and I would like to do this small thing for you. It's what families do."

Alice liked to spend evenings with Opa. She would finish a shift at the newsstand and bring a sketchbook and a novel until he fell asleep for the night.

None of them had to do this. After Opa was released from the hospital, William arranged for him to be moved to his own Midtown apartment and hired round-the-clock nurses to see to his comfort.

Opa's bedroom was flooded with light in the daytime, and his bedcovers felt like real silk. They probably were. He slept well, ate well, though the head injury had weakened him beyond what they expected him to recover from.

Two weeks in, Opa's breathing became particularly labored. A bedroom was made up just next to him for Vera and Alice to use. Vera liked to go home to Angelo, but Alice noticed that Opa slept better when she was near.

Sometime in the night, Alice fell asleep on the window seat and woke to feel William sit down next to her. Lincoln sat at her feet, which had become his permanent spot. Seeing the little pup every day gladdened her in these sorrowful times.

"Shh, shh," William said when she stirred. She rubbed her neck, which felt stiff after the awkward way she'd been sitting. "I just came to switch places with you if you wanted to go to your bed."

She stretched her arms out. Her bed sounded great. It was a feather bed, soft enough to sink into, with down blankets that were like heaven.

"That's very kind, but he seems to know when I'm not here. I'd like to stay a bit longer, at least."

"Do you mind if I stay with you?"

It was lonely sitting here with Opa. William's company would be welcome.

"I would like that."

He walked over to the closet and brought out yet another blanket like the one in her room. My goodness, had he taken stock in whatever manufacturer made these? Or were they as standard to rich people as dish towels were in her kitchen?

He laid it across her knees, and as he did so, he noticed her open sketchbook.

"May I?" he asked, touching its cover.

She nodded.

William flipped through the first few pages, on which she'd drawn places around New York that she'd committed to memory. First, one of the eagles. She was proud of the way that one had turned out. Just the right shading so that each feather on its chest was distinct. The eyes had been difficult—at first her attempts had made it look angry. But she'd erased it enough to thin the paper in that spot until she was happy with the results.

Others were redraws of places she'd been with Emmett. Not all were locations. One was a lone trunk, with all the items they'd found in the luggage room. She practiced rubbing the lead and varying the pressure of the pencil to perfect the details. It wasn't finished, but it was on its way.

The final one was her attempt at a portrait. Emmett. Thoughts of him competed with her concern for Opa, but when she realized that all her worry was not going to bring him back from whatever had happened to him, she acknowledged her helplessness and focused her thoughts on her grandfather. At least her presence here did some good.

As time went on, though, she began to accept that Emmett might be gone forever. She could wallow in thoughts about who he might be and what might have happened to him. Or she could move on with her life. She had so much. A family who loved her.

A man like William.

William's gaze lingered on this last sketch. Alice hoped he didn't recognize it. Faces were a challenge for her, as proven by all the work she'd done on the eagle. In truth, it looked nothing like Emmett, and she'd felt too spent to correct it, preferring to preserve all her memories in her heart rather than in this poor rendition.

She must have conveyed something of her feelings on paper, though, because William said, "Emmett?"

His voice was low at this word, and she hung her head, feeling bad about accepting all this generosity on behalf of her family when her heart had been laid open for all of them to know about that night at Emmett's apartment.

"Do you love him?"

She shrugged. Then nodded.

Why had Emmett never contacted her? With what they had shared, either it had all been a pretense, or . . . he was gone forever.

This simple gesture was the most she'd acknowledged about him in all these weeks, and it pricked her resolve like a pin to a balloon. Suddenly the tears that she'd held back flowed. A trickle at first and then an unleashed flood, enough to make her catch her breath loudly. William sat next to her and pulled her into his arms as he had that night Opa went to the hospital.

As she had then, she felt so secure there. She thought again that William just fit like something that was always meant to be. How could she put into words that Emmett was a dear and wonderful and terrible chapter of her life? But also that she was ready to turn that page? To turn to William.

She let herself rest against his chest until all the tears were spent. All the while, he said nothing. He just held her and stroked her hair.

They must have sat there for half an hour. She didn't look up at him, just remained curled up, staring at the way the moonlight shone through the window. William stood after that and guided her to her feet.

"I think you should go now. Look. He's breathing calmly. Let me stay here with him so you get some sleep. I promise I'll wake you if he stirs."

He walked her to the door, and as he opened the one that led to her room, she had the fleeting thought that it would be nice to be kissed right now. A gentle kiss. Gentle but strong, just like William.

Her dreams became confused, alternating with nightmares of what might have happened to Emmett, taking on a strangeness that included grizzly bears in a forest to falling off the Ferris wheel at Coney Island.

Other nights she thought she felt William slide into the bed next to her, under those magnificent blankets, and hold her all night.

But she woke up alone, knowing that she had imagined it all.

The next few nights passed similarly, with William finding her on the window seat and helping her up and promising to get her if Opa needed her. The only difference was that there were no tears. And that each time he closed the door behind her, her desire for him to kiss her grew stronger.

On the fifth night of this new routine, a gentle knock at her bedroom door woke her hours after William had come to sit with Opa. The door cracked open, letting in a little light. William was silhouetted in it, and she thought that perhaps he was going to join her after all.

"Alice," he whispered, never passing the threshold. "I'm sorry to wake you, but you'd better come."

She jolted up. Opa. She'd changed into a nightgown and now slipped on the robe at the foot of the bed. She tied the sash around her waist and hurried into the other room.

Opa was restless and coughing. She sat next to him and stroked his liver-spotted hands until he settled. She helped him turn to his side, which had sometimes helped in the past.

It took longer than usual, but he fell asleep once again.

She stood up and found that William had not sat the whole time. His arms were crossed as he watched the scene.

She walked over next to him.

"It won't be much longer, will it?"

He shook his head. "I don't think so. I'm so sorry." His voice became deeper. Quieter. "Alice."

She turned to him, his face less illuminated than it had been when the moon was full days ago. But she saw in the shadows of his face a longing that she'd known had been there all along. And her own for him, which had remained dormant among bigger, wilder, more passionate ones, began to bud.

"William."

She faced him now, willing for him to unfold his arms and pull her into them.

"I—" he started.

"Yes?"

"I love you, Alice."

Her heart began to beat faster. It ached like one who had been harnessed and was only now being released. This felt like the kind of love that her parents shared. The kind that could span years.

The kind she realized she wanted.

"William," she said as she lifted her head to his. "I love you, too."

Chapter Thirty-Three

1943 and on

William and Alice were married the following month, and Opa died three weeks after that in as much comfort as possible. William had been a rock to them all, an eagle all his own. Alice recalled that there were twenty-two of the granite statues around Penn Station. Not just the one that looked into their window. Perhaps there were as many kinds of ways to show love, to receive it. Emmett had shown her one that was complicated and passionate. William demonstrated one of simplicity and warmth. With Emmett she felt fiery things that consumed her. With William she felt the peace of gentle waters that calmed her.

Yes, twenty-two eagles. At least that many ways to love.

Angelo and Vera could hardly contain their joy. William invited them to join them in the beautiful white town house he'd purchased for his bride on Fifth Avenue. But both loved their little apartment on Thirty-Third Street and refused nearly every bit of help that he tried to offer.

With the exception of the prosthesis. His quiet voice rose above their protests in that they ceased arguing and allowed him to do this one thing. And it was a miracle. After several poor fittings, Angelo now had one that worked so well that he didn't even limp when he had it on. His new mobility inspired him to expand the newsstand to twice its size and productivity.

William encouraged Vera to leave her place at Macy's and helped her find one at an all-girls' school, where she could teach art lessons. What she did not know was that the school required all their teachers to have graduated from college, but a sizable donation from the Pilkingtons allowed this particular rule to be overlooked. And in time, the faculty was so impressed with Vera's natural gift with both paints and students that no one even remembered that she wasn't formally trained.

Alice, however, did receive her degree. After their daughter, Libby, was born, William insisted that twice a week she allow a nanny to take over so that she could attend classes. It took nearly a decade, but she graduated with honors after completing her thesis on historical architecture.

Her subject was Penn Station.

She covered the story of Alexander Cassatt's inspiration to build tunnels that connected New Jersey to New York. The stories of the demolition of the Tenderloin. Her parents supplied her with an endless number of anecdotes about that time. And while their kinds of memories were not the sort that would fit naturally into a research paper, they did provide hours of conversation around the dinner table.

Alice did not write about watching soldiers kiss their girlfriends as they went off to war, nor about the room that housed the lost luggage. They were not pertinent to her focused analysis of the construction of the station, but more than that, they were memories that she held close to her heart and never spoke of.

The best information that the policemen were ever able to relay to her was that Emmett Fischer seemed to be an immigrant whose father was German and mother was Jewish. There was some reliable information that pointed to his father's death of unknown causes, and while nothing was known of the mother, it was likely that she'd been sent to a concentration camp. Alice hired a private investigator to follow up on some of these leads, and he reported that neighbors of the Fischers said that Emmett's father had claimed to be Jewish so as not to be separated from his wife when she was taken away. Emmett was able to escape, and they assumed he'd succeeded in the plan he'd laid out for himself—to use his father's passport, which showed a striking resemblance, and flee to the United States. They had not heard from him since.

As to what happened after that awful day in the apartment, the police believed that Emmett was not part of any official movement but may have used his Aryan looks to ingratiate himself in some of the Nazi circles that did meet in New York in the hopes of discovering something that might be helpful to the Allies.

At that point, they laughed at the notion that a young man could have aspired to be useful in that way, but Alice knew better. He'd found something that must have been important or they wouldn't have taken him. Whatever the letters were—she would never know—someone had wanted to stop them from being seen.

1959

Vera liked to say that Libby was Pearl's revenge on all of them.

She said so with a smile. Pearl's name might as well have been mentioned right next to God's, considering the admiration with which they all spoke of her. But where Angelo, Vera, William, and Alice were all shades of agreeable, Libby had inherited Pearl's feisty nature.

Ever-new opportunities for women encouraged voices that were increasingly fearless. It was never a question that Libby would go to college or that she would study nearly anything she wanted. She looked forward to voting in the upcoming election, but she treated it as a matter of routine, since women had been doing so for nearly four decades.

Perhaps that was the victory. Not that these things were possible. But that they were commonplace.

But there was still a long way to go. When Alice graduated from college, she'd found few doors available in the men's world of architecture. She always applied for jobs as Alice Bellavia, as she wanted to be accepted on the merits of her ideas. But twelve interviews later, she had to accept that some boys' clubs just weren't ready yet. So she put her visions into motion without them. She and William spent weekends driving around the city finding abandoned properties. They'd measure the spaces, make anonymous offers to owners, and to date had converted seventeen properties into functional, beautiful places that she sold for a profit.

But Libby was going to be another matter. She was wild for Elvis Presley, not merely for his good looks and famous hips but for his innovation. Like many teenagers of her era, she liked everything that was new, new, new. William and Alice regularly invited her to join them on their drives, but she had no interest in buildings full of spiderwebs.

Alice reminded William that this was the very thing his mother had fought for—to pave the way for young women like Libby to have their own ideas about things.

Though Alice was Libby's champion at every turn, their relationship was not without contention. Their latest disagreement was over an invitation to spend the summer in Nantucket with the family of one of her school friends.

"You're quite right to hold your ground on this, dear," Vera said as she and Alice drank their coffee in the atrium of the apartment. Vera had come over early, since they had plans to tour the botanical gardens today. Vera wanted to paint the irises that had just been planted, and Alice was writing an article for *National Geographic* about Lord and Burnham, its architects. “It’s simpler to be poor,” her mother said. “One doesn’t have friends who have houses on Nantucket, and one knows that they will spend their summer working.”

“You’re not poor, Mama,” Alice said as she poured the cream for both of them.

“I didn’t say I was. I said it was simpler to be poor. And I used to be, you know. For many years. So, yes. I do know a little something about it.”

“The truth is,” Alice said, looking right and left to make sure that Libby was not within earshot, “I’m going to talk to William about letting her go. I’ve been invited to speak at a symposium at Cambridge University on the piece I wrote about colonial architecture, and I want to ask William to go with me. He’s been working himself to the bone ever since his grandfather retired, and we haven’t been away together since Maine.”

Every anniversary, William and Alice took a vacation. He only called in to the office once a day, and they’d found it to be the key to keeping their marriage romantic. They outdid each other with surprises. One year William arranged for Alice to take a private tour of the Baths of Caracalla in Rome. Another year Alice took him to the Daimler-Benz factory in Germany.

“And you should,” said Vera. “But you don’t need to ship her off hundreds of miles away. She can come and stay with us. We’re her only grandparents, after all.”

Alice smiled and handed her mother the sugar bowl.

“That’s very generous of you, Mama. But why don’t you and Papa stay here instead?”

“Is that the game you’re playing? You’ve been trying to get us to move in for sixteen years now. So you plan to wine and dine us under the guise of watching Libby and think that we’ll be seduced by the best cook in New York and the great views from the balcony?”

“You suggested it, not I.”

Vera shrugged. "Well, we're not moving. I like our apartment. I like my stove. And I like my Laundromat. The owner is the most interesting Chinese man. But when you live like this, people do your laundry for you. You'd never meet the interesting Chinese man here."

"Well, there's an interesting Turk I buy apples from when I walk by his cart."

"Suit yourself."

Alice leaned in to her mother. "You know that I would be just as happy over on Thirty-Third, if not more so. But the apartment was a gift to us when William's grandparents finally made peace with the fact that he'd married me and that it had actually lasted, against their predictions. So how can I deny him that? It's the only kind of thing he's ever known."

"Not true. He lived with me for a while as a boy. Don't forget about that."

William walked in holding a newspaper. "My ears are ringing. Were you ladies talking about me?" He kissed Vera on the head and then came around to his wife, where he kissed her lips. "Good morning, dear. New scarf?"

At Libby's urging, Alice had tried a hot-pink wrap around her hair. The color complimented her skin tone, but it felt like a juvenile accessory. "Borrowed from our daughter."

"I like it on you."

She didn't answer. Just basked in William's attention to detail. He always noticed new earrings, new shoes.

"Mama has just offered to stay with Libby next month so that you and I can make that Cambridge trip together."

"You know I'd love to, but that's when the buyers from Barcelona are coming in." He poured himself a cup of coffee.

"Why don't you save them the boat ride and have them meet you in London? We could stop there first, and you can have your meetings in those offices."

"They weren't taking a boat trip, Alice. They're flying. It's not as difficult as it used to be."

Vera slumped in her chair and crossed her arms. "Don't talk to me about airplanes. They're ruining this country."

"They're *uniting* this country," refuted William. "One can travel farther and faster than ever before."

"People aren't meant to fly. If we were, God would have given us wings. There's something unnatural about it."

Alice turned to her mother. "There was a day when riding on rails would have seemed unnatural to people who thought the two feet you were born with could get you everywhere you'd need to go. And yet you love train travel."

"Of course I do. You stay on the ground. Let gravity do its work."

"You're a bit cranky today, Mama. Is everything all right? Is it your back again?"

"It's not my back. It's the blasted newspaper."

William asked, "What do you mean?"

"I got my copy this morning before I walked over. I should have seen it coming. The Pennsylvania Railroad Company has sold off their air rights. See, there's progress for you. All the planes and all the cars mean that people don't need the trains anymore. You've seen the plastic sheets they've hung up over there. Closing off parts of the station that aren't even used anymore. Poor Alexander Cassatt would roll over in his grave if he knew."

William and Alice had exchanged glances the minute she said, "Air rights," a particular real-estate term that allowed the owners of a building to sell not only the ground it sat on but also the air above it. One might own a three-story structure but sell the air rights up to thirty-five stories, making an enormous profit. Selling air as if it were land.

It had been talked about in some circles. The beginning of the end for Penn Station. Their worst fears. It would be torn down to build who knew what in its place. William flipped to page three of the newspaper and showed Alice the story that Vera had mentioned.

"There it is right there," he said.

The fate of Penn Station had caused some disagreement in the family, William as the lone neutral party. While he'd been in and out of the station many times, he did not have any particular memories attached to it the way Vera and Alice did. And the dawn of more air travel meant new methods of transportation with which he could send cargo out from their factories.

Libby spoke of Progress as if it were the most vital thing in the world.

But there was one project that grandmother, mother, and daughter were all working on together: a bronze statue honoring suffragettes. Vera had hired the sculptor and was in charge of locating some possible places to put it. Though it would not carry the name of Pearl Pilkington, it would bear her face.

Alice and Libby were in charge of fund-raising. Of course, William and Alice could write one check and not only have the statue built but also grease the hands of the city officials who might consider their top location contenders. But Alice felt strongly that the suffragette memorial needed to be funded by everyday women so that they would feel a piece of ownership over it.

They were just over halfway there.

The progress of women came with a price, in Alice's eyes, and her daughter was a bellwether of that. Combined with an age where technology was allowing people to do things previously unthinkable—it was actually thought they'd be able to put a man in orbit within the decade—young women were keenly focused on the future with little regard for the past.

Alice feared what this meant going forward. Not merely for the rejection of the moral structures of a functioning society—though she acknowledged to herself that she had not exactly adhered to tradition in regard to her affair with Emmett—but to the actual destruction of what was old.

To the Pied Pipers of Libby's world who played the flutes of Progress, there was no coexistence to be had with the ancient or the antique. Out with the old, in with the new. And the young people were marching to the tune without question.

Funny how those who most prided themselves on being revolutionary were often the biggest conformists of all.

"Penny for your thoughts, dear," William said, and Alice grinned. She played out these imaginary arguments with Libby in her head, hoping to build some storehouse of wise sayings when the time came.

But the truth was that she wouldn't rock the boat with her daughter. She was proud of Libby for having conviction.

"I'm sorry, William." She set her napkin on her lap. "I was just lamenting that there are those who want to march so far forward that the things I love—the things of the past—are going to get overlooked. Or worse, destroyed. The idea that Penn Station—you know how much that place means to me—might cease to exist is like telling me that my right arm is going to be cut off and I have to step in line and be happy about it."

"You have to admit that the old girl is fading, though. At the time they built it, they expected it to outlive us all by hundreds of years. They might have been fantastic engineers and visionaries, but they couldn't construct a crystal ball that could tell them that people would fly or that cars would become sophisticated enough that families could travel on their own wheels rather than renting them from the Pennsylvania Railroad. That's the progress that is killing the station. Why travel by rail to San Francisco and do it over days when you can fly and get there in a few hours? We have to face it. Train travel as you and I knew it is dying. And the station is dying with it."

Vera spoke up; Alice had nearly forgotten that she was there. "That's the way of beauty."

"What do you mean, Mama?"

"The way of beauty. We are born shiny and new, and people marvel at us. How we smell. How we look. They celebrate when we take our first step. Fanfare all around. I remember when Penn Station was just like that. Angelo and I watched the opening ceremony from his newsstand together, and it was as magnificent as anything I've ever seen."

She continued. "But then it reached a sort of a middle age. No one lauds you when you take a step, because you have done it several million times before. As much as I love it, I can't say that I'm awestruck every time I enter the main hall. The station became functional rather than fantastic."

William tapped on the newspaper article. "And now this."

"Yes," said Vera. "Without the maintenance it needs, it's showing its age. As we all do. Our wrinkles tell our story, etched out like a road map. That's the way of beauty. Birth, middle age, decline."

"But," interjected Alice, "there are some things that are better as they age. Wine. Cheese. Books. Who doesn't love the smell of an old book? This is exactly *why* I love old buildings. They have history. The things they've seen. A new building is an empty shell. Sure, its plumbing may run smoothly, but has it ever embraced a cheering crowd or housed a dramatic performance or sponsored a ghost?"

Vera smiled. "Exactly, my dear. You understand it. At Libby's age, because they are so new themselves, they embrace what is being birthed right alongside them. But at our age—well, mine particularly—we value that very arc and see the beauty in its entirety. Libby doesn't have the eyes for that yet."

Alice stood up and removed the coffee cups. "Well, I don't suppose there's anything to be done about Penn Station, since the air rights are already sold. But if they can destroy that—that—*masterpiece*, what will be the next victim? Grand Central? The Astor Library? That beautiful post office by McKim, Mead, and White? Something has to be done to save them."

"What do you propose, then?" asked William.

"There must be some kind of commission or ladies' society or something that can get the word out. Do *you* want to live in a world where its history is erased so handily?"

Vera laughed. "It sounds like we have another Pearl in the house."

Alice rejoined them at the table. "Well, maybe I understand her even better now. Maybe we all have to find our cause—our purpose. The thing that makes us get up in the morning with our battle armor on. It's not going to be the same for every person. I promise that this article won't be the hot subject at the barber's today. But believe me, when there's a gaping hole where Penn Station once stood, people will notice, and I, for one, am not going to let it happen to anything else."

She realized that this might have been the most impassioned speech she'd ever given, but maybe it was that fire sparked by her love for Emmett all those years ago, right in the belly of the train station, that made her feel as if an irrecoverable blow had just been dealt to the girl she once was. If bricks and mortar were the flesh and bone of one's past, their destruction was your demise.

If she saved a building, it was like saving a life.

Maybe she *was* the next Pearl, instead of Libby.

And perhaps the way of beauty was not a one, two, three process. Birth, life, death. Maybe there was a fourth stage—renewal. She'd already been through it once. There was a time when she'd thought she would never recover from the loss of Emmett, but she'd gone on to marry William, graduated from college, written about buildings she loved.

But she'd also immersed herself in motherhood. And now that Libby would graduate from high school soon, she was ready to take on a new project that would invigorate her.

The death of Penn Station would be the rebirth of Alice Pilkington.

Epilogue

1963

My dreamer, the note said. *It's been too many years. But I must see you. E.*

"Who gave this to you?" Alice asked the boy at the door. "And where is he now?"

"Downstairs, ma'am. At an outside table in the café. Said he'd give me an extra dollar if I brought you there."

"Why didn't he come up himself?"

"I couldn't say, ma'am. I didn't ask him any questions."

Emmett was here. He was alive. He was *here*. Like someone facing death, scenes raced through her mind. His kisses on her skin, their embraces in the darkroom.

"I'll be right back," she shouted to her mother. It had been an emotional morning. Watching that first eagle come down off the building—the one her father had named Saint Michael—was more than her mother could take. Angelo's death still felt recent, although it had happened nearly two years ago. The dismantling of the station felt like the undoing of both of them, each woman woven so intricately into its fabric. She knew that it brought back the loss of Vera's father as well. She'd always taken such pride in what he'd done as a sandhog.

She'd slipped a sleeping pill in her mother's water. It would be good for her to rest for a while.

She checked her watch. She'd told William she'd meet him for lunch at twelve thirty. An hour to go.

Alice followed the boy downstairs, each step feeling like a brick was tied on her feet. They wanted to fly. When they reached the ground floor, he pointed to the café and ran ahead to collect his extra dollar.

The man sitting with his back to them turned to the boy and gave him the money. Then he stood, and as Alice looked at him, it seemed as if she had seen him only yesterday.

He still took her breath away.

"Hi, there," Emmett said, pulling out a chair for her.

She didn't take her eyes off him as she sat across from him. A waiter set down water glasses.

"You're here," she answered.

"I'm here."

"How?"

"Pan Am."

She laughed, surprising herself. In fact, her chest felt like a knot had grown in it. "I didn't mean *how* did you get here. I meant *how* is this possible?"

He leaned in. "There is so much to catch up on, Alice in Wonderland."

Those magical words. She'd never forgotten that name.

"No one has ever called me anything like that except you." How slowly they were both speaking. Dancing around the things they both wanted to say.

"It's how I've always thought of you."

"Have you thought of me?" she whispered.

"Every day."

Her heart clenched.

She would not cry. She would not cry.

"I thought of you, too." She crumpled a napkin in her hand just in case. "What happened, Emmett? The last time I saw you, those men were dragging you from your apartment. I didn't know where you were. I didn't know *who* you were. Emmett Fischer."

His eyebrows raised, and he sat back. "Emmett Fischer. I haven't heard that name in a while."

"What do you mean? I hired a private investigator to find you, and he confirmed that Adler wasn't even your real name."

She saw him ball his hands into a fist. "Is that what you did with your rich husband's money? You tried to find your old lover?"

His bitterness was palpable, and it felt like she'd been slapped.

"That is not a fair thing to say."

"That's how it looked to me at the time."

"What on earth do you mean?"

"Look"—he leaned in—"let me just knock this all out for you so that we don't spend all day rehashing what happened. The tale of Emmett Adler. Or Fischer. It's Schwartz now, by the way, but that will come later."

The waiter interrupted. "May I take your orders?"

Alice didn't think she could eat anything. But it wasn't the waiter's fault that a memory had turned into flesh and blood and walked back into her life.

They each ordered black coffee.

Maybe it would calm the nerves she was feeling.

"So," he said. "Here it is. I was born Emmett Fischer. My German father was a tailor; my Jewish mother was a seamstress. They worked together. You've never seen anyone so in love. When the Nazis came and took her away, my father sewed a yellow star on his sleeve and claimed his name was Schwartz so that he could follow her to the trains that we later learned went to the concentration camps. I'll never know if he found her or if they died there or later. But at the time I knew that I needed to leave or I would be sent there, too. I always resembled my father, so I made myself look older and was able to escape with his passport. I didn't think I could get a job, though, so I bought a camera with everything I had and began selling pictures. You know that part."

She couldn't imagine. To have lost his parents in such a way. Alice wanted to reach out to him, but too many years had passed. Too many things had happened.

"You found a real passion for it."

"I did. I could look through a lens and see the world I wanted to see rather than the world I was in." He leaned in and took her hand. A jolt shot through her.

But it was the reaction of a girl from long ago. The woman was married—happily—to the man who'd stayed.

"My heart was black, Alice. Black with hate. Bent on revenge. And then I saw you through that lens—my dreamer—and it felt as if the cloud that had been consuming me was lifted and there was beauty and light and it would be possible to live again."

Her lip quivered, and she took a deep breath. These were the things she'd wanted to understand for so long. It felt like he was mining a place she'd closed up. "Why—why didn't you tell me this before?"

"I was already playing a fool's game," he continued. "I'd gotten it into my head that as a German I could infiltrate those circles convincingly and see if I could find out anything that would help to bring those devils down."

"Emmett Fischer takes down the Nazis." She said the words slowly, rolling them around her tongue to see if it felt as naive as it sounded.

The coffee arrived. She closed her eyes and inhaled its steam. The sound of jackhammers behind her was drilling into her heart. And Emmett sat in front of her squeezing it. She felt she'd go crazy in the middle of this tug-of-war.

She breathed out again.

Emmett folded his arms. "I suppose that's what I thought. I was young and stupid."

"You weren't stupid. You had a very large chip to remove from your shoulder," Emmett." His name rested on her tongue. It had been so many years since she'd spoken it out loud.

"By the time I met you, they'd already begun to suspect that I was up to something, and I knew I was being followed. In hindsight, I don't think they realized that I was just a boy with a mission. They must have thought I was working for the US government. Really, they paid far more attention to me than what was warranted. In a moment of panic, I gave you a different last name for me. If they ever saw me talking to you, I wanted you to know as little as possible."

He'd been telling the truth. He'd left so that she would be safe.

"Why did you pick Adler as your name?"

"The eagles. I always liked looking up at the eagles when I entered the station, and it was the first thing that came to mind when I started submitting my photographs to magazines and newspapers."

She smiled. The birds had had that effect on so many people.

"Well, speaking of young and stupid," she said, taking a breath and trying to return it to a normal cadence. "The first time I realized that Adler meant *eagle* in German, I took it as some kind of cosmic sign that I was supposed to be with you."

She saw his jaw tighten.

"And yet that's not what happened. No sooner was I gone than you married. You married well, I see."

"You don't understand, Emmett. I thought I'd lost you. I'd even begun to think that those men had killed you. Not a word from you."

"Are you saying you didn't love him, then?" Emmett held her eyes and challenged her.

Tears welled up, and she dabbed them with a napkin. Dear William. She loved him deeply.

"Of course I loved him. I still do. I wasn't an opportunist, if that's what you're implying."

"Well, you have to know that I escaped from those guys after a few days. When they realized that I really didn't know anything, nor did I even know what those damn letters were that I was photographing, they lightened their watch on me, and I got away."

"Why didn't you contact me?"

"Because I didn't want to endanger you. They knew about you, Alice. Not by name, but they had been watching my apartment, and they'd seen you coming and going. I heard them talking about how they had to *find that girl* in case she knew anything."

She put her hand to her mouth. Yes, Emmett had been protecting her. Poor Emmett. How lonely, how brave. He'd stayed away to save her, and she'd—she'd married someone else.

The old wound rose in his voice. "So imagine my surprise when I came across a copy of the *New York Times* to see the 'wedding of the year' in a headline, and how William Pilkington, the clothing heir, had married Alice Bellavia—*my Alice in Wonderland*—in so quick a time. I even harbored hopes—silly, romantic hopes—that you were perhaps pregnant with *my child* and that my staying away had forced you into this. But I watched the papers. I saw you in pictures in these society rags. But there was no child. Not until later, so she couldn't have been mine."

Alice bent her head in apology. "Her name is Elizabeth. We call her Libby."

"I didn't stick around long enough to know that. I returned to Germany with as much blackness and hate in my heart as when I'd left."

She clutched the napkin on her lap under the table. She'd done that to him. She'd exiled him with her actions. Guilt was a suffocating force, she realized.

"Did you ever marry?" she asked. She had to hope that he'd found happiness. The tragedy of Emmett's life had to come around to something better.

He leaned back, and his voice softened. "I did. Her name is Heidi. She is a wonderful woman."

Alice was so relieved, though a bit envious. It didn't negate all that she felt for William. But Emmett had a way of opening things she kept hidden. She hoped the woman he'd married realized what a good man he was. "Where is she now?"

"She is here with me, as is our daughter. We live in Munich, but she's always wanted to see New York. The girls went shopping today."

It was just as well. Alice wasn't sure she could handle meeting them.

A cheer rose from the crowd behind them. Alice turned around and saw another of the eagles being pulled down, ripping her heart out. It was like living the deaths of her opa and her father all over again. Suddenly, she couldn't hold back the tears any longer. She wrapped her arms around her waist and bent over.

Emmett pulled his chair over to her and pulled her in. She soaked the shoulder of his shirt as he stroked her hair. He was no longer the man she was in love with. But he was the one who knew her better than anyone in this moment.

It was not only Penn Station that was being torn down. It was the wild optimism of youth. The tie she had to the love she'd lived within those walls.

She tried to speak, but the words wouldn't come.

"I know," he whispered. "You don't have to say anything."

It was nice to be in Emmett's arms again, but as she started to breathe, a peaceful feeling washed over her. It wasn't Emmett's arms that she wanted to lie in at night. It was William's. A first love might be the most intense, the most passionate kind one would ever know. But it wasn't the love that was enduring.

It was William who laughed with them as her family sat around the dinner table. William who surprised her with her first trip to Rome. William who walked the ruins with her and bought the pistachio gelato her father had always talked about. William who held back her hair as she retched with the sickness of pregnancy. William who was there when Libby cut a tooth, when Alice graduated, when Vera had her first gallery showing.

It was William who'd held her hand as her father breathed heavily from pneumonia.

"Why did you return today of all days, Emmett?" She pulled back and rubbed her hands across her cheek to wipe away any mascara that might have stained her skin.

Emmett looked at Penn Station as he spoke. "The happiest time of my life was spent in that building. When I heard about its destruction, it was like being at the bedside of an old friend."

She knew what he meant. "Why did you decide to send me a note? And how did you know I was there if you thought I was married and living in a different part of town?"

He squeezed her hand. "Why did you rush down when you received it? Because despite everything, I know this about you, Alice. If you are anything like me, then the best days of your life were also spent inside those walls, and there was no way that you were not going to be here watching it. And your old apartment, sadly, had the best view for it."

She nodded, but he was wrong about one part. At the time, she would have said that those were her happiest days. But in fact, it was what came after—the life she'd built with William—that she would never exchange for anything.

But that didn't diminish the very real pain of the memories.

"My daughter is over in that crowd," she said. "She's among the supporters. Excited about the new sport arena that will go up in its place. And maybe that's what the city needs. What do I know? I'd hold on to every old brick and gutter pipe of every edifice ever built, but I suppose nostalgia, like anything else, has to be balanced out with progress. I just wish this particular place did not have to be the sacrificial lamb."

"I know what you mean."

His eyes told her what he didn't say in words. That he would hold on to her if he could.

She pulled away from him and smoothed the folds of her skirt. "I'm actually working with the mayor on creating a landmarks commission so that this kind of catastrophe doesn't happen to other important places in New York. We'll have architects, historians, and real-estate agents all advising on which buildings should be saved and preserved and which can be let go of in this path toward modernization."

She realized that she spoke more quickly as she talked to him about her favorite topic. "Believe it or not, Grand Central is on the chopping block, but I think we're going to manage to save that one. Good thing. Bertie moved his little business over there, and he's rallying the troops to preserve it. People are already realizing what we're losing here at Penn Station. They ignored our warnings, but it's awakened a sense of respect for the past, and I suppose if this one loss saves hundreds more, then it's a cost worth bearing."

"Spoken like a girl who's found her purpose."

She smiled. "I suppose I have. Your dreamer, two decades later."

"I always knew that about you." He smiled at her, and she couldn't help but return it.

They turned their chairs to face Penn Station. The coffee had gotten cold, and the waiter poured new ones.

Just like memories. They cooled in time, and fresh ones took their place.

Their story was just one of millions that had played out under the grand ceilings of Penn Station. And in its place would be an arena that would create new stories for the Libbys of the world. The concerts she would see, the rallies she would attend, the sport teams she would cheer for. Her young path was illuminated with possibilities that hadn't been open to Vera and Alice, its pavement laid by Pearl and many nameless women who imagined a future for granddaughters they would never know.

Alice thought of all these things as she watched the past fade stone by stone in front of her eyes, and she grabbed Emmett's hand. What was beautiful was coming to an end. What would rise would be a new kind of beauty. She would serve as a bridge between the two. Preserving what had been dear in times before her. Championing her daughter in the opportunities. That was the way it was meant to be. Birth, life, death, renewal, repeating over endless years.

She stood up and released Emmett's hand for the last time. He joined her and pulled her into a prolonged embrace that eliminated the need to say anything else. Then she slipped her purse over her shoulder and walked to the curb. She hailed a cab and asked the driver to take her uptown, where William was waiting for her.

Author's Note

In my research, I did not find any records of suffragettes dying during their hunger strikes. However, many of them became gravely ill, and the force-feeding by tubes was unspeakably painful. I also don't have any evidence that suffragettes went on a hunger strike in Albany particularly, let alone at the real-life former police station on Pearl Street. (The real street name of the station! Authors love such coincidences.) My intention here is to merge real-life occurrences with the details that propel the story in order to honor the sacrifices of the suffragettes and all who rally so selflessly for the causes they believe in.

As my stories often do, this one started with an image in my head: of a soldier kissing his girlfriend goodbye in a train station as he left for war. For whatever reason—providence's hand, I suppose—I put Penn Station into a search engine instead of the more famous Grand Central. I'd been through Penn Station before, and its ugly, dark halls that make the description of a rat in the opening quote seem apt. But I had no idea that a remarkable, timeless station had once stood on top of it where Madison Square Garden is now. I pored over pictures, and as its story unfolded, I imagined three women whose lives intersected with the station. I saw a parallel arc of the rise, heyday, and fall of the station, much like our own stories as humans. But we get a say in our own renewal, unlike edifices. The way of beauty.

I decided not to go deeply into the history of the station—there are many informational texts for you to read if you'd like to learn more. But I wanted to tell the tale of it through the stories of the women. Because buildings, after all, are still bricks and mortar, while we are flesh and bone.

It is true that Penn Station was the sacrificial lamb in a movement in the 1960s that valued modernization over nearly everything else. The Landmarks Preservation Commission was established in 1965 in direct response to the loss of such a beautiful building. Since then, it has designated about thirty-six thousand landmark properties and has protected about fourteen hundred. Among those directly saved have been the Astor Library, Grand Central Terminal (with large assistance from Jacqueline Kennedy Onassis), the Guggenheim Museum, Stonewall Inn in Greenwich Village, and several Broadway theaters.

As of this printing, plans are under way to create a new Penn Station inside the grand post office building that is located just across the street. McKim, Mead, and White designed both the original Penn Station and the current post office building, and I am personally ecstatic that the city is embracing a way to combine the old with the new.

Acknowledgments

This story owes its roots to an afternoon when I was sitting on my bed with my daughter Gina, brainstorming about what I would write next. We came up with secret journals, a father/daughter story, hidden letters, and all sorts of things that didn't become a book. But there was one image that we loved—the idea of soldiers kissing their girlfriends goodbye in a train station.

So, big thank-yous to Gina and the rest of the brood who give me tremendous support and encouragement as I write—my husband, Rob, and the other kiddos, Claire, Mary Teresa, and Vincent.

Sadly, they're barely kiddos anymore. They're almost all taller than me. That's not saying much, though.

Thanks to my agent, Jill Marsal. If I write a hundred books, I will always be thanking you for taking me on and guiding my career.

To Danielle Marshall, my acquiring editor—I'm so happy that you're at the helm, and I marvel at how you do it all. It's been a joy to get to know you and continue to work together.

To Chris Werner, my primary editor—thank you for being in my corner. I've been told many times over how lucky I am to have you as my editor, and everyone is right!

To Tiffany Yates Martin—oh, girl, you handle the hard work like nobody's business! Two books in together, your words haunt my dreams and my writing sessions—"But what is she *feeling*?" You make me better in many, many ways.

To Gabe Dumpit—you are a flawless champion of authors and a beautiful person to know, inside out. What a blessing it was to spend your birthday together along with Goofy and Pluto and quotations and friends. You are family.

And thank you to Sara Brady for incomparable copy edits that ushered me through a time period that is a world of its own.

I wrote this book in the middle of a huge cross-country move. It was terribly difficult to leave friends and family behind, but new friends in a new state made me feel welcome immediately. Thank you, Susan Schlimme (you are *awesome*!), Joyce Hoggard, Mary Clare Sabol, Amber Spivey, Andrea Erskine, Kaylie Lane, Lauren Wittig, Sharron Warren, and Erin Gross for embracing a frazzled woman and showing her the ropes here. Erin—God's hand was *all* over introducing us.

The writing community is unbelievably awesome. Thank you to Rochelle Weinstein, Emily Bleeker, and Heather Burch for an unforgettable week in Florida. Friendships can bloom quickly and grow deep roots when women like you are in the picture. To Fiona Davis—can't wait to see our books side by side in New York! To Barbara Davis—what fun we had in Camden! Thanks for driving up for lunch and for making me a fan of your books and of you as a person. To Aimie Runyan—why do I get the feeling that we're going to be partners in crime someday?

To the Ladies of the Lake (and a few lads)—you are the most amazing tribe. I can't name you all here, but each and every one of you is a treasure to me, and I smile every time I have a new Facebook notification from our group.

To those who promote books and the readers who read them, I would not be living this dream if it were not for you. I am particularly grateful for Andrea Peskind Katz, Suzanne Leopold, Ann-Marie Nieves, Kristy Barrett, Lisa Montanaro, Cindy Roesel, Jennifer Gans Blankfein, Jennifer O'Regan, Kristine Hall, Elizabeth Silver, Sharlene Martin Moore, Barbara Bos, Peggy Finck, Sylvia Denisse Cuervo, Tasha Seegmiller, Hailey Fish, Dianne Guevara, Amy Voorhees, Pam Carpenter, Gisela Riddle, Marie DeGennaro, Melissa Khadimally, Linda Zagon, Sandra Gomez, Susan Cunningham Roberts, Marisa Gothie, Alicia Kendall Krick, Marilyn Grable, Lauren Blank Margolin, Becky Kunasz, Gwen Score, Trina Burgermeister, and Beth Sullivan Cheshire.

To Max Tucci—thank you for the research help! Can't wait to see your book on shelves.

And, as always, to my parents, Pete and Chris, for their support of me my whole life.

About the Author

Photo © 2015 Gina Di Maio

Camille Di Maio always dreamed of being a writer, and those dreams came to fruition with her bestselling debut novel, *The Memory of Us*, and her second novel, *Before the Rain Falls*. In addition to writing women's fiction, she buys too many baked goods at farmers' markets, unashamedly belts out Broadway tunes when the mood strikes, and regularly faces her fear of flying to indulge in her passion for travel.

She and her husband homeschool their four children and lead an award-winning real estate team in San Antonio, Texas. They split their time between Texas and Virginia. Connect with Camille at www.camilledimaio.com.